SHADOW KING

SUSAN K. HAMILTON

This is a work of fiction. Names, characters, organizations, places, events, and incidents are either products of the author's imagination or are used fictitiously.

Published by Inkshares, Inc., Oakland, California
www.inkshares.com

Edited by Lizette Clarke
Cover design by Charlene Maguire
Interior design by Kevin G. Summers

ISBN: 9781947848986
e-ISBN: 9781947848474
LCCN: 2018937934

First edition

Printed in the United States of America

PROLOGUE

GRIPPED BY THE feverish dream, the little girl tossed restlessly, some of her unruly dark hair sticking to the patina of sweat on her forehead. Her head rolled on the pillow, and the delicate point of her ear peeked out from under her tangled locks. Her eyebrows furrowed, and a frown pinched her face.

Two men stood on the crest of the hill. One with chestnut hair and haunted, dead eyes, the other nearly alabaster skin, white-blond hair, and eyes so pale and blue they looked like ice. The blond leaned forward and whispered into his companion's ear, and then he pointed. Below them, at the bottom of the hill, were several homes, including a large manor with green gardens and enormous windows. Her house.

The man with dead, haunted eyes started to chant, and as he did, he conjured a windstorm so hot and fierce that it scorched the leaves on the tree that it swirled around. Bark blackened and withered, and the alabaster man laughed, vicious and cruel.

"They helped take her away. They're hiding her from you. Kill them . . . Kill them all," he hissed.

In her bed, the child whimpered and clutched her favorite stuffed toy, a lamb that her father had brought back from his travels.

With a savage cry, the darker man opened his hands and flung them toward the manor. Unleashed, the windstorm coalesced and started to roll across the ground, following his invisible direction. Everywhere it passed, nothing remained—everything was burned and consumed, leaving only bones and ash to mark its passing. The storm grew and darkened as it closed in on the manor, feeding off the screams and the fear. It surrounded the house, enveloping it.

After an eternal moment, the screaming stopped, and in the resonant silence that followed, the cloud contracted and blackened. From deep within its core, a wail of anger and despair erupted, so terrifying the very ground recoiled. When the cloud moved on—still seeking the prey it had not found—all that remained of the manor were some beams and tiles, and the charred bones of the family who had lived there.

The young Fae girl woke up screaming, her violet eyes filled with terror.

CHAPTER 1

FROM A DISCREET place across the street, Aohdan considered the run-down split-level house. Moss mottled the asphalt roof shingles, and the siding was faded and dented. As a growl of thunder rumbled in the distance, a threadbare curtain was pulled back a few inches and then fluttered closed before a tall, lanky man came out the front door. Skiffle jiggled the doorknob and then jogged lightly down the front steps. Twirling his keys in his hand, he headed down the sidewalk toward the end of the dead-end street where he'd parked his car.

Aohdan's eyes narrowed. *Your good mood's not going to last, you little shit.* He glanced to the side and nodded. Rory got the message and crossed the street, ready to cut Skiffle off in case the skinny man spooked and bolted. Aohdan glanced up as another rumble of thunder sounded; the sudden and fierce storm had done little to alleviate the summer humidity in Boston. Skiffle stopped to say hello to his neighbor, and when he did, Aohdan moved behind the cab of a pickup truck, where he could watch and listen without immediately being seen.

"How's it hanging, Sorley?" asked Skiffle.

The squat little Leprechaun hooked his thumbs into his pants. "Wee bit to the left, but the wife never complains. Where you off to?"

"Meeting my cousin at the race track. Play the ponies a bit," Skiffle bragged.

"Ah, found a bit o' money, did you?" The thought of money added a glint to the Leprechaun's green eye.

"You could say that," Skiffle said without trying to hide a self-satisfied grin.

Aohdan ground his teeth but forced himself to relax as five of Sorley's eight children tumbled into the miniscule front yard. Unclenching his fists, Aohdan took a half step out from behind the truck and managed to make eye contact with the stout Leprechaun. Sorley's eyes rounded and his mouth sagged, and when Aohdan made a gesture toward the house with his chin, Sorley didn't hesitate.

"Well, best o' luck to you, Skiffle. Okay, rug rats, back in the house." The order was met with a chorus of disappointed voices. "Nay, I promised yer ma we'd help with something, and you know, the faster we get it done, the faster I can take you all for ice cream." The disappointed moans turned to excited squeals at the promise of ice cream treats, and the young Leprechauns charged back into the house.

Skiffle ambled down the sidewalk, so caught in his own thoughts that he never noticed Aohdan quietly stalking him. Skiffle's car was a beater of an old Toyota Corolla—not worth much and butt-ugly, but it ran. The lock was sticky, so he jimmied the key a little, and just as he started to open the door, Aohdan's deep voice filled his ears.

"I'm really disappointed in you, Skiffle. Really disappointed."

Skiffle spun and backed up a few steps as a cold sweat broke out all over his body. Aohdan towered over him. "Oh, man. I can . . . I can explain . . ."

"Explain what?" The white T-shirt only emphasized the definition in Aohdan's arms and shoulders as he waited for an answer. For a minute, all Skiffle could do was stare at those muscled, tattoo-covered arms until Aohdan asked again. "Explain what, you little weasel?"

"That, uh, I . . ." Skiffle's mouth went dry as he tried to come up with a plausible lie. Aohdan pushed some of his long black hair behind one tapered ear while Skiffle fumbled under the Fae's angry, intense stare.

"I think you're trying to explain why I have to waste part of my Saturday in Dorchester tracking your sorry ass down. When you came to me for that loan, what did you tell me? You needed to cover some bills, just a little something to get you by until the next job. Five grand was all you needed. That about cover it?"

Skiffle nodded miserably.

"And when I gave you the money, I told you it was a loan, not charity. A loan with interest. Remind me again what you do with a loan?"

Skiffle stayed silent until Aohdan slammed his hand on the roof of the car, denting it, and the skinny man recoiled, shaking.

"You pay it back," Skiffle whispered hoarsely.

"You pay it back," Aohdan repeated. "So, when you were late and I sent Rory to collect your payment, what did you tell him?"

"I don't . . . I don't remember."

"Don't lie to me." Aohdan drew himself up to his impressive full height. At a hair over six feet five inches, he dwarfed Skiffle.

"No, no! I wouldn't lie to you! I wouldn't. I remember now. I remember! I kinda told Rory to fuck off." Skiffle stuffed his hands in his pockets to stop them from shaking.

"And?"

Skiffle sighed heavily. "And I, uh, I told him to tell you that you could fuck off, too . . . because I didn't have the money."

Pulling one trembling hand out of his pocket, Skiffle ran it through his stringy, damp hair.

"Because you didn't have the money," Aohdan repeated Skiffle's answer.

"I'd been drinking, man. I was being a tool, just sayin' stupid shit." Skiffle kicked at a clod of crabgrass growing out of a sidewalk crack.

"From what your cousin told me, it took less than four races at Suffolk for you to blow almost all the cash."

A strangled noise came out of Skiffle's throat at the mention of his cousin.

Aohdan ignored the lanky man's discomfort and continued, "I actually don't really care what you used the money for. I *am* concerned about your refusal to pay me back. That's essentially stealing from me, Skiffle, and I don't like it when people steal from me." Aohdan's voice grew darker and more ominous. Skiffle whimpered. Everyone knew bad things happened to people who crossed Aohdan Collins.

Finally overwhelmed by the thought of what Aohdan might do to him, Skiffle bolted, nearly falling as he raced around the front of his car and started to careen down the street, only to run blindly into a nasty stiff arm from Rory. Aohdan shook his head when Rory's arm slammed across Skiffle's chest and the skinny man collapsed in a heap on the pavement, wheezing and gasping. Rory picked him up by his stained shirt, hauled him back to Aohdan, and smashed him into the side of the Toyota. A rag muffled the scrawny deadbeat's pleas for help and mercy.

"Shut. Up." As he bit the words out, Aohdan opened the passenger door, stretched Skiffle's arm out, and in one swift motion, slammed the door shut, crushing Skiffle's hand. Even with the rag, his agonized scream filled the street, and when Aohdan opened the door, Rory let go and Skiffle crumpled to the ground, weeping. He spit out the dirty scrap of cloth and cradled the ruined mess of his bleeding and disfigured hand close to his chest. Bones poked through the skin at odd angles. Aohdan grabbed him by the hair and forced him to look up. Snot ran out of Skiffle's nose and down his face.

"No one steals from me, you worthless shit. Rory's going to come back in a week or so, and when he does, you'd better have *all* of my money." Aohdan walked away, leaving Skiffle huddled against his car, bleeding and crying.

After a half block, Rory said, "Worthless fucking human. We should have just left him in his trunk. This summer heat would have taken care of everything."

"I don't get any money back if he's dead," said Aohdan. From behind his sunglasses, Aohdan carefully looked up and down the street. As far as he could tell, no one but Sorley was home. Stopping at the Leprechaun's house, he grabbed his wallet and fished out two crisp hundred-dollar bills before walking to the front door. A little Leprechaun girl, probably no older than six, with wild curly red hair answered when he knocked.

"Is your father here?" asked Aohdan.

"Da! Someone wants to talk to you." She stared at Aohdan, then out at Rory, who was still standing on the sidewalk, then back at Aohdan again. When he got to the front door, Sorley swallowed hard. He shooed the little one back into the house.

"What kin I do you for, Mr. Collins?"

Aohdan handed Sorley the money. "This should cover ice cream for the kids and a nice dinner for you and your wife."

"Oh, that's not necessary . . ."

"I insist." Aohdan pressed the money into Sorley's hand and gave the Leprechaun a knowing look. Sorley swallowed hard and took the money. Without another word, Aohdan walked back down the concrete walkway to meet Rory.

CHAPTER 2

BY THAT NIGHT, Aohdan had erased Skiffle from his mind. Standing in his spacious living room, he stared out toward the city. *I don't care if there are bigger, fancier places in other parts of the city—this view is worth every last penny.* With an expansive and open living room that flowed into a gourmet kitchen and dining area, the penthouse condo also sported a master suite with a private balcony that looked out over the water, two additional bedrooms, three and a half baths, an office, and a private area Aohdan used as a small gym. The living room had its own separate balcony and a bank of windows that afforded a gorgeous view across Boston Harbor toward the financial district, and the city was lit up against the night sky.

He glanced at his watch. *Too nice of a night to drive; I'll just walk to Underworld.* Aohdan went into his bedroom and took a quick look in the mirror. The difference was night and day: he'd exchanged his T-shirt and ripped jeans for dress pants and a gray silk button-down shirt that looked like it had been tailored just for him. He grabbed a pair of shoes and then took the elevator down to the lobby. Fan Pier's cobblestone and concrete walkway led from the condos, around the federal courthouse, and to the city. The breeze coming off the water carried with it the aroma of salt-spray roses.

A man in a suit slouched on one of the benches that normally afforded tourists a place to relax and admire the city skyline, and the man's voice followed Aohdan as he walked by. "Nice night for a walk, Collins."

Aohdan turned back. "Do I know you?"

"Nope, but I know you." Light glinted off a gold detective's shield.

Pain-in-my-ass cops. "Something I can do for you, Detective?" Aohdan looked him up and down as the detective tugged at the tie around his neck to loosen it. He only managed to knock the whole thing off-kilter.

"You can tell me what you know about who gave Joey Terrazzi a beatdown today. Mangled his hand pretty good."

"Joey Terrazzi?"

"Don't play games, Collins. You know exactly who I'm talking about. You probably know him as Skiffle?"

He's just fishing. Skiffle—that little bastard—wouldn't have the balls to talk to the cops. "Oh, him. Met him a few times, but don't really know him. He lives in Dorchester, right? Pretty tough neighborhood if I recall."

"So . . . you don't know anything about what happened? Nothing at all? I heard he owed you money." The detective fiddled with his tie again.

"Owed me money? I don't know anything about that. But wouldn't Joey be able to identify who attacked him? I'm not sure what information I can give you." Aohdan smiled pleasantly at the detective and brushed a nonexistent piece of lint off his sleeve.

"Nice shirt," sneered the cop. "Fancy. Probably cost you, what? A couple hundred bucks?"

"More, but who's counting?" Aohdan's answer was sharp and snide.

"Makes me wonder, you know? How does a guy like you, who works in a tattoo shop, afford a shirt like that? Or live in a place like this?" The detective gestured back toward the condominium towers.

"I *own* the tattoo shop," corrected Aohdan, his temper starting to fray.

"Whatever. You can't possibly pull in enough income from that to afford to live like this. The money's coming from somewhere." The detective stepped close to Aohdan, full of bluster, but given that he was several inches shorter than the intimidating Fae man, his attempt at bullying fell short.

"Where my money comes from is none of your damn business, but I will tell you this: investing early in Apple, Amazon, and Facebook really paid off."

"Right. Investments. That and your bookmaking, extortion, pimping, and blackmail."

"Those are a lot of ugly words and accusations, Detective." *And you don't have shit to back them up, or I'd already be in handcuffs.* Aohdan started to turn away, bored with the unpleasant banter between them.

"Typical Fae," spat the detective. "Can't trust any of 'em. Pointy-eared fucks."

Aohdan's back stiffened and his jaw set in a hard line as he slowly looked back over his shoulder with narrowed eyes.

The detective smirked and shrugged. "I can't wait for the day you or your crew finally fuck up. It'll be Christmas for me no matter what time of year it is. You might think you're the godfather in this city, but you're not. You're not above the law, Collins. No one is."

As the detective taunted him, Aohdan forced himself to walk away. *That asshole isn't worth the jail time.*

Underworld was one of the hottest new clubs in Boston. It had been open for just six months, but word of the venue's great bands and great drinks had spread quickly. When Aohdan arrived, the line was already twenty-five deep, and at least half of the people waiting to get in were young women in tall heels and short dresses. They preened and flirted under his appreciative gaze as Aohdan bypassed the line and walked directly up to the bouncer. Bald, stern, and clearly a bodybuilder, he pulled the admission rope back as soon as he saw Aohdan.

"Welcome back, Mr. Collins."

"Good to see you, George." A fifty-dollar bill appeared in Aohdan's hand and then vanished into the bouncer's shirt pocket.

"Thank you, Mr. Collins. Always a pleasure to see you. Enjoy your night."

Inside Underworld, the music was pounding. Often, the club featured popular local bands; tonight a DJ was providing the entertainment. An expansive bar ran the length of one wall and curved for more seating. Made of dark cherrywood, the bar, chairs, and tables gleamed. The hanging teardrop lamps were made of deep red and gold blown glass and gave the dining area around them a warm feeling. The burgundy theme continued to the tables and seating—the chairs at the high bar tables and regular dining tables had deep and comfortable seat pads. Aohdan stopped for a moment and looked around the club. The dance floor teemed with people—an agreeable mix of human and faerie. It hadn't always been that way.

Faeries had lived in a parallel dimension to the ones inhabited by humans, and visited the human realm through what came to be known as "faerie rings" and other sacred sites. But over six hundred years ago, one faerie—the Seelie king's brother, Luan—had unleashed a spell so foul and dark that it destroyed the entire Faerie realm. That spell became known as the Desolation, and to escape it, the faerie races, or what was left of them, fled to the human realm, sealing the portal doors behind them. The arrival of faerie-kind had thrown human civilization into chaos, and the first response had been to treat the faeries like warring interlopers; it had taken some time for the insular faerie races to assimilate into their new world and learn to comingle comfortably with humans. It had taken the humans some time to adjust as well, and some—as Aohdan's encounter with the detective proved—hadn't adjusted at all. As far as Aohdan was concerned, there were still too many who clung to old, outmoded ways of thinking, and that was exactly why he'd abandoned the Seelie Court.

The Seelie Court used to be the heartbeat of the Faerie realm, the Seelie king someone you wanted to pledge your loyalty to. Now it is nothing but a pale shadow of what it used to be. The Seelie king should have established the Court as a center of power and culture here in the human realm, become an equal to kings and presidents, but he's done nothing, thought Aohdan.

Aohdan made his way along the edge of the crowded dance floor toward the VIP area, then stopped when a voluptuous blond stepped in front of him and started to shimmy, trying to entice him into a dance. He let her grind on him for a moment, enjoying the show, before he stepped around her and continued to his regular table. Waiting for him—all grinning like fools—were his closest friends and the captains of his crew: Galen, Oisin, Kieran, and Rory. As he arrived, a waitress brought him a double shot of his favorite whiskey.

"There's glitter on your shirt," Galen observed before Oisin interrupted him.

"You seriously don't want to tap that blond? Seriously?" Oisin smiled devilishly and ran a hand through his dark blond hair as he eyed the woman who'd flirted with Aohdan.

"Yours if you want her," said Aohdan, "but she's already sloppy drunk. She'll be throwing up before midnight."

"Don't need to wait—she can be the warm-up. And that drunk, it would be even easier to bend her over the bar." Rory's smug comment was nearly lost in his beer.

"If that's how you want your women, Rory. But drunk or no, she does have a verra nice ass," said Kieran with just a hint of Scottish brogue.

"I'll drink to that." Galen raised his glass. "Here's to a good night, good food, and beautiful women."

The others echoed his toast, and as they all took a deep drink, Aohdan got comfortable in his seat. Two other waitresses arrived with more cold beer and platters of appetizers. Plates of stuffed jalapeños, meatballs stuffed with mozzarella, hummus and fresh vegetables, and Thai lettuce wraps covered the table, and the scent made Aohdan realize how damn hungry he was.

After downing a few of the lettuce wraps, Oisin leaned over to Aohdan. "How was your day? Your errands turn out okay?"

"I think that little loan problem has been addressed. I did get a little visit from one of Boston's finest on my way here."

"Those fucks?" Oisin shook his head. "What now?"

"Nothing but annoying bullshit, and frankly, I'm starting to get a little tired of it." Aohdan finished his whiskey and gestured to the waitress for a refill as a petite brunette stopped at the edge of the VIP area and waved to Oisin. He raised his glass to acknowledge her, and she offered a coy, flirtatious look before she disappeared into the crowd.

"Who's that?" asked Rory.

"I think I hit that a couple weeks ago . . ." While Oisin tried to remember her name, Aohdan scanned the establishment with a critical eye. The dance floor was crowded, and drinks seemed to be flowing steadily out of the bar. As if he'd read Aohdan's mind, Galen moved closer to his boss so they could talk.

"Club's doing very well. We're on every hot list in the city and, most nights, there's a line to get in. I'm looking at ways we can increase revenue and traffic on the typically slower nights, like Sundays and Mondays." Although his demeanor was serious, there was a gleam in Galen's eye that told Aohdan his second-in-command was happy with Underworld's progress.

"Has there been any trouble?" Aohdan still hadn't quite let go of his earlier conversation with the detective.

"Nothing of consequence. Some cops stopped by the other day asking about a mugging," Galen told him.

"Here?"

"No, I would have taken care of that myself. Happened about three blocks from here. I offered them our security tapes, but it happened too far away to make a difference. I have some ideas for security upgrades to the back offices that I want to talk to you about."

"Do what you think is best. I trust your judgment."

Muriel—one of the regular waitresses in the VIP area—came up carrying a tray holding five shot glasses of Glenlivet whiskey. She put them down on the table.

"The good stuff. Verra impressive. Where did these come from, Muriel?" asked Kieran.

"The young ladies over there." She gestured toward a knot of six women at a nearby table. They all waved and smiled when they realized Aohdan and his companions were looking.

"What do you think, Aohdan?" asked Rory. "Ready for company?"

"It's Saturday night; we're here to play," said Aohdan, and he started to smile as he gave the women another appraising look. Unlike the one who'd started to grind on him earlier, these women looked sophisticated and clearly weren't drunk—at least not yet.

"Well, then, why don't I go invite them up and we can show the ladies how much we appreciate a shot of good whiskey? Come with me, Kieran. They can never resist that voice of yours," said Oisin.

"Verra true," Kieran said, letting the rolled *r* linger as he stood up. Despite both being about the same height, the two Fae men were very different. Kieran had dark brown hair that he kept liberally streaked with blond highlights, and had tawny eyes. Over the centuries before the Desolation, he'd spent a tremendous amount of time in the human realm, particularly in Scotland, and he had the accent to show for it. Oisin, with his rich blond hair and dark blue eyes was quick to laugh and drink and shoot his mouth off, and had been Aohdan's friend since childhood. He sported a diamond stud in his left ear.

They walked down to the table, and it didn't take long for them to convince the ladies to join them in the VIP area. The women sat down in and among Aohdan and his captains. Once they were settled, Aohdan ordered another round of shots and a bottle of champagne for the table and soon found himself with a woman on each side.

One had light brown hair, and as she shifted, her dress gaped, giving him a tantalizing glimpse of the lacy red bra she wore underneath. She moved closer and put a hand on Aohdan's chest. "My name's Cindy. That's my friend Sonja. You're Aohdan Collins, right?"

"That depends who's asking."

"People say you run this town," Cindy purred.

"People exaggerate," he answered, but his grin said differently. "But let's not talk about me. I'd much rather hear about the two of you. Girls' night out?"

"It is," giggled Cindy. "Just got a promotion at work, so we're out to celebrate."

"Congratulations," said Aohdan, not really caring what Cindy did for work. He turned to look at Sonja, who was staring at his pointed ears, a clear hallmark of his Fae heritage.

"You're Fae," she said.

"I am. Pointed ears kind of give it away." He masked his annoyance with a grin. "Is that a problem?"

"Oh, no." Sonja gave him a coy look as she rested her hand on Aohdan's thigh. She squeezed. "I've just never been with a Fae before."

"Neither have I," added Cindy. "Is it true you can have sex for hours?"

"You'll just have to wait and see." Aohdan pulled Cindy closer to him and kissed her. She yielded, opening her mouth to let Aohdan do whatever he wished. Watching, Sonja ran her fingers along his thigh, and after leaving Cindy breathless, Aohdan looked at Sonja and smiled. He poured some more champagne. It was shaping up to be an excellent night.

CHAPTER 3

BRIGHT MORNING SUN streamed through Seireadan's bedroom window. She slowly opened her eyes, cursed, turned back over, and squeezed them shut, willing it to be nighttime again. A moment later, she sat straight up in the bed with a grouchy sigh.

"It's your own friggin' fault," she muttered to herself. "'Just work on the site for a few more minutes,' you said. 'Just another half hour and then you'll go out.' Famous last words. You wasted yet another Saturday night working."

And now Seireadan had only half of Sunday to herself because she'd promised to take an extra shift at Sacred Circle, a New Age spirituality shop where she worked part-time reading tarot cards. She didn't need the money; her web design business was doing quite well. But being self-employed meant being alone for long stretches of time. Sacred Circle gave Seireadan a chance to actually interact with people other than her clients.

The shop's owner, Julia Orlando, had been thrilled when Seireadan joined the team since Seireadan was one of the few Fae who possessed the Sight. That meant, on rare occasions, she actually could See glimpses of someone's future. Fae with this particular talent were called Ravens, in homage to the birds that represented wisdom in their culture.

"Next weekend, you *will* take Saturday off," Seireadan said to her reflection in the mirror. "You *will* go out Saturday night and try having a life. And on Sunday, you'll spend the day doing absolutely nothing related to work." Her dark mahogany hair was a mess, so she caught it back in a thick elastic band. After fishing a pair of running capris and a T-shirt out of the laundry, she pulled on her sneakers and headed out for a run to clear her head.

At the Intercontinental Hotel, Aohdan glanced into the bedroom of the suite he used most weekends. The manager, who owed him a favor or two, always kept it open for Aohdan to use whenever he liked. Cindy and Sonja were sprawled in the king-sized bed; they'd been eager enough sex partners, willing to do just about whatever he asked, and Aohdan had kept both women up until nearly sunrise. As a rule, he never brought any of his hookups back to his place; too many complications and implications. He closed the door quietly when he left, and headed out the back of the hotel for a stroll along the Harborwalk on his way home.

From her apartment on Emerson Street, Seireadan headed to East Broadway and then up L Street until it became Summer Street. She followed Summer Street all the way to the Fort Point Channel and then ran the Harborwalk over to the federal courthouse. As she looped the court, she passed the 22 Liberty condominiums before turning onto Fan Pier. Keeping up a steady pace, she crossed Seaport Boulevard and cut through so she could run the other side of the Harborwalk, which threaded behind Independence Wharf, the Intercontinental Hotel, and eventually the Federal Reserve building. From there it would be a final sprint back to her apartment.

As Seireadan jogged down the steps at Independence Wharf, she noticed a man coming toward her, and as she got closer, she could tell he was Fae. His clothes were too nice and his shirt far too rumpled for so early on a Sunday morning. That plus the disheveled hair, sunglasses, and air of arrogant satisfaction told her he was heading home after some sort of one-night stand. Despite that, she still caught her breath slightly as she looked at him. *Shit, he's good-looking.* Given her pace, Seireadan passed him in a moment and continued on her way. She didn't see him turn to give her ass an admiring and appreciative glance, but she felt the weight of his gaze and it sent a thrill through her.

After her run, Seireadan showered and made sure she'd arrive at the shop fifteen minutes before it opened. She took a sip of the coffee she'd bought at the little café next door to Sacred Circle, appreciating the sweet, creamy flavor; she'd never cared much for the bitterness of black coffee, preferring hers extra sweet and extra light. She liked the little New Age shop. It was a welcoming, inclusive place, and Seireadan had always felt at home there.

Julia smiled when Seireadan came in. "Hey, Seireadan. Thanks for covering for Lanna today. I know it means a lot for her to go see her niece's ballet recital."

"Not a problem. Just us today?" Seireadan pushed her hair back over her right ear, revealing seven amethyst stud earrings cascading along her ear up to the elegantly tapered tip. They were a lovely complement to her eyes, which were also a deep violet, a trait that ran in certain Fae families.

"Only for the start of the day. Nick and Carrie will also be in. Those are great earrings, by the way. Perfect color to highlight those gorgeous eyes of yours," said Julia.

"Thank you." Seireadan appreciated the compliment. She let the coffee warm her from the inside; in the summer Julia kept the air-conditioning fairly high and the shop was always a bit chilly. Seireadan flipped through the appointment book as she waited, then helped Julia unpack a new shipment of tarot and oracle cards. Satisfied with the display, Seireadan glanced at the clock; she preferred to get her first impression of a client in her reading room, where there weren't a lot of outside distractions.

Her reading room was small and cozy. In the center was a circular table covered by a plush green cloth with a pattern of leaves and vines woven into it. Several soft lights illuminated the space—four were embedded in Himalayan salt lamps—and Seireadan made sure there was just the smallest hint of sandalwood in the air. The midweight drape that served as a door was pulled back, and Julia let the client walk into the room before drawing the "door" closed. The young woman stood for a moment, looking around, and Seireadan watched her quietly. She was probably in her midtwenties, no older, and looked uncertain. Pretty, but not remarkable, she had short chestnut hair, hazel eyes, and a smattering of freckles across her nose.

"Hello," said Seireadan. "Please, sit down. You must be Anna."

For a moment, Anna froze, looking stunned. "How . . . how did you know my name?"

Seireadan smiled. "Sweetie, it's in the appointment book out front."

Anna flushed and offered a self-conscious laugh. "Wow, that was probably the dumbest question ever."

"Not at all. You'd be surprised how many people ask that exact same thing," Seireadan reassured her, hoping she'd feel less awkward.

"This is the first tarot reading I've ever done," Anna said as she sat down and continued to look around the room.

"Really? Wonderful. Then before we start, I want to tell you a couple things. First, this is your reading. You can share whatever you like, but I won't tell anyone about what we discussed. Second, the future is not set in stone. If you don't like what we see in the cards today, then it's up to you to make deliberate, thoughtful choices to change it. The cards offer advice about the future, they don't dictate it. Does that all make sense?" As she was talking, Seireadan pulled a deck of cards out of a velvet pouch and started to shuffle them like she was dealing poker in Las Vegas.

"Yes, it does." Anna stared at the cards as Seireadan put the stack down right in front of her.

"Now, you shuffle them, and as you do, think about your question."

Anna picked the cards up tentatively. "How long do I shuffle them for?"

"Until you feel done. Now concentrate."

Shutting her eyes, Anna took a deep breath and shuffled while Seireadan watched and waited, wondering if she'd get the sharp tingle that preceded the Sight. She exhaled softly when nothing happened. *If I were going to See anything connected to Anna, I would have Seen it by now.* The realization was a relief for Seireadan; as far as she was concerned, the Sight was more burden than blessing.

Within the Faerie world, each faerie—regardless of type—had the capacity for magic, but as with intellect, athletic ability, and beauty, each had it in different amounts. Within the Fae, a small number possessed the Sight—with the ability manifesting in adolescence—and they were often sought for counsel. But the Sight was a fickle thing, coming and going as it pleased. It could not be demanded or commanded. Ravens, as these gifted Fae were called, tended to have sharper intuition and insights even when not engulfed by the Sight. It was one of the reasons Seireadan was so good at the readings she did for Julia's shop.

Anna's reading proved to be smooth and straightforward. The young woman felt like she was being left behind by friends who were getting married and starting to have children, but based on the cards, Seireadan assured her she wouldn't lose her friends and that she'd find the relationship she was looking for, but not before some upheaval in Anna's life. The Fae Seer was glad she could put Anna's mind at ease, but found it made her think about how long it had been since her own last meaningful relationship.

Ignoring the thoughts about her very solitary life, Seireadan collected the loose cards and shuffled the deck a few times before tucking it into a velvet pouch. She walked Anna to the front of the store so she could pay Julia, and then found something to do until the next appointment. She ended up doing five readings. Three were scheduled; two were walk-ins. To her immense relief, none resulted in a true Seeing.

After helping Julia close the store for the night, Seireadan headed home. As she cut through the shop's small parking lot, she realized she wasn't alone. A Fae man with wheat-brown hair and the shadow of a mustache watched her with contempt, and her lips pressed into a thin, unhappy line.

"Why are you here, Cavan?"

"You didn't come to the last Gathering of Ravens."

"Gatherings have never been mandatory. I was busy." It was a small lie. Seireadan hadn't been busy, but the thought of spending time with Cavan was always reason enough to stay away. The critical look he gave her made Seireadan's hackles rise even more.

"Say it," she said. "Say whatever it is you're thinking."

"You have that look about you . . . that unseelie taint."

Seireadan straightened. In her native language, the word *seelie* meant "shining or bright," and that was what the entire Seelie Court stood for. Built around the Seelie king, the Court was the center of sophistication and culture, lightness and beauty, for all of Faerie. At least, it had been before the Desolation. To be called *unseelie* was the equivalent of being hidden by shadows at best, and—at worst—dirty and vile, and to be officially named as Unseelie was almost unheard of.

"Watch your mouth," she warned.

"You spend too much time away from your people."

Her voice frosted even more in response to the loathing she heard in his words. "Away from my people? Please. There are precious few of 'my people' that I care to associate with, especially ones that fling derogatory names at me."

"You waste yourself among these humans." Cavan said "human" with the same bitter distaste as he did "unseelie," and Seireadan knew from past experience that he detested both.

Seireadan shrugged slightly, loosening her shoulders, as she felt a spark of anger stirring. "The humans have proven more trustworthy than many Fae. Like you. Like the one who lied and murdered my family during the Desolation—" Old pain bubbled up inside her, flaming the anger.

Cavan interrupted her with a disgusted sigh. "Are you still clinging to that ridiculous idea after all this time? That someone deliberately set that spell against your family?"

"I Saw it. I Saw *him*." She ground the words out between her teeth.

"You had a nightmare, nothing more," Cavan said with dismissive superiority.

"It was the Sight," said Seireadan stubbornly.

"You just feel guilty that you weren't there to die with your parents, so you make up stories about Seeing. Stupid, stupid girl. Everyone knows the Sight doesn't manifest until puberty. Your father opposed the prince; he got what he deserved, the disloyal—"

In a heartbeat, Seireadan grabbed Cavan by the collar with her left hand and pulled a hidden knife from the back of her belt with her right. She slammed him back against a car and pressed the tip of the blade between two ribs. Cavan's eyes rounded in shock, which quickly shifted to fear.

Her voice was a low growl. "Don't ever talk about my parents again, or I will tear your throat out. Yes, I was a child, but I Saw it, and someday, I'll find the Fae I know is responsible. The one who LIED about my parents hiding Bryn and Conlan from Luan." In her mind, Seireadan could see the pale eyes and cold, alabaster skin of the Fae man she knew was responsible. She could still hear the words "kill them all" echo after all these years.

She dropped her knife hand and let Cavan go. He drew in a ragged breath and glared hotly at Seireadan, but she didn't move. She kept the hilt of the knife in her hand, pressing the flat side of the blade against her arm in case Cavan did something unexpected and stupid.

"Feral little bitch," he hissed.

"Best you remember that," she snarled as he walked away.

Back at her apartment, Seireadan went to her closet and rummaged in the back, finally pulling out a long wooden box. Inside, wrapped in a tattered bag, was an ancient-looking sword. The scabbard was worn from use. Seireadan put her hand on it lightly.

"You belonged to my father, to my family. Someday. Someday, I will find my Alabaster Man and I will use you to run him through for what he did." She whispered the promise to herself and the sword before she tucked it back in the closet.

CHAPTER 4

AT ASMODEUS INK, Donnie and Wharf Rat were working with clients and Kerry had run out for coffee. In the back office, Aohdan's eyes skimmed over the ledger. Business was up 15 percent in the past three months. While Aohdan had many other business ventures in the city—all of which he ran to be as profitable as possible—he owned Asmodeus because he loved it. Making a profit here was a bonus.

Nearby, Jimmy McLaren lounged in a chair playing a game on his phone, and Aohdan's smile faded. *He should be running errands for Galen, not sitting on his ass doing nothing.* Before he could say anything, the bell for the front door rang and Aohdan went out to the front of the shop. A young man started to browse the shelves and displays, and Aohdan was about to help him when Rory and Oisin came in. With a nod, Aohdan sent them to the back office.

"Looking for something in particular?" he asked the customer.

"Thinking about getting a piercing—probably the nose."

"Well, have a look at these." Aohdan steered him toward a glass case where there were trays full of piercing options for ears, noses, navels, nipples, and any other body part a person might be interested in ornamenting. The customer bell rang again as Kerry bustled in with a tray full of coffee. She had multiple piercings in each ear, a ring and stud in her nose, and through her shirt, it was evident she had some sort of belly button piercing as well. Aohdan took his coffee, turned the customer over to Kerry, and went back to his office. Oisin and Rory were sitting in front of the desk, and Jimmy was still fiddling with his phone.

"I saw Skiffle today. He returned that stuff he borrowed from you," said Rory.

"Maybe he's not as dumb as he looks," Aohdan replied. He fell silent, intently watching Jimmy, who remained completely absorbed by his phone.

"Hey. Jimmy Boy." Aohdan's voice was sharp, and Jimmy looked up furtively like he'd been caught napping in class.

"Yeah, boss?" He tried to look like he'd been paying attention, and Aohdan raised his eyebrows before he glanced at his captains and then back at Jimmy. Jimmy Boy should have left the office the instant Rory and Oisin came in. His lack of attention, plus the fact that he was sitting on his ass playing games, wasn't winning him any points with Aohdan.

"Get the fuck out of my office and go make yourself useful!"

Jimmy Boy scrambled out of his seat and left the room so fast he nearly forgot to close the door behind him, but managed to recover before Aohdan said anything else.

"I don't know why you keep him around," said Rory. "Weak-minded, lazy son of a bitch, that's all he is. Fucking humans."

Aohdan didn't answer Rory; he just looked at the door. *If you were anyone else's son, I would have cut you loose a long time ago, Jimmy.* But if it hadn't been for Jimmy's father, Aohdan would have been found dead in the harbor ten years ago. In an instant, he could taste the blood in his mouth again . . .

Aohdan's lungs burned, desperate for air, and the coppery taste of blood lingered at the back of his throat as he grabbed futilely at the two pairs of arms holding him under the water. He clenched his teeth; having his lungs fill with Boston Harbor water was going to be a shitty way to die. A moment later one set of hands disappeared and then the other, and Aohdan broke the surface of the water, gasping and gulping air into his starving lungs. He grabbed one of the dock posts, but it was slick with algae and he couldn't get a grip. Exhausted, he felt himself start to sink back into the water until two strong hands grabbed the back of his shirt and hauled him up onto the dock. Aohdan lay there, coughing up water, and pushed himself up to his knees, hoping he wasn't going to have to fight off anyone in the next five minutes.

Aohdan stood and his rescuer, who wasn't a small man, had to look up at him. "Damn. You're a big son of a bitch, aren't you?"

"What happened . . . ?" Aohdan was still getting his bearings.

"Pipe to the side of the head for one and a good, swift kick in the balls for the other. I'm Danny McLaren. Work here on the docks. Just didn't seem right to me to stand by and watch a man get drowned. Plus, cops would close this dock down to investigate and I'd lose a day or two of pay." The dockman's grin was genuine and showed he was missing a few teeth.

"I'm glad you feel that way." Aohdan held out his hand. "Name's Aohdan Collins. Very nice to meet you, Danny. I owe you one."

Aohdan pulled himself out of the memory. "Forget about Jimmy Boy. I need you both to take a little road trip."

"What's up?" Oisin leaned forward in his chair.

"Rory, your cousin Moira still live down in Rhode Island?" asked Aohdan. As he talked, Aohdan took a container of milk out of the mini-fridge he kept in the office, poured a little on a small plate, and left it by the cracked window. There was an orphan Pixie in the area, and Aohdan felt bad for her. In return for the milk, the Pixie would bring him news from around the neighborhood. Several times the information had been quite valuable.

"In Warwick. Why?"

"I've been hearing some rumors that Matriarch Baibin is unwell. Unwell enough that she might seriously be looking into succession within her *fréamhacha agus brainsí*," said Aohdan.

The Fae organized themselves in loose family units similar to clans. In Faerie, they were called *fréamhacha agus brainsí*—literally "the roots and branches"—but it was a simple term for a complicated institution. Each *brainsí* was ruled by a single Fae, a triarch. Aohdan was patriarch in Boston. In the Faerie realm, a triarch acted as a chieftain who was loyal to the Seelie king or queen, and the faeries within a triarch's *fréamhacha agus brainsí* were loyal to their triarch. But things had changed after the Desolation, with many of the triarchs moving away from the Seelie Court, lured by the opportunity of wealth, power, and independence.

"Hmm." Oisin rubbed his chin. "That would be quite a change, even for a small *brainsí*."

"She has a son," said Rory.

"A loud-mouthed idiot of a son who has no business becoming a patriarch," snorted Aohdan.

"You've met him?" asked Oisin.

"No, but I've seen the aftermath of a few of his ill-conceived escapades," Aohdan answered.

"Even with her adherence to the old ways, I can't imagine Baibin being willing to turn her *brainsí* over to him," said Aohdan. "Rory and Oisin, I want you both to go to Providence and find out how sick the matriarch really is and what the rumors say will happen. I'm sure Moira can put some questions in the right ears. And find out if Matriarch Teresa has been sniffing around."

CHAPTER 5

IT WAS SATURDAY night and, true to her promise to herself, Seireadan was going out. Unfortunately, she was going solo. Her best friend, Lia, was out of town on a long-term consulting gig, but Seireadan wasn't going to let that stop her. She pulled two dresses out, then quickly discarded them. *Too light. Too frumpy.* She grabbed the next one and immediately tossed it on the bed. *Way too slutty. What was I thinking when I bought THAT? Oh, right. Lia talked me into that one . . .*

Thinking of Lia made her smile. Seireadan picked the dress back up and gave it a critical look before dumping it on the bed. Slutty was not the look she was going for. She pulled out one more dress and held it up. This would do; it was a relatively simple black dress, but it was covered with a light smattering of black sequins, giving just a hint of flash and sparkle. The neck was scooped and the sleeves were long, and the clingy material fit well through the body and hips until the cut of the skirt allowed it to flare as she moved. She hung the dress on the closet door and grabbed a pair of shoes: black heels with faux diamond accents. Satisfied the outfit was suitable, she pulled her shirt over her head and stepped out of her yoga pants.

She indulged in a hot shower, letting the water cascade over her as she scrubbed herself with a new lemon essence sugar scrub she'd found at Sacred Circle. She inhaled deeply, enjoying the bright, tart scent. Once she was dried off, she blew her hair out so the natural wave relaxed a little, and put on just a touch of makeup. If there was one thing she couldn't stand, it was seeing a woman try too hard by caking on the makeup. She pulled on the dress, cursing at the zipper, and then slipped on her heels. Lastly, she decided on a set of diamond studs to run up the edge of her ear.

She took one last look at herself in the mirror. "You don't clean up half-bad. Not half-bad at all." With a final nod, she deemed herself presentable for a night on the town and headed out for her evening.

"The Seaport area," she told the cabbie when she got in. As they pulled away from the curb, she saw him glance at her in the rearview, look away, and then glance again. It wasn't uncommon; she attracted enough appreciative glances from men of both races on a regular day, but when she dressed up, there was always a noticeable increase.

She settled back in her seat and watched the city pass by. Like many parts of Southie, the Seaport District was booming with new businesses, condos, restaurants, shops, and clubs. She went to Club Zee first. There wasn't much of a line out front, but as she got closer, a pack of loud, well-inebriated young men arrived. They hooted and hollered at her and made a few lewd comments. Because of that, she decided Zee was a bad idea. Being hit on was one thing; getting hounded all night by drunk frat boys was another. Underworld, a new club she'd heard good things about, was only a few minutes away. She put a touch of swagger in her step and walked down the sidewalk.

Once she arrived, Seireadan knew Underworld was a good choice. She found a seat at the bar and entertained herself by watching the eclectic crowd. She guessed nearly a third of the people there had origins in Faerie. A group of Leprechauns and Clurichauns toasted one another and chugged their beer, while two Undines and a Rusalka with their blue-tinted skin chatted with several humans. And a determined Korrigan made his best efforts to convince one of the human waitresses to give him her number.

A young Selkie, barely old enough to be in the club, approached Seireadan and offered to buy her a drink. Based on his frequent glances at his three equally dumbstruck companions, Seireadan guessed that they'd dared him to chat her up, assuming she'd shoot him down. While Seireadan wasn't necessarily looking for someone to take home with her tonight, she also wasn't opposed to the idea. But the Selkie was far too young.

She told him a gentle lie about waiting for her boyfriend, but that if she were single, she absolutely would have let him buy her that drink. He retreated to his friends, and she was glad he hadn't pushed his offer; she'd had to fend off aggressive suitors before and it was never fun, especially on the few occasions she'd had to demonstrate her rather formidable right hook.

Underworld's bartender, an Asian man with a shocking stripe of blond in his dark hair, asked if she wanted a refill on her "white-hot peach sangria," but she declined. A few minutes later, he returned and put a sour apple martini down in front of her. Seireadan eyed the neon-green drink with suspicion.

"Not a real vodka fan," she told the bartender.

"From Romeo down there at the end of the bar," said the bartender. "I told him you were drinking the sangria, but he *insisted* on this."

"I see." Seireadan looked down the bar and saw a thin human man staring at her. He looked young, barely twenty-one by her guess, and he was hurrying to tuck in his shirt and smooth back his hair. Then he started to nervously twist the claddagh ring on his finger.

That one will have trouble taking no for an answer. Seireadan offered only the slightest nod and took a drink of her sangria, not wanting to encourage him at all.

Galen was pleased with the night's crowd, and the line outside the door was halfway down the block. As he got closer to the bar, he noticed Jimmy Boy fiddling with his clothes and then nervously twisting the ring that had belonged to his father. Looking down the bar, it didn't take long to see the very lovely Fae woman with the extra drink in front of her.

I give him credit for trying, but Jimmy will never land a woman like that. Not in this lifetime. Galen handed Tommy two bottles of rum to replace the ones that were running low.

"Don't get your hopes up, Jimmy. That one will disappoint you," he said.

"Screw you, Galen. You don't know that."

Galen slapped him on the back of the head, hard.

"Ow! Fuck, that hurt."

"Then watch your mouth when you talk to me."

Jimmy looked sullen. "I'm going to go talk to her."

"She's not interested," Galen told him.

"How do you know? She didn't send the drink back, did she? She didn't leave."

Galen knew there was no talking to the bull-headed young man. *You're an idiot. She hasn't sent it back, but she hasn't taken a sip, either. And she's deliberately not looking down here anymore.* In fact, based on her body language, Galen surmised she actually was getting ready to leave. Jimmy started to walk toward her, but Galen caught his arm.

"You're shit out of luck anyway because you have some things to take care of," Galen told him.

"Things? What things?" He tried to step around Galen, but Galen moved in front of him so Jimmy had to look up to see him.

"Things," Galen said with emphasis.

"Oh." Jimmy deflated a little. That meant Aohdan wanted something done. "What's up?"

"Apparently your last conversation with Dimitri about the importance of paying back a gambling debt wasn't persuasive enough. You need to have another discussion with him—a much more serious one."

"I'll take care of it tomorrow." Jimmy tried to look around Galen toward Seireadan.

"Now. You'll take care of it now," Galen said firmly.

"Jesus, fine. Yes, I'll fucking take care of it now." Jimmy rolled his eyes and stalked away from Galen, and on his way out, he stopped next to Seireadan. She glanced at him and took another drink of her sangria.

"Hey, beautiful. I'm Jimmy. Enjoy the martini. I have to take care of something important for my boss, but I'll be back. Then we can have a drink together." He gave her a wink and a smile and sauntered out of the club.

Seireadan was about to push away from the bar when a Fae man appeared next to her.

"I'd like to apologize if he bothered you, miss. I'm Galen Grey, the manager here. Jimmy's an employee, and not only should he not be bothering guests, he should also be gone for a couple hours. Please don't feel like you need to leave on his account. In fact . . . Tommy!" Galen called the bartender over. "If this young lady would like another drink, it's on the house."

"You got it, Mr. Grey." Tommy put a small red chip on the bar in front of Seireadan.

"Thank you," she said to both of them.

"My pleasure. If you need anything else, let Tommy know." Galen offered a polite nod and returned to his work.

CHAPTER 6

AOHDAN SLIPPED IN through the back door of Underworld and went to the office. His last client at Asmodeus had taken much longer than he'd anticipated. He'd considered going home since Oisin and Rory were still in Providence, but Galen and Kieran would certainly be up for a Saturday night of fun if he could get Galen to stop working long enough to enjoy it.

He waved at Kieran when he reached the main floor of the club, and as he wove through the crowd toward his regular table, he shook hands with and said hello to several people. There were, as always, a number of beautiful women on the dance floor. Galen was walking toward him when a sparkle at the bar caught his eye. A burly Pooka walked in front of him, and Aohdan stepped back for a better look. When his eyes landed on Seireadan, he nearly forgot to breathe.

His eye wandered over her elegant black heels and up her legs until they disappeared beneath a sequined dress, and then he followed the curve of her body until it vanished beneath a fall of glossy dark hair. There was an understated elegance and confidence about her as she turned slightly to look out at the dance floor, and he drank in her high cheekbones, her violet eyes, and the diamonds accenting her lovely tapered ear.

She's stunning.

"Aohdan?" Galen knew exactly whom his patriarch was staring at.

"Now that's what a Fae woman is all about."

"You aren't kidding. Jimmy Boy already took a run at her."

"Our Jimmy?" Aohdan laughed but never took his eyes off Seireadan. "He's got some balls, I'll give him that." *Too bad he doesn't have the brains to match.*

"She wasn't interested. I sent him to take care of a couple errands before she left on his account."

Aohdan didn't answer Galen, but rather excused himself and went to the bar. With a subtle gesture, he brought Tommy over. They talked for a minute and Aohdan slipped Tommy a fifty-dollar bill.

Seireadan raised her eyebrows at Tommy as he put another drink down in front of her. This one was the same sangria she'd been drinking plus a shot of whiskey, and she said, "I already had my on-the-house drink. And I didn't order a shot."

"From the gentleman—and not the same one as last time. The whiskey's the good stuff, too." Tommy grinned. That brought a smile to Seireadan's face, but when she looked down the bar she gasped softly. *Oh, shit. That's Aohdan Collins!*

Aohdan was well known in the city, especially within the Fae community, and Seireadan's breath hitched when she saw how intently he was watching her with his dark eyes, waiting for her reaction. Even from this distance, he radiated a raw masculinity and confidence. His dark hair brushed his shoulders, and a very neatly trimmed beard—in the Vandyke style, with the sides extending back just along his jawline—shadowed his face. It was cliché, but not only was he tall, dark, and handsome, but he also had that dangerous, bad-boy air about him that Seireadan found so irresistible.

She hesitated. She'd heard the gossip and the stories about Aohdan and the harem of women he left in his wake. Still, she raised the shot glass and smiled at him before downing the whiskey in a single gulp. She felt the burn slide down her throat as Aohdan walked toward her.

He moved confidently, completely self-assured, and when he reached her it took only a moment under his serious stare for the college kid in the seat next to her to take his beer and move elsewhere. Aohdan sat and leaned an elbow on the bar.

"Thank you for the drink." Seireadan took a sip of the new sangria and studied his face. He had high cheekbones and a generous smile.

"You're very welcome. I'm—"

"Oh, I know who you are," she interrupted with a laugh.

He smiled, too. "Oh, you do, do you? Tell me, then, who am I?"

"You're Aohdan Collins, and you're not just any Fae." She dropped her voice to a whisper. "You're the patriarch of the city."

Other than the slight widening of his eyes and the smallest twitch in his smile, Seireadan would have never known she had surprised him.

"Then you have me at a distinct disadvantage . . ."

"Seireadan. Seireadan Moore," she answered.

"Well, it is a pleasure to meet you, Seireadan." He held out his hand and she shook it, desperately trying to ignore the spark when their hands touched.

"Same." She smiled and sipped the sangria.

"Are you here with anyone? Friends?"

She smiled. "No, a long-overdue night out for myself." *Not smart telling him you're alone, Seireadan,* her pragmatic brain warned her. She ignored it.

"And what do you do, Seireadan?"

"Do you mean in the Fae world or here?" She gestured around at the teeming club.

"Both. Either." Aohdan took a drink of his beer and waited.

"I'm a web designer. I own Moore Creative Media. I also read tarot cards at Sacred Circle."

"A fortune-teller?" He grinned at her.

"I'm not just a fortune-teller; I'm a Raven," Seireadan said.

Aohdan tilted his head slightly and scrutinized her face. "A Raven? Then you *are* far more than just a fortune-teller."

Seireadan didn't answer, flustered inside by the intensity of Aohdan's gaze, by the desire clearly evident in his eyes, and she had to force herself to not stare back. Seireadan wet her lips, feeling hot and flushed under his scrutiny. They continued to talk, bantering about safe subjects like the club, the DJ, and why Seireadan was such a fan of the peach sangria. As they talked, they drew closer to each other, leaning in to catch subtle words.

If I don't leave now, I'm going to go home with him. Seireadan stood up from her chair and tucked her small clutch under her arm. Aohdan stood as well, a single fluid movement that kept him very close to her.

"Leaving? There's still plenty of night ahead of us, Seireadan. We could go somewhere more private." Aohdan slid his arm partly around her waist as he stepped a little closer. It was a bold move after so short a conversation. Seireadan took a deep breath, secretly delighted by his masculine confidence; he clearly was a man accustomed to getting whatever he wanted. The implication of a night filled with breathless, wanton sex hung between them.

Seireadan closed her eyes as her insides twisted, and she tightened her grip on her wine glass to keep her hand from shaking as she took the last swallow of sangria. For a moment, she thought the Sight was going to consume her, but it didn't.

Nonetheless, she couldn't shake the feeling that despite how badly she wanted to share a bed with Aohdan, being a one-night stand with him was a mistake.

Listen to your intuition; it's there for a reason. She repeated the lesson she'd learned from the Ravens: intuition was ignored at your own peril.

"No. I don't think so."

At the refusal, Aohdan stiffened.

I bet he doesn't hear that word very often. But Seireadan knew he could read her the same way she could read him. They both wanted each other; the chemistry between them was intense.

"Believe me, it is a very tempting offer, but waking up alone at your favorite hotel tomorrow to an empty bed and a hot breakfast? Not something I'm interested in." *Did I really just say that to him?*

"My favorite hotel?"

Seireadan forged ahead. "People talk, and I've heard them say that's where you take your women. A hotel, not your home. If I'm going to wake up alone, it's going to be in my own bed."

"If it is your own bed that you want . . ." He smiled at her.

"No, you're not coming to my place." She shook her head and laughed softly.

Clearly frustrated but undeterred, Aohdan pressed his suit. "I want to see you again. Will you come back to Underworld? Maybe we could have dinner?"

She looked at him through her thick eyelashes. "Maybe."

Having made short work of his errand, Jimmy Boy pushed through the Underworld crowd, jostling several people, including Kieran, who cursed at him. His face fell when he saw Aohdan having a very intimate conversation with the Fae woman he'd tried to impress. She laughed at something

Aohdan said, and Jimmy realized the sour apple martini was still on the bar, untouched.

Goddamn it. I saw her first. He's going to fuck my girl.

From behind him, Jimmy heard Kieran's voice. "Do no' feel too badly. She was out of your league anyway."

"I saw her first," Jimmy whined, sullen, as he turned back to watch Aohdan and Seireadan. His fists clenched when they stood and Aohdan pulled her closer. All Jimmy could think about was her naked in bed with Aohdan and not him. But then she walked away, leaving Aohdan standing by the bar.

"Look!" he crowed. "She's leaving . . . without him. The mighty Aohdan isn't going to get the girl tonight." Jimmy sauntered away, acting smug and somehow vindicated, but no one really paid attention. Kieran and Galen were much more interested in watching their patriarch, who still stood at the bar looking confounded. Aohdan waved down Tommy and got another shot of whiskey, which he downed in a swallow, and then he stared at the door as if willing Seireadan to walk back in. Abruptly, he turned away from the bar and headed back to the offices.

CHAPTER 7

A BEAM OF afternoon sun wandered through the window of Seireadan's home office as she tapped her finger absently on the desk. She squinted at the screen as if that would make whatever was bothering her about the design suddenly come into focus. It didn't work, and she rolled her shoulders to try to loosen them up. The office phone rang.

"Hello, this is Moore Creative Media. How may we help you?"

The voice on the other end was male. "Seireadan Moore, please."

"Speaking." She started to smile.

"Hi, Seireadan. It's Aohdan . . . from the club," he added when she didn't answer right away.

"Oh, I remember you, Aohdan-from-the-club."

Seireadan could hear the smile in his voice when Aohdan answered, "Good, I'm glad you remember. I really enjoyed talking to you. Maybe we could continue the conversation over dinner on Saturday?"

"I can make that work. What time?" She tried to ignore the thrill that raced through her.

"I'll come get you at six. Dinner at seven?"

"Perfect. Do you want my address, or would you prefer to track it down yourself?"

"Might be easier if you just told me." There was a rumble of humor in his voice.

Seireadan gave him her address, and they chatted about where they might go. After they hung up, Seireadan looked back at the screen and then elected to ignore it—daydreaming about Aohdan was far more appealing.

At 5:45 p.m. on Saturday, Seireadan glanced in the mirror again, checking the combs that held the sides of her thick hair back. *Enough! You'd think I'd never been on a date before. I need to pull my shit together.* While she hadn't had a serious boyfriend in a very long time, Seireadan hardly lived a cloistered life. Still, she couldn't remember ever being this nervous about a date. *And it isn't just because Aohdan is the patriarch. I like him. I hardly know him at all, but I really like him.*

Anticipating he'd be prompt, she went to the front door and pulled back the corner of the sheer curtain. Aohdan was halfway down the walkway, adjusting his tie. He stopped when Seireadan shut the door behind her and started down her steps. Her deep-blue dress slid along her curves, and to her satisfaction, his eyes rounded.

"You look amazing."

A blush tinged Seireadan's cheeks. In his tailored gray suit, Aohdan made her breath catch. "The same can be said for you." She took his offered arm, and Aohdan walked her to his sleek Audi RS7. He opened the passenger door for her.

They exchanged a few mild pleasantries on the way to the restaurant. The maître d' escorted them to a quiet table in the corner where they had an uninterrupted view of the city and the world beyond. They kept the conversation simple and light, mostly discussing her work at Moore Creative Media, as they waited for the rib eye steak and shrimp scampi to arrive.

Aohdan poured some more wine into her glass. "You're not like other Ravens that I've met."

"How so?"

He hesitated for a moment. "You have the confidence of one, but not the arrogance. To be honest, the few I've met have been either pretty standoffish or pretty conceited . . ." When she didn't answer immediately, Aohdan tried to recover. "But you're neither of those things. Do you know a Raven named Cavan?"

"Cavan's an ass." Seireadan's voice turned hard. "*Conceited* is the kindest thing I would say about him." As she watched Aohdan lean back a little in his chair, Seireadan realized how harsh her response had been. "I'm sorry. I shouldn't have reacted like that. Cavan and I have some unpleasant history."

"Then he is off-limits unless you want to talk about him. But I'm still curious: What's it like to be a Raven? Do you have the Sight often?"

Seireadan paused, her mouth set in a thoughtful line. "Often? Not really. That's probably the biggest misunderstanding about the Sight—that I can simply turn it off and on at will. I have no control over when I See something. I could See once a day for a week, and then not See anything for decades. Sometimes people will demand that I See something for them, and I can't. It just doesn't work that way."

"And there's no one thing that triggers it?"

Seireadan pushed her hair back over her ear, and the sapphire studs she wore sparkled. "No. It's completely random. I've had it happen after watching a child play in a sandbox, and I've had it happen before . . . large events." She hesitated for a moment. *I can't tell him about that first Seeing; he'd just dismiss it like everyone else has.* Seireadan hurried to speak again before

Aohdan could press her for any details about the "large events" she referred to.

"What makes it even harder is often the images are abstract or jumbled. It isn't like watching a movie. Images can layer over one another and be fuzzy, or small details might be emphasized. Then I need to figure out what it means, or at least what I think it means. Sometimes I can't even do that."

"It sounds like a bit of a pain in the ass." Aohdan smiled at her.

"You really have no idea." She laughed.

"Do you like having the Sight?"

Seireadan's brow furrowed a little more before she looked up and met his eyes. "No, I don't, actually. It's painful and confusing, and sometimes knowing what's going to happen to others is really hard."

Aohdan nodded and took a drink of his wine, becoming lost in his own thoughts. The silence lingered until she finally said, "There must be something quite fascinating in your wine."

Aohdan's cheeks colored slightly. "I'm so sorry, Seireadan. Lost in my thoughts for a moment."

Great, now I've made him self-conscious. Good job. "You said earlier you owned a tattoo shop?"

"Yes, Asmodeus Ink."

"I think that's awesome, but I have to say, if you can afford an Audi like yours on what you make running a studio, I'm in the wrong line of work."

Seireadan realized what she was saying a fraction of a second too late, and her heart jumped into her throat. *For the love of . . . You're out with the patriarch of the city and you make a wiseass comment about where his money comes from? Now* that's *how you ruin a date.* Her eyes rounded as she watched his face darken, and she put her hands in her lap so Aohdan wouldn't see them tremble.

"I've offended you."

"No, not at all. I've just had a lot of people make digs about where my money comes from. The sour face is for them, not you. Asmodeus does very well for me, but I've also made some good investments—not just stocks, but clubs like Underworld, restaurants, things like that. I do dabble in other businesses."

Aohdan didn't elaborate on the other businesses, and Seireadan didn't ask. *I've put my foot in my mouth once. Not going to do it twice.*

"But of all my businesses, Asmodeus is my favorite."

Seireadan brightened a little, happy to move the conversation along. "I'm sure you've done lots of different pieces, but is there one tattoo that stands out to you? That's special?"

"Not sure I can pick one." He pondered for a moment. "If I had to, it would be a full chest piece I did to cover a woman's mastectomy scars. When she came to me, she told me she wanted something beautiful there again so she wouldn't think about what she'd lost. She wanted a bird of paradise surrounded by vines and leaves. We put flowers and butterflies in the greenery to get some color in there, but the bird was the focus."

"It must have looked amazing."

"Her sister cried when she saw it. She cried when she saw it. She told me it completely changed how she felt about her body." He had a distant look in his eye as he talked.

"That's wonderful you can help like that. How many tattoos do you have?" She'd seen the edges of a few when they were at Underworld.

"Quite a few. Mostly on my arms, back, and chest." He drank the last of the merlot in his glass and gave her a cheeky grin as he leaned forward a little. "And what about you? Any ink?"

"Some. Two raven feathers." She met his eyes and matched his grin.

"Really? I can't wait to see them."

She swallowed the sip she'd taken of her wine and laughed. "We'll see about that."

They talked for another hour, the conversation growing more comfortable and relaxed with each passing minute. By the time Aohdan paid the check, they were the last ones in the restaurant and it was nearly midnight. The kitchen had closed, but the manager—helped by an extremely generous tip from Aohdan—didn't see the need to kick them out. When they finally did walk to the car, Seireadan was nearly doubled over with laughter as Aohdan regaled her with stories of the trouble he and Oisin had gotten into as youngsters.

Standing at her front door, Seireadan said, "I had a really good time tonight. Thank you."

"I did, too." Aohdan moved ever so slightly closer, resting a hand softly on Seireadan's waist, and closed his eyes as she ran a hand up his arm. When he opened them, Aohdan let his eyes search her face, glad she didn't seem intimidated by his hungry gaze.

Leaning closer, he let the prospect of a kiss linger between them until Seireadan tilted her head up to brush her lips against his. The kiss started softly, but quickly turned more passionate, and as he felt her mouth yield to his, Aohdan pulled her even closer. He let one hand roam over her back from her waist up to the nape of her neck, and then moved his head to the side and kissed her neck, the sound of her breath catch spurring him on. A groan rumbled in his chest when she tangled her fingers in his hair, and he covered her mouth with his again.

"Continue this inside?" he asked, relaxing his arm just enough to move his hand to her elbow and steer her toward the door.

"Not tonight." Seireadan put her hand flat on his chest, stopping the step forward he was about to take.

No? This was the second time she'd refused him. *No* wasn't a word Aohdan often heard, and he didn't care for it one bit. For a moment, the tight leash on his frustration slipped and his grip on her elbow tightened. The instant Seireadan felt the pressure, her entire demeanor changed. Her body stiffened, immediately on alert, and her expression darkened.

Aohdan let go as soon as it happened. The realization that Seireadan wasn't going to let him just do what he pleased made her even more attractive, but it also served as a stern rebuke for the patriarch. Despite all his power, he didn't own the world, and he certainly didn't own this confounding Fae woman. *And the fastest way to lose her will be trying to control her.* He felt her relax as soon as he gave her some space.

"Just because you bought me dinner doesn't mean I'm going to jump in the sack with you, Mr. Collins." Her voice was frosty.

Despite his deep disappointment and frustration, Aohdan smiled. The skin at the corners of his eyes crinkled. "I am not sure what to make of you . . . Miss Moore."

"Then maybe you should spend a little time figuring me out. Call me." Seireadan gave him a quick, unexpected kiss and disappeared into her apartment before he could say anything else.

Inside, Seireadan leaned back against the door. It had been so tempting to say yes when she was pressed up against him, and her mind rifled through all the things she wanted to do with him, to him. A primal part of her brain screamed at her to abandon her reservations, to call Aohdan back, to take him to bed immediately. He was all lean muscle and fire, and she pressed her fingers to her lips. After another moment, she heard Aohdan's footsteps disappear down her stairs.

I can't believe I sent him away. Am I completely insane? People don't say no to Aohdan Collins. He's the patriarch of Boston. The patriarch!

If the news headlines were true, that meant Aohdan was not exactly a law-abiding citizen of the city. Surprisingly, she didn't really care what the headlines said or about the rumors that swirled around Aohdan's businesses—or even about his reputation as a playboy. What did worry her, however, was the possibility Aohdan wouldn't call her again.

CHAPTER 8

SEIREADAN HUMMED TO herself as she put out the new shipment of crystals at Sacred Circle. She loved the textures of the different stones in her hand. She adjusted a moonstone on its Lucite stand, frowned, and then moved it to the side, where it picked up more of the light. A sphere of labradorite went next to it, the iridescent gray bands giving it a mysterious sparkle.

"You're humming," said Julia. She put another box down next to Seireadan.

"Am I?"

"So, who is he?"

"What are you talking about?" Seireadan kept her eyes on the crystals in front of her.

"You don't fool me, Seireadan. The only reason I've ever known a woman to hum like that is when she's got a man on her mind. Who is he?"

"Someone I met recently. We went out last night," said Seireadan, unable to repress a smile.

"And it went well, I take it."

"It did. I hope we can go out again. I told him to call me." Seireadan put the rose quartz pyramid on one of the lower shelves. *What if he doesn't call?*

"Have you done a reading about him?" asked Julia.

"No, I never read for myself. You know that. Too much opportunity for me to interpret the cards the way I want."

"Do you want me to do one for you?"

Seireadan stopped unwrapping the sphere in her hand and thought for a long moment. "No, not right now, but thank you for the offer. I want to just let this develop on its own."

"As you wish. You really like him, don't you?"

Seireadan looked up. Julia's smile was warm, and there was mischief in the older woman's gray eyes.

"Yes, I do."

"I heard a hesitation there."

"We've only just met," said Seireadan. "We hardly know each other, and he's got some baggage."

"Oh, sweetie. We *all* have baggage. But bring him by the shop sometime and I'll give him the once-over. Make sure he meets with my approval." The door to the shop opened, and Julia turned to help the new customer.

Seireadan put the obsidian crystal on the shelf next to the three different-sized ocean jasper samples. *I'm not entirely sure he's going to meet with your approval, Julia. Not sure at all.* But Seireadan's concerns vanished as she started to daydream about Aohdan.

Several hours later, on the other side of the city, Galen—tumbler of Glenlivet in hand—walked into the back office at Underworld in time to hear Aohdan mutter something under his breath as he tossed his phone on the desk.

"He's going to be a real pain in the ass," growled Aohdan.

"You mean Crogher?"

"Yes. The little bastard thinks he's saying all the right things, but he's a lying little weasel."

Galen couldn't disagree with that. Crogher was notoriously selfish and shortsighted, and Aohdan's second had heard of more than one time when Crogher had backed out of deals or changed terms at the last second. And his mercurial temper didn't add anything good to his reputation. One way or another, Crogher was going to be a problem.

"If Crogher becomes Providence's next patriarch, he's going to want to make a name for himself." Galen took another sip of whiskey before he continued. "And what better way than taking out the patriarch of Boston? Although, I find it hard to believe he'd have balls quite that big."

"Sometimes you don't need balls if you're just stupid," answered Aohdan.

"What do you propose?"

"It would be expedient for him to have an accident, but Baibin's been a friend for many years, and he is her last remaining child. I thought proposing to merge our *fréamhacha agus brainsí* would be a way to avoid any extreme action."

"You'll also need to think about the Conclave."

"I need to worry about Baibin first; she very much adheres to the old ways," said Aohdan.

"Everything in your proposal was proper," said Galen. "I don't see how she could take offense to it, although clearly her son has. If she doesn't accept, that will just embolden him, and you'll be in a position of having to take control of Providence by force after she passes." Galen downed the last sip of whiskey and put the glass on the desk.

Force isn't the way to take care of this if we can avoid it. "Force is a last resort. Too much blood, too many bodies, and too much resentment. Plus, nothing makes the cops pay attention more than a turf war." Aohdan brooded for a moment, turning over in his mind what to do with Baibin's son. *Nothing to decide yet, not until he shows his hand.*

They moved the conversation from Providence and Crogher to other business before they each turned to their own work. Eventually, Aohdan picked up his phone. It rang twice before he heard Seireadan's voice.

"Hi. It's me," he said.

"Hi, Aohdan."

"Are you busy on Friday night? We could have dinner again . . ."

"I'd like that."

Her agreement—or maybe it was just the sound of Seireadan's voice—made Aohdan's smile widen. "Great. I'll pick you up at seven."

"I'm looking forward to it. See you then."

"Definitely."

"Same woman from the other night?" Galen asked once Aohdan ended the call.

"Yes. Seireadan."

"You don't usually try again if you get shot down."

"I don't usually get shot down."

"Very true. So why take another swing?"

An odd smile crossed Aohdan's face. His entire body tightened as he remembered the pull he felt when he first spotted Seireadan in the bar, the anticipation that tore through him when he'd touched her hand. "This one . . . This one's special."

"Why?"

"I don't know yet."

Aohdan didn't say anything else after that. Galen might have been one of his most trusted friends, but he wasn't even certain himself what made Seireadan so different, and if he didn't understand it, he wasn't going to bother trying to explain it to Galen. *How do I explain that jolt simply from hearing her voice? The first time I saw her, I thought it was lust, pure and simple, but it isn't just that. She's a kindred spirit—I can feel it—and I have to find out more.*

CHAPTER 9

ON FRIDAY NIGHT, Underworld was packed. Galen had managed to book an up-and-coming local band called Dovetail to play three separate weekend shows throughout the summer and fall. He tapped his foot absently to the beat as he watched the crowd. The band wrapped up the song and promised the enthusiastic crowd they'd be back after a short break. Galen took several bottles of beer and headed over to the VIP table where the rest of Aohdan's captains were hanging out, along with a human man.

"Chris. Good to see you. When did you get back?" asked Galen. "How's your grandmother doing?"

Galen gave him a quick appraising glance. Chris Cervenka had started out running errands and being a lookout when he was nine years old, and over the next fifteen years had worked his way up in the organization, earning both Aohdan's trust and respect during a time when the patriarch was actively weeding out threats and opposition from other crime organizations in the city.

Some days it seems like he went from boy to man overnight. Galen still struggled sometimes with how short human lifespans were compared to Fae ones. "She's doing much better, thanks. I flew in a few hours ago. Is the boss around? I wanted to talk to him."

"Nope, boss man's on a date," said Oisin with a smirk.

"Date? Yeah, sure. He's just chasing a piece of ass," snorted Rory.

For the next twenty minutes they bantered and joked, toasted and debated. Oisin was lounging in his chair when he suddenly sat up a little straighter. "I don't fucking believe it."

"What?" Galen glanced around but didn't see any immediate issue.

"Look." Oisin started to point but then thought better of it. "Aohdan's here and he's alone."

Aohdan saw them all staring at him as he threaded his way through the crowd to the table. Flopping down in a seat, he put his foot up on the low table without saying hello. He flagged down Muriel and said, "Get me a whiskey, a double. I need more than one friggin' drink tonight."

"I'll bring it right over." Muriel disappeared into the crowd.

"She didn't put out, aye?" asked Oisin.

Because they were childhood friends, Aohdan only gave him a dirty look in response to the comment.

Galen was more tactful. "So, the date didn't go well?"

Aohdan didn't answer right away as Muriel brought his whiskey, which he drank in a single swallow. After letting the alcohol burn his throat and pool in his stomach, he took a deep breath.

"The date was great. We went to Marcello's, best table in the restaurant. We had a great time. She's easy to talk to, and certainly not afraid to speak her mind. Then we went out to a show at Laugh Factory. Kid headlining was excellent. Very, very funny." Aohdan picked up his empty shot glass and waved it at Muriel so she'd bring him a refill.

"And then?" prompted Oisin.

"Then I took her back to her apartment . . ."

"Not the Intercontinental?" asked Chris.

Aohdan blinked for a moment. He'd been so focused on his date with Seireadan he hadn't really paid full attention to who was at the table.

"Chris! You're back. How is everything in Chicago? Your grandmother?"

"She's going to be fine, and came home from the hospital yesterday. I wanted to thank you for helping us."

"Family's important." Aohdan drank his second double of whiskey before he continued. "To answer your question, Chris, when I first met Seireadan, she made it clear she wasn't going to get taken back to a hotel and left to wake up alone. So, after the comedy show we went back to her place and I walked her to the door—"

"Such a gentleman." Rory laughed.

"Shut up, you dick. We started kissing and she was into it—and shit, can she kiss." Aohdan shook his head. Just thinking about kissing Seireadan, running his hands over her body, made him feel hot and flushed.

"And?" asked Oisin.

"And then she sent me home." Aohdan ran a hand over his face, clearly baffled.

"Seriously? Fuck that," said Rory cavalierly. "You don't need that, Aohdan. There are plenty of beautiful women here tonight who would line up and beg you to fuck them. If this bitch doesn't want to play, screw her. Ditch her and move on."

Glasses crashed to the floor, spraying a few people at the table with spilled beer and whiskey, as Aohdan surged out of his chair. He grabbed Rory by the shirt and dragged him halfway across the table. Everyone else backed up as Aohdan got right in his captain's face.

"I don't want just anyone; I want Seireadan. Just because she isn't easy doesn't mean she's not worth the effort. Maybe it's nice to be around a woman with a little self-respect for a change. I think of you as a friend, Rory, so I'll warn you this once: don't ever call her a bitch again."

He pushed Rory, and his captain stumbled back into his seat. Seemingly out of thin air, a busboy appeared and started cleaning up the drinks and glass as if nothing had happened.

"Shit, Aohdan. I was just playing around." Rory readjusted and smoothed his shirt.

"Well, I'm not." Aohdan lapsed into a brooding silence.

Not long after, Oisin and Rory disappeared into the crowd to pursue two flirtatious Selkie women. Aohdan glanced at Galen, who had a faraway look. He knew his second had something on his mind, but he was content to wait; Galen was probably the most circumspect of his captains. Aohdan always appreciated the thought his second put into any comments he made, unlike Oisin, who had no real filter and was liable to blurt out the first thing he thought, regardless of what it was.

"I got some information today," Galen said finally, "from one of my contacts in Boston PD."

"Am I going to need another drink when I hear this?"

"Probably. And it's probably best we talk in the office."

Balls. Just once, I'd like for a week to go by without something going sideways. Aohdan stood up. "Chris, I'm expecting something from Greer. He should be here in a few minutes. Back door. Get the package from him and bring it to the office."

"Sure thing." Chris took his beer, and Aohdan and Galen followed him down the hall.

In the office, Aohdan leaned back on his desk, arms folded. "So what's the bad news?" he asked his second.

Galen didn't dissemble. "Skiffle's been talking to the cops."

"Fuck me," Aohdan cursed. "That rat-faced little bastard."

"They promised him some protection if he'd come clean about who mangled his hand."

Aohdan's face hardened. "Has he talked to them yet?"

"No, he called them from out of town. His cousin's house out near Albany. He's going to meet the cops on Monday."

"Son of a bitch," Aohdan cursed. Putting the palms of his hands on the desk, the patriarch shook his head and looked up sharply at the knock on the doorframe.

"Sorry, am I interrupting?" Chris asked.

"No, come in."

"Greer just brought this." Chris handed Aohdan the package and turned to leave.

"Stay." It was an order. A polite one, but an order nonetheless. Aohdan studied him, pleased that Chris didn't seem overly concerned by the pointed attention.

"Something you need me to do?" Chis asked, glancing between Aohdan and Galen.

"Yes, but before that—Galen, can you ward tonight?" Aohdan asked.

Aohdan hated to ask Galen to use his magic. Before the Desolation, most faeries had some capacity for magic. Some could cast only the smallest of glamours, designed to change one's appearance, while others had the ability to work great feats of magic. The Desolation itself was the result of a spell gone horribly wrong. But the Desolation disrupted the fabric of the natural universe, and now, very few faeries could use their magic without enduring significant physical pain or exhausting themselves.

Galen had somehow managed to retain some magical ability, and his spell allowed Aohdan some privacy that no one could penetrate. He used it when he wanted to discuss his most sensitive business decisions, to make sure there were no eavesdroppers, but it always came at a price for Galen.

"Yes." The second sat down and closed his eyes, and his lips began to move as he murmured the words of a spell. As soon as the first few were spoken, Galen started to breathe harder, sweat beading on his upper lip. Spells like this were routine before the Desolation destroyed the Faerie realm; now, for the few faeries who could still wield magic, casting spells was a dangerous and usually painful proposition. And the more sophisticated the spell, the greater the chance the power would maim, or even kill, the caster in the process.

Galen grimaced harder and leaned forward in the chair as a quartz crystal in one corner of the room began to glow and a stream of light raced across the floor to another crystal, and then another, until the perimeter of the room was connected by a band of glowing light. When the final connection was made, there was a sudden, eerie silence as every outside noise was shut out. Galen relaxed slightly, but his forehead was still creased and his mouth pinched. He nodded to Aohdan.

"No one can hear us," Galen confirmed through clenched teeth.

"There is something I need you to do, Chris," Aohdan said. "Skiffle's big mouth is going to create some big problems. I want you to handle it."

Chris's eyes widened slightly. In Aohdan's lexicon, to "handle" something meant to take care of it—permanently. He nodded and asked, "Are you sending a message? Or does the problem just need to go away?"

"Just needs to go away. As tempted as I am to make an example out of him, it would be more trouble than it's worth. It needs to be done before Monday morning."

"Whatever you need," Chris said.

"Good man." Aohdan looked over his shoulder at Galen. "We're good."

With another whispered word, Galen released the spell and the glow disappeared. While all of the outside noises rushed back in, Galen put his head between his knees and tried not to throw up.

On Monday morning, Skiffle was at the bottom of a lake in Maine and his police contact was waiting at a Dunkin' Donuts in Mattapan for a complaining witness who would never show up.

CHAPTER 10

SEIREADAN WAS STARING at her computer screen critically, as she absently caught her lower lip in her teeth. *Something's not quite right.* She let her eyes travel the screen, looking for whatever was nagging at her on the nearly finished home page, and let out an aggravated sigh. Aohdan had called her on Monday to let her know he'd be out of town for a few days, and then, to her surprise, had hired her to revise the Asmodeus Ink website.

She got up and went to the kitchen. Rather than dirty a glass, she stuck her head under the faucet for some water.

Back in her office, Seireadan picked up her phone and tapped out a quick text message to Aohdan: Flight go OK? She was surprised when a text came back immediately.

Meeting in Providence ran late. Had to get different flight down to Philly. Should still be back Saturday morning.

Good. You busy that night?

Hopefully with you, beautiful.

I bet. Pick me up @7:30. Don't dress all fancy.

OK. What are you doing up? It's late.

Working.

At this hour? On what?

Some guy gave me an unreasonable deadline to revise the site for his tattoo shop.

Funny girl.

Why are you still up?

Just got to hotel. Was about to shower when you texted.

Seireadan paused, images of what Aohdan would look like naked, with water running over his broad shoulders and tight abs, flooding her head. She closed her eyes as her body tightened with anticipation and barefaced desire. There was no question about it: she wanted Aohdan Collins in her arms and in her bed. *So why am I being so stubborn about it? I've proved my point that I'm not some random hookup.*

Her phone chimed again with another text. You still there? Or too distracted imagining me naked?

Seireadan turned scarlet.

Wiseass. Go to bed.

Sweet dreams, beautiful. See you soon.

Seireadan stared at her computer screen for another five minutes before she saved and shut down. After that conversation, there was no way she was going to get any work done until morning. Once she climbed into bed, she lay awake, thinking about Aohdan and wishing he were there with her.

Much later, she started to twist restlessly. As her breathing increased, Seireadan's fingers flexed, clutching the sheets, and her head rolled on the pillow. The vivid, sharp dream tore at her with images of fire and hot wind, cruel voices, and terrifying, ice-filled eyes that turned to look directly at her. With a scream, she bolted out of her bed, her stomach roiling.

Over the years, the Sight had brought her only a few images of the Alabaster Man she so desperately wanted to punish. This dream, while vivid, hadn't left her with the splitting headache that accompanied the Sight, but the memory of those eyes turning on her still left Seireadan cold. In the bathroom, she splashed a little water on her face and glanced back into the bedroom. The clock read four thirty in the morning.

"Well, no getting back to sleep now. May as well get a little work done before I'm due at Sacred Circle."

Seireadan actually accomplished more than she'd expected on the new Asmodeus Ink site and emailed Aohdan a link to the test site. After a short run and a long shower, she got to Sacred Circle a few minutes before her first appointment. Seireadan had three readings in quick succession and then a break. Leaning on the counter near the register, she browsed some of the earrings Julia had out on display. Julia leaned back in her chair and put her feet up on the edge of the counter, quietly shuffling her own custom blended deck of tarot and oracle cards.

"Careful you don't fall over," Seireadan cautioned.

"Seen your honey lately?" Julia asked.

"No, he's in Philadelphia on business."

"But things are going well?"

Seireadan smiled. "Yes, they are. We're going out again when he gets back."

"So are you ever going to tell me his name?"

That brought Seireadan up short. "What do you mean?"

"What do I mean? You've talked about him several times, but you've yet to mention his name at all. Why is that?" Without waiting for an answer, Julia handed Seireadan the card deck. "Shuffle."

Seireadan hesitated, but then did as she was told and handed the cards back. Julia peeled the top three off and put them down on the counter: Knight of Cups, Hermit, and King of Swords.

"Well, then," Julia mused. "Your young man is certainly occupying your thoughts. But as much as he brings excitement and romance, he's bringing you introspection, soul-searching. You very much need to have clear thinking around him."

"You are; as always, very accurate," said Seireadan. "And his name is Aohdan. Aohdan Collins."

One of Julia's eyebrows arched, and she pulled out one more card, an oracle card that showed three closed doors: one wood, one metal, and one stone. "He'll be a doorway for you, Seireadan. But a doorway to *what* remains to be seen."

Promptly at seven thirty on Saturday night, there was a knock on Seireadan's apartment door. She opened it and smiled. Aohdan looked relaxed, casual, and infinitely sexy. His shirt fit snugly over his broad chest and arms, and Seireadan was tempted to have him turn around so she could admire his backside in those faded jeans. In that instant, all she wanted to do was drag him inside and get him out of those clothes.

"Am I unfancy enough?" he asked.

"You look perfect. Come in, have a seat. I just need to grab my boots out of the other room."

It was the first time she'd let Aohdan past the front door, and he looked around as he sat. The kitchen was small but welcoming, with a circular table in the center and counters along two of the walls. There were a few dishes piled in the sink, and the window above it sported a sheer white curtain. A small vase filled with flowers rested in the center of the table. Off the kitchen was a cozy living room with a sofa, chair, and large television.

"Where are we going tonight?" he asked.

"You'll see," Seireadan called from the bedroom, where she was staring at herself in the mirror. She had on an unbuttoned white shirt with the sleeves rolled up over a rich blue tank top. Her slim black jeans hugged her hips and legs down to the ankle boots she'd just pulled on.

When she came back out into the kitchen, she said, "Ready?"

"More than ready." Aohdan let his eyes roam over her. Unable to resist, he pulled her in for a kiss and groaned as he felt Seireadan's body press against his. Her lips parted, welcoming his kiss and responding in kind. A moment later, he gently pulled back.

"I missed you," he said.

"I missed you, too."

"And I've been looking forward to tonight, so lead on—I'm in your capable hands."

They went to Viga, Seireadan's favorite pizza place in the city. The original location on Stuart Street wasn't typically open late, but they'd recently added a second location that catered to more of a dinner crowd. Aohdan managed to snag them a table, and when Seireadan brought the box to the table and opened it, the savory aroma of the four-cheese white pizza surrounded them both. Once they were finished, she slipped her arm through his as they strolled along the sidewalk.

"Where are we off to now?"

"We're going to the movies," said Seireadan. "Two choices. We can either see the new asteroid-destroys-the-planet action flick, *Launch Sequence*. Or we can see *Voices*. That's a comedy. Your choice."

"Okay." Aohdan pretended to seriously mull the choices over. "I think I'd rather see *Voices*. I'm up for a good laugh."

They took the scenic route to the theater, walking through the Public Garden on the way to Boston Common. The night was clear and warm, and the winding roads took them through lush landscaping, around ponds that reflected the evening lights of the city, and past giant weeping willow trees with their bulky, gnarled roots trailing down into the earth. She stopped on a bridge that arched over a small, undulating pond and leaned on the railing.

"Can I ask you something?"

"Of course," said Aohdan.

She looked out at the water. Dots of light from the streetlamps skipped across the ripples on the water's surface, and Seireadan tried to track them as she wondered whether or not she really wanted to ask her questions.

"Seireadan?" Aohdan leaned on the rail, too, his forehead creased with concern.

"Are you Prince Faolan's son?"

"Where did you hear that?" Aohdan's knuckles whitened on the metal top rail.

"I was looking for some background information for the Asmodeus site. I think the bios of all the artists could tell much better stories, so I was browsing around Google before I started asking for information," she answered.

Aohdan was quiet for a long time, but finally he said, "I don't talk about my father very much, but yes, I am Faolan's son."

"Which means Fionvarr—the Seelie king—is your uncle," said Seireadan, hoping Aohdan couldn't tell her heart was racing. *Aohdan is a prince of the Court—he might know who the Alabaster Man is!* Her moment of hope was wrecked as abruptly as it appeared when another thought blasted through her mind. *Shit, what if he's friends with the Alabaster Man? Related to him?*

Aohdan touched her elbow, and she flinched. "Seireadan, why do you want to know? Does it matter?"

"No." She felt a pang of guilt at the white lie. "It just made me curious."

"I have little use for the Seelie Court." Aohdan's voice turned dismissive. "When Faerie was decimated and we realized we could never go back again, Fionvarr failed us. Rather than lead or be decisive, he retreated into a shell, and he's stayed there for over five hundred years."

"Given what . . . ," Seireadan started to say, but she stopped as she suddenly realized that Luan, the Fae who had unleashed the spell—the spell that destroyed her entire world, destroyed the entire Faerie realm—was Aohdan's uncle.

"You can say it. My uncle, in his jealousy and hate, destroyed Faerie. I'm not saying Fionvarr had no right to mourn, but eventually life goes on. He's sunk into a morass of grief and regret, allowing others to rule in his name while the Court just hovers around, impotent, waiting for their king to lead them. They cling to the old ways, and those ways no longer serve us in this world." Aohdan fell silent, but Seireadan knew he still had more to say.

"The Court thinks we just have to go on as we always did," he said, "but this world . . . this isn't ours, not really—we're interlopers and we have to change, to adapt, if we're truly going to survive here. I got tired of watching them rot from the inside and decided to make my own way, my own life. This world is what I make of it, and frankly, I won't have them—any of them—dictate how I live my life. I will not serve a man I do not respect. In that one way, I am my father's son."

Seireadan's voice was soft. "Thank you. I know that was a very personal question."

Aohdan slid his arm around her waist and pulled her closer before giving her a soft kiss. "You can ask me anything, Seireadan. I can't promise you'll always like what I have to say, but I will answer. I don't want any secrets between us."

Secrets. Seireadan thought about her Alabaster Man and the sword—Claíomh Solais—hidden in the recesses of her closet, and quickly said, "We should go; otherwise we'll be late for the movie."

Seireadan had always liked the area around the Loews Theater on Tremont Street. Adjacent to Boston Common, it wasn't far from Emerson College, and she enjoyed the students with their outlandish ideas of what made each of them unique. There was always something interesting to see. Aohdan tried to buy the movie tickets, but Seireadan put a stop to that, reminding him that the date was her treat. He acquiesced after a brief discussion, and once they were inside, Seireadan bought a bag of gummy bears, and they found two seats near the back and settled in. Seireadan ripped open the gummy bear bag and popped a couple into her mouth. She was barely done chewing when she had a few more.

"You're clearly a gummy bear junkie."

Her chewing slowed and she glanced at Aohdan out of the corner of her eye. "Uh-huh," she said around some half-chewed candy.

"May I have one?"

"Maybe."

"Come on," he cajoled. "You know you want to share."

Seireadan sighed, looked at the bag, looked at Aohdan, and then looked into space. Aohdan shifted in his seat and rested a hand lightly on Seireadan's thigh. As he started to move his thumb in a gentle circle, she closed her eyes. *That feels way too good. I'm never going to be able to pay attention to the movie.* She held the bag of candy open for him, and Aohdan took a few out.

"Thank you," he said and gave her leg a squeeze. The lights dimmed as the screen lit up for the coming attractions reel.

As the movie progressed, Seireadan found she was smiling as Aohdan laughed out loud at several of the scenes. Just seeing him relax and enjoy himself made the date a success as far as she was concerned. She started to run her fingers along his leg. He stilled and sat up a little straighter. He may have kept looking at the screen, but the glance she caught from him and the grin on his face told her he didn't object in the slightest. He put his arm around her shoulder, pulling her a little closer to him while she continued to feather her fingers on his thigh.

After the movie, Aohdan put his arm around Seireadan as they walked outside. She slowed and turned to face him when his hand moved to her waist. She looked up through her lashes, her expression a little coy.

"I'm glad you liked the movie," she said.

"I loved it." Aohdan brought his hands up to cup her face, and held it gently so she couldn't look away. As they stared at each other, people walking along the sidewalk parted and went around them, like water flowing around rocks.

"Aohdan . . ." She'd wanted so badly to kiss him during the movie; it had almost been physically painful.

"Kiss me," he said and dropped his head down until their lips met. It started softly, but Seireadan responded by kissing him harder, with more passion. So consumed with the kiss, they practically forgot where they were until someone wolf-whistled at them.

"What's next on the agenda?" asked Aohdan, laughing.

I am so done with playing hard to get. "Well, I had a couple things in mind, but now? I think I've changed my mind." Seireadan's lips were still tingling from the kiss, and a smile spread across her face as she watched Aohdan try to read her expression.

Seireadan stretched up so her lips were next to Aohdan's ear when she whispered, "We're going to go back to my apartment and get naked."

Aohdan's knees nearly buckled. "You're sure?"

She gave him a lingering kiss, catching his lower lip between her teeth for a moment, and ran a single finger down the front of his shirt. "You have no idea how sure."

His hand shot up in the air. "TAXI!"

Aohdan's heart nearly stopped when Seireadan said she wanted to go back to her place. As they climbed into the cab, she gave the driver her address, and before they'd even pulled away from the curb, Aohdan had drawn Seireadan into his arms again, kissing her fiercely. With a glance in the rearview mirror, the cabbie just shook his head as Seireadan twisted and straddled Aohdan. Tangling his fingers in her long hair, he drank in her face, nearly losing himself in her deep violet eyes.

"I've wanted you from the very first time I saw you. You're all I think about," he whispered.

"I know. It's the same for me."

He let go of her hair as she leaned forward. The long, slow kiss made him ache, and he ran his hands up her sides and lightly over her breasts. His hips moved involuntarily when he felt the rise of her nipple through the tank top, and he groaned softly. She shifted in his lap and he gripped her hips, fighting to regain a modicum of control over himself. *Otherwise I'm going to strip you down right here in this cab.*

"Why tonight?" he said softly. "Not that I'm complaining." He kissed the base of her throat while he waited for an answer.

"Because I'm tired of waiting," she finally said.

"And you're not afraid I'm never going to call again?" He brushed his fingers over her breasts again, relishing how she responded when he traced a finger around her nipple. She tightened her thighs, and all Aohdan could think about was how that would feel while he was buried inside her.

"I'm ready to take the chance. You might not, but I think you will." She ran her fingers down his chest, tracing the outline of his muscles and feeling them clench under her touch.

At her apartment, Aohdan practically threw the fare and tip to the cabbie before he and Seireadan stumbled their way up her front steps, unable to keep their hands off each other. She untangled herself long enough to unlock the door and let them in. Aohdan flicked one of the light switches and nothing happened.

"Oh, that switch is broken," Seireadan said. "I keep meaning to get that fixed."

"Put a light on—I want to see you," Aohdan said.

Seireadan flipped on the kitchen light and came back to Aohdan. She hooked her thumbs into the waist of his jeans. "Now, where were we?"

"We were done wasting time," he said. With no additional preamble, he pulled his T-shirt up and over his head and tossed it on the kitchen floor. He watched Seireadan as she drank him in. Lean, fit, and muscular, Aohdan watched Seireadan look at his body, his tattoos, and all he saw in her eyes was want. He reached out and pushed her button-down shirt over her shoulders, and she shook her arms to toss it away.

As he kissed and gently nipped the area where her neck and shoulder met, she whispered, "You'll have to tell me the stories behind the ink . . ."

"Later." Aohdan tugged at her tank top, pulled the waistband of her jeans, and ran his hands underneath. Sliding them along the smooth curve of her body, he started to work the shirt higher. Seireadan raised her arms, but rather than yank, Aohdan moved the material slowly, savoring every inch of bare skin that was revealed until Seireadan stood in front of him in her black bra and slim jeans. Her hair was messy and she took a few steps back. Slowly she pulled one bra strap off her shoulder and let it hang down her arm, and then she reached across and pulled the other one down. Aohdan shifted, his jeans painfully tight.

"I think we'd be much more comfortable in the bedroom." She strolled down the hall, and when she reached the bedroom door, Seireadan looked back over her shoulder. "You going to come or not?"

The laughter in her voice said she was completely aware of the double entendre, and Aohdan answered by covering the distance between them in a heartbeat, pulling her to him and then pressing her back against the bedroom wall. She smelled spicy, like there was a touch of cinnamon on her skin, and he kissed her throat and shoulders. He was on fire, and the sensual moan that escaped Seireadan's lips as he pushed against her just drove him closer to the edge.

"You are so beautiful," he murmured.

She put her lips to his ear. "You know what else I am?"

"What?"

"I am so ready for you . . ."

Aohdan made a strangled noise as his entire body responded to her words, savoring the fact that she had no hesitation to express herself. Without breaking eye contact, he hooked his fingers into her jeans, unbuttoned them, and pulled the sides apart, forcing the zipper down. She shifted her hips from side to side, but Aohdan grabbed her wrists and shook his head.

"Wait," he said.

Wait? He's got to be kidding me. The irony of waiting for him now was not lost on Seireadan. She acquiesced and put her hands on top of her head as Aohdan traced a single finger along the elastic of her panties before letting his hands travel up again to trace the edges of her bra. He tugged it, drawing the cups down. Exposed, Seireadan moaned, dropping her hands down so she could tangle her fingers in his dark hair as he lowered his head to run his tongue over her skin until she was breathless.

Seireadan had never wanted a man as much as she wanted Aohdan. His fingers and lips on her skin were intoxicating. She whispered his name as he tugged the sides of her jeans down a few more inches. He slid his hand inside the pants to cup her, and she pushed against him, eager for more and unwilling to be put off. He pushed his fingers past the edge of her panties, and a moan of desire rumbled through him when he felt how wet and ready she was. All Seireadan could do was gasp and let her head fall forward onto his shoulder as he explored her.

"Yes . . ." Her voice trailed away as she felt her body coiling with anticipation. She wanted to spread her legs wider, but the jeans restrained her, and she moved restlessly. Aohdan moved one hand to her sable hair and tangled his fingers in it, and her voice caught in her throat as she looked directly into his dark eyes.

"Do you know what I want?" he asked. "I want to make you come, and then I want to fuck you until we're too exhausted to get out of bed."

Even in a whispered hush, his voice was fierce and commanding, and the bald candor of his words caught Seireadan completely off guard. Her breath hitched, and she started to say something, but it was incomprehensible as his fingers stroked her again. Seireadan's entire body trembled, aching for him to finish her.

Abruptly, he took his hand away and Seireadan nearly gasped. "Aohdan . . ."

"Patience," he murmured, kissing her. "We're not through yet; take those off." Aohdan gestured at her jeans.

"Bossy . . ." Seireadan smiled; she didn't normally take well to being ordered around, but for some reason she couldn't fathom at the moment, she wanted to do exactly what Aohdan said, to allow him to be in control. She hooked her fingers into the belt loops and slowly shifted from side to side, sliding the jeans down until they were at her ankles. She reveled in the way his eyes darkened as he watched her; he made her feel irresistible.

Her lace panties matched the bra, and she moved to the edge of the bed where she could lean back. Lifting her legs, Seireadan pointed her toes so Aohdan could pull the jeans off completely. He tossed them aside and stepped closer. Seireadan ran her palms up his waist and over the hard muscles of his abdomen until she reached his chest, where she gently fingered the gold ring that pierced his left nipple. He closed his eyes and ground his teeth as she moved her hands from his chest up to his shoulders and down his arms. Everything about him was hard, muscled, and magnificent.

"Are you inked below the waist?" she asked, reaching for the top of his faded jeans. He didn't answer, so she unfastened the button and slowly pulled the zipper down, feeling the hardness hidden behind it. With a few tugs, Aohdan's pants crumpled to the floor, and he stepped out of them. Seireadan made sure to skim her body along his boxer briefs as she stood up from the bed's edge.

"No tattoos," she said, answering her own question.

"Not yet."

With a firm pull, Aohdan spun Seireadan so she faced the bed, and anchored her body against his with one arm. He started to kiss her neck, and she let her head tilt to the left, wanting to feel his lips on every inch of her skin. He paused briefly when he noticed the tattoo between her shoulder blades: two crossed raven feathers.

"The ink suits you," he said as he used his one free hand to unhook her bra. It fell, unnoticed, to the floor.

Seireadan made a soft noise in the back of her throat as he slid his hands across her breasts, down her stomach, and down to her panties. This time, he didn't make her wait. As his fingers stroked her, explored her, Seireadan pushed back against him and ran her hands over her own breasts. Closing her eyes, she let the sensation fill her until she was nearly gasping as Aohdan brought her to the edge of release, and then backed off, letting her cool down for a moment before sliding a finger inside her, spiraling her desire even higher. Nearly incoherent, Seireadan let her head fall back on his shoulder when he began to move his hand again.

"I need . . . I . . . !" Nothing else existed for Seireadan except Aohdan.

"I won't stop," he promised. "Not until you come for me."

In that moment, Seireadan slipped over the edge, everything inside her tightening and releasing as her climax churned heat throughout her body. She dug her nails into the bed's comforter, desperate to kiss Aohdan, but he held her tightly as the orgasm washed over her. When it finally subsided, and Seireadan felt his arm relax, she turned and kissed him brazenly before yanking down the boxer briefs. She stared at Aohdan shamelessly, and with one smooth motion, she dropped her panties to the ground and leaned back on the bed. She looked up at him through her thick lashes.

"You said you were going to fuck me after you made me come."

Aohdan tumbled Seireadan onto the bed, kicking his briefs away from his ankles. He searched her face, looking for any hesitation, and unsure of what he'd do if he saw any fear in her eyes. The only thing he found was desire. His body demanded that he take her, ravage her, but as he settled between her legs, he forced himself to stillness. *She deserves more than that, better than that.*

"I want you, Seireadan. All of you," he whispered to her.

Seireadan reached up and pushed his long hair back behind his ears and then ran one finger along his jawline. Aohdan stared into her beautiful eyes, feeling her warmth, so close to him, so tempting, but he waited, wanting this to be what she wanted.

"Yes," she murmured, and once she answered his silent question, Aohdan didn't hesitate.

Seireadan gasped, her back arching, as he entered her, filled her, and the pleasure in her voice nearly made Aohdan come. He kissed her, hard, wanting to taste her lips, her skin, as he started to move, savoring the sensation of being surrounded by her. For that moment, his world was nothing but the sound of her pleasure in his ear and the sensation of being welcomed into her body every time he thrust forward. He was pulled out of his reverie as she dragged her fingernails up his back.

"Give me more of you," she said as she shifted, opening herself to him even more.

A thin sheen of sweat covered them both as Aohdan increased his tempo, and as he felt his own release building, he struggled to master himself. He looked down at the beautiful woman beneath him, with whom he was so intimately joined. *She's beyond everything I've ever wanted . . .*

"Seireadan." He said her name as if it were something sacred as he thrust forward again. He could feel how close they both were, and knew Seireadan could, too. Bracing himself on his elbows, Aohdan slowed, trying to draw out the pleasure even longer. Her fingers gripped his arms, the nails digging in.

"I want to feel you come inside me," she purred.

There was no more waiting, and Aohdan's head spun as she tightened around him, consumed by her own orgasm. He thrust forward one more time, shouting as he came, a primal, savage sound, his body shuddering with release. They collapsed, still tangled in each other's arms, overwhelmed by the sheer force of their passion.

CHAPTER 11

AS THEY LAY together in her bed, still overcome, Seireadan pulled the tangled sheets up. *That was* . . . She paused. Adjectives like "amazing," and "mind-blowing" seemed not only cliché but completely inadequate to describe how it had felt to be with Aohdan.

"I'm getting some water. Do you want some?" she asked.

"Please."

In the bathroom, Seireadan grabbed a dark green camisole hanging behind the door and pulled it on. She splashed a little water on her face and then studied her reflection in the mirror. Something had happened back in her bedroom, something unexpected, when she'd given free rein to the magnetic pull between them—she'd given herself fully and completely to Aohdan, given him a level of control that she never allowed. *And I loved it. Every. Damn. Second.*

Holding the edge of the sink to keep her hands from shaking, Seireadan lost herself in the moment. Just thinking about being with Aohdan made every part of her respond, even now. Out in the bedroom, she heard him start to move around.

Is he leaving? I don't want him to go. She bit her lip, and when she left the bathroom, she deliberately avoided looking toward her bed, afraid she'd see him getting dressed. In the kitchen, she drank a full glass of water before she filled one for him.

The tension in her shoulders dissolved instantly when she saw Aohdan was still in bed, sitting up with some pillows propped behind him. Her camisole barely fell below her hips, and he watched every step she took with a look in his eyes that made her want him all over again.

Aohdan emptied the glass in a few gulps. A few drops spilled and ran down his chin before he put the glass on the nightstand and grabbed Seireadan around the waist. She shrieked in pleasant surprise as she was toppled down on the bed next to him.

"You are so beautiful, Seireadan."

She reached up and traced from the tip of the ear down to his face and along the well-trimmed beard on his jaw. "I usually don't like men with beards, but I love this on you." She couldn't imagine him without the Vandyke. She let her eyes wander, taking in the different tattoos, before she reached out and touched the image on his right pectoral. It looked like a stone with an upright arrow carved into it—a Nordic rune stone. The texture was so convincing she expected it to feel rough to the touch.

"I love this one," she said. "What made you get this?"

"You're the fortune-teller. Tell me what it means and you'll know why I got it," he said as he twined a few strands of her hair between his fingers.

"It's a rune called Tiwaz," she answered immediately. "It's a symbol of courage and fearlessness, success through sacrifice. As patriarch, you'd need all those qualities."

He nodded; she was absolutely right. "I've always liked the idea that ancient people believed physically putting a symbol on your body meant you inherited its qualities," he said.

"And it is a very, very potent male symbol." She slid a finger up the shaft of the arrow, and as Aohdan pulled her closer to kiss her, there was no mistaking exactly how male he was.

She turned her attention to the other side of his chest. Just over his heart was a crowned heart protected by a circle of intertwined thorny vines. Inked in a tribal style, it was dark, bold, and fierce. She reached toward it and then drew her fingers back slightly, but Aohdan took her hand and placed her palm directly over the image. His skin was warm and Seireadan could feel the strength of his heartbeat under her hand. The connection was so powerful it bordered on frightening.

"This one's special . . . powerful."

"It's the symbol of my *fréamhacha agus brainsí*," he said.

I wish I could wear it. The thought startled her. She let her hand linger for a heartbeat or two before she started looking at his other tattoos. There was a pentacle on his left shoulder and a scarab on his right. A tribal armband encircled his left bicep, and a Chinese dragon wrapped his right arm from shoulder to elbow. On the ribs under his right arm was a Celtic cross, and on the left were some kanji symbols along with some initials.

"What are the kanji?" she asked while he ran his hand from her knee up past her hip until it reached her waist. His palm was warm, and she realized she was breathing a little harder.

"One is for loyalty and the other, courage. The initials are my closest friends: Oisin, Galen, Kieran, and Rory. I want you to come to Underworld tomorrow and meet them."

"I'd like that." She wiggled in his arms, and he let go enough for her to sit up straighter. Then he held out his arm so she could see more of his tattoos. On the top of the left arm were a Leviathan cross and a Mexican Day of the Dead skull. His right forearm was mostly a blank canvas, and she considered the expanse of skin.

"Nothing for this arm?"

"All of my ink means something to me," he said. "When the next piece of my story falls into place, I'll add more."

She nodded, agreeing. "That's good. If you're going to make it a part of your body, it should mean something to you. My friend, Lia, has a tattoo that matches mine. We're both Ravens, and if you look closely, you'll see my name hidden in one of the feathers and hers in the other." She turned a little so Aohdan could look at the image on her back. The artist had done impressive work to camouflage the names. He kissed the feather and pulled down the straps of her camisole.

"What are you doing?"

"Getting a better look."

"The camisole didn't cover it." Her laugh turned into a sigh as one of his hands cupped her breast.

Aohdan's voice was low when he answered. "My mistake." He took his hand away, and Seireadan's sigh turned to a groan, wanting to feel his hands on her again.

"If you liked the rune on my chest, you'll appreciate the work on my back." He turned on the mattress so Seireadan could kneel behind him. On the back of his left shoulder was an eternal spiral, and between his shoulder blades were three more runes, all clearly done by the same person who had inked the Tiwaz.

"What do you make of those, my lovely fortune-teller?"

"The first represents physical strength and speed, and untamed potential. The middle one is for protection, like a shield. Those are pretty straightforward. The last one? That's a little more complicated." Unable to resist, she planted a lingering kiss on his shoulder and pressed herself against his back.

"How so?" he asked.

"The rune's name is Kenaz, and it is for vision and knowledge. It gives the power of transformation and regeneration, the ability to create your own reality."

Aohdan twisted to look at her, and Seireadan saw approval—and respect—in his expression. She knew then she'd read the symbols correctly. He caught the hem of her camisole and pulled it down, exposing one of her breasts. His dark eyes smoldered.

"You left one thing out about Kenaz."

"The part about physical love and passion?" Her laugh was low and sensual. "I didn't think I needed to point that out."

Aohdan pulled the rest of the camisole down and pressed Seireadan back on the bed. She went willingly and wrapped her arms around his neck as he kissed her. This time there was no preamble, no foreplay; they both just wanted to feel their bodies together and Seireadan moaned each time he drove forward until they both cried out, consumed by their desires. After, Aohdan toyed with the ends of her hair as they lay in the bed.

"Are you going to kick me out?"

"What?" Her voice was sated and sleepy.

"Are you going to kick me out of your bed so you can get some sleep?"

She looked at him and then at the bedroom door. With a smile, she shook her head. "No, I think you should stay right here in my bed." *Where you belong.* Seireadan pulled the covers up higher and moved closer to him, and as he wrapped her up in his arms, she drifted off to sleep.

CHAPTER 12

GALEN IGNORED THE chair's squeak as he leaned back and looked at the two invoices in his hands. The first one looked fine, and he tossed it onto the desk. The other one? Not so much. *That is way too much of a price increase for pizza cheese; I'm going to need to make a few calls about that.* The office door opened, and he glanced up to see Aohdan stroll in. It took Galen only a moment to notice the wrinkled T-shirt and unkempt hair and ascertain his boss's evening had gone well.

"Take it she didn't send you packing again last night?"

"No, she did not." Aohdan flipped open the cover of the laptop on his desk and started to scroll through a few emails.

"You could at least say if it was a good night or not," Galen finally said.

Aohdan leaned back in his chair, an odd expression on his face. "Good? It was fucking amazing."

Clearly. Galen returned to his work and looked up again about twenty minutes later to see Aohdan staring out the window, utterly lost in thought. It wasn't that Galen didn't consider his patriarch a thoughtful man, but he'd never seen him quite so taken with a woman. *From the second he saw her at the bar, something's been different. He's been different.*

"You coming to the club later?" Aohdan asked Galen as he closed the laptop, stood up, and stretched.

"When do I ever leave here?" His second laughed.

"I'll be back later, and Seireadan will be here, too. I asked her to come and meet all of you."

Galen's eyebrows went up. *Meet us? After, what, three weeks? Four? You hardly know her.* "Are you sure you want to introduce her to this band of fools so soon?"

"I want her around for a very long time; she may as well meet you all and understand my life sooner rather than later."

Knowing what he did about all of Aohdan's various enterprises, Galen had to wonder exactly how full a picture Seireadan was going to get. And whether or not she could be trusted with that much information.

After Aohdan left, Galen took a break and went home to shower. He lived in a renovated warehouse; it looked modest on the outside, but inside was an open, airy loft. He really loved the apartment, but sometimes wondered if he should just have a little studio near Underworld, given how much time he spent at the club. He was back at Underworld in less than two hours, and Tommy did a double take.

"Did you even leave?" asked Tommy.

"Only long enough to shower and change. Are you good running the bar tonight?"

"Absolutely. I got this," Tommy assured him.

Galen went to the back office to do more of what seemed to be a never-ending river of paperwork, but by seven he was feeling cross-eyed. He checked in with the chef, then went out to the main floor. Kieran and Oisin were just coming in.

"Can I get either of you a drink?" Tommy asked amiably.

"Shit, yes," said Oisin.

"I'll take care of it. Can you give us a minute, Tommy?"

"Sure thing, Galen." Tommy threw a bar towel over his shoulder and headed back to the kitchen.

"Good day?" Galen asked as he poured a beer and slid it over to Oisin.

"Verra good day," said Kieran. He took three envelopes filled with cash out of his jacket and put them on the counter. "Crew did no' have any trouble for a change."

Smooth business is always good business. "What about you, Oisin?"

"Fine." He took a drink of his beer. "I did catch up with Oona the Unlucky, and look how she paid." Oisin took a velvet bag out of his pocket and spilled four strands of pearls onto the bar. Three were white and one was black, and each strand was about twenty-four inches of knotted silk.

"They look like the real deal," said Galen.

"She said they were authentic and worth about six grand each; black strand might be worth more. It doesn't cover her whole debt, but it will buy her a little time." Oisin let one of the strands run through his fingers as he talked.

Kieran changed the subject. "Where's Rory? Unusual for him to no' be here."

"He texted me earlier," said Galen. "One of the people he needs to see today ended up out in Worcester. I think he's still there."

"Stuck in Worcester? Well, he'll be in a piss-poor mood later, the redheaded bastard," snorted Oisin. "Anyone seen the boss today?"

Galen had been waiting for that question since the moment Oisin sat down. "Saw him earlier. He'll be back a little later."

Oisin sat up a little straighter. "You've seen him? And?"

"And what?" Galen didn't look at him.

"And what," snorted Oisin. "You know exactly what: Does he still have huge blue balls?"

"Based on how he was acting this morning, they're definitely not blue anymore," Galen answered.

"Really?" Oisin pressed for more.

"And that was all he said, other than she's coming here tonight because he wants to introduce her to all of us." Galen let that bomb drop and waited. He was rewarded when Kieran's head snapped up.

"Here? Specifically to meet us? He's no' brought a woman to meet us, let alone after, what, three dates? He must be verra taken with this one."

"Jimmy still talks about her," said Oisin. "All self-righteous about how Aohdan stole his woman."

"Aohdan needs to kick the shit out of that kid and put him back in his place," snapped Galen. *He cuts Jimmy way too much slack.*

"Whatever. Screw Jimmy Boy," said Oisin. "I'm curious to meet her, but it seems like Aohdan's getting serious about her pretty fast. Not questioning his judgment, but . . ."

"Can no' say I disagree," said Kieran.

Galen glanced up. "Speaking of the devil himself."

"What's this?" asked Aohdan when he reached the bar. He picked up the black strand and looked at it with a critical eye.

"From Oona the Unlucky," said Oisin as he scooped all the strands up and put them back in the bag. "It doesn't cover all of her debt, but it's a good start. I'm having the pearls appraised on Monday. Figured Louis and Greer could do it."

Aohdan nodded. "They're smart enough to do a fair assessment."

"And I told her how pissed I'd be if they were fake, and that her debt would go up 50 percent. Plus, I told her you'd take it as a personal insult if she tried to fleece the house."

For the next ten minutes they talked business before Kieran pushed back his chair. He picked up his envelopes of money and said, "I'm going to lock these up and then head home for a quick shower. I'll be back later."

"I'll be here," said Galen.

"I hear the lovely Seireadan might make an appearance tonight?" Oisin raised an eyebrow as he looked at Aohdan.

"She will." There was a note of satisfaction in his voice that they all noticed.

What an interesting evening it will be, thought Galen.

CHAPTER 13

THE DAY DID not go as planned for Seireadan, and it hadn't helped that she'd been a little late for work after spending the night tangled up in her bed with Aohdan. Julia had immediately seen through her lame excuse, but was kind enough to wait until they were alone before she began interrogating Seireadan about her night. By the time she got back to her apartment, it was already nine. She pulled out her phone and sent a quick text.

Things ran late. Showering now. Be there asap. Sorry.

She turned on the hot water and jumped under the spray without waiting to see if Aohdan answered. She scrubbed herself down with a loofa and rinsed before washing her hair. While the conditioner sat, she turned the temperature up and just enjoyed the hot spray. It was wasteful, but there was something about the decadence of a truly long, hot shower that she found irresistible. After she toweled off, she rummaged through her closet before settling on a pair of dark slim jeans and a burgundy silk tank top. She looked in the mirror and nodded, satisfied.

Grabbing her phone, she found a text waiting for her: OK. See you when you get here.

Leaving now. Be there soon.

Good. Was starting to worry. Line crazy. Go to back door of club—ask for Galen.

Any other evening, Seireadan might have considered walking, but she was already late enough. When the cab dropped her off, she raised her eyebrows at the line, glad Aohdan had told her how to get around it. She found her way to the back only to be stopped by a burly, imposing bouncer. His brass name tag said "George."

"Sorry, miss. All guests need to go through the front." He picked his bulk up out of the little chair he was sitting in and gestured toward the front.

"Hi, George. I'm supposed to come to this door. I was told to ask for Galen?"

"Oh, hang on a sec." He sent a text, and a moment later his phone pinged. "Sorry for the confusion, miss. They didn't let me know to expect anyone tonight." He opened the door and held it for Seireadan.

"No trouble. Thank you."

Inside, George saw one of the waitresses. "Muriel! This young lady is a guest of Mr. Grey. Would you take her to his table?"

"Sure thing. Come with me, sweetie. Right this way." Muriel bustled down the hallway, and Seireadan had to hurry to keep up with her. On one side of the hall were some darkened offices, and on the other was a locker room for the workers. At the VIP table, Galen saw them come out from the back.

"Aohdan, I think your date is here."

Seireadan paused as every head at the table turned to look at her, but then she saw Aohdan and smiled. He came down to the main floor and kissed her. Seireadan melted into him; she'd been waiting to taste those lips since the morning.

"I'm glad you made it. You look gorgeous," he said as he escorted her up the four steps to the VIP area.

"You're so sweet, thank you. I'm sorry I'm so late. I meant to be here earlier," she said, savoring the taste of whiskey that lingered on her lips from his kiss.

"You're here now, that's all that matters. Let me introduce you to everyone. Seireadan Moore, this is Oisin O'Neill, Kieran West, Rory Molloy, and I believe you've already met Galen Grey?"

"Yes," she said, shaking Galen's hand. "But only briefly. It's nice to meet you officially." She shook hands with each and took a seat on the banquette that surrounded the backside of the table. Muriel appeared with appetizers and some drinks.

"Can I get you something from the bar, miss?"

"Please." Seireadan glanced around the table. "A shot of whiskey and a Sam seasonal. And a round of the same for the table."

Oisin did a double take, and a huge smile split his face. "A shot and a beer, and a round for the table? Aohdan, I LIKE her!"

A few days after meeting Aohdan's friends, Seireadan was cooking dinner for the two of them. Aohdan lounged in a kitchen chair watching her cook. Seireadan had refused his offer to help; although Aohdan could hold his own in a kitchen, this was *her* kitchen. She stirred her marinara sauce and brought a spoon to her lips for a taste. She frowned absently, threw some more oregano in, and tried again.

"Better?" asked Aohdan.

She smiled at him. "Yes, I knew it was missing something."

"Did you have a good time the other night?"

"What part of the night are you referring to? Underworld? Or back here after?" An image of Aohdan, naked while she straddled him, flashed into her mind. Suddenly warm, she tugged at the collar of her shirt.

"Oh, that second part was more than a good time, but I was actually asking about the first part, meeting everyone."

"That was great. They seem like a great bunch of guys . . ." She stirred the sauce again and balanced the spoon on the edge of the pot.

"I hear a 'but' in there," said Aohdan.

"But you didn't just introduce me to your friends. I met the captains of your *fréamhacha agus brainsí*."

Aohdan, his dark eyes unreadable, finally said, "You're right, they are my captains."

"They're all quite different," she observed as she remembered the night. "Galen is very thoughtful; he's quick to smile and laugh, but he watches everything. Nothing ever gets by him."

"No, it doesn't, and that's why Galen is my second."

"Your second?" Seireadan tapped the sauce spoon on the edge of the pan.

"Second-in-command. If something were to happen to me, Galen would become patriarch of Boston."

"Are you related? I thought being a triarch was inherited."

Aohdan shook his head and leaned on the kitchen table. "The practice of familial inheritance has become less common over the centuries. A few smaller clans still hold that tradition, but I disagree. I think it leads to a feeling of entitlement, and that can turn into laziness very quickly."

"That makes sense, but why isn't Oisin your second? I don't mean any disrespect to Galen, but you and Oisin have been friends since you were children. Even after only spending an evening with all of you, it's easy to see that he'd walk through anything with you." Seireadan turned up the heat on the pot of water, and a small spot of sauce on the counter disappeared with a swipe of her dishtowel.

"He would. We don't share the same parents, but Oisin is the brother of my heart." Aohdan paused for a moment, giving the term of affection the gravity it was due. "We grew up together, escaped the Desolation together. He'd do anything for me, and I'd do the same for him. But as much as I love him, he's not a triarch. You saw him the other night. What did you see?"

Seireadan thought for a moment, remembering the laughter, the toasts, and the bawdy jokes. "I saw someone who watches out for you, but who certainly has his fun. He loves to laugh, to drink, to tell dirty jokes. And he certainly loves to flirt!"

Aohdan laughed. "That he does. And it is all of those qualities that make him a less-than-ideal choice for second. He's loyal, no doubt, but he has a smart mouth and he can hold on to a grudge. Galen is pragmatic and circumspect, and he understands long-term thinking. He's also a good negotiator because he stays cool no matter how much pressure he's under."

"Oisin would shoot first and ask questions later," said Seireadan. *And "shoot first" may be frighteningly literal.*

"Exactly."

"How did he feel when you didn't choose him?" Seireadan put the garlic bread into the oven and then dropped the tagliatelle into the boiling water.

"He wasn't happy. In fact, he was pretty pissed. Eventually, he understood, and he's told me on a couple occasions—when he's watched Galen really have to operate under pressure—that he thinks I made the right call."

Stirring the pot, Seireadan said, "But it takes more than business smarts and negotiation skills to be a triarch."

"It does."

When it was clear Aohdan wasn't going to elaborate further, Seireadan changed the conversation. "I liked Kieran, and I think my friend Lia would *really* like him. He seems a lot like Galen. Pragmatic, unflappable. But Rory . . ." A flash of a frown crossed Seireadan's face.

"But Rory what?" asked Aohdan.

"There's something about him. Something much more overtly dangerous." She gathered her thoughts so she could articulate the feelings that Rory stirred up in her. "He holds part of himself back, keeps it hidden. And he doesn't like humans very much at all."

She remembered Rory's loden-green eyes roaming over the crowd at Underworld and the blatant disapproval and outright disgust that filled them when he watched a Fae woman dancing with her human lover. And she clearly remembered looking up to find Rory watching her with an enigmatic expression that finally ended in a judgmental smirk before he looked away.

"No, he doesn't. Rory had a very difficult time when we first came to the human realm, and his first real interactions with humans after the Desolation were bad. Really bad. He's never forgotten—or forgiven—what they did to him."

Aohdan didn't elaborate, and Seireadan didn't ask. Using two red potholders, she dumped the pasta into the colander to drain. "Do you want some wine with dinner? There are a couple bottles on the counter near the refrigerator."

While she mixed the sauce and the pasta and pulled the bread out of the oven, Aohdan considered the wine and chose the pinot noir since it would stand up to the acid in the marinara. While Aohdan poured the wine, she put the meal on the table, then they both sat down.

Aohdan raised his wine glass. "To loyal friends."

"To loyal friends." Seireadan clinked her glass against his. After they took a drink of wine, they tucked into the meal and, briefly, the conversation took a back seat to dinner.

Finally, as they were finishing, Seireadan put her fork down, and said, "I'm not keeping you a secret, you know that, right?"

"What are you talking about?"

"I've met your friends—your important friends. But you haven't met mine. I don't want you thinking that I'm hiding you from them."

"I don't think that at all, Seireadan. I figured you would introduce us when you were ready. I'm not exactly the boy next door," said Aohdan.

Her voice softened. "I don't have a lot of close friends. I've been alone for a lot of my life. I'm fairly close with Julia, who owns Sacred Circle, but Lia is my best friend. She's been on a consulting assignment out in San Diego. It was only supposed to be for a few weeks, but then it turned into four months, and now it might get extended again."

"Then I can't wait to meet her once she's back," he said, covering Seireadan's hand with his own. "Now, I trust there is a delectable dessert to go with the fabulous home-cooked meal?"

"I have whipped cream."

"To go on top of what?"

"You," she said with an audacious laugh as she picked up her plate and brought it to the sink. Aohdan followed, crowding up against her from behind, his thoughts totally and completely on his dessert.

CHAPTER 14

FOLLOWING AN INVITATION from one of Aohdan's business associates, Seireadan, Aohdan, and his captains spent Labor Day weekend at Crane Beach, with its miles of gorgeous shoreline, dunes, and trails. An epic clam bake with cold beer and all the trimmings punctuated a weekend of relaxing in the sun, and after a leisurely return on Monday evening, Seireadan felt utterly relaxed and refreshed.

Knowing Aohdan would want to drive her home, Seireadan had her light jacket over her arm and was standing on Aohdan's balcony, looking out at the city, when he came up behind her. She closed her eyes and smiled as he wrapped her up in his arms.

"Thank you for taking me this weekend. I had so much fun."

"Me too. I don't get the chance to really relax all that often," Aohdan said.

Across the water, the buildings of Boston's financial district were lit up in the soft twilight, their reflections bobbing in the harbor waves.

"Your condo is gorgeous. This view is amazing," she said.

"One of the reasons I bought this place," he said as he pushed Seireadan's hair to the side and kissed her neck. With a sigh, she turned and looked up at Aohdan. He tilted his head closer, until their lips were nearly touching, and they stayed that way for a moment, hesitating, feeling the pull between them grow stronger with every passing second, until Aohdan finally closed his mouth over hers, drawing her in for a deep kiss.

"But I have to confess, I had an ulterior motive in stopping here tonight," he said quietly when they paused to catch their breath.

"And what's that?" Seireadan gave him a sideways look.

"Because I want you to stay here tonight," he answered.

She looked up sharply, wondering if she'd heard him correctly.

"Stay with me tonight. Here," he murmured in her ear.

Goose bumps peppered Seireadan's arms, and she realized she couldn't hide the hope in her voice, or the trepidation. "You've never let anyone stay . . ."

"I haven't wanted to share it with anyone before." Aohdan pushed her hair back and let his thumb feather her cheek. "I know this seems sudden, Seireadan, but I want to be with you. Only you. I want everyone to see that a woman like you would be with someone like me."

"Someone like you?" Her brow wrinkled.

He shook his head, his long hair brushing against his shoulders. "I'm the patriarch. I didn't get where I am without making some hard decisions. Some of them very bloody decisions."

"We're Fae. Bloody decisions are part of our heritage whether we like it or not." As she spoke, a vision of pale, cold eyes materialized in her mind and vanished again. "The Seelie Court was rife with plots and schemes, and blood feuds that ran for millennia. Some that refuse to die, even today."

"Maybe so. But there's a difference between understanding the concept and living with the reality. Would you really want to be with someone who makes those kinds of choices? Could you live with that?"

She heard the worry—and the hint of self-loathing—in his voice, and it pained her. "From what I've seen, you don't make capricious decisions, ones for your own amusement at the expense of others. You make decisions that need to be made. I would never be ashamed to be with someone like you."

"Seireadan, I'm not a good man," he said, his voice somber.

"Bullshit." There was no trace of doubt in her voice, and Aohdan kissed her again, hard.

"Stay here tonight," he repeated.

"You hardly know me . . . ," she whispered.

"I know enough."

No. No, you don't . . .

CHAPTER 15

SEIREADAN'S EYES OPENED slowly. She shifted, sinking deeper into the mattress, and sighed as memories of the night before washed over her, memories of a passionate night in Aohdan's arms—and in his bed.

His bed. His place . . . His woman? She thought back to the conversation they'd had as they looked at the city skyline. She didn't regret anything she'd said; she would never be ashamed of being with someone like Aohdan. *But what am I doing? Aohdan isn't just any Fae man. He's ruthless. He's dangerous . . . But he's generous, and thoughtful . . .*

All the other thoughts disappeared in an instant, crowded out by another, and Seireadan's fingers anxiously curled in the sheets as she wondered again if Aohdan might know the ice-eyed monster from her dreams. She squeezed her eyes shut as she forced the thoughts down and locked them away—that possibility was too much to consider. She stretched once more and slid her hand across the sheets, disappointed to find them cool on Aohdan's side of the bed.

With a sigh, she rolled over and flailed at the nightstand until she found an alarm clock. It was just after ten. She managed to find the switch for the small lamp on the nightstand and sat up, gathering the sheets around her, wondering where her clothes had ended up. *They're probably all over his condo.* In the end it didn't matter. At the foot of the bed, Aohdan had left a pair of his flannel pants and a soft fleece shirt. Laughing a little, she rolled the pant cuffs up so she wouldn't trip and cinched the waist. She had to do the shirtsleeves as well, so they wouldn't hang past her fingers. Her hand was on the doorknob of the bedroom when she heard voices.

He has company? Should I go out there? She took her hand away from the doorknob and then put it back. *Screw it. He said he wanted the world to know we're together. This will tell me if he's bullshitting me or not.* She opened the door and walked out. At the kitchen island, Aohdan was leaning on his elbows talking with Galen and Oisin, and he smiled when he saw her come out of the bedroom.

"Good morning, beautiful," he said.

"Good morning."

Galen and Oisin turned and said good morning as well, and neither looked surprised to see her there, although Seireadan did notice that Galen's smile was a little distant. She shrugged it off; they'd been having a pretty serious conversation when she came out. She stood at the island, and Aohdan kissed her.

"Am I interrupting?" she asked.

"Not at all. Are you hungry? I make a respectable omelet."

"You're going to cook for her? When are you going to cook me Sunday breakfast, Aohdan?" Oisin offered a cheeky smile and raised his coffee mug in a toast before taking a deep drink.

Seireadan, as she walked around the island to take the seat next to Oisin, leaned down and whispered in his ear, "When he thinks you're better than me in bed, then he'll cook you an omelet."

Oisin nearly blew coffee out of his nose.

After Aohdan took out the skillet, eggs, and cheese, Oisin and Galen said their goodbyes and left the condominium. In the elevator, Galen stabbed the lobby button on the keypad.

Oisin gave him a look. "Who pissed in your cereal?" he asked.

"Call Kieran and Rory and tell them to get their asses to Underworld," said Galen.

"What the fuck's bothering you?"

Galen pointed up, back toward Aohdan's penthouse. "That's what's bothering me."

"That Aohdan got laid?"

"No, you jackass. I don't really care who the boss humps. That's his business. But Aohdan's known this woman for what, a month? She's all he thinks about, and now he's brought her here to spend the night? *Here?*" Galen folded his arms and shook his head.

"What's your beef with Seireadan?"

Galen stared at Oisin like he was an idiot. "My point is that we don't really know a single fucking thing about her, and I don't trust what I don't know. She could be working for Crogher. For all we know, she's related to Matriarch Teresa and she's here to cut his throat in his sleep."

"Maybe she is, but maybe she's also just a woman he's fallen hard for," said Oisin.

"I hope that's all it is. I like her, Oisin, I really do. But we need to vet her out and make sure. I'm not going to take chances with Aohdan's safety, especially not now with Providence."

"Are you going to tell the boss what you're doing?"

"No."

"No?"

"If we find something, we can tell him. If not . . ." Galen stared at the doors, waiting for them to open as the elevator reached the lobby.

"Aohdan will be bullshit if he finds out we're doing this."

"I know," said Galen. "And that's why I'm making this an order. I'm his second and I'm supposed to watch his back. If he gets pissed off, he can be pissed off at me—I'm doing exactly what a second is supposed to do."

"Which is why I never want your job," said Oisin. "I used to, but now? Not in a million fucking years."

Upstairs, Aohdan and Seireadan made small talk over breakfast, both surprised at how remarkably comfortable it was. After the dirty dishes went in the sink, Aohdan threw her over his shoulder and carried Seireadan, laughing, back into the bedroom. It was nearly 1:00 p.m. when she got out of the shower, dried herself off, and pulled on her clothes. Still naked, Aohdan was lying on his stomach on the bed. He dragged a pillow over and folded his arms on top of it while he looked Seireadan up and down.

"You sure you need to go?"

"Unfortunately, yes. I blew off working on one of my client's sites on Friday, and I really have to show them something tomorrow. Call me later, though? Maybe we can do dinner?"

"Definitely. I may have to be in Providence a few times for business this week. Something's come up, but they shouldn't be late nights."

"Is that why Oisin and Galen were here this morning?"

"It was," said Aohdan. After a moment he added, "I want to merge Matriarch Baibin's *fréamhacha agus brainsí* with mine, but it's a sensitive negotiation and not everyone is happy with the idea. Especially not her son."

Seireadan frowned. "Be careful of him."

Aohdan shifted and sat up. "Why do you say that? Have you Seen something?"

"No. Actually I haven't had a run-in with the Sight for several years. But I just have a funny feeling."

"Believe me, I'll be watching him." Aohdan didn't trust Crogher anyway, but Seireadan was a Raven. Even without the Sight taking her, a Raven's "funny feeling" was something to be taken very seriously.

CHAPTER 16

CRIOFAN SHEA STROLLED through the enormous mansion the Seelie king called home. The Fae he passed in the halls nodded in deference, and the other faeries—Pixies, Leprechauns, Banshees, Selkies, Dryads, and many more—that had business at the Court gave him a wide berth. He enjoyed the respect, the wariness, and even the fear. Having spent countless years gathering influence, he had risen to a position of power: King Fionvarr's chief adviser.

After the Desolation of Faerie, the Seelie king, shattered by what his brother had done, sank into a well of despair and grief, which was augmented when Criofan had sadly informed him that Paidin, his closest adviser, had not only been killed but had been harboring Luan's wife, Bryn, and her lover, Conlan. Sensing his opportunity, Criofan worked his way into Fionvarr's confidences, and when Fionvarr's queen died not long after coming to the human realm, the Seelie king sank even deeper into his morose depression and simply allowed Criofan free rein. It was easier than facing what his kingdom had become. A vocal few had questioned Criofan as his power ascended, but most of those voices were silent now. One of the loudest among them, however, had been Aohdan Collins, before he abandoned the Seelie Court.

Criofan pushed his white-blond hair back over an ear and frowned as he always did when Aohdan crossed his mind. *Thorn in my side, then and now. All his talk of adapting and changing, that our traditions would destroy us here. Our traditions are what gave me all of this power.*

Strangled by their fear of this strange new world, most of the Fae had refused to listen to Aohdan and his message of change, and Criofan made sure to take advantage of that. He played on their fears, offering the comfort of sameness and tradition that made them feel insulated and safe. Aohdan opposed him at every turn, but eventually grew disgusted by the Court and left to make his own way.

I was just as happy to have him out of my hair, but he has quietly and quite ruthlessly accumulated power and wealth. I suppose I have to admire that to a certain extent, but this Conclave he's created with the other outlaw fréamhacha agus brainsí *concerns me. I can't allow a rival center of power to exist.*

Rumors of Aohdan's play for Providence had reached Criofan's ears, and with them, whispers that called Aohdan king. *Regardless of what I think of him, Aohdan isn't stupid. Setting himself up as a king, trying to impose his will on the other triarchs, is just an invitation for them to turn on him. Savages, the lot of them. But there is only one Court, and only one king. It's well past time to deal with Aohdan once and for all.*

A strand of Criofan's white-blond hair fell across his eyes, and he pushed it to the side as he pondered his options. Abruptly, he reached out and grabbed the arm of a Court page. The young Domovoi yelped in surprise.

"You! Find the Pari named Abrezu and Vashti and tell them I want to see them right away."

Both Pari were waiting for Criofan in the gardens behind his own opulent home. It had originally been a guesthouse but was a mansion in its own right, and it was adjacent to the Seelie king's residence. Criofan could see the warm glow from the two fire faeries even before he reached the French doors that opened onto the patio and private garden. Both Pari were lovely with long legs and slender necks. Shimmering, translucent wings sprouted from their backs. As he approached, Abrezu tossed her head, her red-gold hair flowing over one shoulder. Vashti, her sister, had darker red hair and eyes the color of embers. They were both mesmerizing.

"Thank you for coming so quickly," Criofan said as he walked onto the patio. He put the box he was carrying down on the glass-top table. The Pari smiled at him and folded their wings back discreetly, and as they did, some of the glow surrounding them faded. Criofan kissed Abrezu's hand.

"You are as gorgeous as ever." The words flowed smoothly off his tongue, and Abrezu preened under the praise.

"I've missed you, Criofan," she purred. "I've missed our games."

He smiled. The Pari had proven to have not only a voracious appetite for him in bed but an expansive imagination as well. "As have I, but for me it must always be work before pleasure." Abrezu gave him a pretty pout as Criofan looked at her sister.

"You must be Vashti. Your sister has spoken highly of you."

Vashti's expression turned shrewd. "Has she? My sister may work for . . . free . . . but I do not. What is the work, and what will you pay?"

Criofan returned the Pari's appraising look, finding her directness and lack of deference intriguing and exciting. "Vashti, I wouldn't dream of asking for your help without adequate compensation. I want information. About Aohdan."

"Aohdan Collins?" asked Vashti.

"He's delicious," cooed Abrezu as she licked her lips. Both Vashti and Criofan ignored her.

"Yes. But I don't want you bothering with Aohdan himself. Look to those who surround him, his captains, his friends. Someone will be willing to talk about him."

"To what end?" asked Vashti.

"I need information on his ambitions, his plans. Information I can use to bring him down. Aohdan has grown powerful, and I've allowed it to go on too long." *Like all the other Fae, he and the other rogue* fréamhacha agus brainsí *should be obedient to me.*

"This will be exciting," Abrezu said.

Vashti gave her sister a look. "This work is risky, Criofan; Aohdan is powerful and that makes him dangerous. And you are asking us to possibly consort with humans, something I find distasteful. Again, what will you pay for this?"

Criofan went to the table and picked up the box. He held it out to the Pari as he opened the lid, and both Abrezu and Vashti gasped. Nestled on deep navy-blue velvet were twelve large fire opals and several dozen smaller ones. The kaleidoscopic sea green of the gems was shot through with glittering reds and golds.

Generally speaking, most types of faeries loved gems, but in the case of the Pari, opals were particularly prized, and the more a Pari had, the more respected they were among their own kind. Many Pari would kill for opals of the size and quality Criofan was offering, and he knew Vashti and Abrezu would do whatever was needed to acquire them. Without realizing she was doing it, Vashti started to reach out toward them, and Criofan pulled the box back slightly before he shut the lid and tucked the box away.

"Then we have a deal?" he asked, already knowing the answer.

CHAPTER 17

SEIREADAN LOOKED SHARPLY over her shoulder when she heard a knock on her door. She thought about ignoring it, but the knock came again, louder, and she dragged herself out of her chair. *Hold your friggin' horses.* It couldn't be Aohdan; he was down in Providence again, courting the old matriarch, and wouldn't be back until later. She glanced through the security hole and then flung the door open.

"Lia!"

"Surprise!" Clearly delighted by Seireadan's shocked expression, Lia clapped her hands and made no effort to hide her amused smile. Some of her wheat-blond hair fell across her eyes. "I'm not interrupting, am I?"

"No! Come in! You know you can show up on my doorstep anytime, day or night. How are you? What are you doing in Boston? Let me just save this work before I lose it." After saving, and while Lia flopped down on the sofa, Seireadan grabbed two bottles of Leary's Lemonade from the kitchen.

"So, what's going on with you? I've been terrible about keeping in touch." Lia took a deep drink from her bottle.

"I asked you first." Seireadan laughed. She made herself comfortable in the corner of the couch.

"Some last-minute meetings here at the home office. Knew I had to come see you, so I flew in a little early. Thought it might be a fun surprise."

"I'm so glad you did." Seireadan smiled. "I miss having you around." Her phone rang, and she held up a finger to pause Lia.

"Hey," Seireadan said into the phone.

"Hi, beautiful." Aohdan's voice was deep and warm, and she couldn't help but smile. "My meeting is running late."

"That's fine. In fact, I actually need to cancel dinner tonight. My friend Lia is back unexpectedly from San Diego."

"Is she? Good, I know you've wanted to see her. You're bringing her to Underworld later, aren't you?"

Seireadan's smile widened. "I know you want to meet her. Maybe we'll see you there. Is your meeting going well?"

"Better than I expected, so at least it's running long for the right reasons."

"Good. Okay, I'll see you soon—"

"Just you?" There was humor in Aohdan's voice, and Seireadan shook her head.

"Okay, okay, *we'll* see you soon." With a laugh, Seireadan hung up and tossed the phone on the coffee table.

Lia arched her eyebrows. "Well. You've clearly been holding out on me. Spill it! Who is he? Why haven't you told me about this before now? Don't skimp on the details—you've got a look in your eye that I've never seen before!" Lia pulled her legs up underneath her and settled in for a good story.

"Well, I'm seeing someone."

Lia rolled her eyes. "Obviously. Like I couldn't tell that from the smile you had while you were talking to him. Do you mean 'seeing' as in had a couple of dates? Or 'seeing' as in this is serious?"

"The second. We really haven't known each other long, and it's gotten pretty serious pretty fast. There's just . . . something about him."

"How long have you known him?"

"Almost two months." Seireadan tried not to smile but couldn't help herself.

"Shit, two months and you're totally in love with this guy? Who is he?"

"I am not in . . ." Seireadan shook her head to deny what Lia had said, but she knew she was lying. "Okay, yes, I'm in love with him, and I don't know how it happened so fast. Everything between us just clicked."

"Well, then he's clearly something special. What's his name?"

Seireadan sighed and covered her face with her hands for a moment. *What's Lia going to think? She'll know exactly who Aohdan is.*

"This is getting better and better." Lia looked like she was ready to pounce, and she rubbed her hands together. "What, are you dating some Selkie accountant named Wilfred? Or a Parisian Pixie named Pierre?"

"Aohdan Collins."

Whatever other smart-ass thing Lia was about to say vanished on her tongue, and instead she blurted out, "Come again? Aohdan Collins?"

Seireadan nodded.

"Holy shit. Aohdan Collins, the patriarch of Boston's *fréamhacha agus brainsí*?"

Seireadan nodded again. "One and the same."

For a second, Lia just blinked. "So, you and Aohdan are . . . ?" Lia drew the question—and the implication—out.

"Aohdan and I are what?" Seireadan smirked.

"You're really going to make me ask, aren't you? Fine. You're sleeping with him, right? How's the sex?" Lia folded her arms and waited.

Seireadan laughed out loud. "You never do mince words, do you?"

"Not when it's such an important question!" Lia started to laugh, too.

"Here's your straight answer: fucking amazing." There was a wicked look in Seireadan's eyes, and after a moment she added, "But vulgar innuendo aside, it's so much more than sex, Lia. From the moment I met him, there's been something, I don't know, magnetic between us. Something powerful. He is . . . he's . . . I can't even really put it into words . . . but I love him, more than I thought I could ever love anyone."

"Don't take this the wrong way, Seireadan, but love? You hardly know him."

Seireadan didn't blame Lia in the slightest for her skepticism. *Lia's right. I hardly know him. But it doesn't matter . . .* "I know. It's insane. And I haven't said it to him yet. He'd probably think I was crazy."

Lia said, "Well, you certainly don't do anything half-assed, do you? I'm happy for you, I really am, but I hope you know what you're doing, girlfriend."

"Me too. You'll have to judge for yourself: you'll meet him later tonight."

"I can't wait." Lia grinned at her.

They walked to the Rosewood Diner just a few blocks away from Seireadan's apartment, and as they strolled, Seireadan answered all Lia's questions about how she and Aohdan met and what he was like. After finishing some killer cheeseburgers with thick-cut steak fries, they relaxed in the booth while they indulged in splitting a large bowl of ice cream.

"So, I have my own little surprise," Lia said. "Not quite the bomb you dropped earlier, but it's big."

Seireadan paused, her spoon hovering over the cold confection. "You have my attention."

"I'm coming back to Boston."

"Seriously?" Seireadan lit up. "That's fantastic! When? Why?"

"San Diego doesn't need anyone full-time on-site anymore, and my company made some changes here. They had an opening for a senior consultant. Got the job, so now I'm back. I'll still have to travel a lot, but I'll be based here. No more long-term assignments living in crazy places. I'll be back in my Cambridge loft by the start of October."

Seireadan hugged her, thrilled by the news. "That's not long at all! I'm so glad. We are totally having drinks at Underworld to celebrate!"

"I'm not exactly dressed for a club," Lia said.

"You look fine. And if you want to change, you can help yourself to any of my stuff."

An hour later, Lia had pilfered a silvery scarf and belt with a fancy silver buckle that hung down from her hip from Seireadan's closet, and they flagged down a cab.

CHAPTER 18

THE DECOR INSIDE Underworld was sleek and modern. The brushed-steel frames for the chairs were an interesting counterpoint to the burgundy seat pads and the dark cherry-wood. Slim back-lit panels of cream-colored marble ran along the wall behind the bar, giving the whole space a warm quality.

"When you said Underworld, I was expecting something darker," said Lia as she looked around. Seireadan saw Galen and waved him over. He finished giving some paperwork to Muriel and walked over, rolling up the sleeves of his shirt as he did.

"Hi, Seireadan."

"Galen! I'd like you to meet my friend, Lia Allen. Lia, this is Galen Grey, Underworld's manager."

He shook Lia's hand. "Pleasure to meet you. Welcome to Underworld."

"Thank you."

A waiter materialized next to Galen. "Jack, get the ladies whatever they want. They'll be at the VIP table tonight. Put their tab under my name."

"Yes, sir," said Jack. "If you ladies want to make yourselves comfortable and look over the drink menu, I'll be over in just a minute to take your order."

"Is Aohdan here yet?" Seireadan asked Galen after Jack walked away.

"He is. He's in the office on a phone call, but he should be wrapping up. Oisin and Kieran are with him. Chris and Rory are around here somewhere, too. I'll let Aohdan know you're here."

Once they made themselves comfortable and ordered some drinks, Lia looked around. "The VIP table? Very swanky," she said. "This place is really cool. I like it here. Does it belong to him?"

"Probably."

"Probably? You don't know?"

Seireadan gave her a look. "Not for sure. I typically don't grill him on what he owns."

"What? No sexy real estate pillow talk?"

Seireadan rolled her eyes and laughed. "On paper, Galen is owner and manager, but with the amount of time Aohdan spends here and his interest in the club's growth, I'd say it's a safe bet that he is the chief investor. He does own a tattoo shop, and I'm sure he's partners in other businesses."

"A tattoo shop? Seriously?"

"Completely. He's quite a talented artist."

"I'm sure, but . . ." Lia lowered her voice. "The patriarch of Boston? Running a tattoo shop?"

"It's something he loves to do."

"His prerogative, I guess. So let me ask you this. Have you asked him about, you know?" Lia raised a questioning eyebrow but was met with confused silence from her friend. "You know, Alabaster? You don't get to be patriarch without knowing a lot of people."

Seireadan's fingers tightened on her glass. "No, I haven't. Aohdan doesn't know anything about all of that."

"Seems like a pretty important part of you to be leaving out," Lia observed.

"I'll tell him when I'm ready."

Lia made an unladylike noise that expressed in no uncertain terms that she thought Seireadan's answer was a load of crap, but Seireadan covered her annoyance at Lia's doubt quickly when she saw Rory and Chris walking toward the table. As usual, the two men weren't talking to each other, and the silence continued as they sat down. Lia stiffened in her seat, staring at Rory with a wary, suspicious look that he returned with a challenging stare and cocky smirk.

Seireadan interrupted the awkward silence. "Chris, Rory, this is my friend Lia." After quick hellos, Rory remained taciturn, leaving Chris to handle the bulk of the conversation, asking Lia about her work and what it was like living in San Diego. About fifteen minutes later, Aohdan came out from the back with Kieran trailing in his wake. He looked irritated, but when he saw Seireadan at the table, his expression changed.

"Hey, beautiful." He gave Seireadan a kiss, letting it linger for just a moment. "My whole day just got a lot better."

"Mine too. Aohdan, this is Lia."

"A pleasure to meet you," he said as he shook Lia's hand. As he did, Lia swayed slightly on her feet and got a faraway look in her eye. Seireadan caught her arm to steady her.

"Lia?" she asked, concerned.

Lia shook her head. "No, no. I'm sorry. I didn't mean to alarm everyone. It was a long flight from Cali. I must have gotten up too fast."

"You're sure?" asked Aohdan.

"It's really hard for Ravens to hide when the Sight is on them," Seireadan said, hearing the implied question that Aohdan didn't ask. "Everyone would know if it was happening."

Kieran interrupted when he handed Lia a glass of water. "Thank you," she said with a soft smile.

"You're verra welcome," Kieran replied, staring at her longer than he should have, making Lia's cheeks color.

"I've never quite understood this whole Sight thing," said Chris. "What is it, if you don't mind my asking? I mean, I get that if you have it you can see bits of the future, but how? What happens?"

"It's a Fae thing, not really any of your business," barked Rory.

"That's not true," Seireadan responded. "A Raven's knowledge is open to everyone. Chris can ask whatever he likes, just like you or anyone else. But to answer your question, Chris, I don't know if anyone actually knows how, and the 'what' can be hard to explain. There's no telling what can trigger it. A touch, a voice, a smell. But when it does happen, it's different for each of us."

Lia picked up the story. "In my case, I'll go into a trancelike state. I just stop and stare into the distance until the Sight has passed on. It could last minutes or even hours."

"Hours? Shit." Chris shook his head, and then asked, "What are your Seeings like, Seireadan?"

"I see colors and lights," she answered. "And for me, it's painful, almost like I'm having the worst migraine possible, and then there's a moment—inside my head—when everything gets clear and I See whatever it is I'm supposed to. Fortunately, mine usually only last for a few minutes. I've never had any go on as long as Lia's."

The conversation stopped when Jack brought another tray of drinks, including a whiskey for Aohdan. The group talked and drank, pressing Lia for stories about Seireadan while Lia countered with efforts to ferret out stories about all of them. The only one missing was Oisin, who finally appeared out of the back offices wearing the same pinched expression Aohdan had worn earlier.

"What did you find out?" asked Aohdan when he sat down.

"Confirmed what we know. There's definitely more aggressive talk out there."

Aohdan leaned forward and rested his chin on his hands. He shook his head slowly, his expression turning angry. Everyone at the table quieted and just waited, and Seireadan realized Lia was holding her breath and looking everywhere other than at Aohdan.

"Stay close to this." Aohdan's voice was crisp, controlled. "And if he gets tired of hearing himself talk and actually decides to *do* something, I want to know immediately. I don't care what time it is. And if anyone else is stirring the pot, I want to know that, too."

For the rest of the evening, Aohdan was charming and gregarious, but Seireadan could tell that Providence was weighing on his mind. And more than once she caught Lia watching Rory with a pinched, worried expression. Finally, they had a private moment.

"Did Rory do something? You're watching him like he's going to bite."

"I'll tell you later," was all Lia said, and Seireadan had a sinking feeling that whatever Lia had to say about Rory, she wasn't going to like it.

CHAPTER 19

THE NEXT DAY, Aohdan showed up on Seireadan's doorstep with flowers, hoping to surprise her. He knocked on her door, but the stormy look on Seireadan's face when she opened it made him question the wisdom of his decision.

"What do you want, Aohdan?"

"Ah, can I come in?"

"Can't I go twenty-four hours without you checking up on me?"

The anger in her voice shocked him. "Seireadan, what's going on?"

She stepped to the side and gestured for him to come in. Aohdan went to grab a kitchen chair, but Seireadan kept her hand on the doorknob.

"Don't get comfortable, you probably won't be staying."

He put his hands up in surrender. "I just saw you last night. What did I do that pissed you off so much? At least give me a chance to explain."

"You can start by explaining why you have Galen and the rest of your captains rooting through my life and checking up on me." She folded her arms angrily.

"Checking up on you? I didn't ask anyone to . . ." *Galen, you son of a bitch. You're vetting her behind my back?*

"Well, they are. And I don't appreciate anyone digging into my business. This explains about my clients being asked for references. And why I've run across both Galen and Kieran while I'm shopping. And last night, after we left the club, Lia let me know that Rory was following her out in San Diego. You want my damn tax returns, too?"

"Seireadan—"

"That's fucking outrageous!" she shouted.

"Seireadan, I'm sorry. I didn't ask them to do that. I'll talk to Galen and put an end to it. How can I make this up to you?"

She sighed, her anger fading at the sincerity in his voice. "It isn't about making it up to me. Just . . . make them stop."

"I promise they'll stop."

"Okay." She let out a big sigh.

"I'm going to go and take care of this right now. These really are for you." He held out the bouquet of roses, alstroemeria, hypericum berries, and ferns. She took them, drawing in the roses' scent.

"Thank you. They're beautiful."'

"You're welcome." He gave Seireadan a quick kiss. "I'm going to go take care of this . . . situation. I'll call you later, okay?" *And Galen's going to have about ten seconds to explain himself before I rip his fucking head off.*

Less than thirty minutes later, Aohdan stormed into the back office at Underworld. Along with Chris and Jimmy Boy, all of Aohdan's captains were there, and Oisin was in the middle of a raucous tale of some exploit from his most recent trip to Atlantic City when the door slammed open. Those who were sitting jumped to their feet.

"What the fuck do you think you're doing?" Aohdan thundered at Galen.

"Boss?" The voice belonged to Oisin, but Aohdan ignored him.

"Get out," the patriarch ordered, pointing at Chris and Jimmy. Chris instantly headed toward the door, but Jimmy stayed where he was, nearly beside himself with the anticipation of watching Galen get reamed out. Aohdan grabbed him by the shirt and shoved Jimmy toward the door. "I said get the fuck out!"

Jimmy hurried out, and Oisin, Rory, and Kieran moved to follow.

"No, the three of you stay put," Aohdan ordered. He looked from face to face and finally focused on Galen. "Why have you been following Seireadan?"

But before Galen could respond, Aohdan continued on. "And you, Rory—a redheaded Fae following her friend in California? Asking questions about Seireadan? Who told you to dig into her life? And you do it without asking me?" His voice brimmed with anger.

"Aohdan—" Galen started to say.

"Shut. Up." Aohdan turned his attention to Oisin and Kieran. "And the two of you: Fae businessmen asking her professional clients about her? 'Unexpectedly' running into her while she's shopping? This has gone on for a couple weeks, and you never thought to mention any of this? Are you fucking kidding me?"

"Don't yell at them. I gave the order to vet her out. If you're going to be pissed, be pissed off at me," said Galen.

"Trust me, I'm pissed! What the fuck were you thinking?"

Galen got angry. "What was I thinking? I was thinking that we don't know a damn thing about her, and you've got her staying at your condo. Something you've never done with any woman, ever. You are totally willing to talk to her about your business, and you don't even tell Chris about some of the things you're into. So what was I doing? I was doing my fucking job!"

"If you had questions about her, you should have asked me first," Aohdan shot back.

"Maybe. But you would have shot me down, and you need to get your head back in the game, Aohdan."

"My head in the game? Screw you, Galen."

"Screw you!" Galen shouted. "Your head's NOT in the game. You're thinking about Seireadan when you should be thinking about Providence, about the Underworld expansion, about your new arrangement with Louis and Greer. You need to get your head out of the bedroom and back into the boardroom!" Galen didn't look away from Aohdan's furious stare.

"Watch yourself." Aohdan's voice was a menacing growl.

Galen went right back at him. "I will not watch myself. I'm your second, and it's my job to watch your back and tell you the truth, whether or not you want to hear it. Especially when you don't want to."

"If you've got something to say, fucking say it!" roared Aohdan. He knocked a chair to the side as he took a step toward Galen. To his credit, Galen stood his ground.

"Shit, Aohdan. If the roles were reversed, what would you do? You'd turn over every rock to make sure the woman I was practically living with wasn't working for someone else. Teresa. Crogher. The cops . . ."

That made Aohdan pause.

"Don't get me wrong; I like Seireadan. But ever since you got together with her, you've been distracted. If you're not on your game with Providence, things are going to go squirrely. There are plenty of people in Baibin's clan who would love to see this fail."

"That's not Seireadan's fault."

"No, it isn't. It's *your* fault."

"Galen, maybe you should back off a little," warned Kieran.

"No! We need to finish this now before things go to shit!" Galen was still shouting, something he rarely did, which was enough to make Aohdan pause again. "Look, Aohdan, when you made me your second, what did you tell me? That you trusted me. Trusted me to call you on bullshit when you got tunnel vision. You trusted me to keep the interests of your—of our!—*fréamhacha agus brainsí* ahead of everything else. And never in all my time as your second have I ever questioned how you run things. Until now."

"You have an issue with how I'm running things?" Aohdan stopped yelling, but his fists were still clenched.

"I'm starting to worry about it."

"Then tell me, Galen, what's so different about me now?" Aohdan's voice cooled, but no one in the room believed for a moment he'd actually calmed down.

"The truth? I don't think you've ever been in love before. And I don't care if you've said it to Seireadan or not, or even if you've admitted it to yourself. But I see you with her, and I'm not blind. You're in love with Seireadan, for real, and I'm not convinced you've figured out how to balance your role as patriarch with this new relationship."

"You have both gotten verra serious, verra quickly," added Kieran from where he, Oisin, and Rory stood, forgotten and speechless until that moment.

"Don't get me wrong," said Oisin. "I like Seireadan. She's badass . . . but this is crazy fast."

Aohdan's still angry gaze raked over them.

"And I couldn't take the chance she wasn't what she appeared to be. I would have never forgiven myself if I missed something. So if you're going to kick my ass, then kick it, but I'd do it again exactly the same way," Galen told him.

Aohdan folded his arms. "Fine. I'm still pissed you didn't tell me, but I understand. And not another word about being in love—not right now." Aohdan paused, not wanting to ask the question, but finally he did. "What did you find out?"

"Nothing we found says she's a threat to you or the *brainsí*. Her father, Paidin, was an adviser to the Seelie king once, a long time ago, but Seireadan has nothing to do with Fionvarr or the Court," said Galen.

Paidin? I remember him. Luan had about as much love for him as I do for Matriarch Teresa. "What else?" Aohdan asked.

"Not much," said Galen. "She's not connected to any other triarch as far as we can tell, and has no relationship with the police other than a complaint she lodged a few years ago about a neighbor who was beating his kids. The paperwork never went anywhere, and I have a feeling that it was Seireadan—and not the police—who took care of the problem."

"If you found nothing noteworthy, then the investigation stops now, got it?" Aohdan looked around, and they all nodded. "Good. And if anything else comes up, ask me before you do anything connected to Seireadan."

"Holy shit," said Oisin as he sat down. "I'm glad we got that all settled."

"We're not settled yet," said Aohdan, still looking at Galen.

"What's not settled?" his second asked.

"You're going to apologize to Seireadan and tell her why you did it," the patriarch said.

Kieran laughed. "Good luck with that, Galen. You'll be verra lucky if all Seireadan does is slap you."

"Now, let's get down to *business*," Aohdan said with a pointed look at Galen.

CHAPTER 20

JUST BEFORE THE equinox, summer offered up one last gasp and wrapped the city in two days of rank humidity. Eventually, the sky blackened as a front moved through, stirring a wicked storm. Sheets of rain drove across the sky, and black clouds turned inside out, rent by lightning and crashing thunder. Finally, the rain subsided to a gentle patter on the flagstone patio outside, and Criofan's sly smile spoke volumes as he watched Vashti out of the corner of his eye. The Pari had wandered over to the table and was looking longingly at the box of opals that sat, nestled, on a velvet pillow. Her sister lounged in a chair deliberately showing most of her slender leg to the king's adviser.

"Progress?" he asked the two.

"Yes," Abrezu said. "We've found someone. He—"

"Abrezu!" Vashti's voice was a whip.

"What?" The other Pari looked daggers at her sister.

"Our sources are our secret. No one needs to know so long as we bring information that's of value. I would be irritated to go through so much only to have someone else poach our prize. And to lose our opals."

"Through so much?" Criofan asked.

"The one we found is quite lusty." Abrezu giggled.

"Lusty? He's a pig." Vashti rolled her eyes in disgust.

Criofan chuckled. "If the effort is so distasteful . . ."

"No," Vashti backtracked quickly. "He may disgust me, but he's close to the patriarch. I would endure far worse for those opals. They'll change everything for us."

Much later that night, just before Underworld was scheduled to close, Aohdan and his captains were finishing the last of their drinks. Tommy and Muriel had just left, and other than the front door, the place was locked up tight for the night. It had been a working dinner for Aohdan and his captains, with much of the discussion centered on Providence and the effort to integrate Baibin's *brainsí* into Aohdan's. Aohdan pushed his empty glass across the table; he was ready to be done with business for the day, and Seireadan was waiting for him.

With no warning or preamble, Galen asked, "Do you love her?"

Aohdan didn't answer right away. No one had mentioned the word *love* since his fight a couple of weeks ago with Galen about checking out Seireadan's background, but that didn't mean it hadn't been on Aohdan's mind. These were his captains, the people he trusted the most in a world where he trusted very few. But to admit to feeling something—especially something that would make him appear vulnerable—was hard, even in front of them. Aohdan knew the answer to Galen's question, but before he could say anything, Rory added his two cents.

"Love's nothing but bullshit. Messes with your head. We don't love anything but money and power." Rory stood up and pulled on his jacket. "Keep a little something on the side, like the choice piece of ass I've got now, but don't get tangled up."

Aohdan gave him a sideways look as he considered the brash assessment. In the past, he might have agreed with Rory, but since meeting Seireadan, Aohdan wanted no part of that life. In fact, he realized, he hadn't so much as looked at another woman since meeting Seireadan.

"You're full of shit, Rory." Oisin sounded offended by Rory's cavalier dismissal of the entire emotion. "Are you saying we can't love? I love all the ladies that I'm with. And we love each other—we're brothers!"

Kieran's voice, soft, weighed down with pain, broke into the conversation. "Aye, we're family, and we love each other like brothers. But it is no' the same, no' the same. No' when you're talking about your woman."

Rory rolled his eyes. "Oh, fuck me. You both know what I mean. And Aohdan hardly knows her." A dismissive scoff punctuated the statement. "Come on, Oisin, let's go. The night's young, and we've got a poker game to get to before I go get my rocks off." He laughed and grabbed the front of his pants.

Before he got up, Oisin looked over at Aohdan. The patriarch gave him a nod and a wave; he didn't care if they left. They were done with their business for the night.

"You never answered my question," Galen said after Rory and Oisin disappeared.

"I do love her," said Aohdan. *More than you could possibly realize.* "But no, I haven't told her that yet."

"Then I'm happy for you, and terrified," said Kieran, pain still woven through his words. "If you truly love her, and she loves you, then Seireadan will bring you a joy you can't even begin to understand now. She'll also have the power to destroy you—to gut you—with a single word or look, and even when she does, you'll love her anyway."

"What do you mean, 'truly love' her?" Aohdan asked.

"It's easy to confuse infatuation, even lust, with love. Look at Oisin. He does no' even really know what it means to be in love. What would you do, Aohdan, if Matriarch Teresa took Seireadan as a way to get to you?"

Aohdan sat up straighter in his chair, his jaw set in a hard line. "Teresa wouldn't dare . . ."

Kieran pushed it. "But what if she did? What if she took Seireadan and beat her bloody, tortured her? Cut her throat? What would you do?"

The thought of anyone putting their hands on Seireadan shredded Aohdan inside. Barbed wire pulled through every piece of him, leaving him raw and bleeding. When he answered, his voice was ice. "I would end her, and it wouldn't be quick." *And that would mean I would also destroy everything I've built because destroying Teresa would shatter the Conclave.*

"And damn the consequences?"

Aohdan met Kieran's eyes and didn't look away. "Damn the consequences."

"Then you truly love her," Kieran said simply.

"Is that what it was like with Elizabeth?" Galen asked.

With a sad and thoughtful look, Kieran nodded. "I would have let you strip the skin from my living body a thousand times over if it meant I could have saved Elizabeth the pain she went through before she died."

Aohdan sat back, looking out a window at some point far beyond what he could actually see. Kieran had married Elizabeth, a human, many years ago. They'd been happy, at least until Elizabeth had fallen victim to the flu pandemic in 1918. She'd suffered for several days before she died with Kieran at her bedside. *I wasn't sure Kieran would live through the grief. It's been nearly a hundred years, but part of him still grieves for her.* As he mulled over what Kieran said, his captain got up to leave, but before he reached the door, Aohdan asked another question. "Would you do it again?"

Kieran let a little smile twist the corner of his mouth. There was mischief there mixed with the old sorrow. "For a long time I would have said no. That I'd never do it again, never find someone again. But I'm no' so certain now."

"Now that you've met Lia?"

The wider smile answered Aohdan's question.

"I do no' know if anything will come of it, but she is the first one I've felt anything for in a long time."

CHAPTER 21

THREE DAYS LATER, Seireadan met Aohdan and Oisin at a small market a few miles away from her apartment. Papa's was a small family-owned shop, and she wondered why Aohdan was there. A young woman with olive skin and straight, shiny black hair was behind the counter.

"May I help you find something?" she asked while Seireadan browsed.

"No, thank you. I'm actually waiting for someone."

For a moment, the clerk looked confused and then her eyes widened. "Oh! You are wating for Mr. Collins. He is still talking with my father. Please, would you like something to drink? It is on the house." Her voice was slightly accented.

The deference in her tone surprised Seireadan. "That's very kind of you, but really, I'm fine."

The young woman shifted nervously behind the counter, and Seireadan realized that her refusal was making the woman very uncomfortable.

"Actually," Seireadan said, "a little water would be nice."

"Of course!"

Before Seireadan could move, the clerk hurried out from behind the counter and took a bottle of water out of the cooler for Seireadan.

Ten minutes later, Aohdan and Oisin came out from the back room. An older man was with them. He had a thick white mustache, but his skin was the same shade as the clerk's and they shared the same smile. Seireadan realized they must be father and daughter. He shook hands with Aohdan.

"Thank you for your time, Mr. Papadakis," Aohdan said.

"I appreciate your help, Mr. Collins. I feel much better knowing my Sofia will be safe here when she's working."

The three Fae left the shop, and Seireadan offered Aohdan some of her water. He took a long drink and sighed.

"You're still tense," she said. "What's wrong with the shop?"

"They're getting bullied," Aohdan said. "Some punks who should know better want protection money from him, and threatened his daughter if he didn't pay."

"Ah." There was a tightness in his voice that Seireadan didn't miss.

"I've dealt with the crew before, and if this is their way of pushing back on me, then they're in for a very unpleasant surprise." After a pause, Aohdan changed the subject. "Feel like Italian tonight?"

"Sounds perfect," said Seireadan.

"Great. We just need to get my car back at Underworld."

"Mine's in the lot down the street," Oisin said. "I can drop you off."

In the twilight the streetlights had come on, and the three chatted amiably about dinner, Boston sports, and other utterly ordinary things until they got to the lot.

"Give me the ticket. I'll cover the parking," Aohdan said.

"This is a business we should be in," Oisin told him as Aohdan walked toward the automated pay meter. Seireadan laughed. She didn't disagree. Good parking in Boston was worth a king's ransom, and she eyed the cars in the lot, adding up in her head what each of them would have to pay for parking that day.

She felt the presence near her a moment before a rough voice said, "Collins needs to stay the fuck out of our business."

The voice belonged to a human man. He wasn't quite as tall as Seireadan, but he was big and clearly dangerous. His companion was built similarly and kept his eyes firmly on Oisin.

"You're the ones who need to stay out of our business." Oisin's voice was just as low and threatening. "Your former boss learned that the hard way."

"We haven't forgotten what Collins did to Artie—he'll get what's coming to him. You all will," said the first man. He gave his friend a nod, and his companion lunged at Oisin, who managed to catch his assailant's arm midpunch. With a flick of his wrist, he twisted it around until all the pressure was on the other man's elbow. With a scream of pain, he dropped to his knees. Oisin didn't let go.

Everything slowed down for Seireadan. She knew Oisin was there, but he had his hands full. *Where's Aohdan? Do they have him, too?* The first man's hand shot out and seized Seireadan by the wrist, and he yanked her forward.

"C'mon, sweetheart, you're coming with me."

Like hell I am. Seireadan reached for the back of her belt with her free hand, finding the hilt of one of her little hidden knives. In a flash, she pulled it out and sliced the arm of the man holding her. He didn't see it coming, and the blade opened a long gash on his arm.

"You bitch!" he bellowed, but didn't get beyond that as Aohdan careened into him, knocking him off his feet and taking him to the ground. They grappled for a moment, and Seireadan cried out when the thug landed one solid punch to Aohdan's face.

That was the last time he had the upper hand. A moment later, Aohdan had him pinned to the ground and landed at least five punches in quick succession to the man's face. With each blow, the thug's features became bloodier and less recognizable. When he finally went limp, Aohdan got to his feet and backed up. He used the back of his hand to wipe the blood from his lip, his chest heaving from the exertion and the adrenaline. He stepped closer to Seireadan, but didn't touch her, keenly aware of the blade still in her hand.

"Are you okay?" he asked.

She nodded, staring at the huddled form on the pavement. "Yes."

"They didn't hurt you?"

"No, I'm fine."

"Where the fuck did that knife come from?" asked Oisin, his voice a mix of respect and horror.

"My belt." She wiped the blade on her jeans and tucked it away.

"I need to get me one of those," Oisin muttered as he tightened his grip on the man he had pinned.

Seireadan didn't pay attention to him—her eyes were on Aohdan. His shirt had blood on it—some from his lip, but most from their attacker—and his knuckles were skinned and raw. He looked utterly ferocious, without any hint of remorse for what he'd done.

Aohdan grabbed the second man by the hair and pulled him up. Oisin let go and moved away slightly so he could watch the one on the ground and still be close to the patriarch.

"Who are you?" Aohdan asked.

"L . . . L . . . Lonn . . . Lonnie. Lonnie Baker."

"And who is your idiot friend, Lonnie?"

"That's Big Mickey Monroe."

Aohdan's voice was terrifyingly cold. "And who the fuck do you and Big Mickey work for?"

Lonnie looked away and shook his head until Aohdan roared, "WHO?" and drove his fist into Lonnie's gut. He would have fallen to the ground if Aohdan hadn't still been holding him by the hair.

"Don't make me ask you again."

"Joe Hayden," Lonnie wheezed.

It all made sense to Aohdan. When he'd first started to expand his influence in Boston, there had been two major underground networks. Artie Devlin had run the crew that dominated South Boston, and Luca Palladino had worked out of the North End. He'd saved Luca from a particularly nasty demise, and they'd reached an accord that still held. Artie hadn't been so willing to negotiate, and after he made several attempts on Aohdan's life, the police had found Artie floating facedown in Boston Harbor. Joe Hayden had been Artie's second-in-command.

He let go of Lonnie. "Take your friend and get the fuck out of here. Don't ever let me catch you around my business—or my woman—again." The memory of Big Mickey grabbing Seireadan made Aohdan's fists clench again.

Seireadan realized she was holding her breath. *I knew he had a dark side. I knew he was no saint, but I never imagined . . .* When Aohdan turned back to her, the fury had disappeared from his eyes, replaced by concern.

"Are you sure you're alright?"

"Really, I'm fine. I hurt him worse."

"That's not what I'm talking about."

Seireadan remembered what he'd said to her the first night she stayed at his condo: *I'm not a good man.* She remembered him asking her how she felt about the kinds of ruthless—and bloody—decisions he'd made to become patriarch.

"I asked you before if you could live with someone like me, someone who makes the choices I do. Someone who does the things that I do. Now that you've seen it in person, can you still live with it?"

Seireadan thought about it long enough that she felt him stiffen, anticipating the rejection. She looked past him to Big Mickey's ruined face and the pool of blood on the ground. She looked at the blood on Aohdan's face and clothes, and the bruised, bloody knuckles on his hand. The violence had been instant and absolute, and it was part of who Aohdan was. If she was going to love him, she had to love all of him.

"I can live with it," she answered.

CHAPTER 22

AS THE AIR cooled and leaves changed, Seireadan found herself slipping into a happy routine spending most of her free time—and nights—with Aohdan. But nightmares and reminders of the Alabaster Man stained her newfound bliss, fanning her fears. She resolved time and time again to tell Aohdan about her dream—her Seeing—as a child, and each time, she managed to talk herself out of it. Each time, she told herself he didn't need to know, not yet, and put up a thick barricade between her fear and her joy, hoping the fear would curl up and die behind the wall where it was banished. It didn't.

On a blustery mid-November day, Seireadan was curled up with Aohdan on the sofa, watching old movies. They'd both been busy lately, and she was relishing an afternoon with no meetings or responsibilities. Her phone rang and Seireadan picked it up.

"Hi, Lia—oh, Kieran?" Seireadan sat up straighter, her eyebrows arching. Aohdan turned to look at the mention of his captain's name in such a surprised tone of voice.

"I'm at Lia's," Kieran said, "and I do no' know what to do. The Sight has her."

Seireadan's face clouded, making Aohdan sit up straighter. "Just stay with her. She could be like that for a long time. I'll be there as soon as I can."

"What's wrong?" Aohdan asked when she hung up.

"Lia's caught up in the Sight, and Kieran wasn't sure what to do." She paused. "Did you know about them?"

"Not entirely. I knew Kieran was interested but wasn't sure if he was going to pursue it."

Seireadan chuckled. "That sounds about right. Lia was a little evasive about it when I asked her about Kieran the other day. I figured she was interested but didn't want to let on. Anyway, I'm going over—I want to be there when she comes out of it, but it could be a while." She grabbed her jacket.

"I'll come with you."

At Lia's home in Cambridge, Kieran, his face pinched with worry, answered the door and invited them in. "Thanks for coming over. I've just no' seen this before."

"How long has the Sight had her?" asked Seireadan.

"At least an hour," said Kieran.

They went into the bedroom, and just as Kieran had described, Lia sat on the edge of the bed, mouth slightly slack, staring at a distant place in space that no one else could see. A small microfleece blanket was tucked around her.

"I was in the shower, and when I go out, I thought she'd fallen asleep, but then I realized she was just sitting on the edge of the bed staring at nothing. She didn't answer me, didn't even blink. It's verra unnerving . . ."

Both Seireadan and Aohdan's expressions changed when Kieran said he'd been in the shower. Aohdan gave his captain a look of surprise and approval.

"Clearly not a first date, then," said Seireadan. "Lia's been holding out on me."

"How long have the two of you . . . ?"

"A few weeks," said Kieran, a slight flush rising up his neck.

Seireadan laughed. "Oh, I'm not surprised at all, not after the way you two were looking at each other when you met. I figured this was bound to happen at some point." Seireadan sat next to her friend and checked her pulse before she gently touched Lia's cheek. "There's no way to tell how long she'll be like this. Could be a few more minutes, could be hours."

She went and rummaged in the bathroom and found some Tylenol, and brought that back into the room along with some water. She handed both to Kieran and was about to instruct him to keep them handy when Lia started to blink. A groan and a sigh escaped the blond Raven as the rigidity washed out of her body, and her head dropped forward. Kieran steadied her so she wouldn't fall.

"Hey, there you are. Glad you're back." Seireadan ran her hand over Lia's hair. "How do you feel?"

"Fuzzy," said Lia, squeezing her eyes and then blinking quickly. "Confused . . . Why am I in this blanket?"

"When I called Seireadan I thought Aohdan might come over, too, and I didn't think you'd appreciate everyone staring at you in your teddy," said Kieran.

"Well, I guess the cat's out of the bag now," Lia said, her cheeks scarlet.

"Indeed—we'll talk later, but for now, here." Seireadan handed her friend a glass of water and the pills.

"Thank you."

Seireadan waited for Lia to finish her water before she asked, "Do you want to talk about what you Saw?"

"There isn't much to say. It was very simple, too simple. I was in front of a beautiful marble wall. It was gray with streaks of jet black, violet, and soft white mixed through it. You'd think the colors would have been cold, but the way they went together? It made the wall seem warm." Lia's words faded as she focused on her memories.

"So all you Saw was a wall?" asked Seireadan, gently encouraging her to share more.

"As I was looking at all the beautiful patterns, I noticed a tiny little fissure, but a moment later it became a crack. It ran from the base nearly to the top. The wall didn't break in half, but it was so close. I felt so scared and sad when the crack started." Lia pulled the blanket tighter around her as if suddenly cold.

"Why were you frightened?" Kieran put his hands over hers.

"Because I knew that if the wall cracked all the way through, it was going to crumble into nothing. And there would be no way to repair it. Ever. But there was no other context. No action, no people, no things that might show what the wall is, or where it is, or what's making it crack." Lia sighed sadly. "So, there's no way to warn someone that something beautiful could shatter."

Lia's words left a heavy pit in Seireadan's stomach.

CHAPTER 23

SEIREADAN WAS CURLED up on Aohdan's sofa, engrossed in a book, and Aohdan watched her as he adjusted his tie, enjoying the play of emotions that crossed her face as the story unfolded on the pages in front of her. She put a bookmark in the pages and got up.

"You look very handsome."

"Good. I need to impress Baibin."

"If I didn't know better, I'd be jealous."

Aohdan laughed. "No need for that, believe me. But I need to look like everything she expects a patriarch to be. This dinner is the most important one. If she wasn't ready to move forward with the merge, she wouldn't be coming up here, but Baibin has very proper sensibilities. If I look like I'm assuming anything, it could still all fall apart."

"It won't."

Aohdan appreciated Seireadan's confidence. "Assuming things go well tonight, I'll need to bring this to the Conclave, and that will be a whole separate argument."

The Conclave was Aohdan's creation, but it wasn't without its difficulties. After the Desolation, different *brainsí* had drifted from the Seelie Court, setting up their own lives in different cities, and it didn't take long for ambitious triarchs to fall back into old habits. A slight here, a theft there—it all added up to unnecessary conflict, and after three different triarchs were assassinated, Aohdan boldly inserted himself into the middle of the fray. He coaxed, bullied, and demanded that the wild clans come to an agreement under which they could all coexist.

The most powerful of the triarchs made up the Conclave, and so far it had lasted close to one hundred years. Not long in terms of a Fae's lifespan, but significant given the often quarrelsome nature of the Fae. They met twice a year, each time in a different city. The triarchs served as a kind of board of directors while Aohdan, as chairman, managed the meetings. He had adamantly advocated for a democratic process for the Conclave—all decisions were made by majority vote, but that didn't stop all of the infighting, nor did it stop the whispers and rumors that he was some sort of shadowy king, building his empire in the dark.

It was a point frequently brought up by his most vocal opponent in the Conclave, the matriarch of New York, Teresa Aberdeen, and Seireadan had heard enough stories about her to know that she would fight Aohdan's merge with Providence tooth and nail.

Aohdan slipped on his suit jacket, and Seireadan came to meet him at the door. She ran her fingers over the lapels of his jacket and looked up with a smile. "Baibin will never be able to resist your charms," she said. "And if Teresa is a problem, she'll answer to me."

"Now that would be something to see." He laughed.

"Have a good dinner. I'll see you when you get back."

"You'll stay? It might be late."

"I'll stay. I promise."

Aohdan turned just before he stepped into the hallway. He looked into Seireadan's violet eyes and ran a thumb along her cheekbone with remarkable gentleness.

"I love you, Seireadan."

In his entire long life, Aohdan had only said that to one other woman, and this time, he meant it. This time, the words felt right, felt like they were anchored down deep in his soul. He was completely, utterly in love with Seireadan Moore.

"I love—" was all Seireadan managed to say before Aohdan kissed her.

Knowing that Baibin had a fondness for German food, Aohdan made sure the dinner was at the top-rated German restaurant in the city. He personally escorted Baibin to her seat, trying to remember every bit of politeness that had been drummed into him by his mother in his early days at the Seelie Court. Baibin seemed to approve, and talk of business was interwoven with more amiable topics throughout the meal.

"The meal was delightful. Good schnitzel is exceedingly hard to find," Baibin said as she dabbed the corner of her mouth with her napkin. She reached for her water glass, and her hand trembled under the effort. Aohdan made a point to glance away.

"I'm glad you enjoyed it." Aohdan smiled pleasantly, wondering how long she'd draw out her decision.

"I have put a great deal of thought into your proposal," she said after a sip of the iced water. "The future of my *fréamhacha agus brainsí* is very important to me, and I believe it will be vulnerable after I'm gone." As she spoke, Crogher stiffened and curled one of his hands into a fist. The matriarch lanced him with a blistering stare, and for a moment a restless, dangerous tension filled the room. Baibin cleared her throat as her eyes slid over her captains and the tension melted back.

Satisfied, Baibin continued, "And there are some other triarchs I believe would not treat my family well, should they have the honor of leading my *fréamhacha agus brainsí*. I won't let that happen. You've proven to be more than capable, and you are respectful. I appreciate that. Some of the other younger ones?" Her eyes slid to her son. "Pfft. No respect."

Aohdan inclined his head, but remained silent.

"We will proceed with the merging of our *fréamhacha agus brainsí*." She looked Aohdan in the eye and held his gaze. "I trust they will thrive in your care."

"I'm glad to hear that's what you've decided, Matriarch Baibin. And yes, I will treat each member of your *fréamhacha agus brainsí* with the respect and honor they deserve." *Those who show loyalty will get loyalty. Those who don't? They won't bother me for long.*

"Excellent." Her fingers were gnarled and rough as she took Aohdan's hands in her own. "I give you the responsibility for the welfare of my *fréamhacha agus brainsí*. I give you my word that this is my will."

Inside, Aohdan howled at the victory.

"And I willingly accept that responsibility, Matriarch. Now that we've reached an agreement, I will bring this to the Conclave. I anticipate no difficulty there, and after that, we can discuss formalizing the merger," said Aohdan.

"Indeed. Please keep me apprised of the Conclave's thoughts." Her eyes fluttered for a moment before snapping open. "Crogher! I am tired and our business is finished. It is time we went home."

Aohdan stood and helped Baibin out of her chair, then gestured to the waiter, who brought over a clear box tied tightly with pastry twine.

"Something for you to bring home," said Aohdan.

"Oh." Baibin looked longingly at the box. "Black Forest cake. My favorite." She gave Aohdan an almost affectionate smile and handed the box to one of her captains while Crogher nearly oozed hate as he glared at Boston's patriarch.

Aohdan stared back at him, unimpressed. *Do something stupid. All I need is a good reason.*

Crogher stalked away, and Aohdan waited until Baibin and her entourage had departed before he sat back down at the table. The waiter brought them all a round of beer.

"Well?" Aohdan asked.

"Congratulations on convincing her," said Oisin.

"Crogher is just pretending to go along, but he's bullshit," said Galen. "That's no surprise based on how he's behaved until now, but I actually thought he was going to start something at one point."

"Agreed," Kieran added. "The others picked up on his behavior; they were edgy. But I do no' know if it was because they agree with Crogher or are just protective of Baibin."

"What's next?" Rory asked.

"I'd hoped to bring this to the Conclave quietly, but I heard from Aeronwy that Matriarch Teresa has caught the scent of this merger and is working herself into a lather. So, I'll need to figure out how to handle her. Rory, have your cousin Moira keep an eye out for anything Crogher might be up to, especially while I'm at the Conclave. And speaking of which, Kieran and Oisin, you'll both be coming with me for this one. We leave Friday."

"I'll call Moira tonight," said Rory. "You around?"

"I'm taking Seireadan to the Cape for a couple days before I fly out, but call if you hear something."

CHAPTER 24

WITH MUCH LARGER buildings looming over it, the South Street Diner looked oddly out of place at the corner of Kneeland and South Streets. Open since 1947, it was a throwback that served breakfast twenty-four seven. Settled in a booth near the door, Detective David St. John looked up from his coffee as Jimmy McLaren fiddled with a paper napkin in the silence. His partner, Marty Sandhurst, drained the last dregs of coffee from his cup. Jimmy tossed the paper aside and glanced around the little café, his eyes darting to the booths and then to the door as he twisted the ring on his finger.

"I hope you're clear about your situation," David said.

Jimmy's jaw was set in a stubborn line.

"Nice ring," David added, hoping to distract Jimmy.

"It was my dad's. He died when I was a kid."

"Sorry to hear that."

"I'm a dead man if I give you anything on Aohdan. I won't do it." Jimmy shook his head.

"I can appreciate loyalty," Marty said. "But I don't think Collins would appreciate your extracurricular activities, Jimmy." He tossed several photos on the table that clearly showed Jimmy taking alcohol from a truck delivering to Underworld and stashing it in the trunk of his Honda Civic.

Jimmy blanched, and David tried not to get excited. He and Marty had been keeping tabs on Aohdan for over a year, and no lead about anything nefarious had ever panned out. Now they had the chance to get an inside man in Aohdan's organization. An informant could get them all the evidence they needed of criminal activity, and if it was good enough intel, they could bypass Fae law and try him in a human court of law.

"You're going to get me killed," Jimmy bleated.

"Should have thought of that before you stole shit from your boss," Marty told him.

Defeated, Jimmy sagged in the booth. "What do you need me to do?"

In a car across the street, Rory watched Jimmy talk to the two men in the diner. He slouched down when Jimmy left, to make sure he wasn't seen, and then stayed to watch until the two men came out. Between the outfits and the unmarked sedan, it couldn't be more obvious they were cops. They got in the dark navy car and drove away.

Rory turned the ignition in his own car. "Jimmy, Jimmy, Jimmy. What are you up to, you sneaky little bastard?"

CHAPTER 25

IT WAS FIVE o'clock in the morning, and Seireadan looked back at the bed. Aohdan was sound asleep, half-covered by one of the blankets, and he looked peaceful and relaxed. She envied him that, glad that her latest nightmare hadn't woken him. A bit of cold seeped through the windowpanes to chill her bare skin, and she tugged the sheet wrapped around her up over her shoulder. Outside, waves rolled up onto the sand but did little to lull her, and she sat, chewing her lip and staring out into the night.

The drive home from the Cape had been quiet, and at one point Seireadan had nodded off in the car. Once Aohdan dropped her off, she knew a run in the brisk cold would help her clear her head, so Seireadan changed, donned a hat and some thin fingerless gloves, and slammed the door behind her. She followed her usual pattern but made an extra loop around the Fort Point Channel before heading home. Just as she hit the small set of steps by the Children's Museum, Seireadan saw a man leaning on the rail, looking out at the water. He was quite tall, and his silver-blond hair was caught in a tie but still fell to the middle of his shoulder blades.

That hair . . .

Seireadan missed one of the steps and practically fell down the remaining three. Her chest tightened and her hands turned clammy inside the gloves.

"You son of a bitch!" She reached out and seized the Fae man by the coat, spinning him to face her, and without thinking, dug her fingernails into his neck. Her face was livid, but it was alarmed green eyes that met hers, not icy blue ones.

"Get off me!" he shouted. She let go instantly.

"You're not him!"

"I'm not who?" He pressed his fingers to his neck, and when he pulled his hand away, his fingers were bright red. "Shit, I'm bleeding!"

"I'm sorry! I'm sorry. My mistake . . ."

"Damn right it's a mistake."

"I thought you were someone else." Seireadan backed away with her hands up.

"Clearly." He rubbed the bloody scratch marks on his neck. "Crazy bitch."

"I really am sorry." Seireadan turned and ran. Her feet slammed against the pavement as she sprinted down the sidewalk as if she could outrun the salty sting of tears on her cheeks.

Back at her place, Seireadan left her running clothes in a pile on the bedroom floor. Hot water assaulted her cold, bare skin while she scrubbed herself with a loofa and then turned the water up until it practically scalded her. *I was so sure it was him, so sure. Am I starting to lose my mind? But this isn't going to go away until I find him, or find out he died in the Desolation. I have to figure out if Aohdan knows him. But what if he does?*

The thought that Aohdan could possibly be friends with—or even related to—the Alabaster Man was nearly too awful for Seireadan to contemplate, but she knew she couldn't avoid it any longer. *I have to ask. And I have to do it today, before he leaves for Chicago and the Conclave. Not knowing is going to drive me mad.*

Seireadan arrived at the Underworld offices a little earlier than she'd expected. Jimmy Boy was standing in front of Aohdan's desk, anxiously twisting the claddagh ring he always wore, the one that had belonged to his father. Nervous sweat dotted his upper lip.

"I didn't think he was serious," Jimmy whined.

His face incredulous, Aohdan snapped, "Galen's my second. Of course he was fucking serious. Don't ever let me hear about you blowing him off again. Now get out and do your job—and don't be a liability!"

Jimmy scuttled toward the door, his finger nearly raw from twisting the ring. Seireadan swallowed hard as Jimmy Boy scurried by, dashing her hope that Aohdan would be in a good mood. The phone rang and Aohdan picked it up, waving Seireadan into the office while he talked. He held up a finger to show he was nearly done. She laced her fingers and unlaced them again, shifting restlessly in the chair, thinking of how to say what she needed to say, and then second-guessing herself.

"You're kidding me, right?" Aohdan took the phone away from his ear for a moment, stared at it, and then shook his head in disbelief.

Seireadan's stomach clenched. Aohdan wasn't talking to her, but she knew that mocking, dismissive tone. It had been directed at her too many times by too many people whenever she'd tried to convince anyone her Alabaster Man was real. A cold, anxious sweat chilled her skin, and she shivered, all of her fears about confiding in Aohdan worming into every corner of her mind.

Aohdan's skeptical voice cut through the air. "If he thinks we're buying into that story, he's mistaken. No, he's delusional. Yeah. Tell him he'd better come up with a better excuse than that. Friggin' idiot. I'm leaving for the airport in an hour. Make sure he's in line before I get back from Chicago." Aohdan ended his call and smiled at Seireadan. "Sorry about that. Want to just grab a quick bite here before Rory takes me to the airport?"

"Sure." Her answer was slow, distracted. *Why would I ever think he'd believe my crazy story about having the Sight as a child? And if I ask now and he knows Alabaster? That could ruin the Conclave meeting. I can't do that; it wouldn't be fair. There's got to be another way to find out.*

"You feeling okay, Seireadan? You look a little pale."

"What?" She looked up sharply. "Oh, no. I'm fine. Just a little bit of a headache."

Jimmy nervously stepped to the side as a car pulled up beside him, but when he saw Rory behind the wheel, he exhaled sharply.

"Get in," Rory ordered.

"Why?" Jimmy's eyes darted from side to side.

"Don't be such a tool. Come on." Rory tapped the wheel impatiently.

Jimmy reached out and put his hand on the door handle, and then he hesitated. Rory never wanted his help on anything.

"What are you waiting for? You think I'm going to rough you up for your lunch money? Get in the fucking car, Jimmy. Time's wasting. I just dropped the boss at Logan, and he wants us to follow up on something."

"Fine. Jesus, you're bitchy today. What's the hurry?" asked Jimmy as he got into the car and closed the door. After getting chewed out by Aohdan, Jimmy wasn't going to question any order that came from the patriarch, and he knew Rory would make his life unbearable if he didn't help with whatever job Aohdan had given them. He absently twisted the ring on his finger until he realized Rory was staring at it, and then stuffed his hand in his pocket.

"Limited window of time. Extra set of hands will make it go faster. I have plans for the weekend and I need to get this shit done. If I miss my flight to Vegas, I'll be pissed." Rory looked in his side-view mirror, waited for a cab to pass, and pulled out into traffic.

CHAPTER 26

AERONWY TOR WAS the matriarch of Philadelphia and Aohdan's cousin, and he spotted her the moment he stepped into the hotel lobby. With her deep red hair, leather jacket, and black boots that hit above her knee, Aeronwy certainly stood out in the herd of business suits that swirled around her. She tapped her foot and looked at her watch. A barrel-chested businessman walked by and shamelessly ogled her.

"You looking at something?" Aeronwy gave him a challenging stare, and he stammered and flushed before hurrying away. She flipped her red hair back over her shoulder and rolled her eyes in contempt.

"Charming the locals again?" Aohdan asked.

"Always good to see you, cousin. You look great." Aeronwy hugged him and then held Aohdan out at arm's length while she looked him up and down. Aeronwy looked past Aohdan's shoulder and nodded in acknowledgment to Kieran and Oisin. "What? No Rory? I'm disappointed—I was hoping to have a little extra fun on this trip. He's not like that one . . ." She gestured toward the businessman she'd frightened off. "Rory's got balls. I like that. He's not afraid of me."

"He probably ought to be. Most people are afraid of you for good reason, Aeronwy," Aohdan told her, and she smiled smugly. Aohdan didn't entirely approve of his captain's relationship with his cousin, who—if he was being honest with himself—was more like a sister. But they were both adults. As long as it didn't interfere with business, he really had no reason to object. And if Rory was ever dumb enough to screw over Aeronwy . . . *Well, I don't really have to worry about that. Once Aeronwy was finished with him, I'd be looking for a new captain.*

As matriarch of Philadelphia, Aeronwy Tor ran her crew with a steely ruthlessness. She was one of Aohdan's staunchest supporters in the Conclave, and though there were those who warned Aohdan that someday her ambition would prove greater than her loyalty, he didn't believe it. For all her faults, Aeronwy was also a pragmatist—she ruled her kingdom, but was keenly aware that she was far more powerful and influential with Aohdan than without him.

They started to walk toward the front door of the hotel. Kieran and Oisin followed them along with two of Aeronwy's captains, Aileen and Davey.

"Aohdan's got himself a girlfriend back in Boston," offered Oisin from behind them.

"He's got plenty of those," Aeronwy scoffed.

"This one practically lives at his condo."

She stopped dead in her tracks. "What? Who is she, Aohdan?"

"We'll talk about that later." The patriarch gave both of them a blistering look that left no room for dissent.

"Are we getting coffee?" Aeronwy asked.

"I'm sure there will be coffee there. Harbin will be a bastard if he doesn't have at least two cups, and he likes it strong."

"Good," said Aeronwy. "I'll need some to deal with Teresa, the little bi—"

Aohdan cut her off before she could say something utterly unflattering about the matriarch of New York. "I need you to play nice with her, Aer. I can't have her fight me on the Providence merge."

"She's more trouble than any other triarch. She's going to fight you anyway. Think about it: with her out of the way, we could have half the East Coast," Aeronwy answered in a fierce whisper.

Aohdan dropped his voice, too. "Do you think I haven't? And what do you think the others would do? Getting rid of Teresa would destroy the Conclave and start a war neither of us would survive. Everything we've both worked for would be crushed. Is that what you want?"

"No," huffed Aeronwy, knowing Aohdan was right. "Fine. If playing nice with her means you can screw her over, then we'll do it your way."

Trattoria Dolce had an exclusive dining area in the back with enough seating for twenty and a private bar. The bar was elegantly lit and made of a rich, dark mahogany. The glass shelving behind the bar had additional lighting to showcase the top-shelf liquors. In the center of the room was one large round table for the Conclave members, and around the perimeter of the room were several smaller tables with enough room for two or three people each. Each triarch brought two captains, who were there to keep an eye on things, prevent unwelcome guests, and—although no one said it openly—provide protection in case something unexpected happened.

"Aohdan Collins, welcome to my town!" Tuathal Ross, the patriarch of Chicago, greeted him with a booming voice. He gave Aohdan a hearty handshake and insincere smile, and they spoke only briefly before Tuathal encouraged the three of them to help themselves to coffee and the light breakfast that was laid out. Aohdan did a quick scan of the room. Aeronwy was already talking with Gregor Travis and Réamann Stone, the patriarchs of Los Angeles and San Francisco, respectively. She raised her coffee cup to him and went back to her conversation. As expected, Harbin Rua, who had flown in the previous night from Las Vegas, was sitting alone at the bar nursing his extra-large cup of coffee and muttering to himself about early mornings.

Tuathal's thunderous voice dominated all the other conversations when two more triarchs arrived: Sorchae McKinley, matriarch of Miami; and Nessa Valor, matriarch of Detroit. They extricated themselves from him as soon as possible and walked straight to Aohdan and the coffee bar.

"We could have done this in Miami, where it's warm. But no, Tuathal had to insist that it was his turn to host. In Chicago. In January. He's an idiot," Sorchae grumbled as she put some cream and sugar in her coffee. "But enough of that. Aohdan, it's a pleasure to see you."

"Sorchae. Nessa. The pleasure is always mine, and I must agree with Tuathal, you both look lovely."

"He's a big blowhard," snorted Nessa. "How gorgeous we are is the only thing you and Tuathal will agree on for the rest of the day."

Sorchae smirked before she said, "My dear Aohdan. Our good friend Teresa called me before the meeting. According to her, you're the devil incarnate, with ambitions to take over the entire world, and apparently you're going to kill us all in our sleep. Why is she all in knots this time?"

"I want to merge Matriarch Baibin's *fréamhacha agus brainsí* with my own," he answered, keeping it as simple and direct as possible.

"Providence, right? Very small clan, but she's an uptight old bitch, that one," said Nessa.

"And that's what Teresa's going mental over? Merging that little clan with Boston?" Sorchae shook her head.

"Well, with Aeronwy on one side of her and Aohdan looking to expand on the other, I can see her concern." As usual, Nessa was thorough and thoughtful.

"I don't remember anyone bitching and moaning when Teresa absorbed New Haven and Hartford," countered Sorchae with some substantial venom.

That's exactly the point I want to hammer home during the meeting, and it will be so much better if you bring it up, Sorchae. He nodded and listened while the two matriarchs debated the merits of the merger. As they continued, Harbin roused himself from the bar, got another cup of coffee, and joined them, and just as Tuathal was starting to get red in the face, Teresa Aberdeen swept imperiously into the room.

"Teresa," Tuathal enthused. "We were starting to worry."

"No, we weren't," Aeronwy muttered under her breath, and Aohdan had to struggle not to laugh.

"I do apologize," the matriarch of New York said pompously—and insincerely—as she surveyed the room. When her gaze fell on Aohdan, the skin around her eyes tightened.

Aohdan smiled at her. "Well, now that we're all *finally* here, let's get down to business. We have a lot to discuss."

CHAPTER 27

CUPS RATTLED AS Seireadan slammed the cabinet door before she prowled from the kitchen to the living room and back again. Unsatisfied, she stalked back into the bedroom and dug through her closet until her hands felt the rough, old cloth. Her shoulders sagged as she wrapped her hands around Claíomh Solais, an unseen weight pulling them down. The hard side of the bed frame pinched her back as she sat on the floor and held the sword to her chest, resisting the desire to pull it from the leather and watch the gold aura dance on the blade's edge.

Millennia ago, the Fae had been given four magical weapons—gifts from ancient gods, if legends were to be believed—which had been kept safe by certain families who had used them only in times of great peril, when the fate of the Faerie realm hung in the balance. Gáe Derg, the Red Spear, could destroy magic; and its sister, Gáe Buide, the Yellow Spear, was said to inflict wounds from which no one could recover. The sword Fragarch could cut through any armor, and Claíomh Solais glowed in battle, filled with the power of the sun.

Fionvarr's only sister—Niamh—had taken Gáe Derg and driven it into the heart of the Desolation in a desperate attempt to destroy the spell before it consumed the Faerie realm. The last thing she saw before she died was the Desolation spitting out the blackened, charred metal head of the Red Spear before it moved relentlessly on.

"I have to know. I have to find out." Seireadan's voice was less than a whisper.

She sat on the floor for an hour thinking of her parents, the Desolation, the terrible Seeing that had haunted her all these years, and she thought about the disbelief and the mockery. When she finally put the sword away and grabbed her jacket, she was resolute, any shame or guilt overridden by the painful memories. *It's the only way to get the information I need.*

No one at Underworld paid much attention when she walked down the back hall; she was Aohdan's girlfriend and was there frequently. She slipped down the hall, keeping her eyes down, and let herself into the office. Inside she stopped, took a deep breath to steady herself, and looked around. Galen and Aohdan's desks were larger, more sophisticated, and the spare desk that the other captains used was in the far corner.

She walked over to Aohdan's desk and put her hands on the top of the chair. The leather warmed under her fingers. *Am I really going to do this? What choice do I have? I could have asked him . . . And be laughed at again? Told I'm stupid, foolish, or crazy? Even Lia was skeptical, but she never laughed at me. What if Aohdan finds out?* Seireadan argued with herself for over a minute, but found she had no answer to her final question. Sitting down in the chair, she flipped open his laptop and powered the machine on.

Reaching over, she picked up the framed picture of her and Aohdan at the beach. She smiled. *That was a really fun day.* Then her heart tightened and she hastily put the picture back down. Pushing at a few of the pens piled to the side, she picked up one and twirled it through her fingers before flipping it away crossly.

"If you're going to do this, do it," she muttered to herself. She punched in the password, something she'd seen Aohdan do a half dozen times when she'd been there, and opened the computer's directory.

Now what? It isn't like he's going to have a file labeled "Alabaster." She clicked a few random files and nearly jumped out of the chair when she heard a loud bang in the hall. Her blood pounded in her ears, and she stared at the door, terrified Galen or Rory would walk in.

A woman's shrill voice cut through the noise outside. "Jesus Christ, now we have to rewash all of those. Who left the box of cocktail napkins in the hall?"

Seireadan's entire body sagged, and with one more covert, guilty glance at the door, she went back to the computer. She started with a file marked "Photos." There were at least five hundred images, so she increased the icon size so she could scroll through. By the time she reached photo 397, she'd had just about enough.

Then she saw the eyes. *Those! Those are the eyes!*

Seireadan opened up the photo, and as quickly as the hope had sprung up, it vanished. The eyes are right. *Those are the eyes, but the hair. It's all wrong.* The face looking back at her from the screen had closely cropped sandy-colored hair, not the flowing white blond she so desperately wanted to find. She closed the file, noting it was labeled "CShea," and looked through the last photos. None of the others were even close. A quick search of the computer's directory revealed one other file with "CShea" in it.

"I've pushed my luck too far already," Seireadan said to herself. "But the eyes are right. Maybe I've missed something?"

She hesitated for another second and then plugged her USB drive into the laptop's port.

CHAPTER 28

AOHDAN COMMENCED DAY two of the Conclave by focusing on some commerce difficulties between Gregor and Nessa. The issue wasn't particularly difficult to solve once the two of them started talking, but he made sure everything was clear and settled before moving deeper into the agenda. He'd deliberately put Providence near the end of the day. The longer the meeting went without mention of Baibin's *fréamhacha agus brainsí*, the more irritated Teresa became, and that was fine with him.

Let her work herself into a lather. The more unreasonable she sounds, the better it is for me.

Finally, after Harbin and Tuathal had finished negotiating some details over casinos, Teresa took the bait. She slapped her open palm on the table and pierced Aohdan with a cold stare.

"Haven't we avoided the elephant in the room long enough?" the matriarch of New York asked frostily.

"What's on your mind, Teresa?" He didn't let his voice betray any of his emotions. *It took you long enough. Do your best, you bitch.*

"What's on my mind? Oh please, don't play the innocent; you don't wear it well. Your move to absorb Baibin's *fréamhacha agus brainsí*. Would you have even brought it to the Conclave if I hadn't found out about it?"

"That's insulting, Teresa. We all agreed that any expansion being contemplated would be brought to the Conclave. Providence is on the agenda for later, but we can discuss it now if that would make you feel better."

"Don't patronize me," she seethed.

"I approached *Matriarch* Baibin in the traditional manner." Aohdan emphasized Baibin's rank to draw attention to Teresa's disrespect for another matriarch. "I wasn't obligated to inform the Conclave unless she was agreeable to my proposal, which we confirmed less than a week ago."

"But you hadn't mentioned it yet. You've been avoiding it, dealing with everything else. With everyone else's problems. Letting us all get so tired of negotiating that we'll agree to whatever you want so we can all go home." She folded her arms and glanced around the table to see who might be listening to her slant on the story, and saw several frowns.

"Our meeting is far from over. I thought there were other, more pressing matters to attend to before we got to something so minor." Aohdan was careful to keep his voice reasonable.

"Minor?" She snorted. "Of course, adding another piece to your empire is nothing for any of us to be concerned with. You'd prefer we all be distracted by—"

Aeronwy cut her off. "You're so damn paranoid, Teresa. His empire? Please."

"No one asked you." Teresa rounded on Aeronwy in an instant, her hatred for the other matriarch as hot as Aeronwy's was for her.

"Why the concern, Teresa?" asked Harbin, interrupting before the two of them could escalate.

"I see him for what he is. Ambitious. Dangerous. Little by little, he gathers power, and with the unquestioning backing of his little ginger bitch here . . ." She flipped her chin toward Aeronwy with contempt.

Aohdan's cousin was halfway out of her chair when Aohdan raised his hand. He was—as all the triarchs had agreed at the inception of the first Conclave—the chairman, and Aeronwy slowly sat back down out of respect. But she didn't make any effort to conceal the anger or disdain she felt for Teresa.

"I understand that as the closest triarch to Boston, you have concerns, but are we really going to waste our time over this?" asked Nessa.

"I would have to second that question," said Gregor. "This is a trifle."

"Can you both really be that stupid? Does it bother none of you that he's expanding his sphere of power? Providence gives him another set of ports to bring in more cash and more product." Teresa swept her gaze around the table, seeing only Tuathal's nod of agreement and not the affront on the faces of Gregor and Nessa.

"What difference does it make?" asked Réamann. "If he brings in more product, it has to go somewhere. That's better business for all of us, isn't it?"

"Except that Aohdan gains the profits," said Tuathal.

"Yes, exactly," Teresa nearly crowed.

"If it's good business, we all profit," said Gregor.

"Precisely my point, Gregor. You are such a hypocrite, Teresa." Sorchae raised her voice to make sure everyone heard her.

"Excuse me?" Teresa's eyes widened.

Aohdan knew several people at the table were watching his reactions as carefully as they were watching Teresa, and he kept his expression as neutral as possible. He leaned forward a little, resting his forearms on the table, and waited. *Drive the nail in for me, Sorchae. Drive it all the way home. Right into her black hole of a heart.*

Sorchae charged ahead. "Of course he's interested in more ports and more profit. I'm interested in more ports. Almost every single person at this table is interested in more ports, and that includes you, Teresa. You wouldn't be complaining if you were the one getting the ports and the profit. So look me in the eye and tell me, in front of everyone, that you've never thought about annexing Providence. That you haven't approached Baibin yourself about her *fréamhacha agus brainsí*. You can't, can you?"

Sorchae dared Teresa to lie and was rewarded with a glare before she continued, "But I know Baibin, and I bet she thought you were too disrespectful to even consider you as a new triarch for her *brainsí*. This is nothing but sour grapes from you."

"Any business I had with Baibin is immaterial," said Teresa.

"Bullshit," muttered Aeronwy.

"You know, Teresa, I don't recall Aohdan whining and crying like a spoiled child when you annexed New Haven . . . and Hartford," added Sorchae.

"That's very true, and if anyone would have had cause to block that, it would have been Aohdan," Gregor said. "You expanded upward, toward him, and I would consider that much more of a threat. Where else is he going to expand to?"

"Another excellent question," Aeronwy said, turning to face her cousin. "Aohdan, where do you plan to expand to next?"

He gave her a warning look for the sarcasm, but still answered the question. "Gregor's right. Where else can I go? Up through Canada and sweep down into Detroit? For starters, I don't have an army. And why would I destroy the productive relationship I have with Nessa?" He nodded to the matriarch, and she nodded back in acknowledgment.

"Let's be done with this. Bring it to a vote," said Gregor.

"Agreed. And I will abide by the Conclave's decision," said Aohdan.

"Fine," Aeronwy said. "Who is in favor of letting Aohdan proceed with grafting Matriarch Baibin's *fréamhacha agus brainsí* to his own?" She raised her hand before she even finished talking. Gregor and Sorchae raised their hands. When Nessa followed, then Réamann, Aohdan knew he'd won. Teresa's face blackened.

"And who is opposed?" Aeronwy asked, making only a marginal attempt to not gloat.

Teresa and Tuathal both raised their hands. Then everyone looked at Harbin. Even if he sided with the nays, it wouldn't make a difference, but Aohdan wanted to know why.

"You're abstaining, Harbin?"

The patriarch of Las Vegas was quiet but finally said, "I am indifferent. I agree with Teresa that you have larger ambitions than you let on, but then again, most of us do. Gregor also raises a good question: Where else will you go if you want to expand? Your geography limits you. I couldn't care less if you take Providence, a drop in the ocean as far as I'm concerned. But if you ever made a bolder move on a larger city? That would concern me a great deal. We cannot, however, waste energy on maybe and might be. So, do what you will with Providence. I don't care."

"Then it is decided," said Aohdan with a sharp smile. "The majority of the Conclave has no objections. I will move forward with my plan to take Matriarch Baibin's *fréamhacha agus brainsí* as my own. Let it be done."

The weather turned foul, closing O'Hare for several hours and forcing Aohdan to wait at the airport. Once they were in the air, he spent most of the three-hour flight having a much-needed nap. After landing at Logan, Oisin and Kieran headed home, but Aohdan took his car and went to Underworld so he could update Galen on the Conclave.

"I'm glad Teresa wasn't too much of an issue," said Galen. He gestured to let Aohdan precede him into the office.

"She's pissed, though. And I wouldn't put it past her to make the rest of the merge difficult out of spite."

"I think Kieran has some contacts in New York. I'll have him get in touch with them, find out if they hear anything."

"Good." Aohdan swept his eyes across his desk. Something was different, off. Things weren't the way they were supposed to be.

"What's wrong?" Galen picked up on his unease immediately.

"Someone's been at my desk. The picture of me and Seireadan is in the wrong place. My pens have been moved." He rested his fingertips on his laptop. "They touched my computer. Go get the security tape. Now."

It took Galen only a few minutes to access Underworld's security system. There were cameras throughout the establishment, and a secondary system that paid attention to the back offices. It had been installed a week before Aohdan's trip to Chicago, at Galen's encouragement. There was usually sensitive information in the office—especially now, with Providence moving forward—so Aohdan's second had lobbied hard for the extra security. Only Aohdan, Galen, and a few others knew about the system. They started to fast-forward through the footage until they saw Seireadan come into the room.

Aohdan's stomach dropped.

They watched her walk into the office and look around, everything about her radiating unease and discomfort. She walked quickly over to Aohdan's desk and stood with her hands on the back of the chair for nearly a full minute before she sat down. Flipping open the laptop, Seireadan leaned back in the chair, but rather than search for something, she started to look at other things. Picking up the framed picture, she ran her fingers over the image and put it back down. She took some pens, pushed them slightly, and then picked one up and twirled it through her fingers.

Putting the pen down, she seemed to sigh and deflate before she started tapping on the keyboard. Her head snapped up, and she stared at the door, frozen, for about ten full seconds before she went back to the computer. A moment later, her face changed, transforming from worried, to stunned, to angry, to an expression Aohdan could only describe as victory, before melancholy washed back over her violet eyes and expressive face.

He watched the tape, watched Seireadan put a USB drive into the computer, and then simply said, "Enough."

Galen stopped the playback. "I'm sorry, Aohdan. I really am."

Aohdan's expression was bleak and hollow, and inside, the pain in his heart was so searing he was numb. Reflexively, Aohdan's hand went to his heart, touching the *brainsí* tattoo through his shirt. *How could she do this me? Trust and loyalty—they're everything. I loved her . . . I trusted her . . .*

"This stays with us."

"No one will know unless you tell them," Galen told him.

"Good. Now get out."

On another day, Aohdan might have expected Galen to try reasoning with him, but he was just as glad when his second got up silently and went to the door, leaving him to stare at the damning picture of Seireadan taking files from his computer as the numbness gave way to pain and the pain transformed into fury.

CHAPTER 29

SEIREADAN SIGHED HEAVILY and stared at the cracks in the concrete sidewalk as she walked. Snow, half-melted and gritty from sand and salt, lingered along the edge of the street in uneven clumps. The blackness around her deepened as a bank of clouds covered the moon, leaving only the harsh, fake light of the streetlamps and car headlights to illuminate the night. A pickup truck rattled by, a squealing, misaligned belt barking its displeasure. Seireadan didn't notice the noise—or how the cold winter wind froze the dampness on her cheeks.

How could I have not trusted him enough to talk to him? He's trusted me with so much. She shook her head, clinging to her fears, using them as a shield against the guilt. *No, he wouldn't have given me files like that. He has so much going on. He would have laughed. A child's night terror hardly compares to what he's shouldering. It would have gutted me if he laughed and brushed it off like Cavan and the others did. I did the only thing I could . . . didn't I?*

She flinched when her phone buzzed; it was another text from Aohdan, and Seireadan swallowed hard.

Haven't heard back from you. Come to Underworld tonight. I need to see you.

She put the phone away without answering. *I'm out of excuses. He might not know, but I do. I know exactly what I've done. And it wasn't even worth it. There's nothing in those damn files. This CShea is nearly a ghost—just another dead end.* She rubbed the back of her neck and rolled her head. A few more cars slipped by unnoticed. The moonlight brightened and then vanished again, hidden by another band of unseen clouds.

Turning down her walkway, Seireadan fished the keys out of her pocket. She turned them in the lock, and it opened with a dull thud. Door hinges squeaked, and she started to reach for the lights, cursing that she still hadn't called the electrician to fix the damn switch. Freed again from its cloudy veil, moonlight suffused the apartment, pooling on the floor, and lighting the room enough to see but keeping everything else cloaked in a palette of blacks, grays, and midnight blues. In the muted light, Seireadan shrugged off her jacket and was reaching for the other light switch when Aohdan's voice glided out of the living room shadows.

"You used me."

The fury simmering below the words was palpable, and Seireadan's knees nearly buckled. Shadows shifted, and she could feel him coil, a predator ready to lunge.

"Aohdan." Her whispered voice barely registered in the silence.

A second later, his hands were on her, slamming Seireadan back against the wall, forcing the air from her lungs. Terrified, Seireadan shouted and punched blindly, but he knocked her hands away, and she cried out in pain as he grabbed a fistful of her hair. Seireadan clutched at the front of Aohdan's shirt.

"Stop! I'm sorry . . ." Her words disintegrated into a wheeze as Aohdan's other hand wrapped around her throat and tightened. Seireadan's ears started to ring, and she tried to claw at him, desperate for air, but Aohdan pressed his body against her, pinning her arms.

His voice in her ear was raw with pain. "You're sorry? That's all you have to say?"

She tried to answer, but all that came out was a choking, ragged noise. Aohdan tightened his grip on her hair but relaxed his other hand slightly, giving Seireadan the slimmest chance to drag some air into her screaming lungs, and the cold burned all the way down her throat.

"I needed information on someone . . . ," she rasped.

"So you just took it," Aohdan seethed. "To do what? Use it against me? Give it to whoever you're working for?"

Her hands still braced on his chest, Seireadan could feel him shaking with rage and a dozen other emotions.

"I'm not working for anyone! Please, let me explain . . ."

"Explain what? How it was all a lie? I gave you myself, Seireadan. More of me—more of my heart!—than I've ever given to anyone. *Anyone!* Do you even understand what that means? Rory's right; love is just bullshit." The anguished noise that rumbled low in his throat drove another dagger into Seireadan's heart.

She whispered his name one more time, "Aohdan. I love—"

His hand tightened, cutting her off, and Seireadan squeezed her eyes shut.

"Don't even say it. Just don't. You may as well have put a gun to my heart and pulled the trigger," said Aohdan. He kept Seireadan pinned to the wall with his hand at her throat but let go of her hair. He tightened his grip again. Seireadan's head started to swim, and tears rolled down her cheeks. She grabbed at his arm, but it was immovable stone and steel.

"I was just a means to an end for you, wasn't I?" Aohdan asked, each word laced with torment. "I've done some bad shit in my life, Seireadan, but I've never told someone I loved them and then used them like that. But you used me. You. Used. Me."

His words cut deeply, accusing her, condemning her, and Seireadan remembered something that Julia had said when she first started seeing Aohdan: *"Be careful, Seireadan. Bad things happen to people who cross Aohdan Collins."*

Seireadan looked up into his eyes, and even in the low, filtered light, they were bright, watching her with breathtaking intensity, a maelstrom of rage and love, heartbreak and crushed hope. To her surprise, Aohdan let go of her throat, but Seireadan didn't dare move; he was teetering on the proverbial knife's edge.

Her voice was husky and rough. "Do what you have to. But I wasn't lying when I told you I loved you."

Aohdan shut his eyes, his face twisting as if it were painful to hear the hope and the sadness, the resignation, in her voice.

"Aohdan . . ." Seireadan felt his pain and instinctively reached out for him. Aohdan shoved her back into the wall.

"Don't touch me. Stay away from me, Seireadan, and stay out of my business."

He backed away, and Seireadan felt her heart fracturing deeper with each step he took, the pain of her betrayal more evident with every moment. Framed in the doorway, Aohdan looked back over his shoulder, and the pain in his eyes and sadness in his voice crushed her.

"I *loved* you, Seireadan. I would have given you *anything*."

CHAPTER 30

SHAKING NEARLY UNCONTROLLABLY, Seireadan slid down the wall and crumpled to the floor, barely feeling the cold air from the still-open front door. Pulling her knees to her chest, she wrapped her arms around them and started to cry. She wept until her chest ached and there were no tears left. Eventually, she dragged herself to the sofa and called Lia.

"Lia? It's me. Can you come over? I did something stupid . . . I ruined everything." Seireadan started to cry again.

When Lia arrived, she found the door still open. "Seireadan? Your door was open—it's freezing in here. What happened?" Her voice trailed away when she saw Seireadan on the sofa, clutching a pillow and staring straight ahead, eyes glassy and cheeks blotchy. But what caught Lia's eye were the marks—still raw and red—on Seireadan's throat, marks that would blacken as a reminder of Aohdan's wrath.

"What did he do to you, Seireadan?" Lia sat on the center cushion and grabbed Seireadan's hand. "What happened?"

"I ruined everything." Seireadan wanted to cry but she couldn't. "I didn't trust him enough to ask for help finding the Alabaster Man. I was too afraid. Too afraid he'd dismiss me like everyone else has. Too terrified that Aohdan would know who he was—maybe even be friends with him! I thought it would be easy if I just . . ."

"If you just what?"

"I looked through his computer while he was away. I was trying to find out if Aohdan knew . . . *him*. I took a file."

"Tell me you're kidding me, Seireadan. Tell me you didn't steal something from Aohdan Collins?"

Seireadan looked at her friend, profoundly sad. "I did. I was stupid and he found out. He came here tonight. He said that I used him. That I never loved him." She reached up and touched her throat. "His hands are so strong . . ."

"You're lucky he didn't kill you."

"I thought he was going to. I don't know what stopped him. But he left and he told me to stay away from him . . . and out of his business." Seireadan put her face in her hands, unable to forget the bereft expression on Aohdan's face when he left. "What have I done, Lia? I love him. I honestly love him and I destroyed it."

"At least . . . did you find Alabaster?"

Completely miserable and abject, Seireadan shook her head. "No. It was all for nothing. Nothing! He doesn't even believe that I love him. Why didn't I just trust him enough to ask him?"

The tears finally came again, and Lia, unable to answer Seireadan's question, just put her arms around her friend and let her cry.

After walking away from Seireadan, Aohdan went back to his place. He upended a bottle of whiskey, not bothering to put any in a glass, and coughed violently as the fiery liquid caught on the painful lump in his throat. He wiped his eyes angrily with the back of his hand and took another swig of whiskey as he prowled around the condominium.

He picked up a picture that sat on the table by the front door. Surrounded by a frame of polished cherrywood was an image of him and Seireadan from their Labor Day getaway. She sat in front of him on a warm sand dune, wrapped up in his arms. It was late afternoon, and the low sun gave the picture a warm, golden hue. They were both smiling, so happy, so in love.

Love . . .

For an instant, love welled up, only to be trampled by the anger coursing through him. Aohdan flung the picture down, and glass shattered across the floor as the cracked frame bounced to the side. An agonized, nearly incoherent howl tore out of him, and his breath stuttered as he continued to wage his losing war with tears. Two more long swallows of whiskey disappeared in an instant as he stumbled to the windows. Pressing a palm on the glass, the whiskey bottle clenched in his other hand, Aohdan stared out into the darkness. *I trusted her . . .*

"Seireadan!" he roared at the night. "How could you? I loved you. I loved you and I trusted you . . . and you ripped my fucking heart out."

He went to take another drink and tossed the bottle carelessly on the floor when he realized it was empty. The visceral memory of his hand around Seireadan's throat—her stuttered breath, her tears, her acceptance of what she thought would happen—engulfed him. He looked down at his hands, and Aohdan's chest started to heave as he thought about what he had almost done.

She was afraid of me, afraid that I'd hurt her . . . that I'd kill her . . .

In that moment, Aohdan despised himself more than he realized was possible, and regret and shame pooled, bitter, in his stomach. But his shattered heart, furious and hurting, wanted nothing to do with sorrow, and the feral part of him—the part he'd used time and time again to become patriarch—refused to be silent.

She betrayed you, she stole from you. You should have killed her, whispered an accusing voice in the back of his mind.

No! Not her. Aohdan yanked a second bottle of whiskey out of the cabinet. Emptiness would be far better than this brutal aching.

You've killed men for less, but you couldn't do it. You couldn't kill her because you love her. Derision and contempt soaked through the thought as Aohdan remembered what Kieran had told him: *She'll have the power to destroy you—to gut you—with a single word or look, and even when she does, you'll love her anyway.*

"I don't love her! Not anymore, not after this!" Aohdan shouted out loud, pounding his fist over his heart as if that would somehow make the ache disappear.

LIAR! roared the voice.

Aohdan tipped the bottle up. The only thing that mattered was forgetting Seireadan's face and annihilating the pain in his heart.

CHAPTER 31

GALEN SIGHED AND looked at his watch again. Aohdan was never late for meetings. There was a lot to do now that the Conclave had approved the merger between Boston and Providence, and Aohdan had to be part of it. But Galen also knew what he'd seen on the computer monitor a few days before. He grabbed his coat.

"I'll be back," he said to Kieran. "If Aohdan shows up, text me and tell him I'll be right back."

For the entire drive to Aohdan's place, all Galen could think about was how Aohdan had looked while he watched that security tape. When he'd left Underworld the night before, Galen knew his boss was going to look for Seireadan; the plastered smile he wore might have fooled the others, but Galen knew Aohdan was tired of waiting for Seireadan to come to him.

The odor of stale, sour, drunken sweat assailed him as soon as he opened Aohdan's door. Galen took a few steps inside, and glass crunched underfoot. A smashed picture frame lay about three feet away. An empty whiskey bottle was on its side in the middle of the floor.

"Aohdan? Are you here?" Galen called. There was no answer other than a dim snore.

On the sofa, barefoot and dressed only in his jeans, Aohdan was passed out with another bottle of whiskey still clutched in his hand. Galen slapped Aohdan on the top of the foot, not wanting to be anywhere near the big Fae's fists or that bottle when he woke up.

"Hey! Aohdan! Wake up!" Galen grabbed his leg and shook.

"What?" Aohdan stirred, his voice slurred and lethargic. He threw an arm over his face. "Fuck, that's bright. Shut the shades. What time is it?"

"Just after noon. We were supposed to meet at ten to talk about Providence."

The room darkened slightly, and Aohdan swung his legs down and slowly sat up on the sofa. He gripped the top of his skull with one hand and squeezed. "My head is pounding," he said before downing the last dregs of whiskey still in the bottle.

Galen took the bottle away from him. "Probably enough of that for now. You look like shit."

"Fuck off."

Aohdan, his fingers pressing his temples, swung his head slowly from side to side. While the patriarch wrestled with his hangover, and all the pain that came rushing back with a vengeance, Galen found the aspirin and grabbed a glass of water. He handed both to Aohdan, and the patriarch took them without an argument.

"She used me, Galen."

"What happened last night?"

"I was waiting for her in her apartment when she came home," said Aohdan. He wobbled as he stood up but kept his balance.

"And?" Galen held his breath, afraid of what Aohdan would say.

“And? I nearly killed her, Galen. I had my hand around her throat. But I couldn’t do it.” Aohdan’s voice trailed away, and Galen carefully let out his breath.

“I loved her, Galen.”

“I know you do.”

Aohdan’s temper flared in an instant, and he grabbed Galen’s arm. “NO!” he shouted. “Loved. Past tense. She used me, Galen. She used me. I don’t think she ever loved me.”

If you really believed that, she would be dead. “Come on, we need to get you cleaned up a little.”

With some coaxing, Galen managed to get Aohdan to the bathroom and into a cold shower. While Aohdan rinsed a little of the alcohol from his brain, Galen got rid of the empty bottles and swept up the broken glass.

Two hours later, Galen was standing outside the closed door of the Underworld office when Oisin walked up and asked, “Why are you just standing here? He in a meeting?”

“No, but unless you really need to talk to him, I’d stay out.”

“What’s going on? I guess this explains Rory’s piss-poor mood.”

“Aohdan ended things with Seireadan last night. He’s hungover and then Rory just had to put his two cents in about the whole fucking thing,” Galen grumbled.

“He what? Shit. Well, I suppose it was only a matter of time before they had a real fight.”

“I think this was more than just a fight.”

“Really? What happened?” Oisin asked.

“I don’t know. I just know that as far as Aohdan’s concerned, it’s over.”

“Into the lion’s den, then. He’s expecting this in his hands this morning, and if he’s in the kind of mood you say he is, I don't want to keep him waiting." Oisin tapped an envelope in his pocket.

Oisin squared his shoulders, and they both went into the office, only to be greeted with a bleak stare and a frown. To say Aohdan looked terrible would have been a compliment. He was pale, his skin waxy, and dark circles haunted his glassy, bloodshot eyes. He'd clearly been in the shower but really hadn't bothered to comb his hair.

"What do you want?" the patriarch growled.

"Last payment from Oona the Unlucky. You said you wanted it today, no exceptions." Oisin tossed the envelope on the desk.

"Good." It was more grunt than actual response, and Aohdan stared at the envelope without really seeing it.

"Do you want to talk about whatever's got you so ripped? You look terrible," said Oisin, knowing full well he was poking the bear, but he was completely taken aback when Aohdan leaped up from the desk, his chair skittering backward, as his gun seemed to materialize in his hand. Aohdan waved it in his captain's general direction.

"Whoa! Hang on a second!" Oisin cried.

"I'm sure you know exactly what's going on," growled Aohdan. "I don't want to talk about it. I don't want to think about it, and I swear on my mother's own life, I will shoot the next one of you that mentions Seireadan's name in front of me."

"Fine, whatever you want," Oisin said, trying to mollify Aohdan, and the patriarch put the gun down. Galen grabbed some files and his laptop, and headed for the door. Oisin was a few steps behind, but before following Galen out, he stopped.

Turning around, Oisin said, "You haven't asked for my advice, but I'm going to give it to you anyway. Maybe this isn't about whatever you think it's about. Maybe it's about something else entirely. Don't blow this relationship over something stupid or because you're too stubborn to listen."

A blistering trail of curses and epithets followed them out of the room, and in the hallway, Galen just stared at Oisin in disbelief.

"You're as dumb as a fucking stump, you know that?"

"It had to be said." Oisin's voice followed Galen down the hall.

For the next three days, Seireadan avoided the world. She called in sick to Sacred Circle, barely spoke to any of her Creative Media clients, and spent an inordinate amount of time in bed. When she was out of bed, Seireadan sat curled up on her sofa, staring at the USB drive lying innocently on the coffee table.

She also tried to ignore Lia's stream of texts and voice mails, but the more she avoided them, the more frequently Lia tried to reach her, and Seireadan knew it was a losing battle. Finally, she caved and answered her phone.

"What?"

"About time you answered," Lia groused. "Don't you freeze me out, Seireadan."

"Haven't really felt like talking." Seireadan made a face at the phone.

"Well, you're going to talk tonight. I'm coming over and we're going out for burgers at Rosewood, and then we are going to hang out."

"I'm not that hungry."

"Bullshit—yes, you are. And I have an emergency key to your place, so don't get any bright ideas about not answering your door, got it? I'll be there before six. That gives you over an hour to get showered and put on some clean clothes." Lia's tone was utterly no-nonsense. "And I imagine it's going to take a bit to get the tangles out of your hair, so get a move on."

Sitting on her sofa in her old leggings, the same shirt she'd worn to sleep, and a grubby old sweatshirt, Seireadan wondered if Lia could see through the phone.

"Lia, I don't really—"

"I don't care. You're not spending tonight alone. See you soon."

The phone clicked on the other end. Seireadan sighed heavily and slammed her head back on the sofa cushion, some of her tangled hair flopping over a shoulder. *She's right, you know. You can't just sit here and wallow . . . and you do need a shower. You're a mess.* Mustering her energy, Seireadan made her way to the bedroom, where she tossed her clothes into the laundry basket and grabbed a fresh towel from her little linen closet.

In the bathroom, she stopped suddenly as she caught sight of her reflection. Her hair was nothing short of a horror show: tangled and unwashed, half was caught in a loose braid, and the other half just seemed to have a mind of its own. Her face was pale and sad, but it was the necklace of bluish-purple bruises that commanded her attention, and for the first time since Aohdan had stormed out of her apartment, Seireadan got angry. She slammed her palms on the mirror face, nearly cracking the glass, and let out a furious, incoherent shout.

"That bastard!" she yelled, staring at the ugly discolorations. "How could he do this? No one puts their hands on me like that! And he didn't even give me a chance to explain, to tell him why I took the file. He just assumed I did it to hurt him. He just decided what happened without even asking!"

She let the anger run wild, coursing through her as she raged about how Aohdan had treated her, marginalized her, and then she turned the anger inward, berating herself for not fighting harder, for not standing up to him. A moment later, her head snapped to the side and she stormed into the living room, where she grabbed a paperweight from the shelf and smashed it down on the USB drive. After snatching the cracked and dented drive, she stalked back into the bathroom. Seireadan flung the drive into the toilet bowl and flushed, staring at the drive as it disappeared in a swirl of water.

"I ruined everything! Threw all of it away for nothing!" she shouted to the empty room. Seireadan gripped the sides of the sink, staring at the bruises, feeling the anger flare up again. But before long the fury cooled to a simmer. *Aohdan assumed I just wanted to hurt him, but I made assumptions, too. I assumed he wouldn't take me seriously, wouldn't trust me, and that hurt him . . .*

"I opened the door for this mess," she told her reflection. "I hurt him, I broke the trust, but that's no excuse for how he treated me. If he ever tries to put his hands on me like that again, he'd better be ready to kill me because I won't put up with that shit a second time."

CHAPTER 32

OISIN COULD HEAR Rory coming down the hall before he saw him. The tall redhead was on his phone. "Big man's always acted like he's king of the world. Can't even make the hard decisions anymore. I have to handle that shit. Been a week since he dumped that bitch, and he's still stuck in the bottom of a bottle." As he turned the corner, he caught sight of Oisin, and Rory's voice dropped to a whisper, the tenor—and topic—changing entirely. "I'll see you later, baby. Oh, I'll do all that to you and more . . ."

"Someone's got a little honey on the side. Must be why you're not so bitchy about having to go to Worcester lately," said Oisin impertinently.

"Smart-ass. You go do work in that armpit of a city."

Oisin paused. "Didn't you just get back from Philadelphia the other day? I can't imagine Aeronwy is all that good at sharing her toys."

"I'm not hers to share—we have a casual relationship."

The sarcastic snort that ripped out of Oisin made it clear he doubted the statement. "And what about this new little piece on the side? Who is she? And does she know you and Aeronwy bump uglies on a pretty regular basis?"

"She's my little prize to play with, and no, she doesn't know about Aeronwy. When I'm done with her, you can have my sloppy seconds if you're interested. Maybe after this, it will be time for Aer to be my little toy." Rory's laugh was callous.

Oisin just shook his head. *You do that and Aeronwy will slap the stupid out of you—after she punches all your teeth out.*

Inside, Aohdan was waiting for them along with Galen and Kieran. The patriarch grimaced as he swallowed some aspirin. For three straight nights he'd put himself to sleep with a bottle of whiskey, the only thing that erased what Seireadan had done—and how he'd retaliated—from his mind. Unfortunately, the memory was waiting when he woke up—along with the hangover.

"We have a date for the Providence transfer," he said without any preamble. "It will be the last day of February. We'll do it over dinner at DJ's Steak & Seafood. And Baibin's second will handle the official duties."

"Crogher? He'd rather stick a fork in his ball sack than see you as patriarch," snorted Oisin.

"I know. I've spoken with both him and Baibin on the phone, and—on the surface—he's playing sincere," replied Aohdan.

"Sincere? I do no' think he understands the concept," Kieran told them.

"No, he doesn't, and I won't believe it until the whole thing is done. Stay in touch with your contacts in Providence. If there's even a whiff of stupid . . . And speaking of stupid, has anyone seen Jimmy Boy? He's not answering his damn phone."

"You need to deal with Crogher," said Rory. "He needs to be handled before something happens. Just like I—"

"No. There won't be any handling of anyone, Crogher or otherwise." Aohdan's voice was sharp; it was an order—and a rebuke—and Rory flushed. "After the merge, Crogher's mine to deal with however I see fit. Now, let's move on . . ."

Oisin's phone rang, and he did a double take when he saw the caller. He glanced at Aohdan, who nodded, a silent okay for Oisin to take the call. It gave Aohdan a chance to rub his temples for a minute, but every head in the office, including Aohdan's, turned to stare at Oisin when they heard the shock in his voice.

"What? You saw it yourself? You're absolutely certain? No, no. It's good you called." Oisin hung up, stunned, and then said, "Aohdan, we've got a problem."

Still nursing a hangover from his ongoing breakup binge, Aohdan glowered at him. "My entire life is one big fucking problem right now. What's one more disaster?"

"That was Maksim, my friend in the coroner's office," said Oisin. "Jimmy Boy's dead."

The fog cleared from Aohdan's head in a heartbeat. "What? Are you sure?"

"Murdered. Maks says it's a positive ID. And whoever did it really fucked Jimmy up. And . . ."

Aohdan didn't like the sound of the long pause. "And what, Oisin?"

"And whoever did it was sending a message. There was a note stuck to the body. One word, written in blood: 'rat.' And I don't think that's a bluff. Maks said one of the detectives, that Sandhurst guy, was losing his shit in the hallway about losing the opportunity to nail you for good."

Aohdan rubbed the bridge of his nose. It had never been a secret that Jimmy worked for him. Regardless of whether or not the cops had turned Jimmy, with their close association and

Jimmy Boy outed as a rat, there was no way the cops wouldn't have him at the top of their suspect list.

"Shit. I didn't tell anyone to handle Jimmy," said Aohdan.

"You didn't have to ask. When I see a situation that needs it, I take care of it." Rory's voice and smile were smugly satisfied.

"What *exactly* did you take care of?" Aohdan ground the words out.

"What did I . . . ?" Rory shook his head. "Are you all so damn stupid? I can't believe you haven't figured this out. Jimmy was a rat; he was working with the cops. And I *handled* it."

Aohdan's vision turned red the moment the words left Rory's mouth, and he lunged for his captain with such force they crashed into the opposite wall. With an incoherent shout, Aohdan twisted and slammed Rory down on the floor, and the cry of pain that came out of his captain told Aohdan that at least one rib was broken. Practically kneeling on Rory, Aohdan landed three crushing punches before Kieran and Oisin managed to pull him off. They held the patriarch back while Rory rolled on the floor, bleeding heavily from the mouth.

"Not here! Not at Underworld!" Galen bellowed over the din.

"You fucking idiot! What were you thinking?" thundered Aohdan, still trying to reach his redheaded captain.

"I was thinking that you're so far down in a bottle over that bitch, you couldn't have made a decision," Rory shouted back as he spit more blood out and scrambled to his feet.

"I made a promise to his father."

"A promise he shit on. He spit in your face, Aohdan!" yelled Rory.

"You know what? He did. And I shouldn't have cut him so much slack. But you had no right—NO RIGHT—to put your hands on him. Not without my say-so. You should have brought this to me the first day instead of pretending to be patriarch."

Rory looked around the room for support and found none.

"Dead cops and dead associates get a lot of attention—too much attention," Aohdan said to Rory once he had a modicum of self-control again. "If we weren't so close to closing Providence, I'd . . ." Aohdan stopped talking, clenching and unclenching his fist, feeling the sting of his skinned knuckles, and leaving his initial thought unfinished. "But I need to show Baibin a united *fréamhacha agus brainsí*, so consider this your lucky fucking day."

Rory opened his mouth to say something, but Aohdan cut him off. "Not another fucking word. Of all the stupid-ass, brainless things to do . . ."

Livid, Rory flushed an ugly dull red and looked at his patriarch sullenly.

Aohdan put his hand in the center of Rory's chest, shoved his captain back two steps, and snarled, "If you breathe a word of this to anyone, I'll come for you myself. Get out. We're done."

Kieran grabbed Rory by the arm and pulled him out of the room before he could say anything else stupid. Oisin and Galen followed, and the three hustled him out the back of the club and down the street. Galen glanced around, assessing how many people were around.

"How can he be pissed? I protected the *fréamhacha agus brainsí*. Jimmy was going to the cops!" Rory shouted. He rubbed his face, which had ballooned where Aohdan had punched him. "Dammit, that hurts."

"Keep your voice down," Kieran warned.

"I showed initiative."

"Initiative? Rory, you totally fucked the pooch this time," said Oisin. "If I were you, I'd keep my mouth shut and my head down. Take whatever ass-kicking he gives you, and don't turn into more of a problem than you already are."

"Whatever." Rory flung his bravado up like a shield. "Aohdan will calm down in a day or two, and he'll understand I've done him a huge solid."

That was enough for Galen. He grabbed Rory and dragged him into an alley. A punch to the gut doubled Rory over, and before the captain could stand, Galen pressed his nine-millimeter Beretta to the back of Rory's head.

"Galen, this is no' a good idea," warned Kieran as Oisin looked to make sure no one had seen them.

"You're a captain, Rory. A fucking captain!" Galen's voice was laced with fury. "If it were up to me, I'd put a bullet in your brain right now and they'd find you in a dumpster with the rest of the trash. The ONLY thing stopping me is the fact that Aohdan didn't green-light it. You know better than to do this kind of shit. You. Know. BETTER."

"Galen . . . ," Kieran said again.

Aohdan's second leaned in close to Rory and whispered harshly, "Do NOT fuck up again."

Galen tucked the gun in the back of his pants, and they left Rory bloody—and angry—in the dingy, trash-strewn alley.

CHAPTER 33

AFTER HE DRAGGED himself out of the alley, Rory made his way to his car and drove out to Auburn, a city just outside of Worcester, to lick his wounds. He stomped up the stairs to the apartment and found the door already open, and his "piece of tail" waiting for him in a sheer black negligee.

Vashti's face fell when she saw him. "Baby! What happened?" She pulled back her wings and pressed herself against Rory.

"Fucking Aohdan, that's what," he snapped.

"Sit down. I'll get you a beer."

Would be nice if fucking Aeronwy pampered me every now and then—when was the last time she ran and fetched a beer?

While she went to the kitchen, Rory started to rant. "Aohdan's completely out of control. He's out of his mind over that bitch, Seireadan, and I wish I knew what she'd done. Maybe she needs a lesson in how to act around a patriarch. But Aohdan is so twisted up he can't think straight. Dismisses every suggestion I have, and I can't even say all the things I've done to help him because he'll just turn it all around. Someone needs to make the hard decisions, and if he can't, I will. I'm getting sick and fucking tired of not getting the credit I deserve."

"That's so unfair," cooed the Pari as she handed Rory his beer.

"I told him about Jimmy being a rat. You think he'd be a little more fucking grateful that I took the initiative when I did. He's swimming in whiskey; he sure couldn't fucking do it. Then he lost his shit and did this." Rory gestured at his face and winced when the broken rib barked.

"You shouldn't have to put up with that. You deserve better," the Pari told him.

Rory chugged half the bottle of beer. "You're damn right I deserve better. And to top it off? I heard a rumor that he's sending Chris to discuss business with the matriarch of Detroit. A human! Teacher's fucking pet. He's next on my list." He finished the beer.

Vashti, who had smartly brought a second beer, handed it to Rory as well. She hid a predatory smile before she slid onto the sofa next to him.

"That's terrible," she said. "You clearly should be the man in charge. You're smart, and decisive. You know what you want and you take it." She leaned in and nibbled his ear. "Aohdan is a fool for wasting you. You should be with someone who appreciates your talents, and who doesn't think a lowly human is a better soldier than you."

"He doesn't think that . . ." Rory stopped, wondering if maybe, just maybe, Aohdan did have bigger plans for Chris. Vashti let the doubt creep in just long enough to settle before she put her hand on the front of Rory's pants and started to rub.

"Abrezu's coming over, but I think I want you all to myself first."

CHAPTER 34

SEIREADAN PICKED AT the bowl of chicken and rice morosely. The TV was on, but she hardly paid attention, at least not until a familiar name shoved its way past her self-loathing and recriminations. The news anchor's voice floated over a video of flashing police lights and crime scene tape.

"The body, which was discovered in an abandoned auto repair shop in Roxbury, has been identified as that of James 'Jimmy Boy' McLaren. Police are currently questioning a suspect in connection with Mr. McLaren's murder."

Seireadan's mind spun. "Jimmy's dead?" *Who would have done that? Aohdan will have their head for it.* She sat up straighter. *What if it was Aohdan? Is he the one being questioned?*

The thought of Aohdan in a dingy interrogation room squashed what little was left of her appetite, and Seireadan scraped her leftovers into a storage container, still rifling through what-if scenarios in her head, each one grimmer than the last. Just as the lid snapped into place, there was a knock at her door.

"Miss Moore?" called a voice. "This is Detective St. John with the Boston Police. Could we have a few minutes of your time?"

Leftovers still in hand, she opened the door and looked at the two cops suspiciously.

"Pardon us for interrupting. I'm Detective David St. John; this is Detective Marty Sandhurst. May we come in?"

"Of course. Have a seat. Would you like some water?" Seireadan asked. Marty refused, but David accepted a glass, and they sat down in the living room.

"What can I help you with?" asked Seireadan. She had a sinking feeling it had something to do with Aohdan.

"We'd like to ask you a few questions about Aohdan Collins," said David.

"He's your boyfriend, correct?" asked Marty.

Seireadan's voice was tight. "Not anymore."

"Breakup have anything to do with those?" Marty pressed, eyeing the now greenish-yellow bruises on Seireadan's neck. Seireadan's eyes flashed, and she resisted covering the blemishes with her sweater. She knew Sandhurst would take any excuse to arrest Aohdan, and all he saw in her injuries was a potential reason.

"Those are none of your business," she snapped.

"Can you tell us where you were last Wednesday and Thursday? And who you were with?"

This has to be about Jimmy Boy. "Last week? I was on the Cape. A little getaway for a few days . . . with Aohdan."

"I thought you said you weren't his girlfriend?" Marty's sarcasm grated on Seireadan.

"We just broke up a couple days ago."

"I'm sorry to hear that," said David in an effort to calm her. "You said you were at the Cape with Aohdan. Can you tell us where?"

"The Chatham Bars Inn. It was lovely. He got us a room with a gorgeous view of the ocean. The same one we had when we went there for Thanksgiving."

"And he was with you all the time? For the whole trip?" Again, Marty barged into the conversation.

"Yes." Seireadan's voice cooled. *I don't care what happened between me and Aohdan; I'm not telling you shit about him.*

"So, you're saying he was with you every second of the trip?" Marty pushed her.

Seireadan fixed Marty with a hard stare. "Every second? Well, he didn't exactly need help when he peed, so no, I wasn't with him every single second of every single day. Why are you so concerned with where we were?"

"We're just looking for a little information. There's no need to make this adversarial," said David.

"I'm not the one making it adversarial," Seireadan snapped. "Does this have something to do with Jimmy McLaren?"

"You know Jimmy?" asked David.

"I met him a few times, but I just saw on the news tonight that someone killed him. What happened?"

"Your boyfriend—sorry, your *ex*-boyfriend happened to him." Marty dropped a crime scene photo in front of Seireadan. Jimmy had been brutally beaten; his face was nearly unrecognizable under the bruises, bloating, and welts. His throat was chewed up like hamburger, and Seireadan forced herself to not touch her own neck.

"He was strangled with barbed wire after being tortured and beaten," said David.

"And you think Aohdan did this?" Seireadan almost chuckled.

"A man's dead and you think it's funny?" growled Marty.

"No, I don't think it's funny at all. It's tragic, really. What's funny is you actually think Aohdan killed him. Aohdan promised Jimmy's dad he'd look after the kid when the old man passed—he wouldn't hurt Jimmy." *At least not without a good reason. And even if he did, Aohdan would never be that brutal, if only out of respect for Jimmy's dad.*

"Jimmy worked for Aohdan. When we found him, the message 'rat' was written in blood and stuck to his shirt. Sure looks like Aohdan didn't want him talking to anyone." David kept his tone conversational.

"If this happened to Jimmy last week, then you're after the wrong man. We were together on Wednesday and Thursday, and then Aohdan left for Chicago. But I'm sure you've already talked to him about that. I think you should both leave now," said Seireadan as she stood up.

"We're not done," Marty said hotly. "Sit down."

"Sit down? I will not sit down! You don't order me around in my own home!" Seireadan was outraged. "Unless you feel like arresting me, then you need to leave. I was with Aohdan, and we went to the Cape to get away for a few days. We got there late Tuesday night and checked out on Friday morning so he could get back to Boston for his flight. Check with the Chatham Bars Inn; they'll verify everything I've said."

"Oh, we'll check," said Marty.

Seireadan squared her shoulders and looked down at the detective. "You do that. And trust me, once we went to bed, Aohdan definitely didn't go anywhere else."

After the detectives left, Seireadan prowled her apartment for a few minutes, turning over the entire interview in her mind. Finally she flung herself down on her bed and stared at the ceiling. "Aohdan couldn't have killed Jimmy. He was with me," she said to herself. "We barely got out of bed for those two days . . ."

Memories flooded through her: the gorgeous little suite in Chatham, with the windows that looked out over the beach . . . their tangled-up sheets, and Aohdan's arms as he kissed every part of her . . . the sun rising just as they fell asleep. Each vivid, happy memory shredded Seireadan's heart all over again. She blinked back the tears.

"I am such a fool."

February turned into a montage of gray sky and dirty city snow for Seireadan. She put on a good front for Lia and Julia, but inside she was as numb as the ice clinging to the eaves and windows. She worked, ate, and slept, and in between those times she excoriated herself for hurting Aohdan, and swam in the bitter debris of a love shattered on the rocks. She spent Valentine's Day doing tarot readings for foolish young lovers and then went home and obliterated their faces from her memory with far too many shots of rum.

The last day of February was crisp and shiny, with a vibrant blue sky and pale yellow sun—a sharp contrast to the two days before when the western half of the state had been hammered by a major snowstorm. Seireadan took advantage of the sun and went for a run. Normally on the last day of the month, Seireadan dedicated her afternoon to cleaning out her office, but a frantic call from Julia brought her to Sacred Circle instead. Julia needed to meet with a vendor, but Lanna, who was going to watch the store, was still stuck in Florida because of the storm and wouldn't land at Logan until nearly midnight.

After closing the shop, Seireadan grabbed a salad to go at Rosewood and went back to her apartment to belatedly focus on her own office. She spent an hour filing things she needed to save, deleting outdated material, and sorting through the notes she'd left for herself about the different sites she was working on. Satisfied with the office, Seireadan went into the living room and picked up a few old magazines and catalogs, and as she turned to bring those to the recycle bin, she hesitated as everything around her suddenly felt far away.

She managed to say "Oh, shit . . ." before colored lights flashed and popped before her eyes.

Crying out, Seireadan fell to her knees as the Sight engulfed her. She pressed the heel of her hand to her forehead, but it did nothing to dull the pain knifing behind her eyes, which turned from their normal violet color to nearly black before the bright, popping colors faded into shadow and all she could See was a golden light in the center of a black lake. There were people inside the light, swirling, clashing. She could smell fear, and then she gagged as her mouth filled with the tang of blood and iron. Flashes erupted—sharp, staccato—and burned into her body. Seireadan struggled to focus, to See faces on the people in the maelstrom.

Who are you? Where are you? Her breath rushed out, and she coughed and gasped for air, as if she'd been punched in the chest. Then she saw Oisin's face, contorted in pain, and a fancy wooden sign. Darkness followed, and, in a final flash, someone with red hair, and a feeling of betrayal so deep and heart-wrenching, she couldn't breathe. An abyss of black swallowed everything.

Seireadan's eyes flew open, and she dragged in a ragged breath, her lungs burning like she'd been underwater too long. Disoriented and covered in sweat, she lurched to her feet and stumbled backward toward the sofa. She slammed her shin on the coffee table and bit her lip as white-hot pain raced up her leg. *How long have I been out of it? Where's my phone?* She managed to hop to the kitchen and grab her phone from the island. Hands shaking, she struggled to find a number. *Dammit, I don't have Oisin's number . . . Aohdan. I have to tell Aohdan!*

Even after Aohdan ended things, Seireadan had never taken his number out of her phone, even though she knew she should have. She tapped the patriarch's number. *Pick up, pick up, pick up . . . Dammit.*

Shaking her head in a vain effort to dislodge the ferocious headache, Seireadan grabbed her leather jacket and belt with the hidden knives out of the closet. She tried Aohdan's phone again as she left the apartment, but he still didn't answer, and she fought to stay calm. *He's fine. He's fine. I didn't See Aohdan. I'm the last person he wants to talk to; he's probably ignoring my call.* When his voice mail picked up, she struggled to keep her voice from shaking.

"Aohdan? It's me. Something's wrong. Oisin's in trouble. I Saw it . . . Find him before something terrible happens!"

Seireadan didn't dare drive because of the searing pain in her head. She was halfway down the block before she saw a cab, and she nearly threw herself in front of it. She ordered the cabbie to take her to Underworld—hoping that Aohdan would be there—and sat in the back seat, arms folded tightly, cold to the very core. There was no line at the club, and Seireadan rushed inside, her hopes crushed when no one was at Aohdan's usual table. She flew to the bar.

"Tommy!"

"Hi, Seireadan. Been a while . . ." Citrus from the squeezed lemon sprayed into the drink he was mixing.

"Is Aohdan here? Galen? Any of them?" *Please let one of them be here.*

"No, they all went to dinner, I think. Some business thing; they were all dressed up, but I don't know where they went. I'm sure they'll be back later if . . ."

Seireadan didn't bother saying goodbye, and on the sidewalk she forced herself to stop, to think while her heart beat desperately in her chest. *Calm down! Think, THINK about what you Saw.* She pinched the bridge of her nose, the headache and her fear making it hard to think clearly, but then she froze. *The wooden sign! It was DJ's, that hot new steakhouse . . . Son of a bitch, that's where they are!*

DJ's Steak & Seafood was only two blocks away. She called Aohdan's phone a third time as she sprinted down the street.

At his table, Aohdan glanced down as the phone rang. *Seireadan again? A third time?* He frowned, torn between anger and concern, and sent the call to voice mail. This dinner was going to seal the deal with Providence, and nothing was going to distract him from that. Not even Seireadan.

"Problem?" asked Crogher with a crooked, insincere smile. At the adjacent table, Rory, Oisin, Galen, and Kieran sat with Baibin's captains, and they'd been eyeing one another warily throughout the dinner.

"No, no problem. I know originally you weren't a tremendous supporter of Matriarch Baibin's decision to blend the Providence *fréamhacha agus brainsí* with Boston's. I hope we've put that unpleasantness behind us," said Aohdan as he watched Crogher fidget with his tie and suit jacket.

"That's exactly why I asked my mother, the matriarch, if I could represent her at this meeting. She is unwell as you know. I have come to understand the benefits of the merger, and I thought it was important that you and I meet, man to man. On behalf of Matriarch Baibin, I offer you our *fréamhacha agus brainsí* to care for and protect."

His words sounded almost genuine. Aohdan, who had been watching every detailed expression on Crogher's face, managed not to frown. *Crogher must have practiced that statement for weeks. Lying sack of shit. This is killing him.*

Crogher stood and offered Aohdan a small branch, gilded in silver, with several tiny gold leaves hanging from it. It was beyond ancient and had been in Baibin's family for hundreds of centuries. Aohdan accepted it graciously and carefully, and set it in a lined box where it would be protected. Then he shook Crogher's hand.

"I accept the responsibility willingly," said Aohdan, using the formal response Baibin would have expected. "Be welcome, be family."

Crogher gestured and the captains all stood. "Thank you for the dinner. I will give your best to the matri—my mother."

"Thank you. I hope you enjoyed the meal."

"Perhaps next time we can meet in Providence. Boston isn't the only city with great steak," said Crogher with another forced smile.

"I look forward to it," Aohdan lied.

At one more gesture from Crogher, Baibin's now former captains each offered Aohdan a bowed head—a gesture of respect—and said, "Patriarch," as they acknowledged his position in the new *fréamhacha agus brainsí.*

Aohdan responded to each just as formally, saying, "Be welcome, be family."

As the Providence cohort left, Aohdan's phone rang again. His eyes flashed angrily, and his captains tried to look occupied with other things as he excused himself. He walked through the adjacent hallway toward the bar, which was separate from the formal dining room at DJ's. He was about to call Seireadan back when he saw her come tearing in through the bar's outer door. She raced up to Aohdan, and he grabbed her roughly by the wrists, pulled her into the hall, and spun her to face him.

"Why are you here, Seireadan?" he asked, knowing she could hear the anguish in his voice.

"Aohdan! Just listen. LISTEN!"

As much as he didn't want to, there was a note of fear in Seireadan's voice that grabbed him deep down in his gut. Something was wrong. He stayed silent, his jaw set in a grim line, and let her talk.

"The Sight! I Saw . . . something. Chaos, blood. Someone with red hair . . . And Oisin. Oisin is right in the middle of it, and he's in pain. So much pain and blood. And it's here. Whatever it is, it happens here!"

A horrible feeling of dread filled Aohdan, and he bolted back to the dining room before she could say anything else.

CHAPTER 35

SEIREADAN TORE DOWN the hall after Aohdan, only to be met by screams and gunfire when she reached the dining room. Throwing herself to the floor and covering her head, Seireadan crawled to the waitstaff station, which offered a slight bit of cover. She put her hand behind her back and ran her fingertips along the hilt of one hidden knife, finding a modicum of security in the smooth wood.

She peeked around the corner: the room was chaos—overturned tables, fleeing patrons, screaming—and right in the middle of it was Aohdan. Seireadan nearly choked on her heart when she saw Crogher level his gun, and then the world turned into slow motion as she watched what she Saw turn into a horrible, bloody reality . . .

Oisin lunged at Aohdan, knocking him sideways as Crogher ripped off at least four shots. Seireadan screamed for them both as Aohdan sprawled across the floor, his gun knocked from his hand. One bullet ripped across the outside of Aohdan's shoulder, while the rest of the bullets slammed into Oisin. The captain's screams were excruciating as he lay on the floor, dark red blood pouring from his middle.

Over the brawl, Crogher shouted, "Go ahead and hide, Aohdan! Coward! Face your last day as patriarch!"

Aohdan lunged for his gun but was driven back as a new wave of gunfire pinned him down, bullets thudding into the overturned butcher-block tables, and Seireadan watched in horror as a gloating look of triumph oozed over Crogher's face. Aohdan was exposed, out in the open; there was no chance Crogher would miss his shot.

Don't you touch him, you bastard! Without another thought, one knife drawn, Seireadan charged out from her shelter and slammed into Crogher as hard as she could. His gun went off as he lurched, but the bullet zipped away on some crazy trajectory, shattering one of the large overhead lights. Tangled, Seireadan and Crogher stumbled to the side, getting caught up in an overturned chair.

They crashed to the ground, and Seireadan swung her blade around, slicing into Crogher's side. It wasn't a deep cut, but it was bloody and painful. She twisted her body around, looking for another opening, desperate to keep Crogher's attention on her and not on Aohdan.

"You bitch!" Crogher managed to catch Seireadan's ankle as she scrambled away, and he yanked hard, slamming her down onto the floor. She twisted and kicked, and Crogher grunted as her foot pummeled his shoulder, but it wasn't enough to force him to let go. Falling limp, Seireadan let him drag her closer, waiting for an opportunity.

"I'm going to gut you with your own knife," Crogher snarled.

Seireadan's hand shot out, aiming the point of her blade at his throat, but he grabbed her wrist, twisting it painfully, and she screamed as the knife clattered to the floor. Still holding her arm, Crogher surged to his feet and kicked Seireadan in the stomach, hard, and then raised his fist. Seireadan flung her free arm up, hoping to block at least some of the blow, but then a thundering, enraged voice tore through the din. It was Aohdan.

"CROGHER!"

After he realized it was Seireadan who had knocked Crogher down, Aohdan lunged for his gun and grabbed the nickel-barreled Colt from the floor. The light above him shattered, struck by Crogher's stray bullet, and he ducked as shards of glass rained down. When he could finally look up, it was just in time to see Crogher slam his boot into Seireadan's stomach and raise his fist.

He'll kill her! Seireadan!

Everything inside Aohdan twisted, stripping away the mistakes and the lies and the stupid, prideful anger of the past month, making one simple fact gut-wrenchingly clear: he still loved her more than he'd loved anything in his life. It didn't matter what Seireadan had done; he didn't care. All that mattered was her.

Crogher heard Aohdan bellow his name and locked eyes with the patriarch. Aohdan didn't hesitate; fire flashed from the gun's muzzle, and Crogher jerked back, blood blooming on his chest. The impact forced him back, but even with blood staining his shirt, Crogher managed to stay on his feet. Seireadan yanked her wrist out of his grip. Crogher glanced at her and then back at Aohdan, hate glittering in his eyes.

This ends here and now. Aohdan squeezed the trigger one more time, and his gun roared for blood. This bullet blew out the back of Crogher's skull. He dropped to the floor, an empty sack of bones and viscera, and blood and brain matter pooled around him on the elegant wooden floor. Seireadan stared at the body where it had fallen next to her for a moment before she scrambled away and climbed shakily to her feet.

Not noticing the shooting had stopped, Aohdan grabbed Seireadan and abruptly jerked her around. Staring down at her, Aohdan searched her face, trying to convince himself that she was fine. He didn't care that she saw the fear in his eyes, the terror knowing that she could have been the one bleeding out on the floor.

"Are you insane, Seireadan? He would have killed you!"

"He was going to shoot you . . ." Her voice trailed away as panic washed over her.

"Seireadan?"

"Where's Oisin?" she screamed. "Where is he?"

At the mention of his friend's name, Seireadan's words in the hall, the details of her Seeing, crashed over Aohdan.

"Oisin!" Aohdan shouted. "Oisin!"

"He's over here," Galen yelled as he struggled to stand; his light pants were stained dark with blood where he'd taken a bullet to the thigh.

"The bastards put iron powder on the bullets," growled Galen.

"I know." Aohdan's voice was cold. He'd felt the iron burning in his blood from where Crogher's bullet had grazed him.

Partly hidden behind some overturned furniture, Oisin lay on his back, a gaping wound in his shoulder, and another in his abdomen. His eyes were glassy and his breathing was labored. Kieran was doing his best to slow the bleeding, his hands pressed hard on Oisin's bloody shirt. Oisin moaned as Aohdan took his hand; his skin was clammy. Closing his eyes, Aohdan knelt next to his friend, reality crashing down around him—if Oisin hadn't pushed him, that bullet would have caught Aohdan directly in the heart. Outside, someone yelled for the paramedics to hurry.

"Hang on, Oisin," he said. "The ambulance is here."

What seemed like an eternity later, two paramedics shoved Kieran and Aohdan out of the way and started to work; a third materialized next to Galen. While Aohdan stared at the paramedics, Kieran threaded his way around some of the damage to where Seireadan was standing. She was staring at Crogher's corpse with a look of revulsion on her face.

"Come on, lass," Kieran said, gently taking her arm. "It will do you no good to be staring at that."

She allowed him to turn her away and steer her back to Aohdan, and she stood, shaking and shell-shocked, as they loaded Oisin and Galen into ambulances. After the doors slammed and the ambulance tore away, siren blaring, a sob poured out of her, and Seireadan, her clothes spattered with blood, turned her tear-streaked face to Aohdan.

"I was too late. I couldn't stop it . . . I'm sorry," she said miserably, her breath coming in ragged gasps as she cried.

"Seireadan . . ."

She looked at the floor and started to back away. "I know. You don't want me here."

Aohdan caught her by the hand. "No. I don't want you to go. Please stay."

Neither Seireadan nor Aohdan was allowed to leave until the paramedics had taken care of both of them. Just after midnight, they arrived at Mass General to find Galen, Kieran, and Rory in the waiting room, along with Chris. Galen had been relegated to a wheelchair to keep his leg elevated. Surprisingly, there were very few other people there, and Aohdan was relieved; his hold on his rage was becoming more tenuous by the moment.

"How is he?" Aohdan demanded.

"We do no' know. They took him in for surgery as soon as we arrived," said Kieran. "How are you?"

Aohdan touched his bandage. "I'll be fine. Just a scratch. Should have been worse, but Oisin . . ." The muscle in his jaw twitched and he ground his teeth. "What about you, Galen?"

"Going to hurt like a bastard to dance for a while, but it'll heal. I had Kieran call Oisin's father, but it's going to take him a few hours to get here. Chris has a car service bringing him."

"Did you have any trouble with the cops?" Rory asked.

"No. Fortunately one of our friends in the department caught the case and not that ass Sandhurst," said Aohdan. "I'm sure we'll hear from them, but Mark will take care of things."

Aohdan's phone rang and the muscle in his cheek started to clench as he stared. He let it ring and then ignored the beep that said he had a voice mail.

"Baibin?" guessed Galen.

"Yes."

"Do you think she knew about this?"

"Right now, I don't really care." Aohdan's voice was deceptively soft.

They waited in agitated, agonizing silence, jumping to attention each time the double doors at the end of the hall opened. Each time they were disappointed, and the only update they could get was that Oisin was still in surgery. Rory paced the emergency room like a caged animal, while Aohdan and Kieran sat morosely in chairs. Seireadan curled up in a different chair, her feet tucked under her, alternately rubbing her temples or staring into space. Finally, Kieran slammed his hands on the chair arms and stood up.

"I'm going to get some coffee across the street," he said. "I'll bring some back for everyone."

Another few agonizing minutes ticked by, and Aohdan went to stand by Seireadan's chair. "Can we go somewhere to talk?" he asked.

"Sure." She unfolded herself from the chair.

"We'll be back in a minute," Aohdan said to Galen. "Text me if there's any news."

They walked in awkward silence down the linoleum hallway until they found a small, unoccupied waiting room. Seireadan sat, her folded hands between her knees, and kept her eyes on the floor. Tired of the silence, she looked up to find Aohdan leaning casually in the doorway, just watching her. His expression was calm enough, but given everything that had gone on in the past several hours, Seireadan knew it was only the thinnest of masks.

"Why did you come to the restaurant tonight?"

She stood up, offended by the question. "Why did I . . . ? Do you think I'm that much of a monster? That I wouldn't share what I Saw? I don't wish anything bad on you, and certainly not on Oisin or the others. I didn't have his number. The best way to get to him . . ."

She stopped, her cheeks flushing.

Aohdan picked up where her voice trailed off. ". . . was through me. That is what you were going to say, isn't it?"

"Yes," she admitted as the flush turned scarlet.

"That's the only reason? For Oisin?"

Seireadan could tell from the tone of his voice that her answer to this seemingly simple question was exceedingly important.

"No, not just for Oisin. For you. I was afraid that whatever shit Oisin was in the middle of would spill over to you. I wasn't going to let that happen. I know you don't believe me, Aohdan, but I still love you." *There, I said it.* To her surprise, Aohdan's face softened.

"I know. You almost got yourself killed tonight, and you did it to protect me. You don't do that for someone you hate.

When I saw Crogher had you, I . . . everything else disappeared. The idea of him hurting you? I couldn't live with that," said Aohdan.

Regret shadowed his voice, and as he talked, Aohdan got closer to Seireadan until he could tilt her head up to look at him. Seireadan, her eyes red and puffy from crying, wiped away the dampness on her cheeks and tried to read all the different emotions in Aohdan's dark, expressive eyes.

"I've never stopped loving you, either," he confessed.

Seireadan's entire body relaxed, suddenly free from the invisible pain she'd been dragging with her. "I'm so sorry, Aohdan. The file . . . I should never have . . ."

"We don't need to talk about that . . . ," he started to say, a hint of tension creeping into his voice.

"Yes. Yes, we do. I don't want this between us for the rest of our lives. I need to tell you why. After that, if you still want me, I'll stay, but I'll go if you don't. I promise."

"Okay," he finally said.

Seireadan took a deep breath. "Do you understand how Luan's spell worked?"

"The one that caused the Desolation? Generally, yes. He was so angry that his wife, Bryn, had taken Conlan as her lover that he created a spell that would consume and kill both of them, but something went wrong. What do Bryn and Conlan have to do with this?"

"Something didn't exactly go wrong." Suddenly agitated, Seireadan pulled herself free from his arms and started to move restlessly around the little waiting room. She owed Aohdan an explanation.

"What are you talking about?"

"The spell was corrupt from the moment it was conceived. You know how important intent is for Fae magic, and Luan threw all his bitterness and hatred at being betrayed into the spell. Because of his hatred, the spell was rotten from within almost as soon as it was created. And the most efficient way to destroy Bryn and Conlan was to release the spell near them and have it fulfill its purpose and vanish." She rubbed her temples.

"That would make sense," said Aohdan. "And my uncle would have wanted to see them suffer. I didn't know him well, but I know he could be cruel."

Seireadan nodded. "Someone told Luan that my father was hiding them at our home. It was a lie. I know because I'd seen Conlan and Bryn just the day before, near the palace, right under Luan's nose." She took another deep breath before she continued. "So, Luan set the spell loose, but when it didn't find its quarry, it consumed everything it could find . . . starting with my family and my home. And when it was done there, it was so rancid it started to consume everything else in an unquenchable thirst to find the two it was born to destroy."

"Could it have been a mistake? Releasing it near your family? Luan wasn't in his right mind."

Finally Seireadan dropped her shoulders and sighed sadly. "I don't believe it was a mistake. When I was very little, I had a dream. A terrifying, vivid dream about my home being swallowed up by a wind so hot and fierce, it scorched the ground it touched. Two Fae men were there, and the one with brown hair created the wind, but the one with blond hair and pale skin—I call him the Alabaster Man—he was the one who pointed out my house and said to kill them all. I woke up, terrified and crying, and I told my father about it. He comforted me like a good father should, but I never forgot it. Never.

"When my Raven abilities fully manifested, I came to believe the dream was the first time the Sight took me, but no one would listen because the Sight typically doesn't show up until adolescence. But I Saw him. I Saw what the Alabaster Man did to my father and my family, and no one believed me." She paused and took a deep breath. "They all laughed and said what a vivid imagination I had. As I got older I was mocked by other Ravens, especially Cavan. I know what I Saw, but they didn't believe me, either. No one, except Lia, has ever believed me."

"Seireadan—"

She plowed ahead, the words tumbling out of her, afraid to stop until she said everything she'd been holding in. "I'm sorry for not asking about your files. So many people have dismissed my Alabaster Man, said that I was making excuses for my father, and that if he'd just turned Bryn over, Luan wouldn't have unleashed that monstrosity. I thought if I could look through some pictures of your contacts that I might see him, and then I would have a name to go with those damn eyes."

"Why didn't you just ask me?"

Her voice was laced with shame. "I was afraid. What if you know him? What if he's a friend of yours? What if the man I'm going to kill someday is someone you love? And even if you don't know him, I didn't trust that you'd believe me. I couldn't bear that you might laugh at—"

Her words were cut short as Aohdan took her by the shoulders, forced her to look at him, and said, "Seireadan, of course I believe you."

Until that moment she hadn't realized how worried she'd really been about what he would think. Seireadan threw her arms around Aohdan, her "thank you" muffled in his chest.

"And I don't care if we find out he's a friend of mine. For what he did to your family, if he survived the Desolation, I'll find him, and I'll—" Aohdan started to say.

"No," she said in a cold, grim voice that offered no room for disagreement. "I will find him, and when I do, I'll handle it. I don't want you fixing this. I have to do this. They were my *family*. I know you understand that."

Aohdan glanced over his shoulder, back toward the waiting room where the rest of his crew sat waiting, worrying, hoping for a miracle. He took her hand.

"I do understand," he said. "And I'll support you, no matter how you want to handle it."

She nodded softly, knowing he'd stand by his word. They stood in silence for a moment, neither quite seeming to know what to say. Finally, after the silence had stretched almost too long, Seireadan asked the question hanging between them.

"Are we starting over?"

"I hope so."

She closed her eyes. "I want to . . ."

"But?"

She heard the worry in his voice, and looked up into Aohdan's dark eyes. "I have never asked you to be anything other than what you are. Never asked you to change, to move differently through the world for me."

"No, you haven't."

"And I never will. I love you for who you are. But you hurt me." She paused, struggling with her words as her hand went to her throat. "You hurt me."

"Seireadan—"

She heard the pain in his voice. "And I hurt you, too. I'll regret that forever. But you will never—never—put your hands on me like that again. Ever. If you do, we'll both regret it. Do you understand me?"

He reached out and cupped Seireadan's face between his hands. "Never."

"Looks like they've made up," Chris said to no one in particular.

Galen, Kieran, and Rory all glanced up, immediately noticing the same thing Chris had: Aohdan and Seireadan walking down the hall holding hands, their fingers loosely interlaced.

"Any news?" Aohdan asked as they sat down, despite knowing the answer.

"Nothing yet," said Galen.

Seireadan curled up into the chair next to Aohdan's and stayed quiet, her mind far away. Now and then, she'd gently put a hand on Aohdan's arm when he got restless. Rory bought a deck of cards from the gift shop and distracted himself playing solitaire and Forty Thieves after unsuccessfully trying to coax Kieran into a poker game. Galen barely moved in his chair, focusing most of his energy on managing his own pain. Chris disappeared to the hospital chapel for a time, to pray. The minutes ticked by in slow motion, and after another hour, the double doors at the end of the hall opened. A doctor in green surgical scrubs, her stride purposeful and determined, walked toward them.

"Are you Oisin O'Neill's family?" the surgeon asked. "I'm Dr. Lynwood."

"Family and friends," said Aohdan.

Dr. Lynwood took a deep breath. "I'm very sorry. Mr. O'Neill died a few minutes ago during surgery. The excessive blood loss and damage done by the bullets and the iron was very extensive."

There was a deep collective groan of agony from the group, and Seireadan covered her face with her hands as the tears started.

"No. That is no' possible," Kieran said firmly.

"Mr. O'Neill sustained two different gunshot wounds to the chest and abdomen, both from bullets coated in pulverized iron. One of them fragmented significantly, sending particles not only into his bloodstream but also into one of his lungs.

The other damaged an artery before deflecting and lodging in his liver." The doctor paused. "I'm very sorry for your loss."

The utter silence in the room was shattered by Aohdan's roar of grief and pain. A waiting room chair crashed into the wall before Aohdan overturned one of the tables, scattering tattered and worn magazines across the floor. Chris and Kieran intercepted the security guard, and Galen softly explained to the head nurse what had happened, promising there would be compensation for the damage. And after his initial outburst, Aohdan stood, shaking, in the middle of the room. Tears stained his cheeks.

"Aohdan." Seireadan's soft voice brought him out of his black thoughts when she touched his lower back with her fingertips. He shifted very slightly under her touch, but didn't move away.

Rory cracked his knuckles, his voice frighteningly eager. "What do you want us to do about this, boss?"

"Not here," said Aohdan tightly. "Come back to the condo. We'll talk there."

CHAPTER 36

INJURED AND MOURNING, they gathered at Aohdan's. He went to the bank of windows and stared out at the horizon. It was morning but the sky had yet to turn pink with the rising sun. In the ghostly reflections in the glass, he could see the others moving around the room. Chris brought a kitchen chair into the living room so Galen could elevate his leg, and Aohdan saw his second grimace in pain when he raised his foot.

We almost lost Galen tonight, too.

A few moments later, Seireadan's reflection appeared over his shoulder. He turned when she caught his eye, and saw Kieran putting the last crystal into a tight circle under Galen's careful direction. Aohdan sat next to Galen while Chris and Kieran settled on the sofa. Rory stood at the far end of the coffee table, and Seireadan leaned on the sofa arm.

"Before we start, Seireadan, tell everyone what you Saw," Aohdan said.

"Ah, that's why you came to the restaurant," said Kieran.

"I did See," she said. "It was confusing, chaotic. But I Saw people fighting, there was shouting, screaming. You could smell the fear. Then there were these sharp, erupting flashes, and my body felt like it was on fire. I could taste blood—and iron—and then I Saw Oisin's face, and he was in so much pain." Seireadan's eyes filled, and she gestured to her chest and her abdomen. Aohdan's stomach clenched—Seireadan didn't realize those were the very same places Oisin had been shot.

"I saw a wooden sign, the one outside of DJ's bar. After that, things flashed black for a moment, then I Saw the back of someone's head. Someone with red hair . . . and . . ." Her voice trailed away as Seireadan's breath caught in her throat.

Aohdan put a gentle hand on her leg. "And what, Seireadan?"

"Betrayal. I felt it down into my bones, and I thought my heart would break from it. I wish I could have found you sooner."

"This isn't your fault," Aohdan reassured her.

"It seems like most of your vision was accurate," said Galen. "The fight, gunshots, Oisin being hurt. Even the betrayal; that other captain from Providence—Fearg—has red hair."

"Be careful," Seireadan warned. "I didn't see a face with the red hair. Maybe it was Fearg, but maybe not. It could be anyone with red hair—"

Rory leaped to his feet. "Are you accusing me of something?"

"I never—!" Seireadan snapped angrily.

Galen cut in, "Enough. No one's making accusations. We need privacy for the rest of this, Aohdan. I'm exhausted, in too much pain. Everyone needs to be inside the circle, so we're limited to the living room."

I hate asking him to do this. He's in so much pain already. Aohdan took a deep breath. "Galen's right. I want us all to hear what Baibin has to say, and then we decide what to do. Are you sure you're up for this, Galen?"

Galen set his jaw in a hard line and said, "I have to be."

Aohdan's second grimaced as he started to murmur the spell. Light shot from one crystal to the next until they were surrounded by a line of energy that shimmered up into a glittering curtain until it reached a single point above them. All outside noise suddenly ceased. Galen pressed the heels of his hands to his eyes and moaned. Everyone crowded together to make sure they were all within the confines of the circle, and Aohdan didn't miss the look Rory threw Seireadan's way, or the bleak stare he offered Chris.

"They shouldn't be here," Rory said to Aohdan. "Chris isn't a captain. And there's no need for your woman to be here."

"This is no' the time, Rory," Kieran said.

Rory looked at Seireadan. "Go in the other room and wait," he ordered.

Slowly, Seireadan's eyebrows went up. "Excuse me?"

"You can't help. Just go wait to take care of Aohdan after we're done." Snide and dismissive, Rory tried to wave her away like an errant child.

"How dare you," she hissed with such venom that it stopped Rory dead, and he stared at her as if he were seeing Seireadan for the first time. "How DARE you talk to me like that?" After lancing Rory with a withering stare, she turned to Aohdan and said, "Oisin was your best friend. I know how much he meant to you. To all of you." She turned her gaze back to Rory and locked eyes with him. "But he was my friend, too. And I have no problem getting bloody for the right reasons. Don't you EVER underestimate me on that count."

Out of nowhere, Aohdan kissed her in front of everyone, and the sheer unexpectedness of the gesture was the only thing that saved him from being slapped.

"I don't doubt your willingness, Seireadan—and believe me, I never underestimate you—but this is going to be bloody and brutal. I want to spare you that."

She looked up and into his eyes. "And I love you for wanting that. But they tried to kill you; I want their heads."

"For fuck's sake, GET ON WITH IT!" Galen pressed his fingers to his temples, pain etching his face. It was obvious to everyone how much strain Galen was under, and Aohdan put his phone on speaker and accessed his voice mail. The voice that came out was dry and ancient, and it trembled.

"Patriarch. I just heard what my idiot son and treacherous captains tried to do. I had no knowledge of this plan, none. We had an agreement, and I keep my promises. If my son is dead, he earned his fate. If he isn't, please give me the privilege of killing him myself. But please, tell me what I can do to make this right before you do anything. Please."

The message ended.

"Is she telling the truth?" asked Chris.

"Doubt it, the old bitch," snapped Rory.

Kieran shook his head. "I disagree. She gave her word—her formal word. I have a verra hard time believing she would have broken a promise that serious."

Aohdan didn't say anything, but nodded, agreeing with Kieran. He touched the "Call Back" button, and the phone rang only once before the same wizened voice answered. He left the phone on speaker.

"Patriarch. Thank you for returning my call."

"Your son is dead, Baibin." His voice was flat and cold.

"I know." The old matriarch's voice was resigned and defeated. "I am ashamed of him."

"My captain, Oisin, is also dead. My second was wounded badly. Crogher tried to kill my girlfriend." He paused. "Two of yours got away. Fearg and Lanty. I want them found."

"I will find them for you, Patriarch. You have my word. I will do whatever it takes to prove to you that Providence is loyal."

Aohdan was silent for a moment, and then said, "I'll accept your word for now, Baibin, but if I find out you had a hand in this, I will destroy your entire *fréamhacha agus brainsí*—everything you value and love." *There will be nothing left but rubble and bones.*

"Your will, Patriarch." Baibin's voice was little more than a whisper.

"You can expect Kieran and Rory to help with the search for them. If you find them before my captains arrive, make sure nothing happens. I want Fearg and Lanty alive, and I want no other questions asked."

"Of course," she said.

Aohdan didn't even say goodbye. He just hung up the phone and leaned back in his chair. Next to him, Galen started to shake.

"Anything else?" Galen groaned. "It has to be quick."

"Kieran, Rory. Get some sleep but get to Providence and bring those bastards back. Rip the city apart if you have to, but I want them back here—alive—before we bury Oisin. And make calls to your contacts; let them know I want these two."

They nodded. Rory was dialing his cousin Moira before Aohdan even finished.

"We're done," said Aohdan.

Galen released the spell and nearly fell from his chair as the strain of channeling the magic vanished. Chris propped him up for a moment until he and Seireadan could help Galen stand, and Rory and Kieran went to get their coats.

"Put Galen in the guest room," Aohdan told them.

The condo was eerily quiet once the others left, and Aohdan went back to staring out at the sky, his forearm braced on the glass. The horizon was dressed in a blushing purple pink along its edge, a color far too cheery for how he was feeling. *Oisin. We've been friends since we were children, since before the Desolation. And now you're dead—all because you tried to save me.* Seireadan put her hand on his back, and Aohdan hastily wiped his face with the back of his hand.

"He was my oldest friend. It should be me in the morgue. Crogher was there to kill me." Grief, thick and heavy, clouded his voice.

"You can't blame yourself. He'd hate that. Oisin pushed you out of the way because he was your friend, practically your brother. If the roles were reversed, what would you have done?"

"The exact same thing." Aohdan drew in a ragged breath and allowed Seireadan to pull him away from the window.

"Come on," she said. "You need to sleep, too. I can lock the door on my way out."

"Your way out?"

She hesitated. "I thought you'd want some space. Sleeping Beauty there in the guest room isn't going to wake up for a while."

Aohdan lowered his eyes and shook his head, his long hair hiding his face for a moment. "I don't want to be alone, Seireadan. Not tonight, not ever again."

Sunlight filled the bedroom. Seireadan stretched, letting her legs extend and her toes point beneath the warm down comforter. Aohdan was right next to her in the bed, and her skin tingled as he slid his palm over her waist. Despite how exhausted they'd been when they went to bed, they'd made love, both wanting, needing, something to focus on other than grief and pain. It had been slow and gentle, and they'd fallen asleep in each other's arms, and for the first time in many weeks, Seireadan felt content.

Aohdan was looking at her when Seireadan opened her eyes.

"Hi," she whispered, smiling.

"Hey, beautiful," Aohdan replied.

Hey, beautiful. How many times over the last month had Seireadan longed to hear him say that? To wake up in his arms and know everything was right in her universe. Then the reality of the past twenty-four hours swamped her, crushing her serenity and contentment into dust. Her smile disappeared, replaced by pressed lips as she tried to hide their tremble while her eyes filled with tears. Aohdan's arm tightened around her.

"Seireadan? Why are you crying?"

"I was so happy when I woke up—being here, with you." She pulled in a shaky breath. "Then I remembered how damn much those few seconds of happiness cost . . ."

Aohdan folded her into his arms and rested his chin on her head while she cried. Eventually, Seireadan rolled onto her back and took a gulping breath. Her eyes were red and she wiped the last tears away. Next to her, she felt Aohdan raise himself up on his uninjured arm. She reached up and brushed some sleep-tangled hair out of his eyes.

"I love you, Aohdan, but if I could trade it all to have Oisin back, I'd do it."

"Stop, that's enough." Aohdan said, his voice still raw with grief. "What happened to Oisin is on Crogher's head and no one else's. This? Us? This is the one good thing to come out of all that shit yesterday, all that pain . . ."

Whatever else Aohdan was going to tell Seireadan was interrupted by a loud thump from the guest room, followed by several obscenities.

"Galen's awake," Seireadan said, "and I bet he tried to walk without his crutches."

"Stubborn bastard. I'll go check on him," said Aohdan with a chuckle. The patriarch got out of bed, pulled on a pair of flannel pants that were crumpled on the floor, and walked out of the bedroom.

CHAPTER 37

SEIREADAN PULLED THE bandage off Aohdan's arm. It had been on for only a few days, but the poultice was doing its job: there was hardly any black residue—a sign that iron had been involved in his injury—on the pad, and Aohdan was in much less pain. She pressed a clean pad down and tore some medical tape from the roll.

"I can do that, you know," said Aohdan.

She made a face. "I saw the bandage the last time you did it yourself. Sloppy, half-assed work, if you ask me."

"I didn't ask," he muttered under his breath.

"Don't really care," Seireadan shot back with a grin.

Satisfied with the result, Seireadan went to the kitchen. Dishes clinked as she pulled some leftovers out of the refrigerator. Aohdan had surprised her by coming home for lunch before he went to Asmodeus for the afternoon. His phone rang.

"Hey. Good. That didn't take long. I'll call you with details."

Aohdan hung up and immediately made another call. Seireadan made a passing attempt to not listen to his side of the conversation, but it proved impossible as he sat down at the island.

"Hey, it's me. We need the boat. Tonight. Let me know where it will be." Aohdan slid the phone into his pocket and pulled a clean shirt over his head before he took the water pitcher out of the refrigerator and poured two glasses.

"Rory and Kieran found your friends?" Seireadan looked at Aohdan out of the corner of her eye as she made two roast beef sandwiches.

"They did. We're going to take them out tonight."

"I see. Boys' night out, then." Her voice was ominously neutral.

Aohdan walked around the island and hooked his fingers through the belt loops of Seireadan's jeans, pulling her back and closer to him. She used a large kitchen knife to slice the two sandwiches in half in a single fluid motion.

"I'd feel better if you put that down," Aohdan said with a soft laugh, his eyes following the motion of the blade.

"I bet you would."

Aohdan sighed. "Baby, I know you're angry over what happened, and I know you want your pound of flesh, but this is something I need to do."

Seireadan's shoulders dropped slightly and she put the kitchen knife down. She did understand; she wished she didn't, but she really did get it. She sighed heavily. "I do understand, and I respect that, even if I don't like it. If you're going to respect how I handle the Alabaster Man when I find him, then I need to stay out of your way for this."

He hugged her tightly and kissed the top of her head. "Thank you."

They were both quiet while they ate. Aohdan finished his sandwich and caught Seireadan around the waist again as she put her plate in the sink. He crowded her against the counter and started to kiss her neck.

"Do you really need to go to work?" she asked, imagining an afternoon naked in bed with him.

"As tempting as you are, I can't. I've already postponed this appointment once; I can't do it again. Want to go out for dinner when I get home?"

"Yes, but someplace close. Barking Crab, maybe?"

"Wherever you want."

It was a busy day at Asmodeus, and Aohdan was grateful for the distraction. Wiping the excess ink from his client's arm, he looked critically at the image: a shining star with angel wings, in the middle of which—sheltered by the wings—was the name Sarah. He was coloring and shading the star when his client started to talk.

"She was my little angel."

"Who was she?" Aohdan was always fascinated by the meanings behind his clients' tattoos. Sometimes the stories were very straightforward, other times they were odd, but they were always interesting.

"She was my granddaughter."

Aohdan glanced up as he wiped away more excess ink. "Granddaughter? No way, Gerry."

"I know, a bit young to be a grandpa," Gerry said with a chuckle. "Well, I knocked up my ex when we were barely seventeen. Grabbed some beer at the packie that night. Next thing you know, we're in the back seat of my car . . . You don't always think shit through when you're seventeen."

"No, you don't," Aohdan agreed.

"When our daughter was eighteen, she went and eloped with her boyfriend. I thought he was a sketchy bastard to start, but he's been good to Emma. They had Sarah the next year, but then when the poor little thing was three, she got sick. Couldn't figure it out for a while, but turns out it was a blood cancer. Doctors at Children's Hospital tried everything, but nothing worked for her."

Aohdan rolled back on his stool to change the needles on his machine. "I'm sorry to hear that."

"Appreciate it. Kid was a trooper. No matter what happened, she'd always smile for me. Always wanted to laugh. She'd yell, 'Gampy, tickle me!' all the time." Gerry's eyes got shiny. "We buried her six months ago and I've been thinking about doing this ever since. Never wanted a tattoo before now."

"I promise you won't be disappointed," said Aohdan. Movement at the door made him glance up. Chris gave him a quick nod and then disappeared as Aohdan wiped Gerry's arm and put his machine down.

"We've got about another hour or so of work. Let's take a quick break. Take a walk, stretch your legs. Bathroom is at the end of the hall if you need it. I'll be back in a sec." Aohdan peeled off his latex gloves and tossed them in the trash can.

"Sounds good. Was just thinking I might need to hit the head soon."

Downstairs, Aohdan met Chris near the front desk. "Hi, Chris. What can I do for you?" He kept a careful eye on the two other customers browsing the shop.

"I have an update for you." Chris also glanced at the other customers. "But before that, I'd actually like to make an appointment. About two weeks from now?"

Aohdan flipped open the appointment book. He was old-school in that sense; even though things were in the computer, he still liked a written schedule book. "Sure. What do you want done?"

"A memorial tattoo. For a friend of mine who passed away."

Aohdan gave Chris a measured look, knowing exactly who the "friend" was. He respected what Chris was doing. *I want to do the work, but I'm not sure I can ink something about Oisin. Not so soon.*

"I think Wharf Rat would be a good choice. He's one of the best artists here," said Aohdan.

"That sounds good—I trust your recommendation."

"Good. He has an opening on the twenty-third if that works for you? At four o'clock?"

"Great."

Their conversation stalled as Kerry ducked behind the counter to get the key for one of the cases. When she was occupied with the customers, Chris leaned his forearms on the counter and dropped his voice lower. "That other thing? South Boston Yacht Club."

Still writing, Aohdan heard Chris but didn't acknowledge the hushed comment.

Chris thanked Aohdan for the appointment and left the shop. Upstairs, Gerry was waiting for Aohdan and watched him stretch a few times before sitting down. Two fresh latex gloves snapped onto his hands.

"Sorry, that took longer than I expected. You ready to finish up?"

"Absolutely."

Gerry watched as Aohdan methodically applied the ink, wiped the excess, and then approached the area from a different angle.

"That looks pissah. People weren't kidding when they said you did monster work. Hey, tell me something, how did you come up with the name for this place? Is Asmodeus some Fae word or something?"

Aohdan laughed as he wiped Gerry's arm. "Nothing like that. Asmodeus is actually from your world. He's the Hebrew devil of sensuality and luxury."

"No shit?"

"No shit."

For some reason, that struck Gerry as funny and he tried not to laugh, but eventually Aohdan had to take the needle away until his client got the laughter out of his system. It made Aohdan laugh, too, and he appreciated the chance to feel something other than the anger and grief he had buried inside.

CHAPTER 38

THE BARKING CRAB was a rather ramshackle-looking restaurant that rested in the shadow of the federal courthouse, or at least it had been until the Seaport area started to boom. The restaurant's owners then put it though a renovation that included a new coat of red paint over the irregular and haphazard shingles, a new roof, and a new tent cover over the outdoor seating area. A lot of locals considered it nothing more than a tourist trap—and several online reviews called the establishment a "hot mess"—but the food was solid and the view was excellent. It was less than a ten-minute walk from the condo on Liberty Pier, and Seireadan had always had a soft spot for the place. The temporary walls were still up around the patio, giving patrons shelter from the chilly March breeze.

Seireadan had an order of fried clams while Aohdan went with a baked stuffed lobster. Seated at a corner table, they chatted about mundane things, and Aohdan told her about Gerry, his granddaughter, and the man's amusement at the shop's name. Once they finished dinner, they took their time strolling home, choosing to go around the courthouse and along Fan Pier. Partway, Seireadan stopped and sat on her favorite bench that looked back toward the city. She pulled her jacket a little closer as Aohdan came to sit beside her.

"It will be nice when the roses along the walk are out again," she said.

Aohdan put his arm around her shoulder and pulled her closer to keep her warm, and for a moment, the depth of her feelings for him swamped her.

"Come on," she said, standing up and pulling his hand. Aohdan got up, but let Seireadan's hand slip through his as he watched her walk ahead of him. She could feel his eyes linger on her jeans and how they curved around her legs.

As soon as they were in the elevator, Seireadan pulled his face down and kissed him fiercely. She moved her hands to his sides and pulled on his shirt until it came out of the waist of his jeans, and then she slid her hands under the material and along the hard planes of his abdomen and ribs. Aohdan closed his eyes and groaned as she ran her fingers over his stomach and up until she reached the smooth gold ring that pierced his nipple. She gave it a gentle tug, and he responded with a moan of pleasure. They practically fell over each other getting into his condo, jackets tossed on the floor, and in a single motion, Aohdan pulled his shirt up and over his head.

Without a word, Aohdan scooped her up and carried her to the sofa, where he dropped her down on the cushions. Seireadan started to move beneath him, but he caught her by the waist and held her still. She stared into his dark eyes, never looking away as his hands found her jeans, undid the button, and slowly dragged them down over her hips and legs. She reached for his belt, but Aohdan blocked her hands.

"Not yet," he said softly.

She subsided, savored the feel of him between her legs, but stretched up to kiss him, keeping Aohdan's lower lip gently trapped in her teeth while she hooked one of her legs around his. Slowly, softly, she dragged her fingernails down his chest, letting the anticipation build. She twisted a little beneath him, pulling her shirt up over her head, and the look in Aohdan's eyes as they roamed over her body, the curve of her breasts, was everything she had ever wanted.

When he kissed her again, Seireadan could feel every ounce of desire coursing through him. She dug her fingers into his arms. He broke away from the kiss, to her dismay, and shifted his weight back. Her eyes heated as he slid his hands down, and she felt his grip tighten on her hips before Aohdan slowly dragged her panties down.

"What are you doing?" she asked with a smile.

"Whatever I want."

Seireadan's head fell back and she cried out when he went down on her, his tongue and fingers teasing and exploring her until she thought she would break. As her hips bucked, Seireadan grabbed Aohdan's hair. The overpowering sensation of his mouth on her dragged her to the edge, and she teetered there precariously. He paused.

"Aohdan . . ." Her voice was breathy, distracted, as her body balanced on a pin.

He flicked his tongue over her, and Seireadan's back arched as he slid a finger inside her. When he tasted her again, Seireadan bucked under his touch, tightening around his finger, as the orgasm crashed over her, and before she was even finished, Seireadan reached for him. Unable to resist her or restrain himself any longer, Aohdan nearly tore the rest of his clothes off, and the noise that erupted from Aohdan's throat as he filled her was primitive and raw with desire.

Seireadan moaned and gasped at his relentless pace, and a moment later she cried out as she tightened around him again, and that was as much control as Aohdan could offer. He exploded with a roaring shout, and Seireadan wrapped her legs around his waist as he buried himself deeply inside her. When she came to her senses, she smiled up at Aohdan, touching his face while he gulped in air, his chest still heaving.

She pushed a strand of hair out of his face and whispered, "You have no idea how much I love you." *No idea what I would do for you . . .*

They lounged in each other's arms until Aohdan reluctantly got up to shower. Seireadan went to the bedroom closet, grabbed something off the shelf, and went back to the kitchen. When Aohdan came out, he absently dropped a jacket onto a duffel bag that was sitting by the door before he joined her in the kitchen. He tugged at the black mock turtleneck's snug collar and drank some orange juice straight from the bottle.

"Here, take this with you." She handed him a brown leather scabbard.

Aohdan looked at it carefully before he wrapped his hand around the carved bone hilt; it was smooth and comfortable in his palm, and he pulled the knife from its sheath. It was a wicked single-edged blade that was nearly nine inches long and clearly Fae forged. The balance was excellent, and he put his thumb against the edge; it drew blood with the lightest touch.

She saw the question in his eyes. "I know I can't go with you tonight. So take this little part of me with you . . . and use it."

CHAPTER 39

IN THE SOUTH Boston Yacht Club's marina, Chris had the engine of the thirty-two-foot sportfishing boat warm and ready to go. From a sheltered, shadowed place in the cabin, Aohdan watched him check some gauges and then examine the smaller AquaSport that was tethered to the larger ship. His eyes shifted slightly when he heard the thump of Galen's cane belowdecks. Finally, in the dim lights dotting the marina, he saw four figures start to make their way toward the boat from the stone-dust parking lot.

When Rory and Kieran reached the edge of the boat—*The Revolucion*—with their guests, Aohdan came out and locked eyes with Fearg and Lanty. They both stopped dead in their tracks. Kieran grabbed Lanty with both hands and practically tossed him, sprawling, onto the boat. He landed with a thud and tried to scramble away, but Chris's boot on his throat put an end to that.

"Give me an excuse to throw you over there, too," Rory said to Fearg. It didn't turn out to be necessary.

"Chris, take us out. Way out," ordered Aohdan.

The boat moved slowly at first while it cleared the marina, and Aohdan watched the two prisoners with his unnerving, silent stare. Bound to the railing, Fearg and Lanty looked at each other, fear painted on their faces, and Lanty glanced over the side of the boat.

"I wouldn't recommend that. Jump and we'll just pull you along all the way out," Galen told them.

The farther away from shore the boat went, the more reflective Aohdan became. Finally, tired of staring at Fearg and Lanty's huddled shapes, he went to the front of the boat to watch the horizon. The wind was bracing, and he folded his arms in front of him. The Fae had strong feelings about concepts like loyalty and revenge. Betrayals were rarely forgiven and never forgotten. *But to turn on your own* fréamhacha agus brainsí*? The only thing I regret is that Crogher is already dead. A bullet to the head was too fast and too clean for him.*

The boat's motor suddenly throttled down, and the vessel slowed considerably. Aohdan looked over his shoulder and up toward where Chris was steering.

"This is as far out as we can go and still be back before dawn," Chris said through the window. Aohdan nodded and walked to the back of the boat. Kieran, Rory, and Galen were sitting on the bench to one side of the rear deck, and across from them, Fearg and Lanty huddled, miserable, on the deck.

"Fearg and Lanty, former captains to Baibin. Traitors and cowards, both of you," Aohdan said. For a moment, neither answered, but they did look at the floor.

"We were loyal," muttered Lanty finally.

"What was that?" asked Aohdan. When Lanty didn't answer, Aohdan gestured to Rory and Kieran. Rory grabbed him by the shirt and hauled him to his feet. The cheap cloth of Lanty's shirt tore under the force, opening a gaping hole at the shoulder. Kieran landed three solid punches to Lanty's middle, driving the air out of his lungs, and he collapsed onto the deck, coughing.

From his seat, Galen tapped the silver head of his cane in his hand and said, "The patriarch asked you a question."

"We were loyal," Lanty wheezed. He tried to struggle to one knee, but Rory kicked him down.

"Loyal? To a backstabbing maggot, not to your triarch." In his mind, all Aohdan could see was Oisin's pale face as he lay bleeding on the floor. Behind him, he heard Galen grunt softly as he got up and put weight on his damaged leg. The second moved stiffly. Aohdan watched him closely but didn't intervene.

"You were two of Baibin's captains. Her captains! You ruined your clan's honor," Galen growled, the loathing clear in his voice.

"No! We were going to restore Providence's status—" Before Fearg could finish, Galen brought his cane down hard, cracking Fearg's collarbone with the force of the swing. The bound man howled in pain.

"Status? You're a fool. Your matriarch formally accepted the merger. How is going against her final act as your triarch anything other than a betrayal? You watched as Crogher offered Aohdan the silver branch, knowing what was going to happen!" Furious, Galen looked at them with disgust.

Fearg raised his head and looked at Aohdan. "What else were we supposed to do? You would have cleaned house in short order. Shipped us off to put our thumbs up our asses in some backwater town. I wasn't going to spend the rest of my life freezing my ass off in Caribou-fucking-Maine!"

Kieran punched Fearg, and a tooth skipped across the deck of the boat. "He would have given you a chance. If there is one thing I've learned about Aohdan Collins, it's that he rewards loyalty. As soon as that branch was passed over, Aohdan became your patriarch. He welcomed you as family. And you repay him like this?"

Aohdan let them continue for a while. *They've all earned their pound of flesh, too. I'm not the only one here to settle a score and send a message tonight.* But when Rory started to talk about the consequences for Fearg and Lanty's families, Aohdan stepped in.

"Rory. Enough."

"Why? They're responsible for all of this. Are you really going to leave children behind who are going to grow up hating you? Wanting to do the same thing to you that we're doing here tonight?" Rory was incensed.

"I don't kill children."

"Then you're a fool." Rory's voice oozed scorn and contempt.

Aohdan's eyebrows went up, but Kieran grabbed Rory by the arm and dragged him back a few steps.

"Shut up, you fucking idiot," Kieran hissed. "With the mood he's in, verra likely you'll end up over the side with those two if do no' watch your mouth."

Rory yanked his arm away. "He leaves too many loose ends," he hissed, giving Kieran a small shove.

Turning his back on Aohdan, Rory leaned on the railing to look out at the black water. The rest of the boat was silent as Aohdan watched him. After a few eternal seconds, the patriarch looked back over at Fearg and Lanty, who were breathing hard and bleeding from the beating they'd just taken. One of Lanty's eyes was swollen shut, and blood poured out of Fearg's now broken nose.

"The fact remains that I accepted the silver branch and then you tried to kill your new patriarch. I won't stand for that." There was a note of finality in Aohdan's voice that was chilling. Fearg and Lanty both moaned.

The patriarch went to his bag and took out a pair of leather gloves. He pulled them on slowly, flexing his fingers. Then he retrieved two small glass vials and handed one to Galen, who sat back down to rest his leg. Aohdan cracked the seal on the other.

"Do you know what this is?" Aohdan asked, holding the vial closer. As the acrid tang of iron assaulted his nose, Lanty panicked and tried to lunge to the side, flailing from side to side as far as the short tether would allow. Rory grabbed the thrashing Fae, kicked him behind the knees, and forced Lanty to collapse before grabbing a thick handful of hair. He jerked Lanty's head back as far as it would go.

Aohdan grasped Lanty's chin in a viselike grip. "Open. Your. Mouth."

Eyes wide with fear, Lanty struggled in vain as the pressure forced his jaws apart. Aohdan dumped the contents of the vial into Lanty's mouth and then pressed a gloved hand down so he couldn't spit the powder out. The former captain's eyes bulged and he started to sweat, his face turning red as the iron burned.

"Swallow it all, you bastard," said Aohdan.

After Lanty swallowed, Rory gave him a contemptuous shove, and Lanty fell to the deck gasping and gagging, convulsions wracking his body as the iron burned its way down his throat and into his stomach. Bloody foam spewed from Lanty's mouth while his eyes rolled back, and Kieran and Chris dragged Fearg past the twitching body to face Aohdan.

Fearg peed himself as Aohdan cracked the second vial and handed it to Galen.

"Please, no. Don't. I don't want to die—not like that. I was just following orders."

"Whose orders?" asked Aohdan, his voice devoid of emotion. "Who gave the order? Who's responsible for all of this?"

"Crogher! It was his idea! He said it was time for a bold move. That there needed to be a changing of the guard. He'd be patriarch of Boston if he took you out after the merge!" Fearg was nearly wailing.

"Not after the rest of us were through with him," muttered Galen.

"Baibin had nothing to do with this?" Aohdan stared hard at him.

"The matriarch? No! No way. Crogher was going to kill her as soon as he was done with you. She'd already made an accord with you; she never would have broken that. Crogher said she was senile, not able to function as matriarch anymore. That he'd be doing her a favor by killing her."

Aohdan knew Fearg was too terrified to even try lying, but that wasn't enough for forgiveness. He grabbed a chunk of Fearg's red hair, forcing him to look up. The trembling Fae's face was ruddy and swollen, and he reeked of fear and urine.

"So, you went along with a plan that violated the wishes of your ruling matriarch? You willingly betrayed her?" asked the patriarch.

"Crogher said it would be worth it . . ." Fearg sobbed, and Aohdan let go of his hair, disgusted. With a gesture from Aohdan, Galen handed over the glass vial.

Aohdan's voice was ice when he said, "Open your mouth."

Fearg's sobs and pleas for mercy dissolved into a painful squeal as Aohdan squeezed his jaw. Slowly, inch by inch, Fearg's mouth was forced open.

"Was it worth it?" Aohdan, fierce and feral, demanded. "I welcomed you into my *fréamhacha agus brainsí* and called you family. You repaid me with treachery and death. Oisin died in agony because you betrayed your own oath, and now so will you. Tell me, Fearg, was it worth it?"

Aohdan poured the black powder into Fearg's mouth, and it immediately started to blister his lips and tongue. As he choked and thrashed, vainly trying to spit out the iron powder,

Fearg managed to bite through his tongue, and blood exploded out of his mouth. Chris and Kieran dropped his arms and let Fearg fall next to Lanty.

Moving to the opposite side of the boat, Aohdan, his three captains, and Chris all stood with unreadable faces and watched the two Fae die.

CHAPTER 40

SEIREADAN MADE A vain attempt to work after Aohdan left for the yacht club, but too many emotions crowded out her focus. Turning off her laptop, she sat in silence, wondering where Aohdan was and what was going on, and she realized that activity was the only thing that was going to keep her from climbing the walls until he got home.

Aohdan had insisted she bring some of her clothes to his place, and she'd barely been back to her apartment since the day Oisin died. Along with clothes, she'd brought her laptop and a few other things that she valued: some of her knives and Claíomh Solais, which she'd tucked away in her new closet.

"No point in having you if I can't use you, and I haven't practiced in far too long," Seireadan said to the sword as she pulled it out from a back corner of one closet. "And it is high time I told Aohdan about you—after everything with Oisin is settled."

She went into the gym and spent a half hour on the elliptical to warm up before moving on to the weight machine. A few sips of cool water went down easily as she wiped her face and neck. She dried her hands and picked Claíomh Solais up. A bastard sword, the black hilt with the twisted band of inlaid gold around it afforded enough room for a one- or two-handed grip. The bezel-set citrine in the hilt glinted as Seireadan deliberately slid the sword from its sheath.

A bead of light ran up the sword's razor edges and rested on the wicked tip as a shimmer of power ran up Seireadan's arm. She whispered to the blade, "Hush. Sleep, Solais. This is only a dry run; there's no blood for you today."

The shimmer subsided slightly, and Seireadan set herself to practicing. Within moments, her stepping and footwork flowed smoothly. Soon she moved on to working strikes and cuts as she imagined an invisible opponent facing her.

"Too slow!" Seireadan berated herself harshly as she pulled the blade back, recovering from her previous effort. "Keep your guard up."

After another fifteen minutes, satisfied she'd improved her responses, Seireadan took a break. She drained the water bottle, tossed it to the side, and wiped her mouth with the back of her hand before closing her eyes. She deliberately looked for the memory of her dream—her first Seeing—and forced herself to look at the Alabaster Man, straining to see clearly features other than his hair and eyes. Flexing her fingers on the hilt, she lunged forward in an attack posture, then struck and counterstruck in various combinations as she imagined herself driving back the pale nightmare before her . . . *The Alabaster Man retreated under a flurry of blows until his blade clattered across the floor. He dropped to his knees, and with a shout, Seireadan swung Claíomh Solais in a wide arc, feeling the moment when it connected with the Alabaster Man's neck and sent his head thumping across the floor, spraying blood behind it.*

Seireadan's eyes flew open and she screamed in frustration, burning to have something solid to drive the sword's blade into. She eyed Aohdan's punching bag for a moment but decided she didn't want to explain why it had been cut to ribbons. At least not yet.

CHAPTER 41

IT TOOK A full fifteen minutes for Fearg and Lanty to die. When it was over, blood caked the dead men's mouths and noses, and had even leaked from their bulging, glassy eyes. Without saying anything, Aohdan went back to the bag he'd brought with him and reached inside.

"Do you want them overboard?" asked Galen.

"Not yet; I'm not finished." When Aohdan turned back, he had Seireadan's knife in one hand and an ornate wooden box in the other. The dull light from the boat's cabin played along the blade, highlighting the edge. Aohdan handed his second the box and went back to the bodies, and the others instinctively stayed well out of his way.

The patriarch shoved the toe of his boot under Lanty's body and flipped him over. Straddling the corpse, Aohdan dropped to one knee and plunged the blade deep into Lanty's chest. Between the sharpness of the blade and the adrenaline coursing through his body, Aohdan had no trouble tearing through bone and muscle, opening a gaping hole in Lanty's chest. Blood pooled on the deck as he made a few more cuts before he reached inside.

When he pulled his hand out, he was holding Lanty's heart.

"Open the box," Aohdan said to Galen.

Aohdan looked at the heart for a long time and without another word, put it inside the box. Galen closed the lid as Aohdan turned back to Fearg. Without any hesitation, he repeated the ritual, using Seireadan's knife to rip Fearg's heart from his corpse. By the time he was done, Aohdan's arms were slick with blood and his chest and face were spattered with gore. He put the second heart into the box and watched Galen close the lid. Still silent, Aohdan went belowdecks. As he descended the stairs, Aohdan heard someone vomit over the railing.

When Aohdan returned, he was completely naked and wet from where he'd washed his face and hands. Still silent, he put Seireadan's knife away and pulled some clean clothes out of his bag. Once dressed, he took the box from where it rested next to Galen, locked it, and tucked it into the bag. Sitting down on the bench, he rested his elbows on his knees and rubbed the back of his neck.

It's been a long fucking night. "They both go overboard," he finally said.

Rory and Kieran grabbed Fearg, chained a weight to him, sliced his abdomen so he wouldn't float, and then tossed his body over the side. The splash echoed loudly in the darkness. Lanty followed his friend down into the deep black of the Atlantic a few minutes later.

When they were done, Chris said, "Any bloody clothes, give them to me. And we'll all need to get into the AquaSport."

He took the small pile of soiled items belowdecks. While he was gone, Aohdan restlessly prowled the deck. Chris came back up, smelling faintly of bleach and carrying two plastic containers.

"Are we set?" asked Aohdan.

"Just about. Can you get the AquaSport going? We'll need to haul ass once I'm done."

Aohdan nodded. "Do what you need."

Five minutes later, Chris jumped in the AquaSport, the pungent scent of gasoline clinging to his sweatshirt, and sent the smaller boat charging across the choppy water. Behind them, *The Revolucion* exploded in a fountain of fire and debris. The breached hull groaned—a final death rattle—as it cracked and splintered. Water rushed in, dragging the bones of the ship under, down into the dark depths to join Fearg and Lanty.

The AquaSport was running on fumes by the time they got back to Boston. Chris pulled up alongside one of the docks just long enough to let the others disembark, then he headed out again to bring the little boat back to its mooring before it was missed.

Aohdan and Galen threaded their way through some side streets until they came out of an alley next to a dive bar, and Aohdan wobbled a little, pretending to be drunk as he hailed a cab. The driver brought them to South Station, where Galen took a different cab home. The horizon was just getting lighter and—even as exhausted as he was—Aohdan decided to walk; he still needed to think.

Now what do I do with Baibin? I'm Providence's patriarch, and I'm within my rights to annihilate her entire bloodline for what Crogher did. But does that create more problems than it solves?

He turned the issue over in his mind several times before he quietly let himself into the penthouse. He didn't hear any noise from the bedroom, and didn't want to wake Seireadan, so he stripped off his clothes and left them in a pile on the floor. He shivered, still cold from being on the water, and crept into the bedroom. Aohdan slid under the covers as quietly as he could and lay perfectly still, afraid he'd wake Seireadan, but a moment later, she pressed against him, her skin molten.

"You're freezing."

"I'm sorry I woke you up," he whispered, his shoulders relaxing as she wrapped her arms around him.

"You didn't; I've been awake for a while. Are you okay?"

"I'm okay," he said softly into her ear.

"Everything taken care of?"

"Yes . . . for now."

"Good."

Across the city, Kieran knew Lia would be angry at being woken up—she'd just gotten back from a business trip to Asia and the jet lag was killing her. He rang the doorbell anyway, and could hear her stomp and curse her way down the hall. With a final expletive, she flung the door open and stopped short.

"Kieran? What happened?"

Kieran pushed by her, not waiting for an invitation to come in, and pulled Lia close. She ran a hand down his hair as they just stood together. He sighed heavily. Fearg and Lanty, as far as he was concerned, had gotten what they deserved, but it was still a heavy burden for him to bear.

"Kieran?"

He pulled her closer. "I know it's verra early. I just do no' want to be alone."

Chris stripped his clothes off and went straight to the shower. Standing under the nearly blistering spray, he swallowed hard. *I've done some bad shit in my life, and I don't regret adding tonight to the list.* The visceral memory of blood, and Lanty's dead heart in Aohdan's hand, made his stomach turn over. *I've never seen Aohdan like that. You'd have to be a goddamn moron to cross him.* He stayed under the running water until his fingers pruned and the water turned cold.

Galen never bothered getting into bed. He'd done too much and his leg was throbbing. He chased a painkiller with a Ben Nevis single malt Scotch, even though he knew it was a bad idea. All he kept thinking about was Crogher. *She was his mother, not just his matriarch.* He still couldn't wrap his head around how a second could betray a triarch like that. *I would die before I did anything like that to Aohdan, but what if one of us . . .* He slammed the door on that thought before it went any further—it was something he refused to contemplate—and he poured himself one more dram of whiskey. He fell asleep sitting up in his recliner.

Rory climbed into bed, pulled the covers to his waist, and then scrunched up his pillow. Vashti slid in behind him and pushed her warm breasts against his back. Rory bit his lip; he was exhausted, but the Pari was impossible to resist. Rolling over, he pinched her nipples, getting even harder as he watched Vashti lick her lips in anticipation.

"Did you take care of your business?" she murmured.

"Yes."

"You don't look happy, baby. Tell me what's wrong."

"The boss brought the human. He saw everything and now he's a big fucking liability," said Rory. "He's not even a captain."

"No!" Vashti gasped in outrage. "Can you even imagine? Him—a human—as a captain?"

"No." Rory slid a finger between Vashti's legs and smiled when she writhed under his touch.

"You'd be a much better patriarch than Aohdan."

"I would be; I wouldn't have all those loose ends lying around." *Like Chris. Or Fearg's brother and Lanty's son. Only a matter of time before someone takes Aohdan's head. And then, of course, I'll need to comfort Aeronwy. She'll be devastated.*

Vashti got up on her knees as Abrezu came in from the other room, climbed onto the bed with them, and started sliding her hands over her own body.

"What do you want?" asked Vashti.

Rory knew it was a bigger question than just his sexual appetite for the night, but he ignored the larger implications, and instead decided to see if Vashti would really do whatever he wanted.

"Whatever I want?" he asked, his eyes glinting.

"Anything," breathed the Pari.

Rory grinned when he said, "I want to watch you make Abrezu come, and then I want to hear you scream my name while I pound you."

Vashti didn't even blink at the request, and said, "Your wish is my command . . . boss."

Rory wasn't sure what turned him on more: watching Vashti go down on her sister or being called "boss."

CHAPTER 42

TWO DAYS AFTER *The Revolucion* disappeared into the Atlantic, they buried Oisin on a blustery March day. By ten o'clock, dark clouds heralding the raw rain to come had rolled in to block the sun, draping the day in its own shroud of misery. Aohdan's tailored black suit was formal and reserved, and he had carefully tied back his long hair. After he got out of the car, he held his hand out to help Seireadan. Over her long black dress, Seireadan wore her Raven's cloak, the colors shifting from midnight black on the hood to a foggy light gray at the hem, where it swirled around her ankles, and the sides of her hair were pinned back with a silver clip.

She gave Aohdan's hand a gentle squeeze as they climbed the steps of the church. In Aohdan's free hand, he carried the ornately carved wooden box from the ship. At the top of the stairs, two elderly women—one a dark-skinned Svartálfar and the other human—approached.

"Mrs. MacAdams, Miss Morke. It's very kind of you to come today," said Aohdan.

Mrs. MacAdams hugged him. "Oh, Aohdan! We were brokenhearted when we heard the news. You and Oisin have always been so good to us. Such nice boys, always making sure we never had any trouble in the neighborhood." She patted him with wrinkled, age-spotted hands. Seireadan smiled as the two old ladies doted on Aohdan.

"Who is this?" Mrs. MacAdams asked when she noticed Seireadan.

"Ladies, my girlfriend, Seireadan."

The Svartálfar looked her up and down, keen, shiny eyes peering out from their deeply wrinkled black skin, and gave an approving nod, but said nothing.

"Oh, aren't you lovely, dear," cooed Mrs. MacAdams as she held out a gnarled hand to Seireadan. "A pleasure to meet you. Now you take good care of our Aohdan."

"I will," said Seireadan.

"We should go in," said Miss Morke. "The service will start soon."

In the church, Oisin's father, Desmond, sat near the front, bent and wrinkled, and near him, Oisin's simple oak casket rested with the cover open. Inside the casket, Oisin was laid out in the traditional manner—naked, save for a blue cloth covering his midsection for modesty's sake. The cloth would be removed just before the coffin was sealed, and Oisin would be buried naked, as was customary for the Fae. His *brainsí* tattoo was bold on his chest, the black ink a sharp contrast to his pale skin and the newly stitched wounds from Crogher's gun.

As they sat, Seireadan nodded hellos to Kieran, Galen, and Rory, and then to Chris, who slipped into a seat behind her. A moment later, Lia, her long blond hair caught up in a bun, hurried down the outside aisle and slid into the seat next to Kieran.

"I'm so sorry," she whispered to them all. "Traffic was awful."

At the front of the church, Reverend DeGrasse stepped up to the small lectern. A short, rotund man with salt-and-pepper hair, he wore round glasses that he adjusted absently. He looked out over the crowd before clearing his throat, and his rich, deep voice carried easily.

"Thank you all for coming. We gather to remember the life of Oisin O'Neill: son, friend, and colleague. While I was not personally acquainted with Oisin, after having spoken to his father and many of his close friends, I feel I've gotten to know him—and wish I could have known him better. He was a devoted, funny man who enjoyed life and wasn't afraid to take chances—as I have learned through several stories about his adventures in Las Vegas and Atlantic City."

A ripple of laughter whispered through the crowd.

"He was also a man of tremendous courage and loyalty," continued DeGrasse. "Someone who, no matter what, had his friends' backs."

Next to her, Aohdan shifted, restless, and Seireadan put her hand over his clenched fist. She knew the fact that Oisin had died to save him still weighed heavily on Aohdan, and that it would be a long time before that feeling faded. She squeezed his hand and felt him relax. Reverend DeGrasse continued speaking for another ten minutes, retelling stories about Oisin that had been shared by those closest to him, blending the serious and sorrowful with moments of humor that truly captured who Oisin was. He paused, looking thoughtful and reflective for a moment, before he continued.

"The Fae believe that when someone dies, their energy—their soul, if you will—leaves the body and moves to a new existence, a new life, but takes with it the emotions, feelings, and wishes of those who mourn its passing. Often, close friends and family leave gifts with the body, representations of something meaningful from the person's life, and these things—along with the emotions attached—give the soul strength as it moves on to whatever and whomever awaits it."

He paused to let the gathered congregation consider his words. "I now invite those closest to Oisin to gift him with the things he needs to take on his journey. They may be physical representations or just the things you hold in your hearts."

A line soon formed as many of the mourners filed up to the casket. Most had thoughts or wishes written on slips of paper, which they dropped in a ceramic jar that would be buried with Oisin. Others, like Oisin's father, left actual items. When it was her turn, Seireadan walked to the front of the church, tall and elegant. She looked sadly down at Oisin as her eyes filled with tears.

Her voice was low so only she and Oisin could hear. "I'm sorry I didn't See things sooner, that my Sight wasn't clearer. Maybe none of this would have happened." She fell silent, knowing what she said was little more than wishful thinking. She'd learned early on that the Sight never gave the full story, only pieces, because the future was fluid. She put a small velvet bag next to Oisin's head. Inside was an unbroken geode she'd found at Sacred Circle.

"The roughest exterior can hide the most beautiful things. May everyone see past the surface and understand what a treasure you truly are." She leaned close, kissed Oisin's forehead, and in the softest voice, whispered, "Thank you for saving Aohdan."

After Seireadan sat down, Aohdan was the only mourner left standing at the casket. He walked with slow, deliberate steps, and as he looked down at Oisin's lifeless, damaged body, he felt the rage kindle again, but the *brainsí* tattoo stirred a wave of pride that dampened the anger and pain: Oisin had lived and died a captain, true to every promise he'd ever made to his patriarch. Aohdan calmed himself before he put the sealed box beneath Oisin's feet.

"Oisin, you are the brother of my heart," he said, resting his hand on the coffin's cool wood, but then fell silent. The rest of what he had to say was for Oisin only, and no one else. *This is between us, my friend. Only us. I've brought you the hearts of our enemies, which I cut out with my own hand. They've paid dearly for taking you from us, from me. On your journey, take with you the power to crush any enemy beneath your heel, and the strength you need to always defend the ones you love. And someday, when I see you again, forgive me for my failures.*

Back at his seat, Aohdan wiped a tear from Seireadan's cheek and put his arm around her shoulder as she leaned into him. When Reverend DeGrasse saw there were no other mourners who wanted to participate in the gifting, he returned to the podium.

"Desmond," Reverend DeGrasse said to Oisin's father. "Will you be sealing the coffin?"

"If they're willing, I'd like Mr. Collins and Oisin's friends to do that. I think he would have wanted it that way." The old man looked across the aisle at Aohdan.

"We'd be honored," said Aohdan. He got up along with Kieran, Galen, and Rory, and he looked at Chris. "You were his friend, too, Chris. Join us."

The five men lined up at the coffin, and Aohdan reached in and removed the blue cloth that covered Oisin's hips, making sure none of the gifts were disturbed. He folded it neatly and tucked it into the coffin.

Once the cloth was gone and Oisin's body was naked, Kieran raised an eyebrow and started to grin before he said, "Well, I'm verra certain the ladies are going to miss *that*."

His voice was soft enough so only his friends at the casket heard him, and his cheeky observation brought smiles to the corners of each mouth for a split second. Together they reached up and pulled the lid of the coffin closed, and Aohdan felt a heaviness settle in his stomach as the dull thud sounded in the church. Rory picked up a tube that looked a bit like silicone caulk from a hardware store and put the tip against the seam between the coffin's lid and body. He squeezed some of the liquid out, and the smell of cloves and orange filled the church.

As it touched the wood, the liquid expanded to fill the space between the lid and the casket and started to solidify. Rory passed the tube to Kieran who, in turn, gave it to Aohdan. Once he was done, Chris took it, and Galen finished the last of the seal. Accompanied by Desmond, the five escorted the casket out of the church and into the waiting hearse.

Reverend DeGrasse shook hands with Desmond and Aohdan. "I'll make sure the burial is carried out according to Oisin's wishes." He got in with the driver, and the hearse pulled into traffic and disappeared.

"Doesn't seem right to just watch them drive away," said Chris.

"Visiting graves is a human practice," Aohdan said. "We don't need to know where Oisin is, only that he's returned to the universe."

The simple words made sense, but Aohdan lingered on the sidewalk in the rain long after the hearse disappeared and the other mourners went home.

CHAPTER 43

THE DAY AFTER the funeral, Seireadan spent the morning working on proposals for two new potential clients. Finally, after lunch she'd had enough. Rolling her neck and her shoulders, she stretched, her back cracking between the shoulder blades. Out in the living room, Aohdan was sitting on the sofa staring at the gray mist outside. She pinched his shoulders from behind.

"What are you thinking about?"

"My *brainsí*," he said simply.

"Because you need someone to take Oisin's spot, don't you?"

Aohdan let his head fall back on the cushion. "I'm still thinking that through, but no matter who takes Oisin's old spot, I'll need at least one new captain."

"Do you have someone in mind?"

"I do: Chris."

His answer didn't entirely surprise Seireadan, and she nodded. "He's a good choice, but you know it won't be a popular choice in some areas." She thought back to the times Rory had disparaged and insulted Chris.

"I know. I'm going to have Chris come here so I can let him know. I'll tell the others tomorrow."

It only took Chris a half hour to get there after Aohdan's call. Seireadan answered the door when he knocked and invited him in. He went to the kitchen, took a seat at the island, and thanked Seireadan when she pulled a soda out of the refrigerator and offered it to him.

"Thanks for coming over. I know yesterday was a long day for everyone," said Aohdan as he came out of the other room.

"No problem. What do you need?"

"Between Providence and Oisin's death, I need to take a look at how things are organized. I'll be running Oisin's crew for now, and Kieran will be taking over the business in Providence; that's one of the big changes. But that leaves Kieran's old spot vacant."

"I get it. Do you need me to check someone out?"

"Not exactly: I want to promote you to the job, Chris." Aohdan rested his elbows on the island's granite top and waited while his words fully registered.

"I'm sorry, what?"

"I want you to be my new captain and to take over Kieran's old crew."

"But I'm not Fae," Chris blurted out.

"I don't give a shit if you're Fae or not. You're smart, you're capable, and you're loyal. I've known you for years and I think you're the man for the job. Are you interested? It comes with a pay raise and perks, of course."

Chris looked stunned. "Yes! I'm absolutely interested."

"You need to understand something, Chris. If you're a captain, you're going to be responsible for things that are beyond what you've done in the past. Once you're in, you're in. This isn't a job you can try for a few months and then quit. Pretty much the only way out is to get promoted or get killed." Aohdan's tone was stone serious.

"I know that, and I understand. You've never been anything but good to me and fair. You've taken care of my family when we needed help. I'm all in for you."

Aohdan nodded approvingly. "Good to hear, but make sure you really do understand. Go home and think about it. If you're still 'all in,' then meet Galen at Underworld on Friday. If you decide this isn't for you, you can stay in your current role. No hard feelings." As he spoke, Aohdan wrote something on a piece of paper and folded it.

"I'll think about it; you have my word." Chris started to stand up, but stopped when Aohdan slid the paper across the island. When he unfolded the paper, his eyes got huge and they flew to Aohdan's face.

"That's your new salary as a captain."

"Holy Mother of God," Chris gasped.

"You take the job and you'll earn every penny of that and more. Remember, once you bind yourself to my *fréamhacha agus brainsí* as a captain, you can't walk away. Ever. Now go home and think about it."

At six o'clock the next morning, Chris sent Aohdan a text: I'm all in.

Later that morning, Galen, Rory, and Kieran met the patriarch at Underworld. Aohdan was leaning on the edge of Galen's desk, his arms folded, and the three captains sat down, waiting for him to start the meeting.

"It's been a difficult few weeks," Aohdan said. "But as painful as everything still is, we have businesses to run, and we need to make sure the *brainsí* is whole and ready to move forward, especially now that Providence is part of it. I've made some decisions about how things will run moving forward. We can't afford to have Oisin's position vacant for very long; that would just invite trouble."

"What did you have in mind?" Galen got comfortable in his chair and put his cane across the desk.

Aohdan looked at the three faces. *I know this is the right decision, but Seireadan's right. Rory's going to be pissed about this. But there is no way I'm having him near the Providence business, not after his comments on the boat about Fearg and Lanty's families. That's far too risky.* "For now, I'm going to take on Oisin's crew," he finally said. "A few months ago, he mentioned that the Svartálfar, Lorna, had a lot of potential, and I want to keep an eye on her myself. If she has the chops, I'll consider promoting her."

Galen and Kieran looked thoughtful, but Rory started to frown.

"I had planned—as Galen's aware—to have Oisin run Providence, but given the circumstances I've had to rethink that," Aohdan continued, "and that area will now be Kieran's responsibility."

"I will no' let you down, boss," Kieran said.

Aohdan watched Rory's frown deepen as his other captain fingered the claddagh ring he'd taken from Jimmy Boy, the night he murdered him.

"Rory, I know you have connections there through Moira, but Kieran is the right pick for the job, and I want you to not only keep running your current crew, but take on a few new assignments west of the city," said Aohdan.

Rory's knuckles whitened as the patriarch continued, "You've done a great job getting the South Shore in line and producing for us. I think you've got some good talent there as well, talent we can use in the future, but I want you to stay with them and make sure they've got what it takes. And you've done some good work in Worcester—you should get the rewards."

"I see," said Rory in a bland, neutral voice. "Who's taking Kieran's crew, then?"

Aohdan gave him a long, appraising look before he answered. "I'm promoting Chris to captain."

"Are you fucking kidding me? A human as one of your captains?" yelled Rory, his cheeks flushed with anger.

"Human or Fae has nothing to do with it," said Aohdan evenly, resisting the urge to punch Rory as hard as he could. "He's proved himself to be capable and loyal. We'll officially bring him into the *fréamhacha agus brainsí* on Friday."

"Un-fucking-believable," Rory muttered as he stood.

Aohdan squared himself to face Rory, ready for the confrontation to escalate and daring Rory to make the first move. He took a step closer to his captain and looked him in the eye. "You'll toe the line on this, Rory. And you *will* be there on Friday."

While Aohdan's voice was level and almost kind, all three heard the order underneath: *Shut your mouth and suck it up.*

"I'll be there. Are we done?" Rory matched the cool, neutral tone and added a layer of scorn.

"Yeah, we're done."

Later, Vashti stayed out of Rory's way and just watched and listened as he raged.

"Fuck him!" shouted Rory. "I can't believe this. You know, I don't really care if Kieran got Providence. He's earned his shot and that city is going to be a shit show to manage for the next decade. But keeping me down, cutting me out of the good territories? That's bullshit. Bullshit! In favor of that insignificant human? Once again, Aohdan doesn't have the balls to make the big decisions."

He quieted for a moment, staring out the picture window in his living room, and Vashti said, "You're right. How can he not see how valuable you are? You're worth more than all his other captains." She came up behind Rory and slid her arms around his waist, pressing against him seductively.

"I am, and he's too busy fucking Seireadan to notice." He held his fist up so Vashti could see the claddagh. "I handle shit when it needs to be handled. This is his way of punishing me for taking care of Jimmy. For doing the fucking job he should be doing!"

"Then you should work for someone who values you. You know I have friends at the Seelie Court who would love to talk to you," she purred. "They would treat you with respect, with honor. They'd appreciate your loyalty.

"He's the patriarch." There was the slightest hesitation in Rory's voice.

"He's only the patriarch if he's the strongest," said Vashti. The words were barely a breath from Vashti as she slinked around Rory and unbuttoned the front of his pants. From her knees, she looked up at Rory through her thick lashes. "He'd be no match for you . . ."

CHAPTER 44

WEARING A BUTTON-DOWN shirt with his best pair of pants, Chris met Galen at Underworld on Friday night. After a brief conversation, they drove in silence to a little nondescript building on Ferrin Street in Charlestown. Chris followed Galen through several halls and finally arrived at a small room where Aohdan, Kieran, and Rory were all waiting for them.

No one smiled at Chris, or greeted him, and the stillness stretched to fill the room until Aohdan's voice broke the silence. "You've come. Why are you here?"

Chris hesitated for a fraction of a second under the scrutiny of those stony faces before he answered, "To become part of your *fréamhacha agus brainsí*."

"You wish to bind yourself to my *fréamhacha agus brainsí*? Once you become a captain, you cannot quit, you cannot leave; the *brainsí* will become your family, your life. Do you understand that? Do you accept it?"

"I do." Chris didn't hesitate with that answer. As he spoke, Aohdan made a subtle gesture with his hand, and Rory, Kieran, and Galen slowly spread out to surround Chris.

"Then we proceed," said the patriarch. "What you see and what you say here tonight will never be shared with anyone outside this room. Ever."

"I understand."

"Christopher Cervenka, you are here to pledge your heart and mind, your honor and loyalty. Your family becomes our family, and our *fréamhacha agus brainsí* becomes yours. What say you?" Aohdan drew himself up to his full, imposing height and waited.

Chris prayed that his eyes didn't betray his uncertainty, but when he spoke, his voice didn't waver. "The *fréamhacha agus brainsí* is my family now and comes before all else." Aohdan gave him the smallest approving nod, and then the patriarch walked behind Chris and took his shoulders, physically turning him to face Galen before returning to his own spot in the circle.

"The triarch's word is law. You do not act against your triarch or *fréamhacha agus brainsí*. What say you?" asked the second.

"I would never act against the triarch or the *brainsí*." Chris's voice was steady as he answered and then turned to face Kieran when Galen gestured in that direction.

"You will no' speak about our business to outsiders, no' ever; our business is ours and ours alone. What say you?"

"I will remain silent when asked about our business," Chris replied before turning to face Rory. The silence was long and uncomfortable, but Chris didn't flinch at the naked resentment in the redheaded captain's eyes.

Rory stayed silent for another heartbeat before he said, "You will be a captain, and the other captains are your brothers, as close as if you were born from the same mother. You will not steal from them, you will not lie to them, and you will not sleep with their lovers. What say you?"

"The other captains are my brothers and my friends—I would not disrespect them by stealing or lying or sleeping with their women," said Chris firmly. Out of his peripheral vision,

Chris saw—and felt—Aohdan step toward him, and as he turned to face the patriarch, Aohdan stared into his eyes.

"Over the years, even without the title, you've acted like a captain. You've proven your loyalty and your love for the *brainsí* many times. You've fought for us, you've bled for us. You are one of us," said Aohdan. "Loyalty is always rewarded; betrayal is always avenged. That is how we live. What say you, Chris Cervenka?" Aohdan's voice filled the room as he pointed directly at Chris.

"I will love the *brainsí*—and my brothers—all of my days." Chris raised his voice, too. "You will never question my loyalty; I'll fight for you, bleed for you. And I'll protect my triarch with my life."

Aohdan offered a slow nod, accepting the promises Chris made, and said, "Don't ever forget the promises you've made tonight. If you violate them . . ."

Chris finished Aohdan's sentence for him: "If I break them, then I will die . . . and die badly."

Aohdan locked eyes with Chris again, and Chris felt his stomach sink when Aohdan's face remained emotionless. *Did I screw something up? Does he think I don't mean it?* Then Aohdan's voice echoed in the room and his words shocked—and terrified—Chris.

"Take him."

"Wait! What the hell?" Chris cried as Rory and Kieran grabbed him by the arms. Out of sheer instinct, he struggled and managed to get one arm free for a moment, but the two Fae men were bigger and even with his martial arts training, he couldn't overpower them. They dragged Chris across the floor and forced him into a chair. Rory held one arm down, and Kieran pinned the other while Galen violently tore the front of Chris's shirt open. Several buttons bounced across the floor.

"Jesus Christ!" yelled Chris. "That was my best shirt! What did I do wrong?"

No one answered him.

I don't know what I fucked up, but if I'm going to die, I'm not going to beg. Chris stopped struggling and fell silent, although his chest was heaving. He raised his chin and forced himself to relax. As soon as he did, Kieran released his arm and—after a hesitation—Rory did the same. Aohdan pulled his own shirt off, and Chris couldn't help but be drawn to the bold tribal-style tattoo over Aohdan's heart. Galen also took his shirt off, followed by Rory and Kieran. Each had the same tattoo over his heart: a circle of intertwined thorny vines that protected a crowned heart.

Aohdan touched his. "This is the mark of my *fréamhacha agus brainsí.* Only those closest to me wear this, and it's time for my new captain to receive his." Aohdan reached out and put his palm on the bare skin over Chris's heart.

Chris's breath came out in a sharp rush. "Holy Mother of God, you guys scared the crap out of me for a minute there."

Aohdan finally smiled as his tattoo machine started to hum. "Chris, you're now my captain and part of my *fréamhacha agus brainsí*'s inner circle. Be welcome, be family."

CHAPTER 45

IT WAS THE sincerity and affection in Aohdan's voice when he welcomed Chris as family that finally broke Rory. He buried the fury and the resentment as far down as he could while Chris was inked, and even managed to offer him a toast at Underworld after. By the time he got home, he was done playing the good soldier, and he took it out on Vashti.

He didn't say anything when he walked in the door. Instead he grabbed Vashti and spun her, pinning her against the wall from behind.

"Rory—"

"Shut up!" He grabbed a fistful of her long reddish hair, the color instantly making him think of Aeronwy. *And she's just like her fucking cousin. Disrespects you . . .*

He unbuckled his pants and roughly pushed her skirt up to her hips before he tore her delicate lace panties and slammed himself into her repeatedly until he came.

"I can't treat that little shit like an equal. I won't be passed over and disrespected like this," Rory growled as he buckled his jeans. With his back to Vashti, he didn't see the hateful look that flashed across her face as she stepped out of her torn and ruined panties and straightened her skirt.

"That's awful. How dare he treat you like that?"

Rory took a deep breath. "You said you had friends at the Seelie Court?"

Her eyes brightened at the interest in his voice. "Oh, I do. I've told Criofan all about you. How smart you are, how decisive."

"Criofan? The king's adviser?"

"Yes, and he's very interested in meeting you. He's looking for someone to work with him—someone trustworthy, who can take charge and make decisions."

"It would be nice if someone showed some fucking confidence in me."

"I know you could do great things with Criofan, show everyone what *real* Fae are like," she said, her voice turning sultry as she ran a finger slowly down Rory's chest. He nodded absently, cataloging all the times Aohdan had insulted or dismissed him.

"Criofan would appreciate you," she continued, "and just imagine the look on Aohdan's face when he sees you're working for the king. You'd be part of the true inner circle, and Criofan would never push you aside for some human."

Vashti layered the word "human" with scorn and contempt, and as soon as she saw Rory's face twist, the Pari went in for the kill.

"I know Criofan; he's a reasonable man. Give him Aohdan and I bet he'll give you the Boston *fréamhacha agus brainsí* for your own. And once you're triarch, then you can bring it—and the other captains—to heel. Show them what a real leader can do. You'll be able to do whatever you want." She smiled when Rory looked at her, the decision evident in his face.

"When can I meet your friend?"

"I'll call him right now." Vashti picked her phone up from the coffee table; she could practically feel the opals against her skin.

CHAPTER 46

THE BLUSTERY MARCH weather gave way to a warmer spring, and close to a month after Oisin's funeral—as life took some tentative steps toward normalcy again—Aghna summoned the Ravens to attend her at the Seelie king's manor. Lia and Seireadan were sitting in an expansive room in the Garden House at King Fionvarr's mansion waiting for the other Ravens.

The Garden House sat in the center of one of Fionvarr's pristine parks, a short walk from the mansion proper. The center of the structure was an airy rotunda with four spacious sunrooms that grew out of the circular center. Around the Garden House were extensive cultivated beds brimming with flowers and plants just starting to bloom. By each entrance to the rotunda, thick trellises supported clematis vines that would blossom into enormous flowers of purple, pink, and white.

Seireadan appreciated the beauty of the location, but she was restless. It had been a long time since she'd attended a Gathering, and she wondered if she should have said no when Lia pushed her on the subject. *Too late now. I would insult Aghna if I left at this point.*

In all, ten Ravens answered Aghna's call for a Gathering, and Seireadan recognized a few. Cavan was there, looking as aloof and arrogant as ever. She hadn't seen him since the day he berated her in the parking lot at Sacred Circle, and time had done little to lessen her distaste. She gave him a cold stare and turned away to say hello to Seanán, who she'd not seen in years.

Aghna, the eldest of the Ravens, stood up from her chair and leaned on a cane as she moved forward slowly. An accident many years ago had injured her hip, and it had never healed correctly; she'd needed the cane ever since. The limp, however, did not diminish her authority and gravitas one bit.

"Let us begin," she said. The other Ravens followed her into one of the sunrooms and gathered in a closer knot, their cloaks all flowing and swirling from their shoulders to their ankles. She slowly lowered herself into a chair with an extra cushion and waited as all of the others took their seats.

"First, thank you for answering my call to Gather. I have not seen some of you for many years." Her eyes didn't linger on Seireadan, but nonetheless, Seireadan felt a little ashamed that she'd not been to see her mentor for so long.

"Why have you called us together, Aghna?" asked Cavan pompously.

"I had the Sight not long ago, and when I relayed my vision to the King's adviser, more questions were asked than I had answers to. This Gathering was requested to find out if anyone else has had a similar Seeing."

Seireadan heard the hesitation when Aghna said "requested" and wondered if it had been an order. She folded her arms, her mood darkening as she started to think this Gathering was not exactly what it appeared to be.

"What did you See that has prompted these questions?" asked Seanán.

"The Sight brought me images of a dark, powerful Fae," the old woman said. Seireadan froze, knowing in her heart it was Aohdan, and she glanced over to see Lia looking at her, wide-eyed and clearly thinking the same thing.

"The face was misty." Aghna closed her eyes as she allowed her mind to comb through the images again. "He is painted in symbols. There is a power there . . . a raw, untamed power. Shadows drift around him, some thin and ephemeral, others solid and anchored. The symbols move, change, transform . . . Powerful. Light and shadow, love and hate. Constant, constant change. Peace and rage." She opened her eyes.

"You Saw Aohdan Collins. The patriarch of Boston. We cannot continue this with *her* here," announced Cavan, pointing at Seireadan and sneering, as if he could smell something foul.

Pretentious prick. Seireadan glared back at him.

"Cavan!" The rebuke came from Lia, but Cavan ignored her.

"She's Aohdan's whor—lover." Cavan stopped himself. "She'll tell him everything that is Seen the next time she spreads her legs for him."

A few other Ravens gasped, shocked by Cavan's crassness.

Aghna's voice lashed the room. "That's ENOUGH! Cavan, this is beneath you. A Seeing is never bound by secrecy. Any of us can share the visions we See with whomever we choose. Whether or not Seireadan and Aohdan are lovers has no bearing on what we do here today."

"My apologies, Aghna. I was only concerned about her relationship with him." Cavan layered sarcasm and derision over the word "him."

"How dare you? You don't even know Aohdan," Seireadan said, fuming.

Perhaps it was the way she said his name, perhaps it was some other whim of the universe, but a moment after Aohdan's name passed Seireadan's lips, Lia cried out and went rigid in her chair as the Sight gripped her, and seconds after, Seanán doubled over, gasping and shaking.

It only took Seanán a moment or two to come out of his Seeing. Lia remained rigid and staring for nearly a full hour before the Sight released her. Seireadan noticed her blinking and knelt down with one hand on Lia's arm to steady her in her chair as her body unclenched. Lia shook her head slowly, trying to clear the fog in her brain.

Lia put her hand on top of Seireadan's. "Thank you. I'm okay now."

Aghna waited until Lia had a moment to compose herself and take a few sips of water before she asked what she and Seanán had seen.

"I saw very little," said Seanán, "but I did see Aohdan, and although I haven't seen him in years, I know it was him. He was in the woods. It was dark. And it was cold—I could see his breath. He kept stopping and looking into the trees. There was a strange wind, a hot wind. It shouldn't have been hot when the woods were so cold. It felt like he was being followed, and he seemed to know it, but I did not See by whom or what."

Goose bumps dappling her skin, Seireadan was riveted, taking in every detail so she could relay the Seeings to Aohdan later. Once it was clear Seanán had nothing more to say, the group turned to Lia.

"Liadain?" Aghna asked.

"I was flying—below me was a blond man; he was on one path, but there were many, many he could choose from."

"Who was this blond man?" Cavan demanded rudely.

Lia stared at him coldly, a silent reproach for his interruption, before she continued. "I only saw him from the back, but the way he was dressed . . . he had the air of the Court about him. What struck me in the Seeing were all of the paths. At the end of each was another man, this one as dark as the traveler was light. It was the same man at the end of each path, but each was different. Some larger, some smaller, some gray, and some deep, deep black. There was one that was bigger than all the others, more powerful. More ominous." She hesitated, thinking, and frowned.

Cavan opened his mouth, but Aghna pointed a bony finger and silenced him with a stern look. "There's more," she said to Lia. "Share it with us, even if it's confusing."

"Then I wasn't flying anymore. Instead, I was looking out through the traveler's eyes. Each time he came to a fork in the paths or a crossroads, no matter what he chose, the road seemed to shift and put him back on a path toward that ominous, dark shape."

"The dark one. Was it Aohdan?" asked Seireadan when Lia seemed to have no more to say.

"I honestly don't know. I never saw his face. He had shadows around him that kept him hidden," answered Lia.

"Could it be more obvious? A towering shadow that's drawing the light into it—can you all be that obtuse? Aohdan is a threat to the Court," Cavan declared.

The Ravens all stirred, and it took all of Seireadan's self-control to not throw herself at Cavan and pummel him. To make a declarative statement about the Sight, especially when so many aspects were abstract and unclear, was not only dangerous; it was irresponsible.

Aghna scowled at him again. "The Seelie king did not appear in any of our Seeings," she said. "Aohdan is wild, ferocious even, but I Saw no malice directed at king or Court. But he loves as fiercely as he hates, and I say woe to anyone who becomes his enemy."

"How can he not be a threat?" demanded Cavan. "He's greedy for power."

"You don't know that!" Seireadan snapped.

"Peace, Seireadan. What you say may or may not be true, Cavan, but I did not See that. If he does lust for power, he doesn't lust for Fionvarr's power," Aghna said.

"He's a savage," sneered Cavan, determined to paint the worst possible picture of Aohdan for the Ravens who didn't know him. Seireadan leaped to her feet, but before she could say anything, Seanán interrupted.

"We are all savages, every last one of us. Look at the history of our race, Cavan. It is littered with stories of ambitions, agendas, betrayals, and revenge. All of them brutal and bloody. We all lust for something; we merely play our games on a different board now—and from behind a façade of civility. Aghna is right. Perhaps someday Aohdan will want Fionvarr's power and come for it, but nothing we've Seen today shows that." As he spoke these last words, Seanán ran a hand through his chestnut hair in aggravation.

"And we can't condemn someone for actions they may never take." Seireadan directed her comment to Cavan. He glowered at her but had nothing to say.

Aghna dismissed the Ravens with her thanks, but not before telling Seanán and Lia they needed to accompany her to Criofan's office to share their Seeings with him. Seanán started to walk Aghna toward the Seelie king's manor, but Lia went to Seireadan before she followed them.

"Promise me you won't go looking for Cavan," Lia said, but Seireadan didn't answer right away.

"If I asked him to, Aohdan would kill Cavan in his sleep without a second thought, but I won't because I would much rather kill him myself," said Seireadan.

"You're not really doing a bang-up job of reassuring me," Lia replied.

"Fine. I'll wait in the gardens for you, and I promise I won't drown Cavan in one of the ponds," Seireadan said with a sigh.

CHAPTER 47

SEIREADAN WAS IN no mood for banter while she waited for Lia, so she pulled her hood up to discourage conversation and found a bench to sit on. She let the sun beat down on her back and shoulders and closed her eyes, but didn't miss the soft crunch of gravel when Lia finally found her almost an hour later.

"Are you ready to go?" Lia asked. "Did you call Aohdan?"

"Yes and yes. I got his voice mail. I told him he'd been in a couple of Seeings and I needed to talk to him when he got home. There wasn't enough room on voice mail to leave all the details. I just said one suggested he might be being followed, and I told him to keep an eye out."

"Good. And I'm happy to go through my whole Seeing with him if that's what he wants," Lia said as they started to walk toward the area where the cars were parked.

"So, what happened?" Seireadan asked.

"With Criofan? We told him what we Saw and he was rude and dismissive. He's the king's adviser, but he acts like he's the king himself. You wouldn't like him at all." Lia stopped suddenly and the color drained from her cheeks.

"Lia?"

"Have you ever seen Criofan?" Lia asked.

"Not in person, only a picture in Aohdan's file."

"What color was his hair?"

Seireadan gave her friend a questioning look and said, "A sandy blond. Why?"

"That may not have been the true color of his hair . . ." Lia turned to look back at the manor and saw Criofan on a balcony, looking out over the gardens. She didn't hide the sarcasm that slipped into her voice. "In fact, there he is now, up on the balcony . . . surveying his domain."

Seireadan, her Raven's hood still pulled up, looked where Lia had pointed and froze, unable to move, unable to breathe. The Alabaster Man was no longer a dream; he was flesh and blood. Seireadan's stomach heaved as the colors and the blackness of the Sight filled her vision and crowded her mind. Only through sheer force of will did she stay on her feet.

"Seireadan! Sit!" Lia steered her toward a bench flanked by two giant catmint plants.

Seireadan's entire body was shaking. In her mind's eye, the vision she had as a child slammed back into her, only this time, faces weren't hidden. She saw Criofan—the Alabaster Man of her nightmares, his face finally crystal clear—whispering in the ear of Luan, who, with a wave of his hand, conjured the foul, hot wind that scoured her childhood home, reducing it to rubble and dust. She gasped as the Sight released her as quickly as it had come. Jumbled emotions reverberated through every part of Seireadan: pain, sorrow, fear, rage, and even a little elation. *I know who he is now! The Alabaster Man is real!*

"It's him, Lia. HIM!" Seireadan's chest was heaving.

"Breathe! Breathe and calm down! What did you See, Seireadan?"

Seireadan gulped in a deep breath and let it out slowly before she said, "Nearly the same as my first Seeing, only clearer. His face, and Luan, and all of the death they created."

She glanced up again, but the balcony was empty; Criofan had gone back inside.

"Come on, let's go," said Lia. When Seireadan didn't move, Lia went back to her and deliberately put herself between her friend and the balcony.

"He's right there, Lia."

Lia took a firm hold on Seireadan's arm. "Seireadan, stop! You'd never get to him through all the guards. Let's go home. You can talk to Aohdan. You have the advantage. You know who he is, but he doesn't know who you are."

Seireadan nodded, knowing Lia was right. As much as she wanted to tear into the manor and shred Criofan with her bare hands, this wasn't the time to be rash. But every step she took as they walked down the bluestone path toward Lia's car was painful. Seireadan turned back once, watching the balcony.

I'm coming for you, Criofan.

CHAPTER 48

AOHDAN ROLLED BACK in his chair. With Seireadan and Lia at the Gathering, he'd used the evening to review a few reports from Kieran about Providence and catch up on some paperwork at Asmodeus. After refreshing the orphan Pixie's milk dish, he thumbed through some portfolios that had been submitted to fill the new artist position he was hiring for, but his thoughts strayed to Providence.

The fallout from Crogher's attempt on Aohdan's life created repercussions that took time to sort out, including several visits with Baibin. During one of them, Kieran suggested the former matriarch mentor him, teach him the ins and outs of doing business in Providence. It wasn't something he needed to do, but Baibin had been grateful to be included. The first thing they did together was select two Fae and one Selkie to be Kieran's first line of contact in the city.

Smart of Kieran to suggest that; it binds Baibin to him, and her brainsí *will respect him because he respects her. She was their matriarch for a very long time. This is the kind of subtle thing that Rory would never grasp.*

Aohdan's attention moved back to the portfolios; there were at least a dozen from very talented artists, but he found it hard to concentrate on them as his thoughts shifted again, this time to the voice mail Seireadan had left earlier. He pulled out his phone and listened again.

"Hey." Her voice drifted out of the speaker. "We need to talk once we both get home. A couple of Ravens Saw you. One Seeing implies someone watching or following you. Nothing was definitive, but keep an eye out. Lia and I are grabbing dinner. I'll give you all the details at home. I love you."

He looked at the clock in the corner of the computer screen. It was nearly 10:00 p.m., but it often turned into a late night when Seireadan and Lia went out, so he didn't expect her home until probably midnight. He opened a few files on the computer and set to work. Surprisingly, the time went quickly, and when he looked at the clock again, he'd made good headway on his backlog. He had just closed the laptop when a floorboard creaked.

Aohdan's head snapped up.

A tingle ran up his spine, the same kind of chill he felt when Galen cast his silencing spell, and a split second later, the door to his office crashed inward. Aohdan leaped up, his hand reaching for his gun, but he froze when he found himself facing four very well-armed Fae men.

He slowly brought his empty hand around and put his palm up. *If they'd wanted me dead, they would have come in shooting.*

"You?" Aohdan snarled when Criofan strolled into the room.

Criofan looked him up and down, taking in the leather and the tattoos. "Savage as ever, I see."

"What do you want, Criofan? I've got nothing to do with the Court anymore." Aohdan shifted and felt a flash of satisfaction as all four of the armed Fae flinched.

"Oh, but you have everything to do with the Seelie Court. They whisper about you, and despite your protestations, I don't believe you've put the Court behind you. In fact, I think you have the Court squarely in your sights. This mess with Baibin and her son? Putting yourself between a mother and son, between a matriarch and her second, in order to expand your territory? Disgraceful, but it shows your ambition. That ambition can no longer go unchecked. There is only one Seelie king."

Aohdan stiffened slightly. There was only one way Criofan could have bypassed the security system at Asmodeus, and only one way he could have known details about Baibin and Crogher. The realization that someone in his crew had betrayed him to Criofan stunned and sickened Aohdan.

Someone sold me out.

Criofan guessed what Aohdan was thinking and gave him a superior smile. "Your people aren't as loyal as you think. Your behavior has been unacceptable for a long time; you dishonor us as a race."

Aohdan laughed. "And your honor is so pristine? The whole Seelie Court is stagnant and suffocating under the weight of your tradition and honor, and you suck your power out of that rot like a leech. Is that really your idea of honor?"

"You don't deserve any answers from me. I'm simply here to deal with you."

"Deal with me? Are you going to have your lackeys gun me down? If not, then dealing with me is the king's prerogative, isn't it? Oh, but wait. You really are the king, aren't you? You've twisted Fionvarr around so much in his grief and pain, he's nothing but a puppet." He saw the eyes of one guard flicker and knew he'd hit a nerve. Aohdan wasn't the only one who disliked Criofan.

"Take him," ordered Criofan.

One of the armed Fae guards moved, and Aohdan spun to face him, but cried out in agony as pepper spray blasted him.

He covered his face with his hands, and a second spray dropped him to one knee. *Shit, that burns!* Aohdan knocked half the papers off his desk as he tried to brace himself and get his bearings, but it was impossible to see.

Hands grabbed at him and Aohdan lashed out with his feet; there was a satisfying crunch and curse as he connected with someone's knee. He scrambled back and knocked his chair over before rough hands grabbed his shoulders from behind. Aohdan threw an elbow back, and his attacker grunted but didn't let go, so Aohdan flung all of his weight backward, crashing himself and the Fae behind him into the wall. Frames and glass cracked, and the little china saucer on the windowsill crashed to the floor.

"It takes four of you to control one Fae?" Criofan's voice sounded flustered, and Aohdan lunged toward where the voice was, but found only empty air before two of Criofan's lackeys grabbed his arms and twisted them behind his back, forcing Aohdan across the desk. A Taser pulsed into the small of his back, and Aohdan screamed in agony before collapsing.

Criofan tucked the Taser back into his jacket while he stared down distastefully at Aohdan's prone body.

"Take him to the car."

CHAPTER 49

SEIREADAN STARED DOWN at Claíomh Solais where it lay, still enveloped by the worn sheath, on the coffee table. She'd been staring at it for hours, imagining all the different ways she could kill Criofan. *Now that I know who he is, I can tell Aohdan about the sword.* She glanced at the clock; it was after midnight. Aohdan should have been home by now.

Thumbing through the directory on her phone, Seireadan found his number. When the call went to voice mail, she started to worry. *He'll let it go to voice mail if he's in a meeting, but all he's doing is paperwork. I'm just being paranoid because of Lia's Seeing; he's probably in the damn bathroom.*

"Hey," she said after the beep. "Was getting late and wanted to see when you'd be home. I need to talk to you about something important. Call me when you get this."

Twenty minutes later, he hadn't returned her call and she took Claíomh Solais and tucked it away on the closet shelf where she kept it hidden. She put on some clean flannel pajama pants before she went back out to watch a little late-night TV in the living room. At 1:30 a.m., Seireadan really started to worry and dialed Galen's number.

"Seireadan? What's wrong?" Galen's voice was muffled and sleepy.

"I'm sorry to wake you—I assume Aohdan isn't with you?"

"Aohdan? No . . ."

"He isn't home and I can't find him. He isn't answering his cell. Something's not right."

"The Sight?" Seireadan heard the sudden alertness in Galen's voice.

"No. Not me. Lia had a brief one that showed him being followed, but nothing else. I just have a feeling, Galen. I just . . ." Seireadan felt cold.

"We'll find him. Just sit tight. As soon as I know something, I'll call you."

Seireadan waited for a half hour before worry and frustration spurred her into action. She grabbed her knife belt and put it on, then headed out into the night. She wasn't about to sit around and wait while Aohdan was missing.

Turning the corner, Seireadan saw Galen and the others gathered outside Asmodeus Ink. As one collective unit they turned to look at her; Galen looked angry, but she didn't really care.

"I said to sit tight," the second said.

She shrugged. "I need to know where he is. Something isn't right. It's not *right,* Galen." Her emphasis elevated everyone's concern. Even without a Seeing, it was never wise to dismiss a Raven's "funny feeling," and it wasn't lost on Galen that she had come ready for a fight.

Seireadan looked at Chris and said, "I know you have the code. Deactivate the damn alarm and open the door."

After a quick glance at Galen, Chris punched in the code and opened the shop doors. Inside Asmodeus, it was dark. There was a whisper of movement, and the men pulled their guns, waiting for a confrontation. Seireadan put her hand behind her back and let her fingers rest on the hilt of one knife. She let her breath out slowly when Chris flipped on the light.

Everything in the main lobby looked normal. None of the jewelry cases were smashed, and the cash register was pristine. Seireadan headed right for the office, but Kieran forcibly bumped her aside so he could reach the door first. She gave him an angry glare but he ignored her. Galen nodded; a moment later they kicked the door in and flooded into the room. It was a mess—papers strewn everywhere, picture frames smashed on the floor, an overturned chair. Panic surged through Seireadan; the only thing keeping her remotely grounded was the fact that Aohdan wasn't lying dead on the floor in a massive pool of blood.

"Where is he?" she demanded, even though she knew none of them could answer her. "We have to find him! Why didn't I See any of this?"

"Probably because there was a spell like the one I cast to keep conversations private." Galen picked up a crystal from just outside the door. "There's still some energy inside it—I can feel it. It would have blocked conversation, noise, maybe even emotions and thoughts."

"I want to know who did this." Her voice got colder and she turned to face Aohdan's captains. "Go turn over every—"

"Stop!" Galen grabbed her by the arm. Angry, she shoved him, and to her utter surprise, Galen shoved her back, hard. Astonished, Seireadan froze.

"I know you love him, but you are NOT the matriarch. And you will NOT bark orders at me or any of Aohdan's captains." There was absolute steel in Galen's voice.

Seireadan softened for a moment. "I want him back, Galen. I want him home. Safe."

"We want him back, too. And we'll find him. I won't let anyone get in the way of that, not even you." Galen's voice was as cold as hers had been, and in that moment Seireadan had no doubt they'd find Aohdan—and she fully understood why he'd chosen Galen for his second.

CHAPTER 50

AOHDAN GROANED. HIS eyes still burned and his body ached. He moved his hands slowly, trying to figure out where he was as his blurry vision started to clear. The air was cool and smelled vaguely of vanilla and citrus. As he inhaled, he became more aware of the heaviness at his throat. *Shit, my head hurts. Where am I? What the hell happened?* He reached up and ran his fingers along the cool steel of a collar and the links of chain attached to it. *Chained like a fucking dog. Criofan.*

He slowly rolled to the side, resenting every chain link that rattled as he moved, and pushed himself up until he was half sitting. He resisted testing the strength of the chain; it would only bring Criofan pleasure to watch him struggle. Instead, Aohdan sat and just listened. Somewhere in the distance there was a wind chime moving in a breeze, but other than that, there was nothing but silence.

Aohdan gingerly touched the side of his head. *I must have hit my head after the Taser made me black out.* He had bruises on his body, and two burn marks where the Taser had bitten into his back, but no bones seemed broken. He blinked several times and was relieved that his vision was improving quickly. Aohdan slowly climbed to his feet and immediately realized he was in a large cage. *Dark gray bars? Solid iron maybe? Or just coated. Bad news either way.* To test his theory, Aohdan let the back of his hand graze a bar. He could feel the iron's cold burn immediately.

The chain attached his collar to a loop in the center of the cage. He had just enough length that he could reach partway through the bars if he stretched, but that brought him dangerously close to touching them. Aohdan paced the inner perimeter of the cage, examining what he could see outside the cell. It looked like some sort of library, and Aohdan guessed he was being held inside Criofan's home.

Generally speaking, the room was open and airy; books lined the wall from floor to ceiling on one side, and on the opposite was a bank of windows. The curtains were closed on most of them, but light still managed to filter into the room. Most of the furniture had been moved, save for a half circle of chairs that looked into his prison. On the third wall, next to the door, was a very large mirror encased in a pretentious and rather tacky gilt frame. Aohdan stopped and stared at his reflection. His bloodshot eyes were surrounded by inflamed red skin, the bruise on his cheek was well on its way to a darker shade of purple blue, and dried blood had crusted on his thin mustache. His shirt was ripped, dirty, and bloodstained.

And based on how my back and shoulders feel, I'm guessing they dragged me to whatever car they threw me in. He paced to the other side of the cage and tried to get a glimpse out the window, but the shades were too well drawn. Behind him, a door hinge creaked and a single set of footsteps crossed the floor. He looked over his shoulder.

"You've rejoined us. Delightful." Criofan dropped himself down into one of the overstuffed leather chairs. He let his fingers slide over the cool material and assessed his prisoner.

"You've no right to keep me here." The patriarch slowly turned to face his captor.

"No right? I'm the king's adviser; I have every right," sniffed Criofan. "You are dangerous and a threat. You should be chained like the animal you are."

"I am dangerous, I'll give you that. But who am I a threat to? You?" Aohdan laughed.

Criofan ignored the question. "You undermine everything we stand for."

"Stand for? You're a fucking idiot, Criofan. We've been banished from Faerie for centuries and all you want is to recreate the old. The Seelie Court is rotting from the inside out. You cling so tightly to your honor, your obsession with light and beauty. You can find beauty in the shadows, too."

"Beauty and honor? You lecture me about beauty and honor? Listen to the vulgarity in your speech, the barbaric designs you've carved into your body, the hair on your face." The revulsion dripped from Criofan's words.

"Who are you to say if they're beautiful or not? What is it the humans say, that beauty is in the eye of the beholder?" For a moment, the memory of Seireadan running her fingers slowly over his ink leaped to the front of his mind. He closed his eyes so Criofan wouldn't see the emotion there. *Son of a bitch will only use it against me.* When he opened them again, his eyes were cold.

"Who am I? I am King Fionvarr's closest and most trusted adviser. If I say they're barbaric, then the Court believes they're barbaric. And if I say you are a dangerous savage who will destroy the Seelie Court, who will oppose me? All this foolishness with your Conclave and the disaster with those mongrels down in Providence? You are a danger to our way of life, and you *will* confess it to the Court."

"Confess to what? I've never acted against my uncle."

"No? I say this Conclave is a slap in his face. And by the time I'm through with you, you'll confess to buggering bunnies if that's what I want."

Aohdan walked up to the bars that separated him from Criofan. "Then you may as well kill me now."

Criofan's laugh was thin and sarcastic. "Kill you? No. At least not yet. First I need to make an example of you. An example sanctioned by the king, of course. And once I've broken you, all of your little minions will see you for what you are."

"My minions?"

"You know they are. You've built quite a little kingdom for yourself, and a lucrative one, I must say. Do you know what they whisper about you? What they call you? They call you a king."

"I have *never* called myself that."

King. That one simple word had moved them onto dangerous ground, and Aohdan watched Criofan warily. He had a good idea of what the king's adviser had planned.

"What you've said doesn't really matter; what matters is what everyone else *thinks* you said. There can be only one king. So is it you, or is it Fionvarr?"

"I'm no king, but I could ask you the very same thing. You accuse me of wielding power from the shadows as you sit there pulling Fionvarr's strings," growled Aohdan, secretly pleased when he saw Criofan's face twist in anger.

"Power matters," snapped the pale Fae.

"You condemn me, but we are exactly the same, Criofan. You just don't have the balls to admit it." Aohdan turned away; he was tired of looking at that smug, irritating face.

"And what are you then, unseelie?"

"Me? I'm a criminal," Aohdan said over his shoulder, ignoring the other remark. "I take what I want, and I'll destroy anyone who gets in my way."

"A threat?"

Aohdan shrugged, ignoring the metal collar's chafe. "Take it however you want."

In the darkness that night, long after the sun had set, Aohdan lay on the hard floor of his cell, his hips and shoulders aching. But it wasn't pain that kept him from sleeping; it was his mind, which had been going a thousand miles an hour since Criofan left.

Who told him about Providence—and what else does Criofan know?

CHAPTER 51

TWO DAYS AFTER Aohdan vanished, Seireadan stood in the police station and stared incredulously at Marty Sandhurst, her blood boiling. Several officers stopped what they were doing to watch her shout at Marty, who offered her nothing more than a banal smile, which she wanted to rip right off his face.

"What do you mean there's nothing you can do?" she shouted. "You saw his office! Clearly something happened! Someone took him!"

"That's just an assumption, Miss Moore. There's no evidence he was kidnapped."

"There was obviously a struggle." Seireadan put her hands on her hips.

"Maybe he lost his temper and trashed the office before he took off. Maybe there was a fight. Maybe he had wild sex with some other woman in there. Maybe someone did take him. And maybe two of his employees were unhappy and trashed the place as a way to get back at him. Right now there is no evidence of an obvious crime," Marty told her as he folded his hands over his paunchy stomach.

"Then tell me this, *Detective*. Where's Aohdan?"

"I don't know where Waldo is. And the forty-eight-hour period for reporting a missing person hasn't expired quite yet, so I can't help you."

Seireadan heard the glee in Marty's voice, his dismissal of Aohdan and any jeopardy the patriarch might be in. "You son of a bitch." Seireadan forced the words out from between clenched teeth. "Even if there had been blood all over that office, you wouldn't really investigate. You don't give a shit what happens to Aohdan. This will come back to bite you in the ass, I promise you that."

"What did you just say?" Marty started to get up.

"You heard me. And I won't forget this," Seireadan said.

As she left the station, Seireadan took a call from Galen, who asked her to meet them at Asmodeus. When she arrived, Wharf Rat sent Seireadan back to the office, which had been cleaned up since Aohdan's abduction. Chris and Galen were waiting when Seireadan arrived, and Kieran joined them only a few minutes later.

Galen muttered a curse under his breath. "Where's Rory?"

"I do no' know," said Kieran. "I got a text saying he was looking into something and would be back later."

"He's getting into a bad habit of not checking in," grumbled the second, more to himself than anyone else. "Fine. I'll deal with him later. What's going on, Chris?"

"I came back here earlier and did some asking around. Made a friend and found out a few things," Chris answered.

"Who?" Seireadan asked, eager for any information about Aohdan.

"You all need to be quiet; she's very nervous," Chris instructed, and then he let out a low whistle.

A flutter of wings flashed in the window as a Pixie squeezed in through the opening and hunkered down on the sill. Frightened by all the eyes looking at her, the Pixie shrank back a little. No more than eight inches tall, she wore a dress made from bits of orange and yellow cloth. Her wings resembled a dragonfly's and were a riot of silver and teal tones. Gathering her courage, she flew from the window to Chris's shoulder, where she dug her fingers into his shirt and stared at the others with large aqua eyes half-covered by shaggy bangs.

"They're all so big," she whispered to Chris.

"It's fine; they're friends. Tell them what you told me."

"They'll be angry," the Pixie squeaked as she trembled.

"Not at you. I promise. You didn't do anything wrong," Chris reassured her.

When she spoke to them, the Pixie's voice was louder than they expected, given her small stature. "Aohdan. The one who works in this office. With all the pictures painted on his arms. He's nice to me. He leaves me milk sometimes, and I tell him things I hear."

"Tell them what happened," Chris urged.

Abruptly, she burst into tears. "They took him! They hurt him and they took him!"

"Who took him?" Seireadan asked as calmly as she could, keeping her hands folded so no one could see them shaking.

"I don't know," the Pixie said sadly. "I've never seen any of them before. They were all Fae, all blond."

That doesn't really help; half the Fae are blond. Seireadan tried not to look impatient; the Pixie was skittish enough already.

"But I heard them before they went in. They were talking. Then there was a funny silence. It hummed. And when it was humming, I couldn't hear them. Then the hum vanished and I could hear them again. One was in charge. Very bossy. He ordered everyone around. They called him Criofan."

Everything inside Seireadan recoiled. Closing her eyes, she tangled her fingers in her hair. *No, no, no! Anyone but Criofan!*

"Are you sure the name was Criofan?" asked Galen.

The Pixie looked at him warily. "Yes, that's what they called him. Criofan. I don't think the others liked him very much, but they did what he said. They tied Aohdan's hands and put him in the car. The trunk. Then they left."

Unable to contain herself, Seireadan slapped a palm on the wall. Startled, the Pixie fluttered her wings and flew up toward the open window. She crouched on the sill for a moment, completely spooked, before vanishing outside.

"Is the Pixie talking about the Criofan I think she is?" asked Kieran. He glanced at Seireadan, who had her hands braced against the wall and was slowly shaking her head back and forth.

"She is," said Galen. "The Seelie king's closest adviser. This could be a big problem."

"Oh, there's a bigger problem than you know," said Seireadan. "As if I didn't have enough reason to cut his throat."

"What are you talking about?" Kieran asked.

"We can't discuss it here. We need privacy. I'll tell you everything at the condo," she said, abruptly realizing how much she sounded like Aohdan.

CHAPTER 52

MILES AWAY, AOHDAN gasped for air as Criofan yanked his head out of the water. His hands shackled behind his back, Aohdan barely had time to pull in a breath before Criofan forced his head back underwater. Just as his lungs gave out and his vision started to blacken, Criofan hauled him out so forcefully that Aohdan toppled backward and slammed onto the floor. He lay coughing, gasping, and spitting up water, and he tried to slow his breathing down.

"Get him up," ordered Criofan.

Two burly Pooka with dark red eyes grabbed Aohdan roughly by his arms.

"Done already?" Aohdan coughed, his throat raw, and then wheezed painfully as one of the Pooka slammed a fist into his stomach.

Criofan smirked. "We're just getting started, but I've been asked to attend the king for a moment. I shouldn't be gone long, and then we'll continue."

Aohdan glared at him, his wet hair matted to his face.

"Take him. Use the large hooks and hang him in the cage. Then wait outside the room until I return," Criofan ordered.

The Pooka dragged Aohdan back to his cage. One hung a large hook from the center of the roof bars before they pulled his hands over the hook, slipping the point through the chains around his wrists, and left Aohdan dangling, his toes barely touching the floor. Within moments, Aohdan was in agony, pain burning through his shoulders.

On the other side of the manor, Fionvarr, king of the Seelie Court, sat at his desk and looked out his window at the garden. In the corner of the room, a young Fae girl played a harp while his butler prepared some fruit and cheese. Two guards stood in the hallway, and Criofan completely ignored them while he gave a perfunctory knock on the doorframe. When Fionvarr didn't invite him in immediately, Criofan's lips thinned. Eventually, the king turned in his chair and waved for his counselor to enter. The music stopped.

"Aya, please continue," said Fionvarr. At his request, Aya resumed, and the clear notes of the harp drifted through the room.

Criofan bowed. "My lord, you asked to see me?"

"I understand you have arrested and imprisoned Aohdan Collins?"

Criofan hesitated for a fraction of a second. "Yes, my lord." *How . . . ? When I find out who told Fionvarr, I'll have his tongue cut out.*

"Why? Aohdan is my nephew. It must be a serious crime to imprison a prince of the Court."

"With respect, my lord, he forfeited that title when he abandoned the Seelie Court to be patriarch of the *fréamhacha agus brainsí* in Boston. As for his crimes, I was verifying some information before bringing the matter to your attention. I wouldn't want to bother you with a mere trifle." Criofan's voice was smooth and soothing as he tried to reassure Fionvarr that everything was under control.

The king's dark hair was peppered with gray, and his gray eyes looked old, a stark contrast to the youthfulness of his face. He nodded thoughtfully, but his response wasn't as meek and compliant as Criofan expected.

"One does not 'forfeit' being a prince of the Court, Criofan," the king told him sternly.

"Of course not, my lord. I misspoke, my apologies."

The king waved away the apology. "No matter. Have you found anything regarding my nephew?" There was a note of authority in the Seelie King's voice that Criofan hadn't heard in a long time, and he didn't like it at all.

"He is obsessed with power and wealth—and, while he has not confessed yet, he harbors ambitions to replace you on the throne, to be the Seelie king himself. He is a clear danger to the Seelie Court. He is, after all, Faolan's son."

Fionvarr's eyes tightened slightly when Criofan said Aohdan wanted to be king. In the silence, the butler padded over and put a plate of fruit on the desk next to Fionvarr and then stepped back, melting into the background to await the king's next request. Criofan, eager to leave, shifted from one foot to the other.

"Aya's playing is lovely, isn't it?" Fionvarr asked as he plucked a grape from the cluster.

"Delightful." With gritted teeth, Criofan listened to the harp for another minute before he said, "My lord? With your leave, I'll take care of this issue with Collins."

"No."

Criofan straightened. Again he heard that note of authority, of decisiveness. *No? What does he mean, no?* He couldn't remember the last time the king had refused him any request or suggestion.

"There must be a trial," said Fionvarr firmly. "Whatever he may or may not have done, Aohdan is my nephew. That blood tie makes him a Seelie prince. If he does plot against me, the confession or proof must be delivered in public to ensure others do not make the same mistakes. It would be improper to do otherwise, just as it is *my* duty to preside over the case and render judgment."

"Absolutely. I'll see to the arrangements." Criofan's voice was tight as he bowed and turned to leave. *Clearly, Aohdan isn't the only thing I need to put a stop to.*

"There are those who . . . dislike Aohdan. I would hate to have justice derailed if something untoward were to happen to him before the trial. Be mindful of that, Criofan."

"Of course, my lord. I'll make sure he is alive for the trial."

When he left Fionvarr's office, Criofan stormed down the hall. *A public trial is the last thing I want, but I can't avoid it now. Not after the guards—and the girl and the butler—heard his specific order. But I promised Collins would be alive; I said nothing about any other damage.*

CHAPTER 53

AS SOON AS they got back to Aohdan's condo, Galen got right to the point. "What's going on, Seireadan?"

"I haven't even had the chance to tell Aohdan about this," she said. "I was waiting for him to come home the night he was taken so we could talk. Let me start at the beginning. This part, Aohdan does know . . ." Seireadan went on to tell them all about her Seeing as a child—the wind, the strange pale man. She took a swallow of the coffee she made during the tale, and offered some to the others.

"I had just finished my training as a Raven when the Desolation happened. My family's home was the epicenter; they never even had a chance to escape. Every last one was devoured, but they shouldn't have been. Luan's spell should have ignored them—it was meant to kill Bryn and Conlan, and the ones who helped them."

Kieran and Galen shifted uncomfortably at the mention of the Desolation; they'd both lost family and friends as Luan's spell inexorably moved through the Faerie realm, an unstoppable cancer that devoured everything. Seireadan was right; the only ones the spell should have sought out were Bryn and Conlan.

"There were rumors," said Kieran. "Rumors your father was sheltering Conlan and Bryn from Luan. His disagreements with the prince were verra well known. Could that be why they did no' escape? Did Luan unleash it where he did because your family was aiding the lovers?"

Seireadan clenched her jaw. "I heard those rumors, too, but only much later. They're lies. Everyone knew there was no love lost between my father and Luan. But he wasn't hiding anyone. I know because I saw Bryn and Conlan the day before the Desolation was spawned."

"You're certain?" asked Galen.

"They had hoods on so people couldn't see their faces well, but I did, and they were hiding right under Luan's nose. I believe Luan was fed lies by this pale man in my childhood Seeing. I believe he deliberately pointed Luan to my father, hoping he'd be disgraced, maybe even killed. But when the spell didn't find Conlan and Bryn, it took on a life of its own and began to consume everything in a blind quest to fulfill its purpose, because it was so corrupted by hatred." Seireadan's knuckles were white from gripping her mug so tightly.

"Why didn't you go to the king?" asked Chris.

"I had no proof. And so many people had tried to discredit what I'd Seen or flatly refused to believe it, I would have been ignored at best. At worst I would have been blamed by association, by those who thought my family caused the Desolation because they helped Bryn escape a horrible marriage. It would have been a fruitless and futile effort."

She took a final drink of her coffee and pushed the stoneware mug aside. "When I went to the king's manor with Lia the other day, we were all asked about Aohdan. Aghna, the eldest of us, had Seen him. She saw the dichotomy of who he is, but nothing else, but the mention of his name alone triggered the Sight in two other Ravens."

Seireadan briefly told them of the two visions and how she had called Aohdan while she waited for Lia in the garden. "What Aohdan doesn't know is this: When we were leaving, I saw a man on a balcony. Tall, white-blond hair, ice-blue eyes . . . and skin as pale as alabaster."

She saw everything come together for Galen just before he said, "Criofan: he's your Alabaster Man."

"He is," Seireadan answered grimly.

"You are certain?" asked Kieran.

"I have no doubts." Seireadan's voice was grim. "He took my family away from me, and now he thinks he'll take Aohdan? Over my dead fucking body."

Utterly exhausted, Aohdan fell when Criofan's lackeys threw him back in the cage. The tile was cool and almost soothing. Knowing Criofan was watching, Aohdan dragged himself to his feet, every movement painful.

"I wonder how long before they give up on you," the blond Fae mused as he walked the perimeter of the cage.

"Who?" Aohdan tracked Criofan with his eyes.

"Your captains, your woman." Criofan shrugged. "Galen's had a taste of being a triarch now. Power isn't something you give up easily once you have it. It's very, very seductive."

"Your point?" Aohdan wanted nothing more than to feel his hands around Criofan's throat.

"My point? You know my point. You already have the images in your head. What's it like to imagine your trusted second taking the woman you love for his own? Because you *do* love her even though you try to hide it." Criofan laughed.

"You're full of shit," growled Aohdan, ignoring the stab of pain in his heart.

"Believe what you want, but I have people watching. He's moved into your condominium, you know. It all belongs to Galen now: your power, your crew, your home, your woman. His sweat and sex all over your bed, all over her. I bet you can hear her calling his name while he makes her come—probably harder and better than you ever did."

"Fuck off." *You're a lying son of a bitch. They wouldn't do that to me. They wouldn't . . .* Aohdan ruthlessly crushed the words *But what if . . .* before they fully formed in his mind.

"Who do you think told me about Providence? The details of your ambitions? Who gave me the code to your shop?"

"Galen would never do that to me." *But someone did; someone in my crew sold me out.* The knowledge of that betrayal had been eating at Aohdan.

"Then you're more of a fool than I thought. Can you hear her calling Galen's name? Begging him to let her go down on him?" The laugh that followed was callous, cruel, and filled with a perverted delight. "Sweet dreams . . ."

Criofan turned out the lights, leaving Aohdan to suffer, alone, in the dark.

CHAPTER 54

WORD THAT AOHDAN was being put on public trial at the king's manor raced through the Fae community, and as soon as he heard, Galen initiated an emergency call with the Conclave. It had been a heated hour of debate, and Galen was beginning to better understand why Aeronwy and Aohdan hated Teresa so much.

"I am not doing this for my own ends," Galen repeated. "As much as you may not believe it, Teresa, I will gladly give the role of patriarch back to Aohdan. But we all need to be prepared for whatever comes from this trial. He hasn't broken any Seelie laws, so I don't know what trumped-up bullshit Criofan will spew, but there is the possibility that King Fionvarr will find him guilty."

"And why is any of this my problem?" sneered Teresa.

Galen stared at his phone in disbelief. *How can she not see what a disaster this could be?*

"It's a *public* trial!" Aeronwy shouted, her voice cracking over the phone line. "He isn't just putting Aohdan on trial; he's putting the triarchs on trial!"

Gregor's comment overlapped hers. "It's everyone's problem! I know you despise him, Teresa, and I frankly don't care, but use your head for a damn minute. Criofan will use him as an example of what happens to those who break from the Seelie Court, and anything he does to Aohdan, he can do to us. Do you really want to take the chance that on a whim, Criofan could come take you, and maybe take your head?"

"He wouldn't dare." There was the slightest hesitation in Teresa's voice.

Nessa bolstered the argument. "Gregor's right. Are you telling me you're willing to take that chance, Teresa? Because once Aohdan is gone, who is the closest triarch to the Court? *You.* Who do you think Criofan will look at next when he worries someone is too powerful? YOU." The phone crackled a few times while Nessa spoke, but her point was clear enough.

"This is our best chance, but we have to be united in our decision," Galen said with a soft sigh of resignation. "Are we agreed?"

"We are," said Aeronwy.

Her affirmation was followed by Gregor, Nessa, Sorchae, and Harbin, and Galen leaned forward in his chair as if being closer to the phone could somehow influence the others.

"I agree as well," said Réamann, who had been silent throughout the call.

"Tuathal?" Gregor asked.

"Agreed," said the patriarch of Chicago, somewhat reluctantly.

"What say you, Teresa?" asked Galen.

There was a long silence on the phone broken only by an aggravated mutter before Teresa finally—grudgingly—said, "Fine. Agreed. I'll be there."

Galen sank back in his chair, relieved and terrified.

Seireadan heard the footsteps and fear clenched its fist around her heart. She couldn't bring herself to answer when the knock sounded. After a pause, she heard Lia's voice.

"Seireadan?" she called. "It's Lia. And Kieran. We need to talk to you; there's news."

Every step toward the door felt like it took forever to Seireadan. She opened the door and let them in, knowing the dread showing on her pale face said everything she was feeling. After they got into the kitchen, Seireadan finally found her voice. "Tell me he's alive. Tell me Criofan didn't do something stupid."

"He's alive . . ."

Seireadan heard the hesitation, the unspoken *but* that hung in the air, but she was so relieved to know Aohdan was alive that her shoulders dropped and she leaned back against the door. Covering her face with her hands, she took in a slow, deliberate breath to steady her nerves.

"That's the good news, so what's the bad?" Seireadan asked.

"The bad news is that he's being put on trial—public trial. The day after tomorrow."

"WHAT? That's bullshit! He hasn't broken any Seelie laws—they have no reason to try him for anything!" Outraged, Seireadan snapped to attention. "What are they charging him with?"

When Kieran hesitated, a coil of fear lanced through Seireadan.

"What, Kieran? What is Criofan accusing him of?"

"Of plotting a coup—killing Fionvarr to take the throne himself," the captain finally answered. Seireadan's mouth sagged open.

"Seireadan . . . ?" Apprehension tinted Lia's voice.

"They're accusing him of treason?" The ghost of Seireadan's voice drifted through the room. "He could be executed for that."

"Aye."

Seireadan nodded, thinking. She saw the worried look that the other two exchanged, and knew they'd be much happier if she exploded; her calm silence scared them. The rage was there, though, waiting to surface, but Seireadan wasn't going to waste it on her friends. No, that was a privilege she was reserving just for Criofan; she just needed to figure out how.

"Seireadan?" Lia asked again.

"Thank you for telling me, but please go. I need to be alone. I need to think," said Seireadan.

"I'm no' certain that's a good idea," Kieran said.

"You worry too much," Seireadan told him, and Lia cleared her throat and arched an eyebrow at her.

"I won't go after him alone. I give you my word. Plus, I know Galen has Chris keeping an eye on me, so you'll be the first to know if I go rogue," said Seireadan. A small part of her found tremendous satisfaction that Aohdan's second was that worried about what she might do.

"It's verra important Aohdan has support. We're all going together for the trial," said Kieran. "Do you want to meet us at Underworld? Or do you want us to get you here?"

"Get me here. Now go, both of you."

Lia and Kieran left reluctantly, and once she was alone, Seireadan retrieved Claíomh Solais from the closet. *It's almost time, Solais. Almost time to put an end to all of it.*

After breakfast the next day, Seireadan went to Sacred Circle. Small white lights winked merrily in the window; Julia kept them there year-round. The shelves were empty and Seireadan knew that meant Julia would be switching the display from her Ostara wares to her Beltaine ones. Inside, a few customers were browsing through the shop, and Julia was behind the counter by the register.

"Hi, Julia."

"Seireadan? You're not on the schedule today." Julia pushed her glasses up on top of her head.

"No. I came to tell you I may need some time off."

"This have anything to do with that Seelie Court trial I've been hearing about?"

"You've heard about it?" Seireadan's voice was tight.

"We have enough Faerie clients here; I listen when people talk. Please tell me you're not going to do anything stupid." Julia gave her a pointed look that dared Seireadan to lie.

"I wouldn't call it stupid. Rash, maybe. Ill-advised? Most definitely."

"Don't get smart with me, young lady."

Seireadan couldn't help but chuckle, considering she was older than Julia by centuries. "I have to do something, Julia. I can't just sit around."

"How about letting the system work?"

"The system won't work when the man holding the strings is the same one responsible for killing my parents."

"Jesus . . . ," breathed Julia, suddenly understanding what was at stake for Seireadan.

"This is my one chance to confront him in front of everyone. To let everyone see what he really is: a monster, a killer." Seireadan put her elbows on the counter and put her face in her hands. She pulled her tarot deck out of her pocket and pushed the velvet bag across the glass. "Keep these."

"Only if you promise to come back and get them."

"I promise I'll try. That's the best I can do."

Julia nodded, her face pinched, and pulled a little box out from behind the counter. "I've been hanging on to this for you. I think you need it now." She pulled out a necklace with a teardrop-shaped pendant of black stone surrounded by silver. Seireadan leaned forward and let Julia clasp the twenty-four-inch chain around her neck, then held the stone in her palm. It was heavy, solid, safe, and it warmed under her hand.

"That's obsidian, one of the strongest protection stones you can have," Julia told her. "It will shield you from all kinds of attacks: physical, emotional, psychic. And it can bring out dark energy from deep inside you—energy that can heal shock and trauma."

Seireadan was humbled by the gesture. "It's wonderful. Thank you."

"Don't you dare take it off. Not until all this business is done," said Julia.

"I won't. I promise."

CHAPTER 55

CRIOFAN SPENT THE days leading to the trial brutalizing and tormenting Aohdan, trying to force him to admit he wanted to be the Seelie king. Aohdan denied him at every turn and suffered for it. He was beaten, deprived of sleep, half drowned, and told horrible stories of betrayal by his closest friends. Criofan told him he had Seireadan in another cage and detailed all of the horrible things he was doing to her. Each word clawed and shredded Aohdan's heart, but he forced the pain down as deep as he could.

I know he doesn't have her. If he did, he wouldn't just talk about it; he'd make me watch. Sitting on the floor, his head resting on his knees, Aohdan looked up when he heard Criofan's now familiar footsteps.

"Back for more?" Aohdan's voice was hoarse, but defiant. *Do your worst, bastard. I'll repay this a hundred times over.*

"After today, you won't be a problem anymore."

"Is that so?" Aohdan was immediately on alert.

"Oh, yes. The king has ordered a very public trial for you, and when he finds you guilty of plotting against him, the only option will be execution. I will gladly swing the sword that takes your head." Criofan watched for a reaction, but got little from his captive.

"Guilty of plotting against him? That's a lie and you know it."

"I can sway Fionvarr to any opinion I wish. I was against this at first, but then I realized it will set a precedent and I'll have the freedom to deal with the members of your Conclave at my leisure once you're dead. Starting with your unseelie cousin in Philadelphia."

Aohdan's expression didn't change. *You'll have your hands full if you tangle with Aeronwy.* "And when exactly will this trial take place?"

Criofan's smile was unkind. "Today. And it will be a packed house to watch you die. Guards, bind him and take him to the Gallery—and make sure he is chained tightly."

By the time the two guards reached the Gallery, half dragging Aohdan between them, it was already teeming with Fae and other faeries that had come to watch. As they reached the Gallery floor, Aohdan managed to get his footing, and he held his head high as he walked, unwilling to look cowed despite the abuse he'd suffered. Those he passed whispered behind their hands.

Near the dais that held Fionvarr's chair, three thick rings were embedded in the floor. The guards chained each of Aohdan's wrists to a ring and took the chain from the third and hooked it to the back of the collar he still wore. He could move about a foot from side to side, but that was all. Feeling the weight of every eye on him, Aohdan squared his shoulders and set his expression to stony indifference. *Let them stare.*

"Chained like a rabid dog."

"Teresa. Here to gloat?" asked Aohdan.

"Fionvarr did this to you?" Her eyes traveled over Aohdan's face and chest, taking in the welts and the bruises, and taking particular note of the distant, dangerous look in his eyes.

"No. It was Criofan."

To Aohdan's great surprise, he thought he saw a flash of pity in the matriarch's eyes before she walked away without another word, her captains closing around her.

Toward the back of the Gallery, Seireadan, Galen, Kieran, and Chris pushed through the crowd. Seireadan carried a bag over her shoulder, and even from across the vast room she could see Aohdan was in chains and that he'd been beaten. A groan of agony started deep inside her, and only Galen's hand on her elbow kept her from rushing to him.

"I hate this as much as you do," Galen said.

I sincerely doubt that. Seireadan, however, didn't have time to voice her thoughts when Rory suddenly appeared in front of them.

Galen was livid. "Where the fuck have you been?"

"Tracking a lead on who turned on Aohdan. It took me down to Jersey and Philly. Turned out to be a dead end," Rory said without remorse.

"Philly? I'm sure Aeronwy enjoyed bossing you around." There was a note of contempt in Kieran's voice.

"Shove it, Kieran. I let Aeronwy pretend to be in charge. But I wasn't with Aeronwy this time . . ."

Rory glanced to the side, a superior grin on his face. They all followed his gaze across the room and saw two Pari wearing elaborate necklaces made from magnificent fire opals. A smirk crossed the face of the one with the dark red hair, but before anyone could ask Rory about her, the main doors of the Gallery were flung open and a half dozen armed Fae dressed in black suits came in.

A voice drifted out of the crowd: "Fionvarr is coming."

Fionvarr's suit was dark gray, and a rich red cloak with gold trim was draped over his shoulders. A thin gold circlet served as his crown, and heads dipped as he passed them and mounted the stairs. As the Seelie king sat on his ornate chair, there was a rustle of fabric as the room bowed to him. Aohdan stood there, shirtless and chained, and didn't offer any obeisant gesture. He was rewarded with a blow to the back of the knees that forced him to the floor.

Seireadan seethed, digging her nails into Galen's arm as Fionvarr looked down at Aohdan, taking note of not only his tattoos but the myriad bruises, welts, and cuts that covered his upper body. The patriarch, despite having been forced to the floor, looked up and met Fionvarr's eyes, defiant.

"Criofan, what is the meaning of this display?" asked King Fionvarr, frowning.

"I ordered him chained to ensure your safety, my lord, for it is his desire to replace you on the throne! He stands accused of plotting to take your crown by force." Criofan's voice rang across the room, and a gasp rippled through the crowd. Many of the assembled faeries looked at Aohdan like he was truly a monster—in the long history of the Fae, as bloody and political as it was, there had never once been an instance of regicide. To even entertain the thought was appalling to them all.

But Fionvarr's voice came back sharp and firm. "Aohdan is the son of Prince Faolan, my brother, and therefore a prince of the Court. Regardless of the accusations against him, I'll not have my own nephew chained like a dog. My guards are more than able to ensure my safety. Unbind him and remove that collar; he is not an animal. His friends may attend him for a moment before we begin."

There was a gravitas and authority in Fionvarr's voice that the Fae hadn't heard in a long time, and many—including

Criofan—took note of it. For the moment, Fionvarr sounded like a king again.

The guards kept a wary eye on Aohdan as the chains came off, half expecting him to lunge at Criofan or Fionvarr. Instead, Aohdan stretched and rubbed his neck where the collar had chafed him, and then he turned to look out over the crowd. The instant he saw Seireadan, all of the lies Criofan told him disappeared, and a moment later he was surrounded by Seireadan and his captains.

"Look at what he's done to you," Seireadan whispered.

"I'll live," he answered. All he wanted to do was sit down and feel Seireadan's arms around him, but he knew he couldn't. *I won't sit on the ground like an invalid. Not in front of these jackals.* He took a deep breath and stood to face the Seelie king.

"You stand accused of treason, which is punishable by death. Aohdan, what say you to these charges?" asked Fionvarr.

"These accusations are lies created by Criofan for his own ends," Aohdan replied.

The king's adviser responded. "Since the Desolation, Aohdan has gathered power, wealth, and influence by any means necessary. He has become a triarch and has organized a court of his own, a court of triarchs. This Conclave will stop at nothing until they control everything."

"Accusations and speculation," said Aohdan. "No evidence."

Criofan's eyes lit up. "If it is evidence you want, evidence you shall have. I have the words of one of your own. Alarmed by your ambitions, your own captain, Rory Molloy, came to me with his concerns."

Criofan gestured grandly toward Rory.

CHAPTER 56

YOU BACKSTABBING SON of a bitch. They'll tear me apart.

Rory looked at Criofan, incensed, but had the wherewithal to step away from the other captains before anyone could react. As he moved, the faeries around him melted away as if they feared guilt through proximity. Two Undines backed away, and a Nix spit at him as the word "treachery" swirled around the room like an unseen riptide.

"You? You did this?" Seireadan pointed at Rory, her eyes blazing.

Rory took one more step back; Seireadan scared him, and not a lot scared Rory Molloy. He looked toward Criofan.

"You promised that . . . ," Rory started to say.

"I made you no promises," said the pale Fae. Rory started to twist the claddagh ring on his finger and looked at Vashti, but she put her hand up.

"You'll never put your hands on me again, swine. I had no power to promise you anything," she said. Behind her, Abrezu mocked him with her laughter. The sudden realization that both Pari had lied to him—that Criofan had used him—infuriated Rory, but he froze in his tracks, everything else receding into the background, when he heard Aohdan say his name.

"Rory."

There was death in the voice, and when he met Aohdan's eyes, Rory's stomach dropped into his shoes. *I'm a dead man. If Aohdan doesn't do it, someone else will.* With nothing left to lose, Rory faced the patriarch and lashed out.

"You never appreciated me. All of the years I gave you, and you never understood what I could do for you. You brought a human into your inner circle. You trusted Chris more than you trusted me."

"Clearly my instincts were right," growled Aohdan.

"I should have taken Oisin's place. You owed me that!" Rory shouted.

"Owe you? I don't owe you shit. I reward intelligence and loyalty; you've shown neither. Quick to anger, quick to judge, quick to act without thinking about long-term consequences. You're a blunt instrument, Rory, nothing more. My next captain needed to see the bigger picture. Have a little more finesse."

More fucking . . . finesse? Rory hadn't realized he could be angrier with Aohdan than he already was.

Criofan watched the two men rage at each other and glanced at King Fionvarr out of the corner of his eye, somewhat surprised the king hadn't put a stop to the chaos already. The king seemed engrossed in the drama, and it served Criofan's purpose just as well—the longer the confrontation lasted, the greater the odds Aohdan would respond. If he did, the king's guard would cut him down regardless of whether Rory had provoked him or not, to ensure there would be no threat to the king.

"Go ahead, Aohdan. Take your best shot. If you've got the chops. Or maybe you're not fit to be patriarch anymore? Maybe you're too weak . . ." Rory taunted the patriarch as he slowly shifted, placing his steps carefully, deliberately, watching Aohdan the entire time. Ready for when the patriarch made his move.

Galen's hand, planted firmly in the center of his chest, stopped Aohdan before he could lunge at Rory. When Aohdan continued to push forward, Galen leaned into him and Kieran grabbed one of his arms while the king's guard shifted restively.

"Steady," Galen whispered. "I know you want his head, but you stand accused before the king. Right now, you can't touch him. He'll get what's coming, but not yet."

Rory continued to goad him. "Why make them wait? You are going to *try* to kill me, aren't you?" *C'mon, come after me. Let Fionvarr's guards do my work for me.*

"Who says Aohdan will be the one to kill you?"

The snarling voice belonged to Aeronwy.

CHAPTER 57

AERONWY STALKED FORWARD as Rory tried to bait Aohdan into doing something stupid. Her captains fanned out, but with a single gesture from her, they melted back. She kept her eyes riveted on Rory.

"How could you?" she growled. "He's your patriarch!"

"Who turned on me when he brought a human into our inner circle!" Beads of sweat dotted Rory's forehead.

"A lame excuse to cover your petty ambitions. You forget, Rory Molloy, that Aohdan's my cousin, the only blood family I have left." Aeronwy flexed her fingers, clenching and unclenching her fists as she took another predatory step forward. "I allowed you into my bed, and this—*this*—is what you do? A betrayal of him is a betrayal of me."

"And when I'm done with him, I'll show you how a real Fae man acts, you bossy little bitch."

No one spoke to Aeronwy that way, let alone Rory, and her head snapped up, furious.

"Aeronwy . . ."

If she heard Aohdan say her name—or the warning in his tone—Aeronwy didn't acknowledge it. As she tracked her prey across the floor, the matriarch of Philadelphia started to murmur, and the air in the room seemed to swirl inward to wrap itself around her like a cloak. Rory started to breathe harder, and a primal fear ran cold through every single faerie in the room, including the Seelie king.

Transfixed by her approach, Rory was stone until Aeronwy grabbed his face with her hands and started to raise her voice, her Fae words getting clearer. In that instant, Aohdan, Galen, and several others grasped just exactly how she planned to avenge her cousin's betrayal, but Seireadan was the one to give voice to the collective realization.

"She's cursing him!"

Of all faerie magic, blessings and curses were some of the most difficult spells to cast. The entire Desolation had been caused by one corrupted curse. Aohdan's shout of denial was echoed by Aeronwy's second, Morgan, and Fionvarr leaped to his feet to forbid the spell. Their protests, however, were too late, and Aeronwy finished, her last sonorous words fading away. Red light glowed beneath her hands as the power of the curse wormed its way into Rory, digging through his skin, and he started to shake and sweat. With an audible crack, Aeronwy was thrown backward, an arc of magical energy spanning from her hands back to Rory, who stood rooted to his spot, screaming in agony as the magic burned into his very bones and blood. On the floor, Aeronwy—despite the searing waves of pain that washed over her—stayed focused on Rory.

"Suffer the consequences of your betrayal, and never again hide your true nature!" Her voice was raw, unnatural in its timbre, and as she released the last vestiges of the curse, blood ran freely from her nose and ears. Aeronwy swayed as she got to her feet, drained, and put a hand to her face. When she took it away, she looked at the blood on her fingers as if she had no idea what it was. Morgan caught his matriarch as she sagged to the floor, semiconscious but—remarkably—alive.

Another excruciating scream erupted from Rory, as if his body were being eaten by acid from the inside out. Still seemingly unable to move his feet, Rory thrashed his arms and clawed at his face. He dropped to his knees, the gouges in his face streaming blood until his skin started to bubble and the bones shifted and snapped underneath. Thickening, his skin took on a leathery look. His cropped red hair fell out in clumps before dingy dishwater-gray hair sprouted from his bald, bleeding scalp.

The Gallery was transfixed. Even when Faerie existed, curses were extremely rare. They consumed so much magical energy, they were exceedingly dangerous. Those who cast them were often changed forever. Almost no one in the room had ever seen someone who was truly cursed, and they were enthralled and horrified by what was happening to Rory. Bones popped, and Rory's fingers grew bonier and longer, his fingernails yellowing and cracking. His eyes transformed, growing more oval while the irises expanded to fill the entire eye, turning it a bright green. His screaming reached a higher pitch as his nose stretched and his jaw shifted, and his body folded in on itself, crushing his tall frame into a twisted new form.

Abruptly, Rory—or what had been Rory—stopped screaming, looked up, and blinked.

Seireadan, as thunderstruck as everyone else in the room, gaped at what she saw: stout of body, Rory now had long and bony arms, with tufts of hair jutting out at the elbows. His short legs were knobby and gnarled, and when he opened his mouth, the teeth were sharp and pointed. He hissed at Aeronwy, grabbed a cap, which was red from the blood that had stained it, and jammed it onto his head. He didn't seem to notice or care that drops of blood trickled down his face.

"She turned him into a Red Cap," Seireadan whispered to Aohdan, although he didn't seem to hear her.

Untrustworthy and deceitful, Red Cap faeries were ferocious and often ate the flesh of their victims. Four other Red Caps pushed through the crowd and leered at him. Instinctively, Rory moved toward them, but recoiled as they growled and gnashed their teeth. Rory turned and fled, shrieking, and a few moments later—after a hissed and snarled conversation—the other Red Caps set out after him, leaving only one behind to watch what happened at court.

CHAPTER 58

DESPITE THE FUROR over Aeronwy's curse, the room settled into silence when Fionvarr stood and raised his hands for quiet. Regardless of what the years had brought, he was still the Seelie king, and the gathered faeries waited on his words.

"Is the matriarch in need of a doctor?" asked the king.

"No, she is not," Aeronwy answered before her second could speak for her. Her voice was remarkably subdued as she leaned on Morgan for support.

"Very well, but note well, Aeronwy Tor, that should you ever attempt to curse someone again, I will have you imprisoned immediately for the remainder of your life. Curses are too dangerous for any faerie to wield, and casting them will not be tolerated. I will have order for the remainder of this assembly!"

The crowd murmured and then grew silent once again.

"Criofan, let us attend to the business at hand. You say there are charges against Aohdan that must be heard and judged." Fionvarr sat down and sighed softly as if his proclamation had tired him.

"Indeed, my lord." Criofan stood and adjusted his linen jacket. "Before the . . . incident just now, I was saying that Aohdan has broken away from the Seelie Court, rejected your authority as the Seelie king, and created his own power base as a triarch. He believes you to be weak and wishes to rule the Seelie Court as king himself."

Attention immediately turned to the patriarch, and all waited for him to react. Aohdan walked a few steps forward so he was on the open floor before the king's dais. He offered Fionvarr a courteous nod, but nothing more, and then he pointed at Criofan. His raw voice didn't waver. "Criofan spins lies. I have never raised a hand against you, King Fionvarr, or the Seelie Court."

Before Fionvarr could say anything, Criofan pressed his case.

"No? What of this Conclave? I see them all here, your supporters. What do you talk about in your meetings? When and how to assassinate those in your way? What you'll do when you attempt your coup?" Criofan made sure to make eye contact with members of the Conclave.

"Our coup? That's an outright lie. You know nothing about the Conclave and what we do. Nothing about how it has *prevented* bloodshed, not called for it. You pile lies upon lies and hope everyone will believe you if you just tell them enough times."

"I lie?" Criofan laughed. "I can put all the pieces together. Your own captain turned on you, came to me and told me of your plots and schemes. You are only hiding in the shadows, biding your time until you can strike. I do *not* lie."

Seireadan saw her opening and seized it. "You don't lie? Everything about you is a lie, Criofan. You accuse Aohdan of ruling from the shadows, the very thing you've been doing for years, keeping the truth from King Fionvarr while you rule in his name. You're more of a threat to the Seelie Court than Aohdan could ever be."

"So desperate to protect your lover . . ." Criofan's voice was snide.

"Do the king and the Court know that you're really the one responsible for the Desolation? That you encouraged Luan to create that spell? That you lied about my father hiding Bryn and Conlan? That just before Luan released the spell, the last thing you said to him was 'kill them all'?"

The room erupted in pandemonium, and for a split second, Criofan's entire expression changed from arrogance, to fear, to a flat, cold-blooded mask that promised nothing but pain and death.

For the first time in a very long time, Fionvarr raised his voice in anger. "Silence! I will have ORDER! You. Who are you to interrupt this proceeding with such an accusation? Speak plainly!" He pointed at Seireadan.

"I am Seireadan, daughter of Paidin, who was once your trusted friend."

"You are Paidin's daughter?" He studied her for a moment. "Yes, I see him in you."

"My lord!" cried Criofan. "This is a vile accusation! I won't stand to be slandered like this. Where is your proof? I demand to see it, if it even exists."

"I am a Raven and I Saw it," said Seireadan, ignoring the scoff she heard from Cavan.

"Oh, yes, the tale of your childhood nightmare about a man made of ice," taunted Criofan. "I've heard that tall tale from Cavan."

Ravens were highly respected in Faerie culture, and a murmur of disquiet skipped through the room as Criofan mocked Seireadan.

The ridicule of his words stung, and for a moment, Seireadan again felt like a little girl being shamed for telling outlandish stories. She centered herself, the promise of Criofan's head on a spike blocking out the anxiety.

"I did have a dream," Seireadan said, "a dream so vivid it could have been nothing other than the Sight, and it was not of a man made of ice, but one with alabaster skin and white-blond hair . . . and eyes so pale they looked like ice." She went on to enthrall the audience with the tale of her first Seeing. When she finished, Criofan started to clap slowly and sardonically.

"Marvelous imagery, and I commend you as a storyteller, but even I know that Ravens don't come into their power until adolescence."

"Just because it has never happened before doesn't mean it's impossible. And it isn't the only time that I've Seen you, Criofan." Seireadan was pleased to see Criofan's eyes narrow suspiciously.

"A few weeks ago, Aghna had a Seeing about Aohdan. Criofan demanded a Gathering to see if anyone else had Seen Aohdan," Seireadan said, directing her comment to Fionvarr and not his adviser.

Fionvarr looked at Criofan. "Demanded? We do not demand anything of the Ravens."

"It was a request on your behalf, my lord," said Criofan quickly. "I wanted to ascertain if there was indeed a threat before I brought that information to you. When his name was mentioned, two other Ravens had the Sight."

"And did you tell the king what Aghna Saw? That yes, Aohdan is ambitious, and yes, he can be ruthless, but also that not one Raven Saw interest in the Seelie throne or malice toward King Fionvarr?" Seireadan's fists were clenched at her sides and her eyes were bright.

"Aghna was your teacher, your mentor," Criofan started to say, and from where she stood, Aghna's head snapped up at the unspoken accusation of bias.

"How dare you accuse Aghna—or any of the Ravens—of such deception?" Seireadan said. "If you are so intent on the truth, then ask Cavan. He despises me and would relish my humiliation here today. Ask him now, in front of everyone, what was Seen."

Fionvarr turned his head slightly toward the knot of Ravens to his left. "Cavan?"

Beads of sweat appeared on Cavan's brow as he looked from Fionvarr, to Criofan, to Aghna. Trapped, he forced his answer out through gritted teeth. "Seireadan is correct. None of the Seeings that we're aware of show Aohdan as a direct threat to you."

Criofan barreled ahead. "Regardless of what the Ravens say about Aohdan, I will not tolerate being accused of something as heinous as being involved in creating the Desolation! What proof do you offer, other than a foolish dream, not even a true Seeing?"

"As I said, I have Seen you a second time, the day we Gathered here as you tried to get information about Aohdan to twist to your needs. It was the first time I'd ever laid eyes on you. The Sight took me, and I saw you whispering in Luan's ear as he conjured that abomination that turned my family and home to rubble, dust, and bones. That horror that destroyed our entire world!"

"Such a simple lie to tell," scoffed Criofan.

Seireadan looked at Aghna. "Lia was with me. I told her."

"It is as Seireadan has said," Lia told them.

"You call that proof? Far from it. None of us can see your visions; we rely only on your word, and who would not lie to protect their friend?" Criofan growled.

Cold sweat chilled Aohdan when he saw the small, sad smile that Seireadan offered him when she glanced over. It was a look of resignation, of apology. A look of someone who was never going home again. He'd seen that look when Fae had given up during the Desolation, and seeing it in Seireadan's eyes horrified him.

"Then we seem to be at an impasse, Criofan. I cannot prove my dream was a true Seeing, and you cannot prove it wasn't. Under different circumstances, I would have been content to put a knife in your heart while you slept, but we are here before the Seelie king. The truth must be shared—"

"Indeed it must. We'll finish this business with Collins and then, then I will deal with you and your baseless accusations," Criofan said, talking over Seireadan, and trying to wrest the conversation away from her.

"But you and the Seelie Court hold our Fae traditions in great esteem. You say that the old ways are best and we shouldn't forget them." The determination in Seireadan's voice swelled. "I respect that, and we will settle this the old way."

A feeling of dread nearly made Aohdan's knees buckle, and he gripped Galen's shoulder.

Seireadan raised her voice to make sure the entire room heard her. "King Fionvarr, I challenge Criofan Shea to prove his innocence or guilt within the circle. I invoke *onóir cath.* Here and now."

"No!" Aohdan shouted as soon as the words were out of her mouth.

CHAPTER 59

"YOU WANT TO settle this the old way? An honor battle?" Criofan smiled savagely. He was a consummate swordsman, and what Seireadan was proposing was literally trial by combat, with the winner being vindicated and the loser being guilty—and quite dead. It had been centuries since the last time *onóir cath* had been invoked.

"I do," Seireadan answered.

"As you wish, then. I accept your challenge. When you're dead, I'll put your head in a jar on my desk," Criofan told her.

Seireadan turned to look at Fionvarr. "This challenge must be accepted. I swear on my own life that Criofan is guilty, and if he is, he cannot be trusted to bring charges against Aohdan. His worth must be assessed before judgment is rendered."

Fionvarr grimaced, clearly uncomfortable with the invocation of *onóir cath*, but Seireadan had followed tradition and offered a formal challenge that Criofan had accepted—there were no grounds to deny her.

With a resigned but determined sigh, the king raised his hand and said, "As you will. *Onóir cath* has been invoked and accepted. The victor will be deemed innocent and exonerated; the Banshees will mourn the loser. The rules are thus: If anyone tries to interfere on behalf of either combatant, that individual will forfeit the challenge and will be executed immediately. As is our tradition, all forms of combat are permitted, barring only the use of poison. Seireadan Moore, Criofan Shea, this is your only chance to withdraw. What say you?"

"I understand and accept," said Seireadan.

"As do I," added Criofan.

"Very well," said the king. "Guards, set the circle."

The room where Aohdan's trial was taking place was originally a massive ballroom, but it had been modified when Fionvarr purchased the mansion. Now it was a number of things: throne room, assembly chamber, banquet hall. And when not being used in an official capacity, the Gallery was often used for sparring and sword competitions, spectacles the Fae had loved for millennia on end. One wall held numerous swords and spears. Some were wooden for beginners to use; others were metal and quite lethal. On the floor of the room, several circles were inlaid in the wood, marking off sparring areas. One was directly in front of Fionvarr's dais—its edge only a few feet from where Aohdan had been chained—and his guards moved the spectators back until the entire circle could be seen.

Criofan made a grand gesture to the wall. "Please, select your weapon first."

"Choose your own. I have mine."

Criofan watched her carefully as she shrugged a tattered old bag off her shoulder and walked over to Aohdan. His smile grew more predatory when he saw the look on Aohdan's face as the two talked in hushed tones. *I will make sure she dies slowly, Aohdan. I promise you that. You will hear her scream and beg, and then, when you hear that death rattle in her throat, it will cut you more deeply than anything else I could do. It will be delicious.*

He took off his jacket and gave it to someone to hold before he unbuttoned the cuffs of his shirt and rolled the sleeves up to the elbows. As the king's closest confidant, he kept his sword on the wall with the others; no one would ever touch it without his consent. It was a clean hand-and-a-half sword that was exemplary Fae work. The hilt was carved bone with gold inlay, and the blade had a razor edge that ran from hilt to tip. He swung the weapon leisurely a few times to loosen his shoulders.

"Don't do this," Aohdan said to Seireadan, taking her hand in his.

She ran her thumb along his cheek. "I have to. I've issued the challenge. There's only one path now. You know what happens if I walk away."

Seireadan opened the tattered, ash-stained bag under Aohdan's watchful eye. The scabbard she withdrew was old and worn, and utterly ordinary and unimpressive. Seireadan took a deep breath as she held it.

"I'm sorry I didn't tell you about this," she said.

"What are you talking about?"

"I was going to show you this the night they took you. Another secret of mine, a family secret I've never shared with anyone. You'll understand," Seireadan said as she touched the ancient leather reverently. Squaring her shoulders, she started to turn away but looked back, her eyes fierce, when Aohdan touched her shoulder.

"As much as you want to punish him, don't toy with him. Put that blade through his heart and be done with it." He leaned down and kissed her, a long, soft, intimate kiss. "Finish it and come back to me."

Inside the confines of the circle, Criofan was impatient. "If you are so keen to prove I'm guilty, let's get on with it. Or do you doubt yourself?"

"No doubt." Seireadan walked into the ring, and once she did, there was no going back.

Everything outside the circle faded away as Seireadan touched the obsidian pendant and tucked it inside her shirt, where it wouldn't interfere. Then she drew in a deep, centering breath and slowly pulled her sword from the scabbard, which she tossed back toward Aohdan and the others. For a moment, the sword was merely a blade, and then Seireadan felt that familiar tingle.

She closed her eyes, her grip tightening on the hilt as she whispered, "I've found him, Solais. Today, you'll have your blood."

The sword responded. A glow started deep in the heart of the large citrine in the hilt, and light from the gem spiraled up and around the blade, illuminating ancient script as it did. The words burned orange against the silver steel for a heartbeat as Claíomh Solais came to life, enveloped by a flickering, shifting, yellow-gold aura.

"Claíomh Solais!" a voice cried. "One of the sacred treasures!"

Even with its flame diminished from the havoc wrought by the Desolation, there was no mistaking the sacred Sun Sword.

Seireadan smiled a wicked smile at Criofan.

CHAPTER 60

CRIOFAN STARED AT the flames twining around the silver blade in Seireadan's hand. "The masses may be impressed, but I am not," he said as a drop of sweat rolled down the back of his neck.

"You murdered my family. You lied to Luan and preyed on his pain to make him unleash that damn spell on top of my home. You could have reasoned with him. Instead, because of your hatred and ambition, all of Faerie perished," Seireadan said coldly. "And now you've tried to take Aohdan from me with more of your lies. I will not let either remain unpunished."

With a cry, Criofan lunged at her, hoping to surprise Seireadan into a moment's hesitation. She brought Claíomh Solais around to block his attack, and the vibration from the blow stung her arms up to the elbows. Criofan would not be an easy kill. Shifting, she struck back, low toward the knee, and Criofan countered. They slowly began to circle each other, assessing, studying, waiting. Seireadan made the next move, a feint that made Criofan bring his guard down. He brought his blade back up a moment later, blocking her second swing. From there, the combatants traded a flurry of blows, each advancing a few steps before being driven back.

Seireadan darted a foot forward, causing Criofan to stumble. Trying to take advantage of the opportunity, she drove the point of her sword forward, aiming directly for Criofan's head—a sure killing blow if she succeeded. At the last moment, Criofan recovered and blocked, but not before the very tip of Claíomh Solais dragged from his lip up to the corner of his eye. He cried out in pain as hot blood poured down his cheek, the wound burning. He backed up a few steps to gather himself.

"No more pristine alabaster skin," mocked Seireadan. "You'll never be able to hide that scar, but I suppose that won't matter when you're dead." She shifted her weight, watching for his next move, and didn't have to wait long as Criofan feinted to one side and lunged. Seireadan slid to the side gracefully, deflecting his sword, and snapped around to face him. She barely had time to block his next attack.

He's fast, but he'll find out I'm faster. She narrowed her eyes and went on the attack. Criofan blocked two high strikes and nearly missed the low one that followed, but Seireadan stepped too far and stumbled on her recovery. Criofan made her regret it on his next lunge as the tip of his blade bit deeply into Seireadan's thigh, her slight turn the only thing that kept her femoral artery from being severed.

Up on his dais, the king observed the deadly dance below him. Like everyone else, he'd gasped and leaned forward when Seireadan's blade had sliced Criofan's cheek, and held his breath when Criofan's blade scored a hit along Seireadan's thigh. At the edge of the circle he saw Aohdan being restrained by a Fae and a human.

And then there is you, Aohdan, son of Faolan. I have also heard stories of you and your Conclave. You have grown powerful—and dark—since you left the Seelie Court. You may not covet my throne, but—like your father before you—you are dangerous.

For a brief moment, Aohdan's eyes flicked up to the dais as if he knew Fionvarr was thinking about him, and the look in his eye left the Seelie king cold.

When Criofan's blade opened up Seireadan's leg, Aohdan felt sick to his stomach. Even now, watching the blood stain her jeans and the painful limp that was growing more pronounced, he could taste the acid at the back of his throat.

"You can't. If you interfere, she'll forfeit the challenge," Galen hissed as he tightened his grip on Aohdan's arm.

"She's bleeding."

"If she's bleeding, then she's alive. If you cross into the circle, she's dead." Galen was blunt and harsh.

"I know." Aohdan's voice was anguished. He shook off their hands and watched the ring, examining Seireadan's moves. *Even with the limp, she moves well. If Criofan thought he'd have an easy victory, he was mistaken.* Seireadan retreated across the floor under a flurry of blows from her opponent; Aohdan's palms started to sweat and his throat grew dry.

As the deadly duel continued to play out. Seireadan twisted her upper body as Criofan's blade sliced through the air. The sword missed its target, her heart, but grazed the outside of her shoulder, leaving a nasty slice in its wake. It was another strike that came far too close for Aohdan's comfort.

"Galen, if she dies . . . ," he started to say.

"Don't even think that," Galen ordered.

Aohdan tore his eyes away from the battle long enough to lock eyes with his second, his expression bleak.

Galen squeezed Aohdan's shoulder. "I know. I know *exactly* what you'll do if she doesn't walk out of that ring, and I promise you—you won't do it alone."

Within the circle, Seireadan blocked Criofan's strike again. Blades tangled, metal scraping and shrieking. As they tried to disengage their swords, Seireadan let go of Claíomh Solais with one hand and hammered Criofan with a hard right hook. Blood sprayed as his lip split and his head snapped sideways. They reset, immediately coming back at each other with a series of furious thrusts and parries. After, they circled again, both winded and hoping for a moment's rest, and Criofan wiped the blood off his chin.

Seireadan took the opportunity to evaluate her foe. Criofan was a consummate swordsman, but his strikes were slowing. The gash in his cheek still bled, and there was gore on his shirt where Seireadan's blade had bitten into his side. Knowing he was doing the same to her, she tried to step lightly, hoping to mask the pain pounding through her leg and shoulder.

When Seireadan's punch landed, Aeronwy cheered and then nodded approvingly when Seireadan and Criofan closed again and Seireadan used an elegant sweep to knock away one of Criofan's attacks. Aeronwy wiped away some of the blood that still lingered on her own face and sucked in her breath when, with a feint and a lunge, Criofan's blade got through Seireadan's defense and grazed her arm.

Aeronwy looked to her cousin, and the level of agony on Aohdan's face was something she'd never seen before. *I suspected that he loved her, but I had no idea. If Criofan kills her, this is going to turn into a bloodbath.*

"Morgan." Aeronwy's voice was sharp, and her second snapped to attention. "Keep an eye out. If something happens to Seireadan, Aohdan won't sit idly by, and we back him no matter what."

Air burned in Seireadan's lungs, and pain clawed up from the wound in her leg where Criofan's blade had sliced open the side of her thigh. Blood soaked her jeans, and with every step, the leg felt heavier and slower. Claíomh Solais's hilt was slick with the blood running down Seireadan's arm. She stepped carefully to the side, watching Criofan and conserving her energy.

"You're getting tired, Seireadan. Give in now, forfeit, and I'll give you a quick death," wheezed Criofan.

Seireadan said nothing as her lips pulled back in a snarl and she brought Claíomh Solais up to the ready despite how leaden her arms and shoulders felt. *I will put my sword through your heart for what you did to my father. For what you've done to Aohdan, I will watch you bleed out at my feet, and regret nothing.*

Sensing her fatigue, Criofan leaped forward. It was a bold, unconventional lunge, but his shoe hit one of the many pools of blood that now painted the floor and he slipped to the side just as he struck. Seireadan managed to block his cut and brought Claíomh Solais around to knock his blade to the side. For a moment, Criofan's chest was exposed: it was the mistake Seireadan was waiting for, and Aohdan's words rang in her head: *Put that blade through his heart and be done with it.* Seireadan thrust forward and up as he tried to recover—driving the point of Claíomh Solais from the bottom of Criofan's ribs upward until it hit his heart.

Somewhere in the crowd, two Banshees began to wail.

Criofan blinked, confused, his sword falling from a limp hand, and he choked as blood gurgled up his throat and spilled out of his mouth. A bubbling scream tore out of him as the yellow aura of Claíomh Solais began to burn him from the inside. Golden light spilled out from his eyes, mouth, and ears as he convulsed, and Seireadan ripped the blade free with a savage shout. His body crumpled, and he fell to his knees and then forward onto the floor, his eyes burned out and charred. Criofan made a futile grasping gesture with his hand as Seireadan watched him die in a pool of his own blood.

He's dead! After all these years, all the pain! Seireadan threw back her head and let out a shout that was both victory and agony as she thought of her father, her family, all of the people she knew who had been consumed by the Desolation . . . and of Aohdan, and how Criofan had tried to break him into nothing. The gathered crowd roared with her, but it sounded very far away.

She turned her back on Criofan's carcass, and as she left the circle, Seireadan thrust the hilt of her sword into Galen's hands. Shocked, he looked at the blade with what could only be described as reverence as Seireadan went straight into Aohdan's arms. She leaned against him, her head on his chest, and fought the tears that threatened to break free.

"He paid for what he did to you."

"It doesn't matter," Aohdan whispered, not caring that every person in the Gallery was staring at him, judging him. "All that matters is that you're alive. I don't know what I would have . . . I love you, Seireadan."

"I love you. Always," she answered softly before Aohdan kissed her as if their very lives depended on it.

CHAPTER 61

A CHAIR MATERIALIZED next to Seireadan and she sat wearily. Aohdan towered behind her, keeping a careful eye on the crowd. As Fionvarr watched them, memories of holding his queen in his arms warmed him but abruptly turned sour as the pain and grief of her death reemerged.

"Bring bandages for our winner," said the king.

Aohdan and Galen took the supplies and did their best to stop the bleeding. Once Seireadan's leg and arm were bandaged, the king spoke again.

"Seireadan Moore, you have honored our ways, and through *onóir cath* have proven Criofan's guilt. He has paid the price, but given his crimes, I wonder if death on your blade was too merciful. You are named the victor, and none can hold his death against you. You are free to stay or go as you see fit."

"I go nowhere without Aohdan," she answered.

Aohdan. "Yes. We must still resolve the matter of the accusations against you, Aohdan, son of Faolan," said the king. A tense silence blanketed the room after he spoke.

"My accuser is dead; his so-called witness has fled," said Aohdan.

"Indeed. But that is no matter. The Ravens say you do not covet my throne, and I take that knowledge to heart. Aghna has always been an appreciated and trusted adviser. However, you have become quite powerful, nephew." The king paused and stared at Aohdan for what seemed like a long time before letting his gaze drift out over the crowd, resting for a moment on Aeronwy, Gregor, and Teresa.

"I've worked hard for what I have," said Aohdan. "I won't apologize for that."

"And what of your Conclave? You rule over them, a king in action if not in name." Fionvarr brought his attention back to Aohdan with the question.

"Rule? No. We are a group of equals, and I serve as a chairman by their leave. I didn't take the position by force, and I don't keep it that way."

Fionvarr glanced at the crowd again, his gray eyes falling again on the knot of triarchs who stood together. *I would do well to keep you close to me, Aohdan. You are powerful, and that makes you dangerous. The same is true of this Conclave, but without you to unite them? They will fracture and destroy themselves.* "Then I will give you a choice, Aohdan Collins. Leave your Conclave and your city. Return to the Seelie Court and take your rightful place here. Return to my side, and all will be absolved. Reunite the splintered Seelie Court."

Of the myriad things Fionvarr could have said, not a single person in the Gallery expected him to invite Aohdan back to the Seelie Court, to tacitly invite him to take Criofan's place, and a hushed murmur rippled across the floor.

"And if I refuse?"

The murmur grew louder, and Fionvarr sat back, caught off guard himself by Aohdan's question. *Refuse an offer of absolution? Refuse to be welcomed back to my Court in a position of prominence?* The king's eyes flashed. "Then you will no longer be Seelie—I will banish you to the darkness and name you Unseelie forevermore!"

A cacophony of voices filled the room at the king's pronouncement, and behind Aohdan, the triarchs whispered among themselves, their conversation muted by the shocked response of the crowd.

"If he returns to the Seelie Court, we will lose everything, and I've worked too hard for that," said Sorchae. "Unless Aohdan is Fionvarr's equal, the Seelie king will slowly destroy us—he sees the Conclave as a threat."

"Aohdan's loss would divide us. We all know—even if we hate to admit it—that he is the only one who can hold the Conclave together. Without him, we'll be at each other's throats in short order," said Gregor. He looked from Aeronwy to Teresa.

"We discussed this possibility already. Are we still decided?" Aeronwy's voice was sharp, and the others looked at her warily; her display with Rory had cast her in a new light with the other triarchs.

"We are decided," confirmed Réamann, who stared hard at Teresa and Tuathal, the two triarchs who almost always opposed Aohdan.

"Deciding between two shit choices," said Teresa. "I'm fucked either way. Yes, we're decided."

While the triarchs whispered just out of his earshot, Aohdan remained silent, weighing the Seelie king's words. The longer he remained still, the more restless the crowd became, and the low buzz of hushed voices grew louder again. Even Galen, Chris, and Kieran began to wonder what his answer might be. Seireadan squeezed his hand.

Finally the king pressed him to answer. "What say you, Aohdan? I give you this one last chance to accept: Leave the Conclave and your city and return to the Seelie Court to serve me. Otherwise, you and those who follow you will spend eternity as Unseelie, those who dwell in the shadows, and not in the beauty and the light. You will have no home in the Seelie Court, and no Fae who claims to be Seelie will aid you, even if you are weeping at his feet."

I can't leave Boston, and I will not abandon my fréamhacha agus brainsí. Aohdan stood taller as he opened his mouth, but Gregor's deep, strong voice interrupted him.

"There is great beauty in the shadows, Seelie king, if you bother to look for it. I will not return to the Seelie Court, and I name Aohdan Collins the Unseelie king!" The Los Angeles patriarch's voice rang out over the crowd.

Aohdan spun to face the triarchs, shocked. "No! When I created the Conclave, we agreed there would be no king or queen, that we would serve as equals. That hasn't changed—I am no king."

Sorchae smiled at him and said, "I welcome the term Unseelie. I embrace it, and I, too, name Aohdan the Unseelie king!" Her voice carried through the hall.

"Aohdan, the Unseelie king!" barked Harbin.

A moment later, the voices of the other triarchs all joined in, acclaiming him as the Unseelie king to whom they would promise their loyalty and honor. Galen and the rest of Aohdan's captains added their voices, and soon his name was being clamored throughout the massive Gallery.

Fionvarr rose to his feet, glaring at Aohdan, and the shouting voices died down.

"I never asked for this," Aohdan said to him.

"No, but you have thought about it. I know you have," said Teresa from where she stood.

"And do you name me Unseelie king as well, Teresa? Would you willingly bend your knee to me?"

Teresa scowled at Aohdan's sharp question, and then said to Fionvarr, "Once, I admired you, respected you, but you have spent centuries wallowing in your grief and your guilt. You disappeared when we needed our king to lead us. You hid, and allowed Criofan to take your power. That is weakness and I have no respect for that. If I must bend a knee, it won't be to you. This is on your head, Fionvarr: I name Aohdan the Unseelie king."

Aohdan knew it took all of Teresa's fortitude to not choke on her own words.

Seireadan realized, even before Aohdan opened his mouth, that he would refuse Fionvarr. She knew he would never abandon his *brainsí* and return to the Seelie Court. Then she watched that fierce determination turn to shock as Gregor named him Unseelie king. Voices joined the chorus of acclamation, and she saw the slightest bend to Aohdan's shoulders as the reality of what they were doing slammed into him.

You can't break! She willed all of her own strength to him. *They're right: you are the only one who can hold the Unseelie together, the only one who can stand in front of Fionvarr as an equal.* And as if he'd heard her, Aohdan straightened and pulled his shoulders back. He started to turn from the crowd, back toward King Fionvarr, and stopped when his eyes met Seireadan's. She mouthed the words "I love you" and he smiled.

"And what say you, Seireadan Moore?" Aohdan asked quietly.

"I say that everything I am, I give to Aohdan, the Unseelie king," she answered and bent one knee to the floor. Her action rippled through the room until nearly a third of those filling the Gallery followed her and paid homage to their new king.

CHAPTER 62

FIONVARR WAS INCENSED. "This is your choice? You—all of you—would turn your backs on the Seelie Court and be named Unseelie, those who walk in shadow? You have acclaimed Aohdan as your king, but what does he offer but chaos and anarchy?"

He stared at those surrounding Aohdan—the newly born Shadow Court that would play counterbalance to his Shining Court—and they terrified him. But it was a surprising and unexpected voice that answered his question.

"He gave me justice." The voice belonged to Desmond O'Neill, and the old Fae hobbled forward, grimacing at the pain in his stiff knee. He looked as if he'd aged a thousand years in the months since they buried Oisin.

"Justice?" the Seelie King asked.

"When my son was murdered, he made sure those bastards paid. What would you have done? Once, in the old days, I could have come to you for justice and actually spoken to a king. Had I come when Oisin died, Criofan would have never allowed me an audience. I would have been sent away and told that my son deserved his fate."

Even Aohdan was taken aback by Desmond's raw honesty, and the skin around Fionvarr's eyes tightened because there was painful truth in the old man's words. Then more voices joined Desmond's, each telling a different story with the same theme: that as patriarch, Aohdan had protected and loved those in his *brainsí*.

"This all may be true, but I doubt you have reached your position purely through altruism. You are no innocent, Aohdan," said Fionvarr.

"No, I'm not. I've made hard choices, harder than you know," said Aohdan flatly. "I have blood on my hands, and I won't insult anyone by denying it. But I have never spilled blood lightly, and I will carry those decisions with me for the rest of my life."

Fionvarr snorted dismissively at Aohdan's words and looked for an ally in the ranks of the Unseelie who would speak against the patriarch. The crowd parted, and it was Baibin who walked through the throng to approach the Seelie king. She came so close to the steps of the dais that one of Fionvarr's guards moved to block her.

It took the king a moment, but then he recognized her. "You. I remember you, Baibin Quinn. What say you? Aohdan killed your last living son, did he not? Took your *brainsí* as his own?"

"He took nothing that I did not freely offer him. My son was a fool, and because of what he did, Aohdan was within his rights to destroy my entire *brainsí*—there are days I wonder why he didn't. Yes, he may be ambitious—show me a triarch who isn't—but he is not blinded by that ambition."

"Your son, your only son, died at his hand," Fionvarr said again.

"Only after he betrayed me, and his new patriarch." Baibin spat the words out. "Had Aohdan not done it, I would have killed the faithless whelp myself. But I will always live with the shame of what my son did. I am dying, Seelie king, and I'll die knowing my *fréamhacha agus brainsí* is well cared for by the Unseelie king."

She took another step forward and the guard tensed.

"And now I will warn you, Seelie king—you and your guard here—that I stand here on purpose. If you move against the Unseelie king, I will stand between you. I will serve as his shield and let my blood, my death, atone for what my son did. You will not touch him while I live." Even in her frailty, Baibin's voice was strong, and there was an echoing silence in the room when she finished. She waved her cane at the guard in warning, the brass skull at the top gleaming wickedly.

Before another word could be said, Gregor's voice boomed across the room. "You are named Unseelie king by acclamation. What say you, Aohdan Collins?"

Aohdan frowned. He looked at the faces in the crowd, at Fionvarr, and finally at Seireadan. "If this is what the Conclave wishes, then I will accept—with one condition."

"Of course there's a condition." Teresa's voice oozed suspicion.

Aohdan held his hand out to Seireadan, and when she took it, he pulled her into his arms. He looked down at her, searching her face and eyes for any sign of doubt. He didn't find one.

"I am no king, not without my queen. Marry me, Seireadan."

The kiss Seireadan gave him made it abundantly clear her answer was yes.

CHAPTER 63

FROM THE DAIS, Fionvarr looked down at them, and Seireadan wondered what they must look like to him: wild and fierce, bloodied by battle, a united front. With a wave of the Seelie king's hand, the guards lining the perimeter of the room moved forward through the crowd and began to close in on Aohdan and the other triarchs. The king's personal guard fanned out in front of the dais as well.

As soon as the first one moved, Seireadan took Claíomh Solais back from Galen and turned to face Fionvarr, taking up a defensive stance. Of the guards she could see, most carried swords, a holdover tradition from the Faerie realm, but she knew very well that at least half would have firearms of some sort with them. If a conflict started, a lot of people would die.

"Don't do this," Aohdan said to Fionvarr.

"I could say the same to you," Fionvarr answered.

"If your guards try to arrest us, we'll fight. Too many people will die unnecessarily, and there will be no undoing that. A civil war will shred what's left of Faerie," said Aohdan.

"Then stand down, renounce the acclamation."

"No."

The Seelie king locked eyes with his nephew. "Then there is no hope for you . . ."

A guard's hand flexed, and Seireadan tensed. She felt Aohdan's coiled energy at her side and the shifting of the other triarchs as they fanned out, along with their captains, to form a semicircle behind Aohdan and Seireadan, ready to defend the newly acclaimed king. Unease infected the room, and Seireadan's violet eyes ranged across the crowd, evaluating faces, and finally fell on the group of Ravens clustered together near the dais. Standing between Lia and Seanán, Aghna began to tremble violently. As the elderly Raven collapsed, Seanán managed to catch her and lower her gently to the ground, where Aghna lay twitching, her eyes rolled up in her head, consumed by the Sight.

"Aghna!" Seireadan cried. Everything inside her demanded that she go to her mentor, but she stopped, fearing her action would be misunderstood and ignite the room.

The old woman's tremors slowed, quieted, and then stopped. Aghna relaxed in Seanán's arms. A moment later, her eyes fluttered open. Lia and Seanán helped Aghna to her feet, and the old woman leaned heavily on Seanán, exhausted even from such a brief encounter with the Sight.

"You have Seen?" asked Fionvarr.

"I have. And you must let them go, Seelie king," Aghna said.

"Let them go? No, they cannot simply secede from the Seelie Court."

"They can and they must. There must be balance, or neither will survive. I Saw a world with no shadows, and the light of the sun baked the earth until it screamed in agony and cracked. I Saw a world with no light, where the shadows were so cold and dark the ground was dead, barren rock," said Aghna. "Light cannot exist without shadow; they are parts of the same whole."

Fionvarr's face was stone as he weighed Aghna's words.

"The choice is yours, King Fionvarr," the old Raven said.

"I don't want to fight you, Uncle," said Aohdan.

Seireadan added her voice to his, keeping it as calm and reasonable as she could. "Please. Let us go, Seelie king. Let us leave before someone does something stupid and starts a war we can't end. We have all lost far too much already."

Aohdan took a deliberate step back, away from Fionvarr, and then another. Seireadan followed him, but the guards continued to press around them, and she kept Claíomh Solais raised just in case. The Seelie king remained silent. With a flash of blond hair, Aya, the girl who often played the harp for Fionvarr, pushed through the crowd and darted out. Completely unaware of the dangerous currents in the room, she stared at Seireadan's glowing sword in delighted awe. She was only a few feet from Seireadan, Aohdan, and the blood-spattered Aeronwy.

His eyes on the little girl, Fionvarr said, "There are too many innocents here, and I will not have their blood on my hands. Take your Unseelie Court and go, shadow king. But know you have put a dagger in the heart of Faerie today; you have divided us forever."

"We were divided a long time ago," Aohdan countered sadly.

CHAPTER 64

AS SOON AS they left Fionvarr's manor, Galen dragged Aohdan and Seireadan to the hospital. It took fifty-two stitches to close the laceration on Seireadan's leg and another fifteen to fix her shoulder. The doctors told Aohdan he was lucky no bones were broken, but the cuts and bruises would heal. What he desperately needed was rest, and Galen assured the doctors someone would be staying with Aohdan and Seireadan to make sure they rested. The pair convalesced for a week under Galen's often restrictive rule, but in the end, it was for the best. Aohdan's injuries faded, and soon he looked rested and strong, and it wasn't long before Seireadan's stitches were removed.

Three weeks later, Aohdan came out of the bedroom, buttoning the cuffs of his shirt. He was a little early, but didn't want to be late for the commencement of this special meeting of the Conclave. Seireadan was standing in the living room looking at the fireplace where Claíomh Solais, sleeping quietly in its scabbard, now hung in a place of honor on the wall.

"Do you like it there?" Aohdan asked.

"I do. It is exactly where it's supposed to be. And exactly where it will stay."

"What did you tell Fionvarr's messenger?"

"I said to tell Fionvarr that if he wanted the sword, then he was going to have to come take it away from me himself." Seireadan nearly snorted in disgust.

"I'm sure he liked that answer."

"I really don't care what he likes. Come here." She adjusted Aohdan's tie. "There, that's better; you were crooked. Are you ready?"

"No, not really," said Aohdan, his answer frank and honest. "I never wanted to be a king, Seireadan. I wanted to live my own life on my terms."

"Who says you can't?" She tilted her head slightly to the side.

"You know everything is more complicated now."

"I know," she said with a nod. "But what was the alternative? The Conclave destroyed and life under Fionvarr's thumb? Now that his eyes are open to what Criofan did, I doubt he will ever be a passive king again."

Flanked by Galen and Kieran, Aohdan paused outside the meeting room. He gathered his resolve, opened the door, and walked in. Seated around a circular table, all of the triarchs waited, looking serious and reserved. At the sight of Aohdan, Aeronwy stood up and the others followed suit, and they all bowed at the waist.

"Let's not get carried away," Aohdan said.

Everyone sat and there was silence around the table for a minute. Finally, Aohdan leaned forward slightly and rested his arms on the table.

"What the fuck were you all thinking?" he asked bluntly.

Gregor had the audacity to laugh before he answered, "You may not have the largest city, but you're the most powerful of us. No one else in this room could hold the Conclave together the way you have—something we all knew, but Galen helped us truly admit it."

"I see." Aohdan raised his eyebrows at Galen, who remained silent.

"And if Fionvarr broke you, forced you back to the Seelie Court, not only would we disintegrate into chaos, but Fionvarr would have come for us as well. We are stronger as a united front, and we needed a leader," added Sorchae.

Teresa cleared her throat, and Aohdan waited for the reaming he assumed he was going to get, but the matriarch of New York's voice was unusually subdued. "I saw what Criofan did to you, and each one of us would have followed you into those chains. It will gall me to call you king, but I am free and I am alive. Sometimes compromises must be made."

As much as he wanted to, Aohdan couldn't argue with their logic. The Conclave spent the next five hours discussing business and the future, and Aohdan surprised several of them by changing very little in the way they operated and interacted. As he had always said, business was good, but it was better when the triarchs weren't fighting. The vote to continue the Conclave unchanged was unanimous.

"One thing I won't have is a Court like Fionvarr's that breeds a lazy pool of brownnosers. You—every triarch in this room—and your captains, you are the Unseelie Court. When the Conclave gathers, we are free to disagree and argue here, but when we are out there . . ." He pointed toward the windows that framed the cityscape. "When we are out there, I am the Unseelie king, and there will be no dissent from what's been decided."

"And if we don't obey?" Teresa leaned back casually in her chair while she asked the question, her eyes narrowing.

Aohdan held Teresa's gaze for three long, uncomfortable heartbeats before he said, "Then you will see exactly what kind of king you've bound yourself to."

The occasionally contentious discussions continued for another hour before the Conclave agreed their business was settled for the time being. But as Aohdan was about to adjourn the meeting for the day, he was interrupted by Nessa.

"We still have one order of business to discuss," she said.

"Which is?" asked Aohdan.

"The wedding and the crowning of the Unseelie queen, of course," said Nessa with an extravagant huff.

Aohdan sighed. "Seireadan and I would like something very small and intimate, but it has been brought to our attention several times that the Unseelie king doesn't have the luxury of a private wedding." He gave Aeronwy a pointed stare.

"The Unseelie need to see their king . . . and their new queen," Aeronwy said simply.

"It will not, however, be some grand spectacle," said Aohdan firmly.

"And when does this small spectacle take place?" asked Gregor.

"We've chosen December 21."

Nessa smiled. "Ah, the winter solstice—the longest night. How very appropriate."

CHAPTER 65

AN *AONTAS*—THE FAE term for a wedding—was typically presided over by a family elder. This individual wasn't an officiant needed to validate the marriage but served more as a shepherd to move the ceremony along. At Seireadan's request, Aghna graciously agreed to fill the role.

Dressed in formal attire with her Raven's cloak over her shoulders, Aghna watched the guests gather in the ballroom. All of the triarchs were there, some with significant others. Their seconds and many of their captains were in attendance as well. Some of Seireadan's human friends were there, along with several prominent humans, including Boston's mayor and the senator from the district. Aghna couldn't help but chuckle when her eye fell on the one clearly uncomfortable representative that Fionvarr had sent from the Seelie Court.

Aohdan's captains greeted the guests and took great care to spend some time with the humans in the crowd to explain the Fae ceremony. This particular *aontas* would start at sunset, and once complete, the celebration would continue throughout the night, ending at sunrise the next morning. The old Raven slowly headed toward one of the side rooms where Aohdan was getting ready.

"You look very handsome, Unseelie king. Are you ready?"

Aohdan was dressed in black pants with a crisp white shirt and black vest. He was finishing the knot in his tie, and his jacket was hanging nearby. Around his head was a white-gold circlet braided in a very intricate Celtic pattern with a large black diamond in the center.

"More than ready." He glanced toward the door.

"Just a little more patience. I'm going to check on your lovely bride and then I will call you both to the *aontas*."

Aghna left Aohdan's room and made her way across the front of the main ballroom to Seireadan's room.

Seireadan was standing in front of a full-length oval mirror. Her strapless gown was made of silver-gray satin and had corset-like lacing on the back, which flowed into pearl button accents farther down the skirt. Following the curve of the gown's train, the silver-gray satin gave way to a lighter, mistier shade of silver about halfway down the skirt, and a strip of crystal and lace designed to resemble vines and flowers lay over the change in color, helping it to flow seamlessly. The sides of her hair were up, but the back remained loose and flowed over her bare shoulders. Diamond studs accented her ears, and around her throat was a gift from Aohdan: a gorgeous deep-blue teardrop sapphire.

"Do you like it?" Seireadan asked.

"You are a vision, my dear. Your parents would be very proud of you, and very pleased today. Just as I am," Aghna said. Seireadan smiled fondly, appreciating her mentor's words. "Now, are you ready for your *aontas*? And your crowning?"

Seireadan exhaled sharply. "Yes, to your first question. Nothing will make me happier."

"But?"

"To be the Unseelie queen? The responsibility that comes with that is . . ." She paused, searching for a word. "Immense. But I will stand with Aohdan and face what comes, whatever that might be."

"Good. Being his queen is not something you should take lightly. Gather yourself, my dear, and I will call the *aontas* to order." The gray-shaded cloak swirled around Aghna as she left.

When he heard Aghna's call, Aohdan came out of his room and felt every eye settle on him, and he heard the murmur that sifted through the guests when they saw the black diamond on his brow. It was the first time he'd worn the Unseelie crown in public. He paused and let his dark gaze roam, nodding now and then when he caught someone's eye, before he strode confidently to the platform.

Seireadan's door squeaked, and the rustle of clothes seemed very loud as all of the guests turned nearly in unison to look in her direction. There was a collective intake of breath as everyone caught sight of the silver gown, the satin shimmering as she walked, and Aohdan found he couldn't take his eyes off her. A phrase he'd often heard Chris use jumped into his head: *Holy Mother of God, she's stunning.*

As she reached the edge of the dais, Aohdan held out a hand to help her up the stairs. Lia slipped out of her seat, adjusted the gown's train, and quickly sat back down, where she threaded her fingers through Kieran's. Aohdan took both of Seireadan's hands in his, raised them up, and kissed them; he was rewarded with a dazzling smile.

Aghna raised her hands in the air. "Aohdan. Seireadan. You have come freely in front of this gathered crowd, two halves of a whole, to complete the *aontas* in front of all and join your lives." She loosely wrapped a braided cord of silver, black, and gray around their joined hands and stepped back.

Aohdan spoke first. "From the moment I met you, there's been no other woman for me. You are smart, fierce, loyal, and caring, and . . ." He paused and looked her up and down. ". . . and you are the most beautiful woman I have ever seen. You're amazing. You understand me in a way no one else does, and you know when to push and when to wait. In front of everyone here, our friends, our family . . . in front of the Unseelie Court, I say that I love you and I willingly bind myself to you for all of my days."

Seireadan squeezed his hands before she spoke. "I love you, Aohdan Collins, and willingly bind myself to you for all of my days. You challenge me; some days you infuriate me . . ."

That comment elicited a gentle laugh in the crowd and a grin from Aohdan.

"But I know there is no one who cares more about me. You are my protector, my warrior, my lover, and my friend. There is no one who is a better match for me, and I will stand by you in everything you do—I will be *your* protector, *your* warrior, *your* lover, and *your* friend for all the days of my life."

Aghna unwrapped the cord from their hands and said, "You came to the *aontas* as two, and you leave it as one, bound together by your love and honor. We love and bless you both."

Aohdan reached into his pocket, and said, "And as we have kept Fae tradition with our *aontas*, I also want to acknowledge the traditions of our human cousins. Seireadan, I offer you this ring as a symbol of what I have declared here today. Will you accept it?"

"Of course." Seireadan held up her left hand for Aohdan. He slid the white gold ring, crowned with three diamonds, onto her finger. It was the first time Seireadan had seen it, and her face softened. It was simple and elegant.

In turn, Seireadan reached into a tiny fold of satin concealed in the waist of her gown and drew out a ring. "I, too, have a ring to honor the traditions of our kin in this realm. Will you accept it?"

"I will." Aohdan held out his hand while she slipped the onyx and diamond band onto his finger.

They joined hands and said in unison, "We were two, and now we are one."

The guests all applauded as the couple concluded the *aontas.* As the noise died down, Aghna took a polished wood box from the small stand next to her. She opened it and held it out for Aohdan. Inside, resting on wine-colored velvet, was a crown. It was a braided band of white gold, the silver tone reminiscent of moonlight, and the entire way around the band were alternating white and black diamonds, each about eight carats in size. Aohdan took it out and held it up for everyone to see. Another buzz ran through the crowd as the light glinted off the jewels.

"I am the Unseelie king," he said gravely as he faced Seireadan. "Today, you become more than my wife and partner. You accept the responsibilities and duties of the Unseelie queen. What say you, Seireadan Moore?"

Seireadan took a deep breath before she answered. "I accept and will serve at your side as the Unseelie queen." She bent her knees to a graceful curtsy, making it easier for Aohdan to put the crown on her head. It was heavier than it looked, but she stood gracefully, never taking her eyes from Aohdan's.

"Now and forevermore, you are the Unseelie queen," Aohdan announced.

He leaned in, gave her a soft, gentle kiss before he straightened and, holding hands, they turned to face the crowd. As they did, Galen stood up from his chair.

"*Sláinte agus sonas*—health and happiness!" he shouted.

There was a rustle and scrape as the next three rows of guests stood. Their voices merged as they all shouted, "*Sláinte agus sonas*—health and happiness!"

Once they were finished, the rest of the guests stood and, for the third time, shouted, "*Sláinte agus sonas*—health and happiness!"

The banquet following the *aontas* was nothing short of magnificent. Guests feasted on pan-roasted prosciutto-wrapped chicken breast, spiced yellowtail snapper, and braised beef short ribs, along with truffle mousseline potato, sundried tomato risotto, petite green beans, and broccolini. Other smaller stations held an assortment of breads, cheeses, fruits, and raw vegetables. The amazing meal was followed by a decadent vanilla cake with strawberry cream between the layers and a fondant frosting with silver decorations that mimicked some of the designs on Seireadan's gown.

Once the meal was finished, dancing and merriment commenced, and sometime during the evening, unseen by most of the guests who danced until sunrise, the Unseelie king and queen slipped away to spend the rest of the night in each other's arms.

EPILOGUE

THE DARKNESS AND cold of winter slowly gave way to a new spring, and by the time the daffodils were out in the gardens around Boston, Seireadan was happy to be outside again. The sun was starting its descent to the horizon, and a gorgeous full moon promised to dominate the night sky. Next to her, Aohdan stood by his Harley and adjusted his leather jacket.

Galen, Kieran, and Chris, all laughing, spilled out of the Barking Crab, followed by Aohdan's two newest captains. The Svartálfar Lorna, with her dark skin, shaved head, and nose ring, had proven to be as exceptional as Oisin had promised, and Cam, a soft-spoken but fiercely loyal Fae, came highly recommended from Kieran's part of the organization. Cam threw a leg over his own motorcycle. They were all headed for the Cape to take care of some business and then spend a long weekend at the beach before the influx of tourists started for the season.

"Time to go. Get a move on, Kieran," said Galen.

Kieran hung up his phone. "Do no' get your knickers twisted. Lia's going to take the early ferry tomorrow, and I'll pick her up when it arrives." He put a few things in the saddlebags attached to his bike.

Looking down to where the pedestrian underpass disappeared into shadows, Seireadan saw something lingering in the semidarkness.

"We have company," Seireadan said to the group. They all turned to look as five Red Caps crept out, and Kieran—who had taken on the role of queen's guard—moved to her left while Aohdan stood at her right.

With their bulbous green eyes, knobby limbs, and bloody hats, the Red Caps skittered nervously down the side of the street, eager to avoid even the last remnants of the sun. A stained bag bumped along the pavement behind the largest one. Aohdan and his captains watched them suspiciously, trying to discern if any of the five was actually the treacherous and cursed Rory Molloy, who hadn't been seen since the day of Aohdan's trial the previous year.

As they got closer to Aohdan, four of the Red Caps stopped while the one with the bag pushed his way to the front. He offered Aohdan an awkward bow.

"Unseelie king." The Red Cap's voice was a hiss.

The captains moved closer so Aohdan and Seireadan were protected—the Red Caps were part of the Unseelie, but they were also mercurial, savage, and unpredictable, and they grumbled, hissed, and snapped at one another as their leader approached Aohdan.

"What business do you have with the Unseelie king?" Seireadan asked. Dressed in black leather for the ride to the Cape, the Unseelie queen looked fierce and pinned the large Red Cap with her stare.

He bobbed his head up and down. "Unseelie queen, we are not here for trouble. We have a gift for the Unseelie king and his queen, a gift we wanted to bring to your *aontas* but could not."

"A gift?" asked Aohdan.

The Red Cap untied the mouth of the sack with his bony fingers, his sharp nails tearing at the material, and then dumped the contents onto the sidewalk. A tattered and ripped red cap, several bones that had clearly been gnawed on, and a gnarled hand still covered in skin and flesh all spilled out onto the concrete. On the pinkie finger of the severed hand was an antique gold claddagh ring. Seireadan's shocked eyes met Aohdan's.

"That ring. That was Jimmy Boy's. Rory took it after . . ." The rest of Aohdan's words were lost as the Red Caps growled and hissed angrily at the mention of Rory's name.

"He looked like us, but he was not one of us. Cursed, foul, filthy traitor," the Red Caps' leader snarled. "We do not tolerate those who turn on the Unseelie king!"

"This ring meant a lot to Jimmy's father," said Aohdan. He picked up the gnarled hand and took the ring, slipping it into his pocket. He dropped the gnawed hand back in the bag, scooped up the hat and bones as well, and then tied the bag shut. He handed it to Lorna.

She took it without question but looked at the grimy sack with distaste. "What are we doing with this?"

"The ring, I keep. The rest? We burn it in tomorrow's bonfire," Aohdan said.

While Lorna stowed the satchel in one of her saddlebags, Seireadan approached the Red Cap. The creature jigged and twitched nervously, clasping his bony hands together, as she bent one knee to be closer to his height.

"Thank you for this gift. The Unseelie king and I will always remember this."

She gave the Red Cap a swift kiss on the cheek, somehow managing to not look repulsed by the fact that he smelled like a dead, rotting animal. Shocked, the Red Cap simply blinked at her in awe. After a moment, he hurried after the other four, heading for the shadows beneath the overpass. Before he disappeared, the Red Cap turned back to watch Seireadan, a strange look crossing his face.

"We love you, Unseelie queen," he whispered softly. "We will do *anything* for the Unseelie queen." He dissolved back into the shadows just as Seireadan turned around.

"What's wrong?" Aohdan asked, putting his hand lightly on the small of her back.

"Nothing. I thought I heard the Red Cap say something. Maybe I'm mistaken."

"If you're worried, I'll look into it when we get back, but for now let's go have a little fun before we come back to our city."

"Our city?" Seireadan's voice was colored with humor.

"Normally, I'd say 'my' city," Aohdan's voice matched hers, "but now I have to say 'our.'" He flashed his left hand so she saw his wedding ring.

"You're impossible." She gave him a gentle shove.

"Let's go," said Aohdan. He gestured to the captains, and they all started to ease their motorcycles down the road toward the Interstate on-ramp. Aohdan threw his leg over his bike, and the engine roared to life. Seireadan buckled her helmet, climbed on, and wrapped her arms around his waist.

Just as he eased up on the brake, Aohdan looked back once more toward the overpass, and into the shadows.

AUTHOR'S NOTE

For those of you who have read this far . . . THANK YOU. Thank you for taking a chance on my book; I am truly grateful. I hope you've enjoyed the story.

People often think being a writer is a solitary job, but that is so far from the truth. Believe it or not, it takes a group effort on many different levels, and there are so many people I need to thank for their love and support throughout this process.

First and foremost is my husband, Jeff, who has always supported my writing and has patiently listened to me fret over it, talking me off the proverbial ledge more than once. I am so ridiculously lucky to have you in my corner; I can't even begin to express it. I also need to thank my parents, Kay and Harry, for always letting me pursue the things that interested me no matter how random they seemed, and for their constant support. You always helped me get where I needed to be but gave me the freedom to do it my way.

Thank you to all of my friends who continually indulge and encourage me, and who—from time to time—kick me in the arse when I need it the most. Special thanks go to Maureen, Jan, Kirsten (and Hannah), Jenn, and Kellie for reading different drafts, giving me feedback (especially the tough feedback), and for being there during the celebrations and nervous breakdowns. They will be very surprised, but this list would be incomplete without thanking Ravin W., Doug W., Toby C., and Robert M.: I couldn't have asked for better supporters—dare I say fans?—throughout the whole Launchpad roller coaster and beyond. You guys are rock stars.

John Robin and Lizette Clark from Story Perfect Editing Services: You're both incredible, and your efforts have helped make this book even better. I am so grateful for your insights and discussion. KL Pereira from Grub Street, your feedback on my early draft made a huge difference and helped give me the confidence to enter Launchpad in the first place. Thank you so much.

I would also be remiss without a shout-out to the fabulous Charlene Maguire, the artistic force behind my cover. I know we went through many more revisions than you expected on this cover, and you took all of my feedback (including my crazy diagrams) with grace, class, and humor, and turned my vague direction into something marvelous. You can find more of Charlene's great work at ShapeShifterStudios.com.

Somewhere out there is the woman who taught my freshman writing class at the University of Massachusetts, Amherst. I remember your name as Sarah, but have—to my shame—forgotten your last name, so I don't even know where to start to find you. But if not for your class, I may not have stepped onto the path of creative writing. I'll always be grateful.

Chris and the Launchpad team and Adam and the Inkshares team: I would not be here in this moment without the Launchpad Manuscript Competition. I entered thinking how wonderful it would be to get feedback from your prestigious team of judges. I never in my wildest dreams imagined I would be in your final top ten. Thank you for the opportunity, opening the door, and helping to turn a dream into a reality.

And last but not least, there are 250 people out there who took a chance on *Shadow King* before I was confident it would actually be published, and your faith propelled me to this point. I don't think I can say thank you to all of you enough. Many of you are friends and family, and I truly, deeply appreciate the support—especially those of you who I literally haven't talked to in decades and who, even after all that time, still said yes to preordering *Shadow King* without even a second thought. You are all amazing.

MAJOR CHARACTERS

Many character names have Gaelic and Irish roots. Pronunciations, however, don't follow a strict pattern. Some are variations of traditional pronunciations, and some merely follow a more intuitive phonetic path.

Abrezu (ah-BREY-zoo) **Hatami**: A Persian fire faerie known as a Pari; Vashti's sister

Aeronwy (AIR-on-wee) **Tor**: Fae, matriarch of Philadelphia; Aohdan's cousin

Aghna (AG-na) **Greenough**: Fae, elder Raven

Aohdan (AYE-oh-den) **Collins**: Fae, patriarch of Boston; Aeronwy's cousin

Baibin (BAY-bin) **Quinn**: Fae, matriarch of Providence

Cavan (ca-VAN) **Laskin**: Fae, Raven

Chris Cervenka: Human, part of Aohdan's crew and *fréamhacha agus brainsí*

Criofan (CREEO-fan) **Shea**: Fae, chief adviser to King Fionvarr

Crogher (KRO-ger) **Quinn**: Fae, second of Providence's *fréamhacha agus brainsí*; Baibin's son

Fearg (FEAR-g) **Hardesty**: Fae, captain in Providence's *fréamhacha agus brainsí*

Fionvarr (FINN-var) **Kendan**: Fae, the Seelie king; Aohdan's uncle

Galen Grey: Fae, second of Boston's *fréamhacha agus brainsí*

Gregor Travis: Fae, patriarch of Los Angeles

Harbin Rua: Fae, patriarch of Las Vegas

Jimmy "Jimmy Boy" McLaren: Human, part of Aohdan's crew and *fréamhacha agus brainsí*

Julia Orlando: Human, owner of Sacred Circle, friend of Seireadan

Kieran (KEER-an) **West**: Fae, captain in Boston's *fréamhacha agus brainsí*

Lanty Soonian: Fae, captain in Providence's *fréamhacha agus brainsí*

Liadain "Lia" Allen: Fae, Raven, and friend of Seireadan

Nessa Valor: Fae, matriarch of Detroit

Oisin (OY-sin) **O'Neill**: Fae, captain in Boston's *fréamhacha agus brainsí*

Réamann (RAY-man) **Stone**: Fae, patriarch of San Francisco

Rory Molloy: Fae, captain in Boston's *fréamhacha agus brainsí*

Seireadan (SER-eh-dan) **Moore**: Fae, Raven

Sorchae (SOAR-cha) **McKinley**: Fae, matriarch of Miami

Teresa Aberdeen: Fae, matriarch of New York

Tuathal (TOO-ah-thal) **Ross**: Fae, patriarch of Detroit

Vashti (VASH-tee) **Hatami**: A Persian fire faerie known as a Pari; Abrezu's sister

FAERIE-KIND

Throughout world folklore there are hundreds of different faeries and mythical creatures, and while only a few are represented in these pages, these are some of the many types of faeries you could encounter in Aohdan and Seireadan's Boston.

Banshee: A faerie who wails when someone nearby is about to die. There are only female Banshees.

Brownie: A Scottish household spirit.

Clurichaun: An Irish faerie resembling a Leprechaun.

Domovoi: A protective house spirit in Slavic folklore. Even the young appear old due to their gray hair.

Dryad: A tree Nymph, humanoid in shape but small. Their hair and skin tends to contain brown and green tones.

Ebu Gogo: A humanlike creature in Indonesian mythology with long hair, a pot belly, and larger ears that slightly stick out.

Fae: A humanlike faerie. Fae have tapered ears and tend to be tall and very attractive by human standards.

Gnome: Typically said to be a small humanoid that lives underground; very shy and not seen frequently.

Haltija: A spirit, Gnome, or elf-like creature in Finnish mythology that guards, helps, or protects something or somebody.

Kobold: A shape-shifting German sprite.

Korrigan: A Breton dwarf or faerie.

Leprechaun: A small, mischievous sprite.

Ljósálfar: A Norse light elf; tends to be light skinned and blond, the opposite of its cousin the Svartálfar.

Naiad: A type of water Nymph. Their hair and skin tends to have blue, green, and teal tones.

Nix: A German shape-shifting water spirit very similar to a Naiad.

Nymph: A female nature spirit. They can be associated with almost any element and tend to have characteristics related to their element.

Pari: Persian fire faerie with a humanoid appearance. Their hair and eyes tend to be shades of red, orange, and gold as do their translucent wings.

Pixie: A benign being with wings resembling those of a dragonfly; very small—about the size of a bird.

Pooka/Pookha/Puck: A faerie changeling that can take a human form or that of a dog or horse. They always have black hair and red eyes.

Red Cap/Redcap: A malevolent, murderous type of faerie with sharp teeth and fingernails and green eyes.

Rusalka: A Slavic water spirit with blue-tinted skin.

Selkie: A faerie that can live as a seal in water or remove its pelt and live as a humanoid on land.

Svartálfar: A Norse elf that typically has dark or black skin.

Sylph: A mythological spirit of the air, they are delicate and elusive.

Tennin: A spiritual being found in Japanese Buddhism; similar to western angels or Nymphs.

Undine: A water Nymph related to the Nix and the Naiad.

GRAND PATRONS

Charlotte McEnroe
Kathryn Hamilton
Kevin McCarthy
Lauren G. Helfman
Mac and Rio

INKSHARES

INKSHARES is a reader-driven publisher and producer based in Oakland, California. Our books are selected not by a group of editors, but by readers worldwide.

While we've published books by established writers like *Big Fish* author Daniel Wallace and *Star Wars: Rogue One* scribe Gary Whitta, our aim remains surfacing and developing the new author voices of tomorrow.

Previously unknown Inkshares authors have received starred reviews and been featured in the *New York Times*. Their books are on the front tables of Barnes & Noble and hundreds of independents nationwide, and many have been licensed by publishers in other major markets. They are also being adapted by Oscar-winning screenwriters at the biggest studios and networks.

Interested in making your own story a reality? Visit Inkshares.com to start your own project or find other great books.